"Is it time?" she whispered.

"It is time," he replied. Her heart leaped wildly in her breast as she watched his face move down toward her own.

The whole world was caught up in that dark, angular face. And then it blurred, and the world became a pair of intensely blue eyes. At the last moment, they, too, disappeared. Later, she never knew if he had closed his eyes or she had closed her own. She knew only that when their lips touched, her soul lifted clean out of her body and soared like a spirit set free.

Dear Reader,

It's hard to know where to begin this month. We have two very special—and very different—stories for you to enjoy, one set in the United States and one taking you as far away as China.

Award-winner Bronwyn Williams brings a half-Indian hero and an orphaned young Englishwoman together for a romance that defies all the odds in *Stormwalker*. Shamed and alone, Laura Gray thinks that no one can ever love her, but John Walker, known to his tribe as Stormwalker, is no ordinary man. He has enough love in his heart for both Laura *and* the child she's carrying. One of your favorites, Patricia Potter, is back with *Dragonfire*, a stirring tale set in the mysterious East. A beautiful British innkeeper and an American soldier find love and safety in each other's arms during the turbulent Boxer Rebellion.

Every month, we strive to take you around the world and into the past, sharing tales of cowboys and captains, pirates and princes. Journey with us in the months to come, because at Harlequin Historicals, there's always an adventure waiting to be lived and a romance waiting to be shared.

Leslie J. Wainger
Senior Editor and
Editorial Coordinator

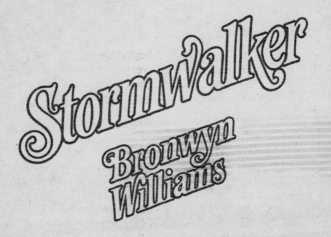

Stormwalker

Bronwyn Williams

Harlequin Books

TORONTO • NEW YORK • LONDON
AMSTERDAM • PARIS • SYDNEY • HAMBURG
STOCKHOLM • ATHENS • TOKYO • MILAN

Harlequin Historical first edition June 1990

ISBN 0-373-28647-3

Books by Bronwyn Williams

Harlequin Historical

White Witch #3
Dandelion #23
Stormwalker #47

BRONWYN WILLIAMS

is the pen name used by two sisters, Dixie Browning and Mary Williams. Dixie Browning had written over forty contemporary romances for Silhouette Books before joining her sister to write their first historical. A former painter and art teacher, currently co-owner of a craft shop in Frisco village on Hatteras Island, Browning divides her time between her home in Winston-Salem and North Carolina's Outer Banks.

Mary Williams is married to an officer in the Coast Guard and has lived in such diverse places as Hawaii, Oklahoma, Connecticut, Virginia and New Jersey. The mother of three grown children, she now lives on Hatteras Island, where both sisters grew up.

Their second historical, *Dandelion*, won the prestigious Maggie Award for the best historical romance of the year from the Georgia Romance Writers.

For our sister.
If Bronwyn Williams had a middle name,
it would be Sara.

Chapter One

September 22, 1711

Hup," cried Edward Gray, and Laura grabbed the end of the long pole in both arms and swung her feet up off the ground. Eyes squinched up tight, she could feel the vibrations as he chopped at the stubborn tap root with his sharpened spade while she pried the root up.

Tough old stump! At times like this Laura wondered if another half acre of corn was worth the backbreaking labor. She sometimes thought her father wondered, too.

"She's a-going! Get set to jump," Edward grunted, and Laura braced herself to leap clear. Otherwise she'd land hard on her backside, the sapling pry bar in her lap. It wouldn't be the first time. Taproots were funny things—some gave up without a whimper, and others creaked and groaned and hung on for dear life. Made a body think the land didn't want to be cleared. But if nobody cleared and planted, then there'd be no farms. And if there were no farms, why, then there'd be no settlements, in which case they may as well give the whole blessed place back to the wild'uns and be done with it.

Ned Gray leaned on the handle of his spade, wiping his forehead and admiring the gaping hole left by the poplar root. Suddenly his eyes narrowed on the woods beyond and he stiffened. "Head on back now, daughter. I'll be in directly."

"Aren't we going to go after that old cedar?"

"Hup!"

Obediently, Laura hupped, although she would much rather have whoaed. Her father used the same commands on his family that he had on his oxen, before they had been driven off by a band of wild'uns, who had likely slaughtered them for food.

Wild'uns, she thought as she picked her way carefully along a path the squirrels had strewn with pine-cone barbs. She knew good and well her father had been friends with at least one of the wild'uns, because she'd heard him mention one named Stormwatcher or Stonewalker or some such. Likely they'd met up when Ned Gray had been hunting and trapping around these parts while he was clearing land and building a cabin so that he could bring his wife and daughter down from Virginia.

There were times when Laura suspected he still preferred the life of a hunter and trapper—not that he ever let on. Still, she couldn't help but notice a certain look in his eyes now and then, when he gazed into the forest or out across the river toward the island where he had once had a fishing shack. As if he'd like to disappear for another few years and not have to worry about stumps and corn ricks and washing up before he came inside the cabin.

Men were strange. They took a lot more understanding than women.

Nearing the cabin, Laura glanced back over her shoulder, hoping to catch a glimpse of one of her father's Indian friends. She couldn't help but be curious. There had been so few of them in the town in Virginia where they had lived before they'd moved south, and Mary Gray had always hurried her daughter inside whenever one of the local Indians had strayed too close to their house.

According to the Harker boys, whose farm lay halfway along the road to Packwood's Crossing, the wild'uns hereabouts wandered in and out of a body's house like chickens if the door wasn't kept shut. Not that they did any harm, at least as far as she'd ever heard. They were more like children, according to Addie Harker—nosing about for sweets, touching anything bright and shiny that happened to catch their eye.

Laura had purposely left the door open once or twice, half hoping one of the strange wild creatures would show its face. Seeing them from a distance, they reminded her of the deer that snuck up to feed on the kitchen garden. She'd always wanted to get her hands on a fawn, or even a full grown doe, but they were too shy and much too quick for her.

She shoved open the door and poked her head inside. "Mama, we're done stumping. I'll be back to help with supper soon's I wash this dust off. Lor', I wish it would rain!"

"Been a while," said Edward Gray by way of greeting. "Almost didn't recognize you, boy."

"You have become a planter." Stormwalker's smile was guarded. He knew and respected this man, but both of them had changed in the three years since last they had met. He had not missed the way his old friend had sent the woman away.

Nor could he blame him. Times were changing, too.

"Aye, I reckon it don't set none too good on your folks, all this clearing and planting, but it ain't about to change back the way it was for no man." Without seeming to, Edward studied the man who had been his companion on many a pleasurable hunt. He was tall for a wild'un, but then, he was half English. Pity he had decided to live wild instead of going on with his schooling. A man like Stormwalker could have gone far if he'd been of a mind to. "No sir, it ain't likely to change back. 'Times I wish it would."

"And I, my friend." Stormwalker's gaze moved beyond the older man to follow the slight, golden-haired figure hurrying toward the cabin. "Your woman?"

"My daughter. Wish to God she'd been a son, but she's a hard worker for all she ain't much bigger'n a tadpole. Your folks faring all right?"

"The hunters must go farther to find game. The women demand salt and cloth and sweets from Packwood's Store. As you say, times change."

"Aye, they do that," murmured Ned Gray, and both men knew that they were speaking of more than the lack of game and the demands of women.

Stormwalker watched as the girl disappeared in the long shadows that reached out across the clearing, only to reappear again in a flood of golden sunlight. He had been silently observing the pair of them for some time before he had let himself be seen, fascinated, in spite of himself, with the stubborn look of determination on so small a face, the glint of laughter in the wide-set gray eyes.

More fascinated than was comfortable by the glimpse of a pale rounded thigh when she had slung one leg over the sapling.

Deliberately, he forced himself to think of Kitappi. Soon he would have to speak to Kokom about her bride price. A man needed a woman to warm his sleeping mat and Kitappi, for all her foolishness, would make a good wife. Both Kokom and his own father would be pleased.

A shaft of sunlight struck the girl's hair, setting it alight as she picked her barefooted way along the edge of the forest. Stormwalker knew he was staring. Men had been killed for less, especially if they happened to be red and the woman in question white. Yet he could not seem to tear his gaze away until the slender figure was finally swallowed up by the long purple shadows.

Reluctantly, he turned his attention to the wiry man with the graying hair. Edward removed his battered beaver hat, mopped his brow and carefully replaced his hat again. If he had noticed Stormwalker's startlingly blue eyes following his daughter, Ned gave no sign. "Trouble?" he grunted.

"Trouble." Wrenching his mind back to the matter that had brought him out of his way to warn his friend, Stormwalker summed up the decisions reached by the latest war council. "Five tomahawks were buried in the council post last night. The upper Tuscarora will stay with Chief Blunt.

Your man in Virginia is once more trying to negotiate a treaty.''

"Spottswood's a fair man. What about the lower Tuskies?" Edward knew something of the ever-shifting loyalties that both divided and joined these complex people. "They're walking awful close to the edge, Stormwalker. Your people ain't fighters and you know it."

"My people are not of the Tuscarora. They will remain friends with the English as long as the English do not renounce that friendship. Hancock controls the Mattamuskeet, the Coranine, all the Bay Tribes—''

"In other words, that mangy old hound controls damn near ever' redskin south of the Pamticoe," Edward Gray put in angrily.

"As you say, damn near, my friend. But not all," the tall, blue-eyed half-breed said quietly. "Hancock is determined to drive the English back where they came from. He will no longer be told that he cannot hunt on lands where his grandfathers hunted."

Stewed salt pork for supper. Laura could smell it as soon as she opened the door, the rich aroma mingling with the scent of firewood and the fresh mud and moss they'd used to chink between the logs. It was a good smell, a familiar one, yet somehow, it didn't seem as comforting tonight.

When her father came in, having scrubbed down at the barrel outside, she waited for him to tell them about his visitor, but he said nothing, and after a while, she forgot. They talked of the corn waiting to be ricked and the chance of rain.

"Dry as a bone all summer and now it's a-gonna rain afore I get that corn put up and covered, you wait and see."

"Leastwise you'll be able to break ground come spring. I declare the dust gets into everything!"

"Pa, you want some more honey for your bread?"

They discussed the new root cellar, which even now was half filled with the last of the fruit not even off the trees yet.

"Feels so cool down there, I might even take to sleeping there. Ned, reckon we could dig it out a little bigger?"

"Not till I get that corn ricked, woman. I laid off to get me another ox come spring. Reckon I'd better see to fencing in a place. Daughter, I'd be obliged if you'd give my spade a few turns of the stone while I check the turtle trap. Reckon we got just about enough light left for one more chore."

Long after the last chore was done that night, Laura lay on her pallet, unable to sleep in spite of being so weary she ached all over. The sound of her father's low voice from the bed across the room drifted in and out of her consciousness as he grumbled about the deer that broke through all manner of fencing to browse on the winter greens and then disappeared as soon as he got his gun.

She heard him say the word *trouble* and shrugged it off. There was always talk of trouble, in good times or bad. If it rained, some folks looked for floods; come a drought, they watched for wildfires. Planters were the worst of the lot, but the womenfolk were little better. Let a woman swell with child and tongues would start clacking like a gaggle of guineas. Counting on fingers. If the poor woman was safely wed, then the talk would be of signs. Three hoots of an owl on a new moon and the babe would be stillborn. If the corn crop failed, there'd be naught but girl babes born until the new harvest.

Hearing the quiet rustle of cornshucks from the double pallet across the room, Laura told herself that seventeen years ago, the corn crop must have been awful. After she'd been born, Ned and Mary had tried twice more for a son, only to be given two more daughters, one of whom had been stillborn, the other having died of fever before she was a year old.

At times, Laura couldn't help but feel guilty for being female, when her pa needed great strapping sons to help clear and tend the land. Not by word nor deed had he ever let on, but it was plain to see the way his eyes followed the Harker boys whenever they stopped by on their way into town. She was too small to be much use, but no matter how much she ate, she couldn't seem to grow any bigger.

Not that Coby Packwood would have been much more help, no matter what Pa thought. She'd felt guilty over turning down his offer of marriage, but it wasn't just because she knew Coby would never have left his parents' store and come to live on the farm.

It was Coby, himself. For all his blond good looks, and he was a stout and handsome young man, she couldn't bring herself to think of—doing *that* with him. And married folks did. It was what made babies. She'd been wanting to talk to her mother about it for a long time now, but whenever she'd brought up the subject, her mother would find something that had to be done right that very minute, until finally Laura had given up.

When the time came that she needed to know, Mary had said the last time Laura had hinted at the matter, then she'd know. Nature took care of these things. It weren't nothing for decent people to talk about in broad daylight.

Bone weary, Laura finally slept. She was up again before daybreak to get the fire hetted up for her mother. After rolling up her pallet, she went outside and splashed off her face in the rain barrel, shivering in her shift and her oldest gown. The mornings seldom varied—while her father went out to check the trotline or the rabbit traps, her mother would commence boiling up the bacon and hominy and Laura would grind the roasted chicory and dandelion roots and set them to simmering for coffee.

They planned the day over the morning meal. "I'll help tote the apples down to the cellar when we get done in the field, Ma. Wait for me, you hear?"

"There's only two more baskets. Ned, if you want one o' them rabbits for supper, you'd best sharpen my skinning knife. I used it to dig up the last of the onions day before yesterday, and that ground's just like a brick. Laura, scrape the last of that hominy into the turtle barrel when you go outside."

Laura wrinkled her nose. Much as she hated the task of scalding and cleaning the wretched creatures, she liked turtle meat above all. There were always one or two snappers in the barrel, being fed on cornmeal and greens to clean out the musky flavor before she cut off their heads.

Would a son do such chores? It was not the first time Laura had asked herself the question. A son might be good for stumping and clearing and even running traps and trot-lines, but it was always the womenfolk who ended up doing the messy work.

Edward Gray had just reached for his hat when he suddenly froze. His eyes went to his musket, which he had loaded and left beside the hearth the night before, somewhat to Laura's surprise. "Some'un's coming," he said softly. "Mary, you'n the girl take them apples down to the cellar. *Now.*"

Laura's eyes widened. She had never heard her father use that particular tone before. Nor had she seen that particular look on his face. It was a guarded look—not exactly frightened, but alert. Aware.

There was the sound of a horse's hooves on the hard earth, and then a man's voice cried out, "Ned Gray! Grab your womenfolk and get out o' there, quick!"

At the trapdoor, the two women looked at each other and then at Edward, who snatched up his musket and opened the door a crack. "Hold a minute," he whispered over his shoulder.

"Isn't that James Burrus?" Laura asked in a low voice.

Ignoring her, Edward called out, "What's going on, James?"

The high-pitched voice was clearly audible to the two women inside. "Find som'ers to hide quick, Ned—them bloody red bastards is burning ever'thing in sight!"

"Which ones?"

"Hell, it don't matter, does it? One lot's as bad as the next! I'm headed for Thompson's, and then I'm going to try to make it back to Packwood's Store. With enough men and guns, we can likely hold 'em off till help comes."

"The cellar?" whispered Mary, her gray eyes stricken.

"Not if they're a-burning," Edward said tersely. "Fetch a blanket and whatever food you can carry, we'll head for the island!"

It was as if Laura were frozen. It was as if she were no more substantial than a shadow, looking on while two strangers rushed around the familiar room, snatching up whatever came to hand.

"Move, girl!" screamed quiet Mary Gray, who never raised her voice.

"We'll be safe enough—ain't no wild'un likely to come sniffin' around Bad Medicine Island. My old huntin' shack'll give us some cover till this thing dies down. Hurry, woman, don' bother with the rest of that meat! I'd rather keep my hair than have a full belly!"

At the last minute, Laura's paralysis broke. Running her hands along the pegs on the wall, she grabbed all the clothes she could lay hands on and then grabbed the still-hot kettle off the hearth.

They burst through the door at once, with Ned practically dragging his wife along with him, trusting his daughter to keep up. The way to the river, where he kept a small open boat, was a well-trodden path that wound crookedly through a stand of giant cypress trees to the dark clear waters of the Pamticoe River.

This isn't happening. It's all a dream. I went to sleep last night thinking about the wild'uns, and now I'm dreaming something awful—something that can't be true. Any moment now I'll wake up and it will be time to go stir up the fire and grind the morning coffee.

Just as she reached the turn in the path that hid the river from the cabin, Laura turned back for one last look in the gray light of dawn. Her lungs were splitting, and she drew in a deep breath, clutching the bundle that held clothing, the kettle and her mother's dull skinning knife.

There was something frighteningly different about the cool gray air. Above the familiar smell of river and sun-baked trees, stronger even than the scent of ripening grapes, she could smell smoke. Not the friendly smoke of cook-fires, but a different kind of smoke.

"Laura! Hurry, child," screamed Mary Gray, and then, before the sound of her voice died away, there came another sound.

It was soft—not at all alarming in itself, yet Laura felt her flesh crawl. *"Mama,"* she whispered; and her feet fairly flew.

She didn't hear the thud of a falling body nor the broken curse and the second thud. She heard only the sound of her own pounding feet, her own half-voiced prayer, and then she heard nothing.

There was the stench; and then there was the pain. And then there was nothing.

Later she would remember clawing at the naked arm that grabbed her from behind when she had run toward her mother's fallen body, choking off her air. She would even remember being swung up off the ground, kicking out wildly and feeling her heels connect with something hard and slippery, but for a long time afterward, she remembered only the stench. And the pain.

Later she would remember biting down hard on the hand that covered her mouth, gagging at the taste of filthy, greasy flesh and hearing a guttural voice grunt something in an unintelligible tongue. She would even remember the brilliant burst of light just before the whole world winked out.

But there were some things she would never remember, which was just as well.

The light was different when Laura opened her eyes again. That knowledge came the instant before she saw him. He was kneeling over her, his face dark and angular and terrifying in its cold anger. His eyes were like the hottest part of a flame, where it burned blue.

His hands were on her shoulders. One of them touched her face.

For a single instant, the fear let go and she felt the pain. Her head—God, what had he done to her head? And her legs—but most of all, the narrow passage between her thighs. She was burning there as if she had been torn apart and rubbed with salt.

He was going to kill her, and she couldn't move—couldn't do anything but lie here and stare up into those cold, burning eyes.

A drop of moisture fell on her face, and then another one. It was raining. *Raining!* And she was lying on the ground with a naked savage bending over her, while her mother...

"Mama? P-Papa?" she cried, only no sound emerged from her lips. Her fingers curled into small fists, one hand closing over the kettle that had fallen from her bundle. She clutched it and, without thinking, she brought it up viciously right into the savage's face.

He fell back and she quickly scrambled away, crawling on her hands and knees. For a moment they stared at each other. He was bleeding. She had cut him. She hoped to God she had killed him!

What had he done to her? Where was her mother? She'd been waiting for Laura to catch up—resting beside the path...

Laura shook her head in an effort to clear it, but the pain only made the dizziness worse.

It was raining. For the first time in months, it was raining, and she was getting all wet—her hair, her clothes, her...

Dear God, she was naked!

"P-Papa?" It hurt to speak. It hurt to move. Carefully, she turned back to stare at the savage, who was still kneeling where she had left him when she'd hit him and rolled away. "What have you done to them?"

He made a move to rise, and she scrambled back, wishing she could lay hands on the knife. "Get away from me! One step closer and I'll kill you! What have you done with Papa? Where is my mother?"

Without waiting for an answer, she managed to get to her feet. She had to get away—back to the house! She ran, stumbling blindly into trees, tangling with vines. She tripped over a cypress knee and kept going, expecting at any moment to feel filthy hands closing around her throat.

If only she could reach the cabin, she would be safe. They would all be safe, she told herself over and over as she stumbled the last few feet to the smoldering cabin. The thick cloud of dark, acrid smoke made breathing difficult, but not until she fell into the open door did Laura realize that it was on fire.

The cellar, she thought with a clarity born of hysteria. Root cellars couldn't burn. They were made of dirt. She would hide here until he went away, and then she would find a boat and go to the island. Her parents had simply gone on ahead. Her mother had been so tired—she'd been lying beside the path, resting.

Somewhere, she could hear a voice crooning over and over, "No, no, no, no, no..."

She rubbed her eyes. They were burning with tears—tears and the thick smoke that was everywhere. The chimney wasn't drawing properly—it never did with an east wind, but it was the east wind that always brought the rain.

And it was raining, all right. After five bone-dry months, it was finally coming down fit to beat the devil. Good thing she was naked as a day-old possum, else her gown would be sopping wet.

Actually, she wasn't really naked, she observed with unnatural clarity. There was a scrap of muslin about her waist and part of a sleeve on one arm. How strange—where could she have been going wearing only a waistband and one sleeve?

Stiffly, she sat there, her gray eyes wide and strangely blank. Overhead, the fire that had smoldered for two hours, slowly went out. A timber fell, shaking dirt down through the plank floor onto her bloodstained hair.

Stormwalker cursed silently as he lowered the two bodies into a single grave. He had warned him—hadn't he warned him? Why hadn't the stubborn old fool left last night while there was time? He could have made it to the garrison in Bath Towne easily enough.

He wiped a forearm across his sweating brow and felt the salt sting the gash above his right eye. He probably should have gone after her, but she'd been too frightened to listen to reason. Like all her kind, she thought one redskin was as bad as another. She wouldn't have known the difference between him and Three Turtle if the two of them had been standing side by side.

He had let her go, knowing she would come to no harm for the moment, and then he had set about burying her parents. No girl, especially one who had just been brutally attacked and left for dead herself, should have to look on her parents' mutilated bodies. It was possible her wits had already been shattered beyond redemption.

Thinking of the golden hair, the clear gray eyes and the smooth slender body that had quickened his heartbeat only yesterday, Stormwalker lifted his face to the rain. That bright hair was now stained with blood and dirt. The gray eyes that had danced with laughter and grown hazy with dreams as she swung on the end of a long pole were now dark with pain. Mindless.

For a long moment he allowed the rain to cool his hatred, and then he set to work covering the wide, deep grave. Tucked under his belt was a beaded headband with two feathers, each distinctly notched and each bearing the dull color of turtle blood.

After a while he went back to the cabin in search of a bit of wood with which to fashion a cross. The girl might find comfort in knowing someone had said words over her parents' grave—although he wasn't sure what the Great Kishalamaquon had in mind for the spirits of his two paleskinned children.

Once the marker was finished, he went to find the girl, so that she could know that her parents had been decently laid to rest.

He would have to take her away, of course, but where? To her own people? It was no longer safe for any red man to show his face near a white settlement. Seven settlers had been burned out, their families murdered in a single night of raids.

He could take her to his own village, but she might not be willing to go. Knowing the danger, they might not be willing to take her in. Even if they were willing, she would probably be terrified by the sight of anyone with skin darker than her own. If she refused to accept his help, all he could do was go to her people, dressed as John Walker, and tell them what had happened. They would come for her. She would be cared for.

And then he would go after Three Turtle.

There was a footstep overhead, and then silence. Laura jumped at the sound of the creaking board. Someone was up there. Who? The man who had done this awful thing or a neighbor—a friend?

She was afraid to call out and afraid not to. Reason was slowly returning, and reason told her she could not stay here alone.

The trap door opened, and she burrowed deeper under the shelf of turnips. Covering her mouth with her hands, she watched the ladder. It was so dark, she could hardly see, but there was no mistaking the gleam of a naked leg that descended into her hiding place.

It was *him*! That savage devil! He had come for her, but she was ready for him. The sharpened blade her father had used to cut through roots when he was digging the cellar had still been here, and now it was clutched in her hand. She would have but one chance before his strength overcame her, but she was not afraid of him.

Come on, you heathen devil—come closer. My mother wasn't resting, I know that now—and Pa would never have gone off and left her. You killed them. Just like you tried to kill me. Come closer, just a little bit closer, that's all I ask.

As the shadowy form descended the ladder and paused to look around, she gripped the iron tool in both hands, raising it level with her shoulders. The moment he turned his back, she would be on him. Wretched, murdering animal, he had crawled all over her and torn at her private flesh. She had waked with his filth in her nostrils!

"Come closer," she murmured under her breath. "One step closer."

Stormwalker saw her almost immediately, her pale flesh glowing in the darkness as if she were lighted from within. He controlled the urge to gather her in his arms and comfort her. He could sense her fear from where he stood.

They stared at each other in the darkness, neither daring to speak. He could not see her eyes now, but when she had first opened them after he had found her, they had been the eyes of a *roccomne*, one whose wits had been stolen away.

He moved a step closer, watching her as he might have watched an animal he was bent on taming. He could smell her fear above the acrid smoke of the smoldering logs.

And then slowly, he held out his hand.

She moved faster than he would have believed possible, unwinding her small body like a snake to strike out at him. There was the flash of a blade, the sound of her indrawn breath, and he stepped back, his arm still extended.

Blood welled from his dusky flesh. For a moment, neither of them moved. And then, without a word, Stormwalker turned and made his way up the ladder, leaving the *waurraupa* woman alone with her fear and sorrow.

Chapter Two

Stormwalker removed the linen shirt. He took off the buckskin trousers and rolled them up in a tight bundle, cramming them into the black, wide-brimmed hat. He despised the garments, but at times they were necessary. Flexing his powerful shoulders, he relished the freedom for a moment, and then he knelt beside the river and dipped his head in the water. A stain of red flowed away with the current, leaving the shoulder-length tresses as black as the wing of a raven.

As John Walker, he had spoken to the elder Packwood, who had promised to go after the girl. Now Stormwalker would go after the man who had raped her.

The rain had stopped, but the swamps would be full. If Three Turtle had crossed the river and gone back to his own village of Seconiac, he would be difficult to follow.

But perhaps he had turned southward, instead. There were fifty-eight fighting men in the town of Raudauguaquank. There were some fifteen more at the place called Island, the Pamticoe's chief town. All were within half a day's easy traveling. And like Three Turtle's people, the Mattamuskeets, all had cast their lot with Hancock.

With no outward sign of emotion, the tall half-breed drew a narrow dugout from its hiding place beneath a fall of thick vines. Kneeling on the stubby bow, he shoved off from the bank and reached for the paddle, deftly turning the canoe toward the opposite shore.

He would go to Seconiac first. He had once walked unafraid into Seconiac, into Raudaugua-quank and Island, as well as many other towns. Once, he had known no enemies. That time was no longer.

In a cellar beneath a half-burned cabin, Laura ventured out of her hiding place. She had no notion of how much time had passed—with every breath she'd drawn, she'd expected to see that gleaming naked leg on the ladder—expected to feel another blow of his fist on her head.

Nothing had happened. No noises—not even the hoot of an owl.

Daylight had come and gone, and finally, knowing she could not remain buried forever, she tiptoed over to the ladder and commenced to climb, her knees trembling so much they could barely support her.

For a small eternity she stood and stared at the gaping hole in the roof. Part of one wall had been burned before the rain had put out the fire. In her shattered condition, it never occurred to her that if it hadn't been for the rain, the cabin would have burned to the ground, the ruins falling in on her head.

How proud her father had been of his handiwork. He had fashioned a real plank floor, because Mary could never abide dust. Now the floor, the shake roof—all those hours of plastering with mud and driving moss into the cracks between the logs, gone for nothing.

Forcing herself to move, Laura slipped out the open door and waited for death to strike. When it didn't, she ventured farther. It was while she was following the trail of scattered garments on the way to the river that she came upon the fresh grave where no grave had been before. She would never even have seen it if the moon hadn't come from behind a cloud and reflected off the wooden cross.

She knew in her heart what it was. Who lay buried in that rich, dark earth. It took another moment for the reality of it to sink in, and when it did, she caught her breath. Dear God, someone had come while she'd been hiding in the cellar! Someone had found the bodies of her parents and buried them!

Kneeling, she reached out to the crude marker, as if to find something of her parents in the rough wood. And then, silently, she began to weep. She wept for a long time. When there were no more tears left inside her, she began to curse. Still kneeling, she cursed their senseless death—cursed the fact that whichever neighbor had come to their aid had come too late.

She neither wept nor cursed that whoever had come to bury them had not taken time to search for her. It simply didn't occur to her.

The moon was beginning to sink in the western sky when she finally rose and dried her eyes. Not bothering with shift or petticoat, she put on her best gown—the only one she had left now—and bundled the rest in the blanket to take with her. It was late. The boat would need bailing, and if she hoped to reach Bad Medicine Island before the moon set, she would have to hurry.

How remarkably well her mind was working now. It was as if the light wind that had cleared the clouds from the sky had cleared the clouds from her mind. She knew what she had to do and felt perfectly capable of doing it. The island couldn't be that hard to find—it was the largest one out there, and the only one that was wooded. If memory served her, it lay on the right, just at the mouth of the river. And although three years had elapsed since the one time she'd visited her father's fishing camp, it should be simple enough to locate once she'd reached the island.

As the moon slipped in and out of the clouds on its westward journey, Laura tossed the bailing gourd aside and reached for one of the crudely carved oars. The wood felt dry and splintery in her hands from long disuse.

The cabin—where had it been located? On the inland side of the island; or the other side?

Never mind, she would find it. Her father had taught her to be self-reliant. He had wanted a son and he had treated her like a son. Thank God she could do more than spin and weave, cook and bear babies. Because until she felt safe venturing on the mainland again, the island would be her home and there would be no Packwood's Store to supply what she couldn't provide for herself.

The open boat, which was broadly built and difficult for one of Laura's slight stature to control, twisted in the tidal current, and she began to curse again, a bit surprised at the length of her vocabulary. But then, she, too, had driven the oxen, who paid no mind to a politely worded command.

Soon she was cursing not only the boat but the loss of her parents, her home—of everything she held dear.

He would pay, she vowed as she pitched her entire weight into the task of rowing. Never would she forget those sharply angled cheekbones, the high-bridged nose, that cruel, twisted mouth.

And the eyes. She had thought all red Indians had black eyes, but she could almost swear his eyes had been blue. The same shade of blue that sometimes showed when a fire was dying.

As he would die. She hadn't seen him the first time—he'd struck from behind so swiftly she hadn't even had time to scream. But she would never forget the look of rage on his face when she'd opened her eyes to find him still on top of her.

Nor had she been able to see him clearly when he'd climbed down the ladder to the cellar. She'd seen enough to know that he was tall—taller even than Coby Packwood. If she ever saw him again she would know him. If not by his height or by those wicked blue eyes, then by the two scars she had given him, one above his eye and another on his forearm.

Perhaps she had killed him, she thought with a lift of spirits. Perhaps the blow to his head had been harder than she realized. Perhaps even now his wounds were festering and soon the poison would eat right through his evil body and he would die a slow and agonizing death.

Twitching her shoulders, Laura bent to the task at hand. There would be time to devise a means of revenge when she had got herself to safety.

The journey was taking longer than she had expected. While she was fairly sure of the direction, with the moon playing tag with the clouds, it was impossible to be certain she was steering a proper course. What if the tide carried her past the island and she drifted out into the middle of the Pamticoe Sound?

By the time she felt the bow of the boat bump against something solid, she was too relieved to care what it was. Her hands were raw, her head was throbbing and her back was fit to break. Instinct alone had guided her for the past hour.

Either she'd reached Bad Medicine Island or she'd run aground on a point jutting out from the mainland. Farther out she could see a streak of silver on the horizon where the moon had broken through the clouds. Behind her was only water, with the south bank no more than a shadow and the north bank not even that.

She had reached the island. Suddenly, she was certain of it. Now all she had to do was locate her father's old fishing shack without getting lost in the woods or blundering into a bog.

Without warning, the intolerable burden of the past nine hours descended heavily on her shoulders. The sheer terror that had driven her for so long deserted her, and she rested her forehead on the rough gun'le and closed her eyes.

Tomorrow. Tomorrow would be soon enough to search for the cabin . . . if there was a tomorrow.

Laura awoke to the gentle motion of the boat, which had slewed around in the tide and was gradually working its way free of the sandy beach. Her mind still befogged with sleep, she pushed her hair out of her eyes, threw off the blanket that had protected her from dew and mosquitos and climbed stiffly over the side, throwing her negligible weight against the side of the heavy craft.

The water was warm—it felt remarkably good and she was tempted to lower herself in the shallows and let the sun bake down on her sore back until she found the strength to go on.

It took no more than the sting of water on her abused palms to change her mind. At least the sharp pain brought her fully awake. Other aches made themselves known as she set about bundling up her few possessions. The lump on the side of her head explained her headache. The unexpected task of rowing explained why the muscles of her back protested each time she bent over.

But there was another hurt that worried her more—the soreness in the most private parts of her body. Yet, even that was nothing compared to the aching emptiness of her heart.

Over the next few days, Laura became familiar with every foot of her island domain. It was shaped roughly like the sole of a boot, with the heel facing the mainland and the toe pointing roughly southeast, as nearly as she could tell from the prevailing winds. On the low end, where she'd hidden the boat, dead trees, driftwood and other debris had washed downriver and collected in an untidy jumble. She saw two muskrat slides and marked them in her mind.

Following the shore on what seemed to be generally an eastward trek, she paused now and then to mark the position of a distinctive tree, so that she would remember where she had left the boat.

She could have rowed around the island and left the boat nearer the cabin, but the very thought made her flinch. She could walk well enough. At least her feet didn't hurt.

Her feet! Lor', she hadn't thought to fetch her shoes from the box where she kept them over the summer. She would have to go back...

No. Her shoes could wait.

She spotted the crudely built chimney first and hurried through the underbrush. Tears threatened as she recalled hearing her father laugh about bartering for a load of ballast rocks to be dumped on the deserted island, and then having to convince the shipmaster that he hadn't lost his wits.

Just before she reached the cabin, she came to the freshwater pond. She had clean forgot about water. What if it had gone dry? Or filled in? It might not rain again for weeks, and this close to the sound, the river water was sometimes too salty to drink, although it did well enough for cooking.

Cooking... First she would have to find something to cook. She'd brought along a few apples from the two baskets waiting to be taken to the cellar, and what was left of the side of bacon her mother had cut for breakfast yesterday.

Had it been only yesterday? she thought as pain nearly swamped her again.

Lifting her chin, she marched on. Apples and bacon. After that she would have to catch fish, using whatever equipment her father had left. There would probably be grapes— and there were oaks in the center of the island, so acorns should be plentiful.

The first thing she noticed on entering the rude, musty shelter were the traps hanging by the hearth. They were badly rusted, in spite of having been coated with lard. But that wasn't the worst of it—they were enormous! It would take a strength far greater than hers to pry apart those jaws.

The first night she couldn't sleep. Standing on the nearby shore, she saw first one and then another fire spring up on the mainland. A low cry escaped her as she realized what that meant.

Hurrying back inside, she closed the sagging door as tightly as it would go, only to have one of the leather hinges give way altogether.

Had anyone survived? Was everyone dead? Had the savages finally driven out all the English?

Or were the soldiers burning the Indian towns?

The next night, strangely enough, her thoughts turned to Coby Packwood. She ate the last half apple and thought of the sweets his mother sometimes made to sell in the store. What would have happened if she'd accepted Coby's offer of marriage? She might have been safe with his family at the store, for surely the savages wouldn't have tried to burn all of Packwood's Crossing. There were seven houses there, with more than enough men to defend them.

But her parents would not have been there with her. Unless Coby could have convinced them to move into town until the troubles died down, they would still have been alone on the farm. And as her father had never cared overly much for George Packwood, that didn't seem likely under any event.

Coby... Laura sighed, wondering if he was all right. Perhaps she should have been less abrupt in her refusal, but she'd been taken by surprise. Her mother and his had been friends, even though her mother seldom got to town, but it had never occurred to her to look on Coby as a suitor. She had never had a suitor, but if she ever had one, she knew instinctively it would not be Coby Packwood.

Marriage. The thought of being touched by a man—any man—made her shudder.

The following days were filled with hard work, which left Laura too exhausted to do more than fall into a deep, dreamless sleep at night. Without consciously dwelling on the matter, she began to come to terms with the loss of her parents. It was hardly the first time she had known death at close hand. First there had been the loss of her three grandparents, the other having died when she was too young to remember. She'd been five years old when her infant sister had died, but she remembered the aching sense of loss.

Gathering fruit and acorns, patiently catching bait and then using it to catch something larger, Laura found she could go for hours without crying. There was so much to be done to make the cabin habitable, for it had been in dreadful repair.

The hard work helped. It kept her from thinking of what must be happening on the mainland. It helped her to sleep through the night without reliving the horror.

As the days passed, she kept a constant vigil along the river, seeing only the occasional canoe, and none that came close to the island. Even the larger schooners that plied between Bath Towne and the Indies or those that carried car-

goes from Europe that came into the deep-water ports of
Virginia seemed to be avoiding the river.

She judged two weeks to have passed—at first she hadn't
thought to keep count—when she saw the fleet of canoes,
some of them enormous, bearing at least thirty or forty
men.

She had risen early to check the net she had just finished
mending and set out the night before where her father's old
poles still stood.

"Always set your net before a changing wind," her father used to say. The wind had not changed—there wasn't
a breath of wind from any direction. The net was rotten, and
her mending less than perfect, but if it snagged a single fish,
it would be well worth the labor.

There was a mist rising from the water, for nearing October, the night air was cool while the water still held the
summer's warmth. It was when a patch of mist cleared that
she caught sight of them—dozens, perhaps more—skimming along silently like ghosts rising from the mist.

Sinking down in the water, gown and all, she prayed for
them to pass on by. Thank God for Bad Medicine Island!
She was safe as long as superstition kept the wild'uns from
coming too near. Soon she was going to have to risk leaving, for she couldn't stay here forever. She had thought the
trouble might be dying down, for there had been no more
fires burning in the night.

Now she was afraid all over again. Afraid to go, afraid to
stay. She had no one to depend on but herself, and with each
day that passed, she had been faced with another of her
shortcomings. She wasn't the greatest hand at fishing—she
couldn't open a trap; she wasn't even sure she would want
to, although she had eaten her share of muskrat and possum and could skin one out as cleanly as her father could.

If only she had been born a man instead of a woman,
none of this would have happened! They would all be safe
at home right now.

She tried to ignore the small voice that whispered that her
father had been a man and that had been no protection.

Another thing about being a woman—she would soon be needing rags for her monthly flow, which was due most any day now. If she'd brought along an overdress or even an apron, she would have been well off, but panniers and aprons and frilled caps were not the least help in swinging from saplings and grubbing up stumps, and so she had put them away for her infrequent trips into town.

She would have to go back home—there was nothing else for it.

Chapter Three

Like most men who lived near the water, Laura's father, Edward Gray, had been a skilled fisherman as well as a hunter and planter. His family had enjoyed all manner of seafood as well as game, fowl and vegetables from their own garden. His daughter, on the other hand, was discovering that she had not learned nearly so much as she had thought about providing for her needs. Oh, there were mussels that tasted of mud, grapes that were mostly seeds and thick hulls—and even those she had to fight the birds for. She had caught one skinny fish in the past two days, and that so bony she could hardly eat it!

It was too calm. Her father had always sworn it took a wind to bring fish into a net. She couldn't even lure them there with bits of mussel flesh. There wasn't a cloud in the sky that might hold a breath of wind that would bring in the fish. At this rate, she would soon be too weak to get herself back to the mainland.

Once ashore, she could walk to the Harkers' farm in less than two hours' time—especially if she left the cart track and took to the woods. They would be shocked to find her still alive, but they would surely welcome her. If it had been their house that had been burned to the ground, Ma and Pa would gladly have taken them in. All seven of them. Charles, the oldest Harker boy, was nineteen—a year older than Laura. Once she had even thought of marrying him, but he'd never asked her. Addie Harker would have welcomed a daughter's hand in the house. With all those boys to look after, she could have done with an army of daughters.

Laura could never marry now, of course. Oh, the soreness had passed quickly enough. Times she could even forget the horror of what had happened to her. But then it would come back and she would remember opening her eyes and knowing that she was somehow—changed.

It had happened. That filthy savage had done *that* to her; and now she could never marry, even if she had wanted to. What decent man would have a woman who had been used by a filthy red savage?

Laura shook off the feeling of depression. What couldn't be changed must be accepted. She'd had that homily preached to her from the time she had first climbed up on top of the fowl roost and jumped off, confident that all she had to do was spread her arms to fly.

She was alive, after all. That was something.

The sky was the deep shade of blue that came only in early autumn, and Laura took a moment to rejoice that it wasn't the dead of winter. Overhead, sea gulls wheeled and swooped, while the whole island fairly bristled with song birds squabbling over the grapevines and the wild seeds that abounded near the marshes.

Before setting out, she took the precaution of wrapping her palms with strips torn off her mother's spare apron. That left her with only one blanket, her gown and shift and a single petticoat.

She had not thought to wait until the tide was with her, and so it took longer than she'd expected before she snubbed the boat down at her father's old mooring post. Before she did anything else, she must see her parents' grave. It had been dark before and she'd been too distraught to take in more than the fact that someone had buried them together in a single grave.

Or perhaps they hadn't. Perhaps old Willy Harker, or whoever had found them, had buried them separately but found only enough wood for a single cross. There was wood a-plenty, but he would have been too frightened to linger.

She was still pondering the matter when she came to the small knoll just off the path. There, shock anchored her feet to the path.

Three crosses? But there had only been one. And there were only supposed to be *two*. Had Willy come back, after all, and brought enough wood to make another marker?

But why three? Who else had died here? Who else would have been buried on her father's land, so close to his own grave?

There were no names, and the crosses were of pine, which wouldn't last out the winter. Poor old Willy—he had never struck her as overly bright, for all he had managed to sire a fine set of sons.

At least it meant that the Harkers—or someone—had survived. As for why anyone would set up three markers when only two people had been buried, she couldn't venture a guess.

Unless the savage had come back and someone had shot him and then buried him alongside her parents.

No! Her mind refused to accept such a thing. No one, not even old Willy, would have buried that evil creature alongside his victims. It was—it was unholy, that's what it was!

Besides, Laura admitted with a certain amount of surprise—she didn't want him shot. She wanted to be the one to see that he paid for his wicked deeds.

Fighting tears, she stared at the three nameless crosses. Already a russet carpet of leaves had fallen to soften the raw earth. Three crosses. Soon she would have to see to proper markers, with the names cut deep enough for all to read. Some day she would have to discover the truth of that third cross, but there was no time now. All the wondering in the world wouldn't bring them back.

Nor would it put food in her belly, she reminded herself firmly.

The cabin had burned to the ground. Somehow, it seemed even more final than those three crosses overlooking the river.

There had been fires all along the shore a night or two after—afterward. Camp fires, she had told herself, but in her heart, she had known.

She stared at the ruins, deliberately fixing the awful sight in her mind. Breathing in the faint acrid smell of things burned that were never meant to be burnt.

There was nothing left. Her home, her parents . . . gone. Nor would things ever again be the way they had been. She must face that fact and go on, or she might as well claim the third cross for herself.

Shoulders braced, Laura set out along the cart track for the Harkers'. Her boots—dammit, her boots had burned and winter was coming on, she thought, irrationally choosing the smaller loss to keep from being devastated by the greater one.

It was a long walk, but she was accustomed to walking. Even before she came in sight of the cabin, she recognized the peculiar sour burnt smell that hung in the air. Dear God, not the Harkers, too! Not sweet Addie and silly old Willy—not Charles with his sweet, slow smile, and Thomas with his squint eye and his clever mind—not the twins, Seth and Joshua, with their gap-toothed grins and their unending love of a good prank.

The Willetts were next, near on three miles down the road toward Packwood's Crossing. Andrew Willett kept the mill, and Pa had always dropped off two sacks of corn on their way into town, one to be ground for their own use and one to trade for flour.

The miller Willett's cabin was only partially burned. From the gaping door, a scrap of once-white cloth, now gray and tattered, stirred fitfully in the breeze like a lonely old woman who had been left behind, waiting for death to return and claim her, too. The mill had been destroyed, and there were still traces of flour on the ground after more than a week.

Laura felt as if she had aged a hundred years in a single day. There was no need to look farther. It had finally come then, after all the rumors—rumors which she had discounted because Pa had always told her the wild'uns were just as civilized as any Christians, wanting only to be left alone to hunt, to fish and to raise their families in peace.

"Now, George," he would say, "it don't do no harm to be civil—how else are they going to learn?" Or, "Now, Coby, them wild'uns is not out to do you no harm. You can't judge the lot of 'em by a few rum-skins or a few who happen to like the taste of chicken, any more than you can judge Tom and Charlie Harker by the way their pa plays cards."

And everyone would laugh because they all knew that old Willy was so foolish he could cheat and still lose every hand at whist.

Pa had been the greatest fool! Those same savages he had defended against town gossip had crept up in the dark just before dawn and murdered innocent people in their beds. Coby had been right—Coby and all those who hated the Indians. Coby had said they would rise up and kill every settler in the territory one dark night, and Pa had argued simply because it wasn't in him to condemn a man without cause.

And now Pa was dead. Pa and Ma and the Harkers and the Willetts—Coby, too, for all she knew.

Dropping down onto a mossy fallen log, Laura stared unseeingly at the sun-dappled ground between her bare feet. They might as well have made a clean slate of it. What good was one woman alone? How could she even hope to survive, much less to avenge the death of her parents?

An enormous weight of inertia settled over her. It would be so easy just to lie down and close her eyes and let the heathen savages claim her body and the Lord claim her soul.

But there was a buoyancy in Laura's spirit that would not allow her to give up. No matter how tired she was—no matter how great the odds—she would not allow those—those red *bastards* the final victory! Not as long as she had the strength to pick up a stick of lightwood and set fire to every heathen village until she'd burned out the whole verminous pack!

But first she had to find them. And even before that, she had to find something to fill her belly. She wouldn't have the strength to say boo to a goose if she'd met one face-to-face.

She could go on to Packwood's Crossing—she had come more than half the distance, already. But what if she got there and found that it, too, had been set to the torch? She would be too tired to make it back to the river, much less to the island.

And suddenly, the island seemed like a haven—a refuge. There, at least, she had a cabin—one built by her own father. And there she could be certain the red savages would not bother her, for they were scared witless of some old tale about fever and a lot of people left there to die.

The man known as John Walker stood in the shade of a large water oak and watched the people go and come through the door of Packwood's Store. He was dressed little differently than any other trapper or hunter come to town for supplies. Better than some. Over a coarse linen shirt he wore a buckskin vest. His trousers, too, were of buckskin, though they lacked the fringe that was favored by his people. His serviceable bearskin moccasins rose nearly to his knees, but those, too, differed little from those of other woodsmen, for they had long since discovered the comfort and practicality of the light, flexible footwear as opposed to their own stiff boots.

His head itched. The damned red powder Kitappi had ground for him disguised the color of his hair well enough, but he would be glad to be shed of it. Among the Tuscaroras, such a coloring indicated readiness for battle.

On John Walker it indicated that underneath his broad-brimmed beaver hat, underneath his buckskins and his dark complexion, he was as English as any man in Packwood's Crossing.

Stormwalker had not wanted to come into town, but it was the quickest place to discover what was going on, short of presenting himself on the steps of the garrison in Bathe Towne. He was bold, but not foolhardy.

Besides, his people were in need of the supplies they had come to depend on, and few of them dared show their face in any white man's settlement.

Not after what had happened. Disregarding those, including Kokom, who had called for coolness, for talks and negotiation, Hancock's hotheads had struck every outlying farm in the territory, finishing what Three Turtle and his drunken friends had begun. They had stopped short of striking the larger towns, but they had burned out more than a dozen planters and their families.

Stormwalker's fists tightened to beat softly against his hard thighs as he watched the settlers scurrying about their business, glancing over their shoulders as if they expected at any moment to see a tomahawk poised to cleave their poor nit-ridden skulls.

God, what a mess! He had lost some good friends, both red and white. A young Coranine brave who had taught him how to capture the horny alligators and how to prepare the sweet meat of the tail. Old Samuel Clayburn, who had taught him to play the white man's game of dice and to appreciate the strange noise of the violin.

Women, children—suckling babes, all slaughtered in their beds.

How could such a thing happen? A raid over a real or imagined offence? The heedless retaliation? And then, before either side could come to their senses, whole villages were being set to the torch, the terrified citizens bludgeoned as they ran screaming out of their lodges.

Red and white alike were at fault. Red and white alike were victims. Where would it end? When there were no more men of fighting age left on either side?

A wry smile touched Stormwalker's lips and was gone before it reached his eyes. Perhaps the Great Kishalamaquon in his wisdom had pitted the one against the other in order to rid his creation of both.

Unconsciously, Stormwalker touched his right forearm. He wished he dared ask what had become of the terrified woman child he had left cowering in a hole in the earth. Her eyes . . . he would never forget the way she had stared at him when he had come upon her lying there on the ground, torn and bleeding. He had found his friend and the woman first, and then the girl, and his anger that such a thing could have happened had verged on madness. If he could have laid hands on the man who had done it at that moment, he would have carved him into pieces so small that not even the buzzards would have found them.

And then she had opened her eyes. She had looked up at him as if he were the devil incarnate.

Yet even frightened, he admitted now with a certain amount of admiration, she had managed to leave her marks on him—one of which he would wear for many seasons. In his hurry to find someone to come to her aid, he had forgotten his own wounds. The search had taken longer than he had expected, for the Harkers' cabin had been deserted. He had followed their tracks as far as the miller's place, but that, too, had been empty. In too much of a hurry to return to his own village, he had stolen a shirt and trousers belonging to the elder Harker boy, and in the ill-fitting garments, with his hair tucked under a sweat-stained hat, he had gone into town and got word to the Packwoods of what had happened.

By the time he had thought to cleanse his arm properly, it had been too late. The wound had already been inflamed. He had washed it in rum and seared it with the heated blade of his own knife.

For several minutes, Stormwalker watched the frightened townspeople hurrying past. None of them spared a glance at the tall, blue-eyed stranger. Their eyes were too busy searching for feathered headbands and painted faces.

His gaze bored into the back of a young woman who had come out of Packwood's and stopped to shift her bundles. Her face was hidden from him, but her hair...

Imperceptibly, Stormwalker straightened. His head lifted, hinting at the pride that was a natural part of his bearing. His breath quickened—and then he sighed.

She was not the one. Her eyes were ordinary—he could not discern the color from where he stood, but he would have known if they were gray. Wide, clear—the color of

rain. Laughing eyes, dreaming eyes. Eyes that clearly revealed the thoughts of their owner, as the dark eyes of his
own people did not.

Perhaps he would return to the place on the river. He had
not been back since he had buried Ned and his woman. Not
that she would have returned—there was nothing for her
there but sadness.

Still, if she had, then she would need someone. And while
she would hardly welcome the company of a red Indian,
especially one she had marked with her knife, he could leave
a gift of food—a fat *welka*, drawn and plucked, some dried
coosauk—perhaps a *rooiune* to keep her warm in the coming cold wind.

And then he drew himself sternly up. The gray-eyed
woman no longer needed him. And God knows, he needed
no white woman to distract him from what he must do. If
she still survived, he told himself, it would be because of her
own kind, not because of anything he had done for her.

She was the daughter of his friend. He had buried that
friend.

Satisfied that he had done all he could have done for the
girl, Stormwalker adjusted the brim of his hat so that it
covered as much of his face as possible and crossed the dusty
road to Packwood's Store.

He did not like the town. He did not like the man Packwood, nor his fat son. Both were as honest as most of their
kind, but it was well known among his people that both men
cheated all those they called "wild'uns." The woman was
not so bad. She did not care to deal with them and had no
unnecessary word to say as she measured out their salt or
molasses, but her weights were honest.

One day, Stormwalker promised himself, he would strip
off his white-man's clothing and show his true colors.

And what, an inner voice mocked, are the true colors of
a half-breed, one who was despised by whites for his Hatorask blood and by many of his red brothers for his white
blood?

A short time later he emerged from the long wooden
building. He filled his lungs once more with the cool, crisp

October air and set off for the edge of town. Kitappi would have her salt and her sweets, Kokom the *matt-eer* for his musket and Gray Otter the rum and laudanum that eased her pain.

At the edge of the woods, he whistled softly for his mount. Another mark of the white man; his people seldom used horses, for they could go more swiftly afoot in the low, dense forests. They prized them as wealth, however, and often used them to pack heavy burdens from one place to another.

Only those who had lived on Croatoan, where the long, low sandbanks abounded in wild ponies, rode well.

Stormwalker smiled as the stallion called Rooiyun, after the gunpowder color of his glossy coat, trotted obediently out of the woods. The son of a great chief, Stormwalker had seldom indulged himself in any great way, yet the horse was pure indulgence. Perhaps he would give him to Kokom as part of Kitappi's bride price.

But later. Not soon. Kitappi was young yet, and there were women enough who were willing to warm his sleeping mat without hampering his freedom.

Yellow hair, he thought absently as, with a subtle pressure of his knees, he turned his mount in the direction of Num Peree. Yellow hair and gray eyes. They were no more memorable than dark eyes and gleaming black hair. Why did they cling to his mind like the seeds of a beggar's tick?

Chapter Four

January 1712

It was the first hard northeaster that brought Laura to her senses. The fact that she'd survived these past few months was a small miracle, for there had been times when the cold rain had kept her holed up inside the cabin for days, with little more to eat than an unpalatable broth made from leaves, roots and dried acorns. The lack of salt had been her greatest hardship, for without it she couldn't preserve meat. Not until a few weeks ago had it turned cold enough so that she didn't worry constantly about sickening from spoiled food. More than once in the past few months had she nearly retched herself inside out from eating food that had set out too long in the heat of day.

And then she'd begun to wonder if perhaps it was more than tainted food. Perhaps she was really ill. Perhaps she had caught a fever and would die here alone with no one to comfort her.

For a while after she had returned to the island she had managed so well. The weather had moderated, the fish had come in great swarms; and she had even grown adept at trapping muskrats by following their slides, discovering their underwater holes and setting a snare fashioned of net and limberjack vines.

The problem had come when she'd had to skin them out and clean the cavity, for her knife had grown almost too dull to use. She had tasted everything that grew on the island. If a single taste didn't sicken her, then she would try more, until eventually she had discovered four quite acceptable salad greens.

It was those, she began to suspect, that had slowly poisoned her. Why else would she feel this awful sickness for the better part of each day?

Not only that, but her whole body had gone strange on her. Here she'd worried so about a shortage of rags that she had torn the hem off her gown and shortened her shift by a handsbreadth, waiting for her monthly flow to begin.

It never had. The nausea that had plagued her, that she had put down to the juicy pink herb that grew along the marshy sound shore, was easing now. Sometimes she went for two or three days without feeling that awful dizziness that made her want to empty her belly.

Perhaps it was only exhaustion. She had almost broken her back dragging driftwood from the snagpile and lugging it back to the cabin. Half of it was too large to get through the door, the other half burned only poorly, giving off little heat.

Surely the fighting must have ended by now, she had reasoned again and again—although she had no way of knowing who had won.

"We English won, you silly ninny," she said, her voice husky with disuse, "else the river would be full of canoes and painted faces."

It wasn't. There were shallops, schooners and sloops beating upriver every few days, heavy laden with cargo from the Indies and points beyond. A day or so later they would head out, laden with hides and lumber.

Laura had lost all track of time, but she reasoned that it must be nearing Christmas by now. Suddenly, the loneliness of her solitary prospect overwhelmed her. It had been months since she had heard the sound of a voice other than her own.

No—that was not precisely true. There had been the fishermen. It had been three days ago—or was it four? She had heard the sound of shouting while she'd been huddled inside the cabin, trying to get a chunk of damp wood to burn.

At first she had put it down to imagination, but then she'd heard it again. With the blanket tied around her shoulders, she'd rushed outside in time to see two fishing boats skirting the island so close she could have hailed them if the wind had been with her instead of against her. With the wind blowing a gale, they had clean missed the channel and were now having to negotiate the shoals that surrounded the island.

She'd shouted until she was hoarse, running down to the shore and even wading out into the freezing water, but not once had they looked back. There'd been five men as near as she could make out, in two boats, each one equipped with a single mast, a jib and square-headed mains'l. Helplessly she'd looked on as they shouted shoal warnings back and forth among themselves until they were too far away for their voices to carry on the wind.

Finally they'd reached deep water, let out the sails and took wing. Thoroughly dispirited, Laura had gone back inside, thrown herself down on her pallet and cried for hours.

She needed someone to talk to. She needed her mother, or at least another woman—someone who could tell her what was wrong with her, why she should be sick as a dog for weeks on end, and then ravenous for anything she could lay hands on.

She was probably dying of some awful fever right this very minute. Pa had spoken once of a legend about some wild'uns who were supposed to have been brought to the island and left there to die of some terrible disease.

She wished now she had paid more attention, but her mind had been on Coby, who, just the day before that, had asked her to marry him.

Well, even if the disease didn't kill her, she couldn't stay on the island forever. There were times when she felt like dying from pure empty loneliness. It was time to go. If fishermen came down the river, that meant there were still people somewhere upriver. All she had to do was find them.

She began to lay plans. There was no point in going by land, following the cart road past the Harkers' and the Willetts'. This time she would take the boat all the way upriver as far as Sawgrass Creek, which led directly into the town of Packwood's Crossing.

Laura's mind refused to accept the awful possibility that the town might not even still be there. Nevertheless, she tucked away in the back of her mind the knowledge that Bath Towne was not too much farther upriver, on the opposite bank. She would be able to go by boat all the way to Bath Towne without even taking to the road.

One thing was certain—her palms would not blister from the rough oar. With all there was to do just to stay alive, she was as tough as a rawhide boot, from the soles of her bare feet to the palms of her callused hands. Pa would have been proud of her, she thought with a sad little smile.

Of course, he might not have recognized her. She had changed considerably from the runt who used to stand on a box to harness the oxen or swing on a pry bar, cursing when a root resisted their combined efforts.

Nowadays she spent all her waking hours fishing, making the rounds of her snares, climbing trees for the topmost acorns and grubbing for any edible root she could find, when she wasn't dragging home rotted branches and driftwood, chinking the drafty old cabin with moss and mud and trying to carve herself a bowl with a dull knife.

That night, Laura set about readying the cabin to leave. It had served her well, and someday, someone else might need its shelter. Some hardy and unsuperstitious soul.

All in all, she had not fared badly here. Perhaps she would consider finding herself a husband, after all. A man could do worse than wed a woman who could do both a man's work and her own.

The weather, which had held passably warm until two weeks ago, turned bitterly cold overnight. Reluctantly, Laura used the rags she had been saving for her monthly flows to bind her feet. A few hours in an open boat in the dead of winter could well do her in, she thought, considering the best way to keep herself warm,

There was a length of rotted canvas she had salvaged from the snagpile and brought home, meaning to fasten it over the door, which had never fit properly. With gown, shift and blanket underneath, it would make a passable cloak.

"Now all I need is a bonnet—perhaps a frontange and lappet of palmetto, wrapped round with a bit of rotted netting." She spoke aloud for the sound of her own voice. She often talked to herself when she was uneasy, and as she carefully closed the door behind her and made her way in the early-morning light to where she kept her boat, she was more than uneasy. She was almost sick with fear of what she would find at the end of her journey.

Stormwalker's presence in the village of Num Peree was always cause for celebration. Even dressed in his white-man's clothing, he drew the eyes of more than one Hato-rask maiden, who gazed longingly at his broad chest in the linen shirt and leather vest, his narrow loins and the powerful muscles of his long, straight limbs in the tightly fitted buckskins and knee-length moccasins.

He was unaware of the soft sighs that followed his progress through the stockaded village, his proud, severe face grimly set as he made his way to the largest of the dwelling lodges.

Why would they not listen to him? How could he make the English see that their own behavior had brought much of the trouble upon their heads?

They would not hear the words of a red man, not even the son of Kinnahauk, who was a great chief. And he could not afford to risk having John Walker's identity become known, for that alone allowed him to move freely among the townspeople, gathering information.

Why would his own people not hear him? He had told them again and again that they must learn the white man's ways—learn to understand their words, to discover why they behaved as they did. Else, how could his people hope to survive?

Only the greatest fool would live among serpents without bothering to learn about them. A man who took the trouble to learn could tame the most savage beast.

Stormwalker's heart was bitterly sore. There were even those among his own people who had turned against him since the troubles began.

"You are not of our people," old Yantoha-yawowa had said.

"My father is Kinnahauk," Stormwalker had replied.

"Your mother is English."

"She is called Wauraupa Shaman by our people." It was a mark of great respect, as all knew, save a few of the old ones whose minds had grown inward over the years.

"She is English," the old man had repeated, and Stormwalker had paid his respects and turned away. A pine tree did not bear acorns.

But they *must* learn! Their very survival depended on it. The old ways would no longer suffice. They must learn in order to gain the respect of the white man or they would be trampled underfoot.

Pausing outside the palisade, he breathed in deeply to rid himself of the smell of fear he had brought from Packwood's Crossing. Without acknowledging the guards, who stood silent as shadows in the nearby forest, he slipped inside and made directly for Kokom's lodge.

Kokom, at least, would hear him out, for the old second chief had lived on Croatoan. He had known Stormwalker's mother, Bridget Abbott, since her first days on the island, and he trusted her, English or no, as much as he trusted his kinsman, Kinnahauk.

"I have brought your *matt-eer*, old friend," Stormwalker said quietly to the figure seated on a bearskin mat near the firebowl. He handed over the flints, a commodity that had lately become scarce, as it did not occur naturally in their lands and trade with the Catawba and the Cherokee had been curtailed since the troubles.

Stormwalker had needed an excuse to mingle with the townspeople. Trading his early pelts for salt and gunpowder, tobacco and flint, had given him that excuse. He had spent half a day at Packwood's Crossing, observing, listening, speaking little.

"Because of your pale eyes, you have once more returned with your scalp still attached to your skull, eh?" The aging chief had lost three teeth, yet his smile had lost none of its teasing quality. Even in his great sorrow, Kokom was able to smile.

Stormwalker accepted a pipe and settled cross-legged on the other side of the firebowl. "It saddens me to see women and children looking over their shoulders as if they expected to be attacked at anytime." Sighing, he shook his head.

"Our woman and children know fear, my friend."

"Whatever the color of their skin, children should not have to live in fear. They must be taught—"

With the arrogance of rank and age, Kokom interrupted. "You have been taught. You have attended the white man's schools. You say the schools are filled with the sons of these men, yet the English continue to fight. They learn nothing. They swarm over our land in increasing numbers each year, while our own kind grow fewer."

"Too few and far too precious to risk in a war that brings glory to neither side."

"I have heard it said," Kokom observed thoughtfully, "that all English speak the same tongue." Both men knew that such was not the case among their own people, whose language tended to differ from village to village, although all could communicate in one way or another for council meetings, feasts and such gatherings.

"We are divided by more than our tongues. Hancock gathers strength daily, and his purpose is not our purpose."

"The head of the serpent inflicts the venom, while the tail is harmless. Yet if the tail is separated from the head, neither head nor tail will live. I speak true."

"You speak true." Nodding, Stormwalker drew on his pipe. He watched the way the smoke curled through the opening in the domed roof, angling low in prediction of rain to come.

After a silence in which little was said but much was understood, Stormwalker laid aside his pipe. "I will sleep here this night, and then I will go to visit with my father's people. You will give Gray Otter the things I brought her, and the sweets to Kitappi?"

Kokom pursed his lips. With a sly look, he said, "You have my permission to give Kitappi the sweets yourself, my son. They would be doubly sweet from your own hand."

For all his twenty-five years, Stormwalker felt the heat of embarrassment stain his cheeks. It was because he knew of Kokom's desire for a union between the two of them that he had taken to avoiding the young woman who had been like a sister to him since he'd first seen her as a fat brown babe. He was not ready yet to take a wife. When the time came, Kitappi would do well enough, but there was much he must accomplish, and he could not do this with a new wife to keep satisfied.

"She is in her mother's lodge. A soft whistle will bring her to your side without disturbing Gray Otter's rest."

Stormwalker mumbled something about bathing and changing out of his town-going clothing, and Kokom laughed. The wily old goat missed no opportunity to throw the pair of them together, thought Stormwalker sourly. Patience was supposed to be a virtue of age. Would that the old man would practice it!

"Hurry, my son, before you grow too old to appreciate such a gentle and obedient creature."

"Gentle?" As tired and worried as he was, Stormwalker had to chuckle. "The last time we met, I threw reeds with your gentle and obedient daughter and managed to defeat her in nine tosses out of ten. The little minx threatened to chop off my fingers, my toes and any other appendage I held in high esteem. There was no mistaking her meaning!"

Kokom let out a whoop of laughter that ended in a cough. "That is my Kitappi, all right," he wheezed, although it was common knowledge that Kitappi had been born in the town of Roocheha Caure. In the year of the frozen water, a great sickness had spread among the people there, claiming the lives of many, including Kitappi's true parents.

Kokom's wife, Gray Otter, a bitter and barren woman for whom Stormwalker had no love, had chanced upon the infant and rescued her, bringing her to Kokom's lodge. Even though it had threatened their entire village with fever, Stormwalker considered the deed unselfish. The only such one of her entire life that he could recall.

"I will take the sweets to your daughter, old man, but if you hear my cries for help..." Grinning, Stormwalker rose and prepared to leave.

Ignoring the small jest, Kokom said, "She would bear you many fine sons."

"There is yet time, old friend."

"Not so much as there was yesterday."

"Not so much," Stormwalker agreed softly, and slipped out, leaving the old second chief alone with his thoughts and his pipe.

The very normalcy of the town seemed somehow shocking. As if the nightmare she remembered had never happened. As if the Harkers and the Willetts—even her own parents—were still back at home, going about their business as always.

They couldn't help but know what had happened. One of them—which one?—had found the bodies of her parents and buried them. One of them—which one?—had even come back later and erected three crosses to replace the single cross she had discovered that dreadful day.

A cart rolled by, creaking under a load of lumber. Laura flinched from the loud rumble of wooden wheels on the rough dirt road.

"Hya-aaa-*rup!*" the driver shouted, and again Laura flinched from the unexpected sound.

A door slammed. Someone called out and someone else replied. Had it always been this noisy? Thank goodness she had not gone on to Bath Towne. She'd likely have gone deaf from the shock of so many people talking and slamming about all at once.

Clutching her stiff cloak about her, she picked her way along the muddy thoroughfare to Packwood's Store. The town was laid out roughly as a cross, with the store being the hub, the landing on Sawgrass Creek one arm, and the few scattered houses, each with its own woodlot and garden patch, making up the rest.

Unfortunately, she had picked a time of day when there was the most traffic about. Two women, so bundled up she didn't recognize them, hurried along with baskets over their arms. The blacksmith came out of his own house and went into the one next door. Children rolled hoops and pitched pebbles at a line drawn on the road until someone's mother called for her child to come eat dinner.

Laura heard a gasp from behind her and turned around, almost tripping over her trailing canvas cloak. "As I live and breathe—is that you, Laurie Gray?"

"Addie Harker? But I thought—" Laura's grasp loosened, and she had to scramble to keep from losing cloak, blanket and all as she stared at her mother's old friend.

"*You* thought! Why, child, the whole town had you dead and buried these past four months. What happened to you? How did you get away?"

They had drawn an audience. Laura could have done without that, but she was so glad to see someone she knew again, it was all she could do not to throw herself into the old woman's arms.

Except that the arms weren't exactly open. They were crossed over Addie's ample bosom as she studied the tattered figure with the ragged cape of canvas and the bound feet. "Did they take your mother, too? Is she with you?"

Suddenly, Laura's throat constricted painfully. Not sure she could get the words out—not even sure of what to say, she simply shook her head.

"Oh, Lor'," the other woman moaned. "Poor Mary. I reckon your Pa's gone, too. They buried some'un out at your place. I never heard who it was, but we all reckoned 'twas the three of you."

By now, Laura's teeth were chattering. For a while, the hard work of rowing the heavy boat upriver had kept her warm, but with the wind off the creek cutting right through to the bones, she was about to freeze.

"Your house—" she managed. "I went there. It had been b-burned to the ground. And the W-Willetts."

"Happened the first day. James Burrus come by to call trouble on us before daylight. Said he'd been by Willetts and was on his way to your place. We come into town. Willy was all for going direct to the garrison, but Charles said we'd be best off not to try to cross the river. We took over the cabin the Shoemakers left. It's small, but Willy, he's planning on building another room onto it come spring."

"And the—" Laura sneezed, was blessed, and commenced again. It seemed so strange, standing here on the street with a woman she had known going on four years, as if everything were back to normal. "The, uh—the Willetts. Are they all right?"

"Moved up some'ers on the Albemarle to Adam's brother's place."

Laura waited for Addie to invite her to go home with her. When the other woman said nothing, she gradually became aware that some half a dozen men and women had gathered and were staring at her as if they had never seen her before. She knew every one of them by face, if not by name.

Trembling, she clutched her rags more tightly about her and ventured a smile.

It was not returned. Heads leaned together. Mouths worked. Eyes remained on her, as if she were the strangest sight ever a body did see. As if she were a ghost.

"I—I reckon I'd b-best be going," she whispered, feeling tears burn the backs of her eyes. Not for the world would she shed them where everyone could stare.

Besides, they would likely freeze her eyes shut if she did.

Not a single person stopped her as she hurried on to the store. No one spoke. *Dear God, do they think I'm dead? Don't they even recognize me? I can't have changed all that much in four short months!*

Grasping the door latch, she jerked it open and practically fell into Packwood's store, her face immediately stinging at the unaccustomed heat. Breathing hard, she leaned against the closed door and stared at the familiar clutter she had thought never again to see.

There were at least five people present—possibly more behind the stacked barrels of flour, rum and molasses. No one spoke.

What's wrong with you, damn all? Don't you care that I'm back? Are you all blind, deaf and mute, or am I dreaming all this?

The windowless room was dim with smoke, from the hearth and the lanterns, as well as the men's pipes. Eyes stinging wetly, Laura forced her gaze away from George Packwood and stared at the counters laden with cheeses, bolts of cloth, smoked joints of meat and crocks of Martha Packwood's boiled sweets.

How many times had she stood here, sucking on a licorice while she waited for her father to finish trading his grain and salt fish for salt and cloth, molasses and nails.

Someone sidled toward the door and she recognized the old woman who sold herbs on the corner near the horse pen every summer. The minister cleared his throat, and Laura shifted her hopeful gaze to him. A body would think she had disappeared into thin air, the way they all looked right through her.

"Hrrumph," the minister pronounced, not quite meeting her eyes.

Laura began to grow angry. If this was all the welcome she could expect from people who had been her friends for nearly four years, and her father's friends for more than that, why then, she might just as well have gone on to Bath Towne. Surely strangers would have greeted her more kindly.

She opened her mouth to tell them as much, but before she could utter a single word, she slumped silently to the floor in a dead faint.

"There now, child, don't fash yourself," Martha Packwood murmured soothingly. "We thought you was dead, and that's the Lord's truth. Why when it come to me who you was, I thought I was seeing a ghost."

Laura clutched the hand that was smoothing a blanket over her chest. A clean, new blanket—not the one her mother had woven, that had served her so well as both bedding and clothing.

"Bad Medicine . . ." she whispered in an effort to explain where she'd been hiding all this time. She felt so weak. Her tongue wouldn't work right. It had been a while since she'd been able to find enough food—and even what she found, she had a hard time keeping down. Plain, ordinary old hunger, that was all that ailed her.

"Bad medicine, indeed, you poor babe. It fair makes my heart ache to think of what you must have suffered at the hands of those wicked devils! Was it awful?"

"Ma and Pa—"

"I know, child. Didn't George and Coby ride out soon's they got word you was in trouble?" Actually, they had taken time to secure their own holdings before they had dared set out. It had been two days—or had it been three?

"Thank you," Laura murmured sleepily. "Thank George and Coby for . . ." For seeing that her parents got a decent Christian burial. And for the markers, she added silently, too sleepy now to remember the confusion of three markers when there had been only one. Later she would ask Martha about it, but for now . . .

"You sleep, child, close your poor eyes and try to forget what you been through. Martha'll take care of you, don't you worry about a thing."

Once, Laura remembered rousing to find Coby standing over her, his sandy hair and flushed face so dear and familiar she tried to tell him not to look so concerned, but before she could find her tongue, she'd drowsed off again. The next time she opened her eyes, Coby was gone and Martha was there to poke gruel into her mouth.

It was three days before Laura felt strong enough to lift her head from the pillow. The sickness had come back, no doubt brought on by having decent food again after so long. She had suffered herself to be scrubbed from head to toe, and Martha had lent her a nightgown, which wrapped around her twice with enough left over to swaddle a small horse.

It felt wonderful. Warm and clean, it smelled of lavender. "I was so tired of breaking my back working with
nothing to show for it," she murmured. "No one to talk to.
So lonely... But the men. There were five of them. I
screamed as loud as I could, but..." She drifted off without seeing the lifted brow or the speculative glance that took
in her work-hardened hands, the scars that came from
working with a dull knife.

And her belly.

After the first day, Martha had kept Coby away. She had
fashioned a place for Laura in one corner of the room she
shared with her husband, George, who grumbled every time
he had to step around the curtained off pallet.

"Hush, now. The poor child's been through enough
without you carrying on, George Packwood! Losing her
folks and then being taken captive by them heathen savages, living in their filth and all... She said there were five
of 'em, and no matter how she screamed, they wouldn't let
her be, the wicked rutting devils. It's a wonder to me she
even lived to tell the tale!"

Later that day, Laura, having heard bits of the conversation, tried to explain what had happened—that she had
not been taken captive, but had escaped to the island, where
she had made out quite well until the weather had grown so
cold. And about the five fishermen.

The older woman only nodded, refusing to hear any details of the unspeakable things that had happened to her
poor young guest. "You just lie there and let Martha look
after you, you hear? If the—uh, the sickness don't let up
after a while, I'll go to the herb woman and see if she's got
something you can take."

"Plantain," Laura murmured sleepily. "Ma always said
it was good for a bellyache."

"Hmm," Martha commented thoughtfully. She'd had in
mind something considerably stronger than plantain tea.
Four months. If the poor child had took right away, it could
already be too late. It would be dangerous, no matter what,
but then, anything was better than whelping a dirty little
half-breed.

Chapter Five

A *baby*! How could it have been possible? She wasn't even wed!

Yet there was no mistaking it, if Martha Packwood was to be believed. And Martha would have no reason to lie to her....

But a *baby*! Dear Lord, she couldn't even care for herself—how would she ever take care of a baby?

The whispering had commenced even before Laura had realized what was wrong with her. She'd been on her feet again soon enough, for Martha had nursed her to within an inch of her life. If she'd have had to swallow one more mouthful of tasteless gruel or another noxious posset, she would have likely died.

As it was, the strange sickness that had plagued her for months had just as suddenly ceased.

"That's the way of it, dearling," Martha told her. "Just when a body gets to thinking she'd like to drown her man and jump overboard after him, why, the whole world suddenly looks bright as a new guinea again. Some women wilts and some blossoms when they're a-carrying. You'll be a bloomer right enough."

But bloomer or not, if she'd had any choice, Laura would have fled the town after the first month. If tongues had wagged to see her standing barefoot in the dead of winter wrapped in a scrap of old canvas, it was nothing to the wagging that went on once word had spread that she was carrying a red Indian's child. She had learned that both the

Harkers and the Packwoods had been back to her place, and finding the grave, had thought her dead along with her parents. It had been Willy Harker, just as she had thought, who had erected the three pine crosses. No one knew who had buried her parents and put up the first one.

Perhaps she would never know.

It snowed on the fourteenth day of February. Most winters they could get by with no more than a dusting, but in the year of our Lord seventeen hundred and twelve, it came down like a windstorm in Willett's flour mill.

Laura took it as a sign that she was to stay on with the Packwoods, at least until after the baby came and she could find some place of her own. She heard of a family out west of town that was planning on leaving come spring, and she hoped to be able to move into their cabin, if no one else wanted it. Until then, she must remain where she was.

At least she was able to work for her keep. George Packwood grumbled, Coby refused to meet her eyes and only spoke to her when it could not be avoided, but Martha stood up for her steadfastly. Settling her fists on her wide hips, she would thrust out her ample bosom and all three chins and glare up at the son and husband who towered head and shoulders above her, daring them to lay a hand on her new chick.

But not even Martha was proof against the wagging tongues of the townspeople.

The tale had quickly spread throughout the territory that Ned Gray's daughter had managed to survive the attack, and after four months had come back, swollen with some heathen's get, to throw herself on the mercy of the decent folk of Packwood's Crossing.

Not until she'd been working at the store for nearly six weeks did Laura learn that in spite of all she had told Martha—and she had finally managed to tell her tale uninterrupted—most of the townsfolk believed she had been taken captive, like so many others, and had lived with the savages all those months before she had either escaped or been released. It was a well-known fact, they whispered to one another, that the wild'uns coveted white female captives, using them for as long as it pleased them to do so and then selling those who survived as slaves.

"I'd sooner die than let myself be used like an animal," whispered a woman to her friend in the store one morning. She was fingering a bolt of calico and staring boldly at Laura, who was busy sorting thimbles. "Every time I see one of them savages, I think of how awful it would be, but then, I was gently brought up."

"Some women is downright shameless, if you ask me. Makes a body wonder what all she done to save her neck, don't it?"

Laura clamped down on her tongue and thought of some of the more inventive methods of torment she had heard tell of. She had discovered early on that it did no good to argue, to deny or to try and explain. No one listened. They had made up their mind about her and nothing she could say would change it. Ned and Mary Gray were dead; their daughter survived. She had a baby in her belly and there was only one way of planting *that* particular crop.

Work helped. No task was too menial, and Martha was glad of a younger woman to take on the work of keeping the store clean. Looking after two great hulking men was enough of a task for any one woman. So Laura worked and she ate well at the Packwoods' bountiful table and she slept the sleep of the just, despite the nasty gossip. By the time nightfall came, she was usually too exhausted to care what a gaggle of small-minded women thought and said.

As time passed, the wild'uns had begun to creep back into town. At first Laura had been so frightened, she had run out the back door and plowed right into Coby Packwood.

"Red Indians!" she had said, panting, and Coby had laughed. Not his old half-shy chuckle, but a nasty sort of laugh. His gaze had wandered down over her belly, which was growing distinctly rounded by now.

"You took a likin' to any one in particular? Say the word and I'll hogtie him and fetch the preacher. Ain't right for you to have to drop a little bastard when there's a whole passel o' them red devils running around loose."

Laura had kept her mouth shut, but Martha had soon noticed her discomfort whenever one of the wild'uns would slip into the store, lay a bundle of furs or a string of shell-beads down on the counter and point to salt or tobacco or sweets.

Gently, the other woman had explained that those who came into town were mostly Hatorask and that they had taken no part in the fighting. "Not that most will credit it. To some, one redskin's as bad as another, but I was brought up to believe that pretty is as pretty does."

Which made no sense at all to Laura. There was nothing pretty about any of the moth-eaten creatures in the shapeless leather garments, the men's heads as often as not bristling with a handful of feathers that had been clipped and dyed, the women often wearing calico skirts under their fringed shifts.

There was one possible exception. From time to time, a girl came in—she was even smaller than Laura and her mouth looked as if she were always on the verge of laughter, even though her eyes remained wary.

Invariably, she traded for the same things—salt, rum, laudanum and sweets, and Laura wondered at the combination.

One day, she looked directly into Laura's eyes and smiled. Laura was on her knees at the time, sanding the floor in front of the hearth. For a long moment she held the young Indian girl's gaze, but finally she looked away—without smiling back. She wanted nothing to do with any of the wild'uns. Hadn't she suffered enough from the hands of "their kind"?

But she was suffering still, and from her own kind. The talk never ceased—the whispers, the knowing looks, the snickers. Forcing herself to ignore the meanness of people she would have once considered her friends, Laura continued to scour, tote, sort and polish what needed scouring, toting, sorting or polishing.

What hurt most was knowing that Martha, who had been the soul of kindness, was having a difficult time defending her to George and Coby.

"I don't like having no Indian's whore around here, Marthie—we got a son to think of. Coby don't need that sort of woman hanging around, flaunting herself before decent folk."

"George Henry Packwood, you listen here to me—that poor mite ain't done no harm to nobody. It ain't her fault the red devils set on her like that—there weren't a blessed thing she could do, and I'm not about to turn her loose in this weather to lie down some'eres and die of the galloping consumption!"

"Come spring, she's gotta go." Laura heard the dictum from her kneeling position the other side of the counter, where she had been scrubbing away the grease left by a badly cured bundle of pelts.

"Come spring, we'll just see about that," Martha snapped.

"Coby—" George began, but his wife cut him off.

"Less than a year ago, Coby was a-fixing to ask that child to marry him! Thank the blessed Lord that boy ain't been poisoned by your wicked heart, George Packwood!"

"Marry!" George roared, and Laura cringed, thankful that the store was closed and that no one else had to hear her being carved up like a joint of beef. "Ain't no son of mine gonna marry no whore, Martha Simmons, so if that's all the reason you're a-keepin' her around, you may as well cut 'er loose and let her drift!"

"It's Martha Packwood, you old goat, and more's the pity! If I'd a-knowed what kind of man you were, I'd sooner married the parson's pet pig!"

Still on her knees behind the counter as Martha stomped off to their living quarters with George on her heels, Laura made up her mind. As soon as the weather moderated—as soon as the baby came—as soon as she could travel again, she would go back to the island. It had served well enough before; it would serve well enough again.

Far better than a place where she wasn't wanted. Except for Martha, she hadn't a single friend so far as she could tell, and she refused to be beholden to those who looked down on her. What sort of life would her son have in a place like this?

Her son, she thought, calming instantly as she settled back on her heels to stroke her rounded belly. She had already decided on a name—she would call him after her father, Edward Gray. Little Ned.

As time passed, Laura comforted herself with thoughts of Little Ned. She would teach him to fish, as her father had taught her—to set snares, to turn the ground and plant in season and to harvest what they had planted. There was enough high ground on the island for a small garden patch, if she could manage to clear away a few trees so that the sun could shine through.

The young Indian girl had a real sweet tooth. Laura got so she looked forward to seeing the door open a crack, watching the slender figure in pale doeskin, with a fringed shawl of the same stuff around her shoulders, slip in, look around and head straight for the crocks of Martha's sweets.

They had both exchanged smiles several times now, Laura no proof against the guileless overtures. But their friendship was firmly established the morning that Kitappi—for that was her name—slipped through the door while Laura was scrubbing the floor, stepped squarely on a sliver of soap and landed flat on her plump behind.

The two girls had stared at each other, oblivious to the elder Packwood, who was counting out musket shot into twopenny lots. Before Laura could find her wits to apologize, Kitappi had burst into giggles.

After the first startled moment, Laura had giggled, too. She'd still been on her knees, and rising awkwardly, she'd held out a hand to help the other girl to her feet.

There'd been only the slightest hesitation before her offer had been accepted, but even before Kitappi had brushed off the wet seat of her doeskin shift, Laura had understood that the hesitation had been shyness and not disaffection.

After that, the tentative friendship had grown rapidly, although they couldn't really talk all that much. Besides Kitappi's rather limited knowledge of English, the Packwoods frowned on Laura's familiarity with one of the wild'uns.

"Reckon that tells the tale, don't it, woman?" George Packwood said to his wife one night after they had gone to bed. Laura, on the other side of the curtain, heard every word, as she was no doubt intended to.

"There ain't no harm as I can see in her being friendly to that girl. It ain't like the folks around here had gone out of their way to show her any kindness."

"All the same, it goes to show she's an Indian lover. Any woman that would—"

Laura stopped her ears with her fingers so that she could hear no more. As soon as the baby came, she would be well rid of this place!

The male Packwoods continued to grumble about the extra mouth to feed and the cramped living conditions. Martha Packwood continued to defend her charge, although after a while, it sounded as if she were growing tired of the need to argue constantly with her own family on behalf of an outsider.

Soon, Laura thought, stroking her belly, which no amount of starched petticoats or aprons could hide. She always managed to be nearby whenever Kitappi came into the store, especially once she became aware that both George and Coby cheated the wild'uns by measuring and weighing short on every purchase.

On a morning in early March, when the weather showed signs of breaking after a long siege of icy rain, Laura had just finished hanging the last of the new lanterns from the rafter when the door opened to admit Kitappi, who, in a mixture of English and her own heathen tongue, immediately set to chiding Laura for climbing up on a stack of boxes in her condition.

"My friend Running Bird fall from a persimmon tree and the Great Spirit take back her baby and won't give her another, no matter how she cry."

"Laura, if you're done hanging them lanterns, stop wasting time and drag that stack of hides into the pack," Coby said coldly. "After that you can see to the dinner—Ma's gone out for a spell."

Chastened, the young Hatorask maiden sidled up to the counter and laid down four beautiful muskrat pelts. "Laudanum?" she whispered.

Afterward, Laura would never know what had prompted her to linger and watch while Coby poured out a stingy measure of laudanum. She knew well the amount due for four pelts of that quality, even though she'd only been working there for a short time. Thank God no one in her family had needed laudanum, but Pa had traded enough pelts for salt and other goods so that Laura knew what Kitappi's prime muskrat should bring in trade.

"That's not near enough, Coby," she murmured as he made to hand the tiny half-filled bottle across the counter.

If looks could burn, she'd have gone up in smoke. "Get on with your work. The whole town knows what you give them heathens, but be damned if you're going to get away with anything while you're under my roof!"

"But, Coby, I'm not—"

He didn't actually raise his hand, but violence was in his eyes. Poor Kitappi cowered there, afraid to speak out, afraid to slip away without Gray Otter's medicine—afraid to move.

That was the tableau that met Stormwalker's eyes as he opened the door and stepped inside, lowering his winter's take of pelts to the floor.

"'Morning, John. I'll see to you in just a minute."

Laura, momentarily diverted, glanced at the tall trapper who stood just inside the door, his hat pulled low over his face. She couldn't allow Coby to cheat her friend—she just couldn't!

"You gave Sam O'Neal twice that much for five mangy old rabbit pelts, Coby. Kitappi's skins are worth a lot more than that."

"If I was you, I'd quit meddling in what ain't your business, seein's how you're beholdin' to me for the roof over your head and every morsel you put in your mouth.'' Threat was implicit in the words.

In the time it took him to loosen the straps around his bundle of furs, Stormwalker had sized up the situation. He saw Kitappi's eyes widen imperceptibly, but knew she would never betray him. There were times when his being a blue-eyed half-breed was a great advantage to his people. And even though many of them would never fully accept him, not one of them would ever betray him, for to do so would put an end to the useful career of John Walker, trapper, hunter, mediator and gatherer of information.

His narrowed eyes returned to the woman, whose back had been toward him when he came in. Recognition slammed into his body with the force of a weighted spear. Her hair was darker now—more the color of winter grass— but there was no mistaking the determined set of her chin or those wide-spaced gray eyes.

She was alive. Those three crosses he had found when he had returned to her father's farm did not mean what he had feared!

But before he could sort out his feelings, the argument between the white woman and the younger Packwood was joined by Packwood the elder.

Stormwalker's heart swelled with a feeling he did not recognize as the tiny woman, her belly swollen with child, stood up to the two towering men on behalf of Kitappi. Few men of his acquaintance, red or white, had ever dared charge them with cheating. It was rumored that the elder Packwood had once killed a man in a fight, and the younger one grew more like his father each year.

But most remarkable of all was the fact that this small, fair-skinned woman had intervened on behalf of one of his people.

Quietly, Stormwalker moved to one side, as if to study more closely the display of guns racked on the split-log wall. Under the brim of his hat, he took full measure of the woman he had last seen cowering under a shelf of turnips, a rusted blade in her hand and fury in her gray eyes.

Garbed in the ugliest clothing he had ever seen, she reminded him of a sparrow in the dead of winter, all drab,
puffed-up feathers, brave spirit and clear, sharp voice. Her
small chin was angled stubbornly up at the younger Packwood, defiance in every delicate bone in her body. It came
to Stormwalker then that, had she been born a son as Ned
Gray had wanted her to be, she would have made a formi-
dable warrior.

Crossing her arms between the slight swell of her breasts
and the more generous swell of her belly, she turned away,
as if needing time to control her anger. Her gaze happened
to collide with his and Stormwalker caught his breath, confused by the mixture of feelings that clashed inside him like
the two great sea rivers that met off his island home of
Croatoan.

Caught momentarily in a shaft of sunlight, the woman's
thick hair blazed as if it were on fire. Something swelled and
came alive inside him, like a seed that had long sought the
warmth of the sun. He neither knew nor understood why
this was so—he only knew that it was.

You have been too long without a woman, my friend.

Feeling Kitappi's eyes on him, he spared her a warning
glance and then turned back toward the gun rack, his side
vision taking in the small yellow-haired woman.

Why, he asked himself mockingly, did the sight of Kitappi not stir his senses in the same way? She was comely
and quick-minded. She was sought after by so many young
braves that Kokom had been forced to raise her bride price
three times in order to hold her until Stormwalker made his
bid.

The Englishwoman was swollen with another man's child.
Her gown was obviously the castoff of a much larger
woman, her apron was stained and had been mended many
times over, and her face was pinched with anger. Why were
his eyes drawn to her ugly garments, her untidy hair and her
shapeless body?

He did not even wish to know the answer.

"Coby, if your mother were here, she'd not countenance your slighting any customer, no matter who it was." Laura's voice had the slightest tendency toward unsteadiness.

The younger Packwood leaned his powerful arms on the countertop and smiled. "Ma ain't got no say. The store belongs to me and Pa, and if you don't like the way things are done around here, you know what you can do about it, don't you?"

His smile suddenly struck Laura as the sort that would make a cautious man cross to the other side of the road. She was beginning to regret getting involved, yet what else could she have done? If she'd watched him cheat Kitappi and said nothing, it would be as good as if she herself were cheating.

Laura stood her ground. "All the same—" she began, but Coby cut her off, his color dangerously high.

"Why don't you just get out? Your kind ain't wanted around here. You come a-suckin' up to Ma, and you with a red brat in your belly—don't tell *me* how to treat them dogs! You're no better than one of them stinking heathens yourself. If you was a decent woman, you'd have ended up like your Ma and Pa, but oh, no! You had to go save your own worthless hide by whorin' for them red bastards! How many was it, Laurie? Ma said you told her there was five. Which one of 'em planted his bastard in your belly?"

Laura swung from the shoulder. The flat of her hand caught Coby across his open mouth and she felt the sickening wetness of his spittle on her palm.

Stunned at the unexpected attack, Coby could only stare for a moment. Before he could recover, Kitappi had slipped out the door, leaving her laudanum behind. Eyes wide with shock, Laura glared at Coby and then dashed out after her.

Coby sidled around the counter as if to follow, but suddenly the door was blocked by the tall silent figure who had been witness to the whole thing.

"I wouldn't, if I were you," Stormwalker said quietly.

"This ain't nothing to do with you, Walker."

Stormwalker said nothing, but something—perhaps the readiness of his stance—seemed to change Coby's mind.

"I ain't taking her back," he muttered. "I ain't having no squalling red pup around here, no matter what Ma says."

Hatred flared, burning intensely in Stormwalker's blue eyes for a single instant before it was forceably quenched. Silently, every muscle in his tall body hardened and ready, he turned on his heel and walked out the door.

Kitappi first—he must find her and tell her that he would bring Gray Otter's medicine and that she was to avoid this place from now on.

But when he caught sight of her hurrying toward the trace that led to their village, he did not follow. She would be on her shaggy pony and halfway to Num Peree before he could catch her, for he had taught her to ride himself.

Instead, he looked for the small sparrow. He did not know if she had other friends or another place to go. He only knew he could not leave her frightened and in tears—not again.

Deep in his heart, the hatred began to simmer once more, the hatred that had begun on the day he had found Ned Gray and his woman dead, their daughter savagely attacked and left to die. Stormwalker had known from the first who was responsible, for Three Turtle had not bothered to cover his sign.

Stormwalker had hunted him for weeks, but the wily Mattamuskeet had disappeared in the swamps where no one not born in that dark, treacherous world could follow.

For months now, in his guise as a trapper, he had met with the Englishman, Massey, of the Ocanechee, and with Eno Will, who was well-known and widely respected among many people. He had met with Blunt of the Upper Tuscarora, and with Spottswood in Virginia, who still worked to bring about an honorable treaty. Personal matters had been laid aside as he had sought to bring an end to the fighting.

Today the hatred had risen to the surface again.

Stormwalker followed the tracks of a small woman until he caught sight of her near one of the houses. It was not the little sparrow. Returning to the beginning, he looked for other tracks and found what he should have seen at the start.

She was huddled behind the store, in the shelter of the horse pen, half hidden by a thicket of bare grape vines. The sound of her weeping cut through him like a dull blade and he moved closer, framing the words he would say.

But no words came. He knelt down beside her and she lifted drowned eyes to stare at him. Did she recognize him? If not as the man who had found her after the attack last fall, then as the man who had witnessed her defense of Kitappi?

His heart melted at the courage it took to stay her tears, at the pride that would not allow him to witness her distress. Head held high, she bit her lip and he wanted to touch it, to touch her.

Yet he dared not. She drew in a deep, steadying breath, her eyes still clouded with tears, and he ached to gather her to him and shelter her from all that threatened her—yet he hesitated. She had been mistreated by one of his kind, he reminded himself, forgetting for a moment that he was in the guise of John Walker.

"W-what do you want?" she whispered.

"Only to help you."

"Can you turn back time?" Her chin trembled as she fought against tears, and the sight nearly unmanned him.

"If I could, I would do so." He watched her struggle for composure, but it was a losing battle. The odds overwhelmed her, and he wanted to tell her to weep until she could weep no more and then to let him take her to her friends. Surely she must have someone to look after her...these were her own people. The English were no more cruel than any other people, except for a rare few, like the Packwoods. They could, however, be stubborn and bloody small-minded.

"You're French, aren't you?"

Kneeling so close he could see the faint scattering of freckles across her short, straight nose, he sat back on his heels. "French? Why do you ask that?"

"B-because of the way you talk. My pa—" She swallowed and blinked rapidly, and Stormwalker clenched his fists to keep from reaching out to her. "My pa had a friend who was French. I heard him talk once. He sounded all stiff and p-proper, like he wanted to be sure to g-get the words right.''

"Your pa had many friends, little . . . little one." He had nearly called her little sparrow. No one else had come so close to unmasking him, yet this small creature, even in her distress, had seen through his disguise.

"My pa . . ." she began, and that was as far as she got. Tears that had been too long held back sprang from her eyes, and she made a small, wounded sound.

Silently, Stormwalker cursed all the gods of all nations, and then he reached for her. A single touch on her shoulder was all it took. As if she'd been starved for arms to shelter her, she toppled against him, burying her face against his buckskin vest.

She cried like a child, whole-heartedly, noisily, her small fists clutching handfuls of his shirt. She was on her knees, leaning between his spread thighs, and Stormwalker fought back an unworthy surge of desire.

God, he was no better than the animal who had done this to her! She shifted slightly, and he forced himself to ignore her warmth, her softness, the sweet woman scent of her skin and hair.

Spirit of the flesh, had he no shame? The woman was with child! Not only that, she was white, and if there was one thing that had no place in his life, it was a white woman. The blood of the Hatorask had been thinned enough, as it was—if he, too, were to take one of her kind to his lodge, he would never be able to reach his people, to teach them what they must know to survive!

The notion was too farfetched to credit. It was only because he admired her for standing up for one of his own people, he told himself. Such fairness was a rare commodity, especially since the troubles.

She moved and he could feel her belly press against him— it was surprisingly hard. His arms tightened momentarily and he told himself that it was only because he felt sorry for her. None of this was her doing, yet she was the one who must suffer.

Gradually it came to him that she was no longer crying. Her face remained hidden, and he slipped his hand between them and lifted her chin.

"Little Sparrow?"

"Kitappi," she corrected, and hiccoughed. "My friend's name is Kitappi. I don't reckon I did her c-cause much good. I'm afraid George and Coby will take out their temper on her, and she doesn't deserve it."

"I know your friend's name. What is yours?" Some deep-seated instinct prevented him from revealing the fact that he had known her father—had, in a way, known her. If she had forgotten, it was all to the good. The road ahead of her was rough and uncertain. It would do no good to look back.

"Laura," she murmured, and he had to lower his head to catch the soft sound. "Laura Gray."

She fumbled for her apron to blot her eyes and then felt under her bodice for a kerchief. At least he thought that was what she was seeking.

"Do you need...?" he began, when she moved away from him, averting her face.

"Never mind, I'll use my apron. It's seen worse than this."

Considerably worse, to Stormwalker's way of thinking. The poor garment was badly stained, and most of the stains were fresh.

Suddenly uncomfortable as his own emotions were harnessed once more, he thought of offering her his sleeve, but it was none too clean. He had spent the morning loading his winter's supply of pelts onto Rooiyun's back, and now he feared he smelled of musk and mud.

What did women of the town use to blow their noses? "Wait here—I'll be right back," he mumbled, suddenly glad of an excuse to escape.

Inside the store, he took time only to note that the elder Packwood was behind the counter, talking in low tones to his son. Stormwalker glanced hurriedly around, fingering first one thing, then another and finding nothing soft enough to wipe the nose of one so delicate. Finally, he settled on a bolt of dusty silk, ripping off an arm's length and striding back outside. He would settle up later.

She was gone. At first he didn't believe it. He began following her tracks, but then he stopped. Shrugging, he stared down at the square of silk and told himself the woman had done him a great favor. With the whole nation seething like a nest of bees getting ready to swarm, the last thing he needed was a weeping woman hanging on to his shirttail.

Jerking his hat brim down over his face, Stormwalker strode back inside the store and began to cut open his bales of prime pelts, spreading them out for the Packwoods to examine. He knew their worth to the last hair and would not leave without his full due in trade goods. His people had many needs, for game was no longer so plentiful now that more and more of their land had been cleared for the white man's planting. They depended on him to provide for them what they could no longer provide for themselves.

He stacked salt, traps, rum, gunpowder and cloth on the counter and, stroking his jaw, considered adding a musket to the lot. He had never used such a weapon for hunting, for it spoiled the pelt and wounded many animals without killing them, but the time might come when he would be glad of possessing such a weapon.

The bargaining was heated. Stormwalker remained unruffled. He added blades and sweets to his stash. Both Packwoods grumbled, but there was no denying the size or the quality of his pelts.

While Stormwalker bundled up his goods for the trip back to Num Peree, the other two men wandered over to the hearth, talking in undertones. Stormwalker, whose ears could hear the shadow of a fox falling upon the snow, had no trouble making out their words.

"Get Laura in here to tote them furs out to the shed," muttered the old man.

"She's gone. Ain't likely we'll be seeing her around these parts no more. Reckon by now she's on her way back to them murdering thieves where she belongs."

Stormwalker laid a musket on the counter. "I'll have this," he said, allowing no hint of his feelings to seep into his voice.

"Cost you extra, John."

"The beaver came from west of the Eno. It is worth the extra."

"Well...seein' how you're a good customer, I'll mark you down for the gun and throw in flint and powder for the beaver. You going out again this season?"

"One more trip west to collect the rest of my pelts."

"You can get your gun then."

"I'll take it with me now," Stormwalker said evenly, and after a moment, both Packwoods nodded.

Slinging his bundle over his shoulder, he let himself out, breathing deeply of the cold, damp air. The haze over the sun told him there would be freezing rain before the sun rose again. He wondered fleetingly where Laura Gray had gone, and then swore as the anger he had been holding back boiled to the surface.

Anger at the man who had used her and left her for dead. Anger at the men who had cast her out as if she were no more than the dirt under their feet.

And anger at himself for responding to her in a way that he could not respond to Kitappi, in a way that made no sense.

He would find Three Turtle, he told himself. Sooner or later, their paths would cross again and when they did, Stormwalker would be ready.

Perhaps then there would be an end to it. Once he had avenged the wrongs suffered by Ned Gray and his two women, he could forget about the yellow-hair.

Feeling more at ease, he strode quickly to the edge of town and whistled softly for Rooiyun. The stallion whickered eagerly, indicating that he, too, had quite enough of the smell of the white man's town.

Chapter Six

May 1712

Pausing beside the stream, Stormwalker inhaled the familiar fragrance of the yellow flowering vine that climbed to the top of the tallest pine in search of light. The land was sweetest here beside the Pamticoe. It was flat, so that a man could walk for days without fear of falling off the edge of the earth. No matter how beautiful were the high hills to the west, with their tumbling waters and their cloud-covered peaks, he could not dwell among them for many days before they began to press in on him.

Having retrieved his cache of pelts, he had turned eastward, pausing to trade with Nathaniel Batts for tools, medicines and weapons for his people at Num Peree, and for similar gifts for those on Croatoan. He had brought special gifts for his mother, his sister, and for Kitappi.

In only three days he would greet the morning sun as it rose from its bed in the Great Water.

The Atlantic. From the English he had learned the proper name of the Great Water. They in turn had learned the names of many rivers from his people. The Pamticoe, the Currituck, the Neusiok and the Perquimans—those names came as easily off the white man's tongue as they did from the tongues of his brothers.

The English had called the broad sound to the north after one of their own chiefs, and now it was called Albemarle by all men.

Was that not proof that all men could live in harmony?

Born on the island of Croatoan, where man dwelt in the open palm of the Great Spirit, Stormwalker had left there in his fourteenth year to come inland only because his father had wished him to travel so that he might learn from all who had wisdom to share.

Stormwalker had traveled far. He had learned much, both from his own brothers and from the English in their great schools. He had met men of many lands and found them to be much the same as his own brothers. Some were wise, some were fools. Some were men of honor, but knaves, he learned, were to be found among men of all nations.

Shouldering his heavy pack, Stormwalker set off at a lope that belied the weight of his burden and the great distance he had come. He moved easily through the quiet woodland, yet his mind was troubled. He thought of the Englishman Massey, who had been made a leader among the Ocaneechee people. He thought of his friend, Eno Will, who was valued by both red man and white for his great skill as a guide.

Were they not proof enough that red man and white had much to teach one another and much to learn?

Why then, he asked himself once more, did so many among his own people despise him for his mixed blood? Was he not the son of Kinnahauk? Had not his English mother been accepted by all as a great healer and a woman of great wisdom?

Yet not even his mother could give him the answer. "Your time will come, my son," she had said again and again. "They are not yet ready to learn what you have to teach them."

When would they be ready? When, if ever, would the time come that the children of each village would be taught the English language, for one day it would be spoken all across the land, and those who could not understand would be left behind.

When would they be taught to read from a book and to write of the things that were important—of the great deeds of their fathers and grandfathers, the legends that had been handed down since the beginning and the wisdom that had guided their footsteps from the land where the sun sleeps to the land where it rises from the sea?

The white man knew nothing of these great deeds, these legends—the wisdom that was the red man's proud heritage. They were too filled with the importance of their own deeds.

Stormwalker knew that he *must* find a way to teach the children of his village so that they, in turn, could teach their children. One day, even the children of the English would hear and read and know of these things.

The sun had fallen from the sky, casting a veil of fire over the land by the time Stormwalker approached Num Peree. He looked forward to a pleasant few hours in the sweat house, a plunge into the cooling river and the feel of soft new buckskin against his skin.

But he had reckoned without Kitappi, who spotted him before he even reached the palisade. She set upon him with a storm of giggling hugs and kisses, and in spite of his halfhearted protests, insisted on dragging him off to her father's lodge where, against all custom, she took her seat and demanded to be told everything he had seen, heard and done since last she had seen him.

"Your daughter grows bold in her old age, Kokom," Stormwalker teased. He had dropped his pack outside and was amused to see Kitappi's frequent glances in that direction.

Kokom laughed. "Her bride price falls with the passing of each moon. If you have not yet bartered away the last of your pelts, perhaps I could interest you in an ugly wife who, though worthless, is not yet too ancient to wash the stink from your clothing and trim that unsightly hair from your face."

Both men smiled broadly while Kitappi made a show of being offended. It was well-known that Kokom all but worshiped his adopted child and could refuse her nothing.

Still chuckling, Stormwalker stroked his rough jaw. He had no doubt that he could hold his own with the striped polecat, for he had traveled hard without taking time to cleanse and groom himself. Due to his English blood, he was hairier than most of his brothers, a fact that, as John Walker, had stood him in good stead more than once.

Not for the first time, he was mildly tempted to consider the old chief's offer—not only for the luxury of having a woman to scrub his body and pluck it of unwanted hair, but also to relieve his desires and thus free his mind of the troublesome dreams that had followed him into the hills and back along the rivers.

Neither hardship nor late nights spent talking and drinking fine French brandy with his friends Massey and Eno Will had held back those dreams. No matter how exhausted he had been when he'd finally closed his eyes, she had been waiting for him. He had even tried staying awake at night and sleeping during the day, but it had done no good. He had but to drop his guard in sleep, day or night, for her to come to him, and no amount of reasoning would keep her away.

She was a stranger, he had reminded himself repeatedly. She was English. She might well despise all red men for what one had done to her, for few among the English could distinguish Mattamuskeet from Hatorask, or Hatorask from Roanoak, being quite blind to the differences of build and demeanor.

He had seen her but twice since that day in the field with her father. The first time she had struck out instinctively, like an injured panther, neither knowing nor caring that he wished only to help her. The second time, she had seen only a russet haired, blue-eyed trapper whose arms had held her for a moment, but whose name she had not bothered to ask.

He should have put her from his mind by now. Dismayed at his own weakness, Stormwalker vowed to be rid of her spell. Perhaps Kitappi . . .

"Three Turtle has offered for my daughter."

That statement brought Stormwalker's wandering mind to an abrupt halt. He glared at the old chief. "Three Turtle led the first raids. He killed a man and a woman and left their daughter for dead."

"He was drunk. A man cannot be held responsible for what he does when rum steals his wits."

That had always been the way of their people. It was no longer enough for Stormwalker. Barely controlling the icy fury that gripped him, he said, "She must not go to him. He will mistreat her."

"He offered five horses—"

"Which you can no longer ride."

"Five bearskin robes—"

"Which will keep you no warmer than the ones you already possess!" Stormwalker would marry Kitappi himself to keep Three Turtle from claiming her, for she was as dear to him as his own sister.

"And three hands of peak," the old chief went on. "That is as good as the white man's gold for trade."

"He would take her to Seconiac. You would not see her again."

"It is the way of a man and a woman. Three Turtle was once your friend."

"No more! He has broken the laws of our people. He has murdered and raped those who have done him no harm."

"He is at war," Kokom said, the calmness of his voice in sharp contrast with the unusual anger of the younger man.

"Those people were not at war! Edward Gray was my friend. We hunted together. His daughter defended yours when Packwood would have given her half measure of laudanum for her skins."

Kitappi's eyes widened. Stormwalker had forgotten she was still present, for as a rule, such matters were not discussed in the presence of women.

"Laura?" she demanded. "Is that the woman you speak of?"

"The yellow-hair who worked at Packwood's Store."

"The baby—it belongs to *Three Turtle*?"

Kokom rebuked his daughter for the interruption and turned once more to Stormwalker. "The laudanum was for Gray Otter. It is time her spirit was made free," said Kokom, and with visible effort, Stormwalker forced himself to let go his anger.

To his great shame, he had not even thought to ask after Gray Otter, who had been ill for a long time. Out of respect for Kokom and kindness toward Kitappi, he attended the recital of Gray Otter's illness and learned that she now slept in the lodge of the healing woman who cared for her. When his mind would have strayed back to Laura Gray, he turned to Kitappi and asked if she would fetch in his packs.

He immediately saw his mistake, but as it lightened the atmosphere, which had grown tense and uncomfortable, he allowed her to spill the contents on the floor of her father's lodge before he singled out a packet and handed it over to her eager hands.

She opened it suspiciously and fingered the misshapen brown lumps it contained. And then she held one to her nose and sniffed. "What is it? Paint?"

Some of the tension disappeared from Stormwalker's face. "It is called choc-o-late. It is used like tea or coffee in many of the finest taverns. Break off a bit and place it on your tongue."

Using her flashing eyes and long lashes to a great advantage, the young maiden said, "I would rather have *you* break off a bit and place it on my tongue, Stormwalker."

Kokom leaned back and chuckled, and Stormwalker reached for the bundle, a tired but teasing smile on his face. "My mother will like them. I will give you the beads I brought for her instead."

"No!" Kitappi clutched the things to her breast. She had more beads than she would ever use, for her father was a wealthy man.

Stormwalker began to smile, and the smile broadened as he watched her dismay on finding the stuff melting on her hands and her shift. Cautiously, she touched the tip of her tongue to one finger, and then, her eyes widening, she began to lick in earnest.

* * *

Stormwalker's stay lengthened, for there were more gifts to hand round and the tools and flints to parcel out among the men. Kokom insisted on hearing all that had transpired on the long journey, and they spoke well into the night of Hancock's restless braves, of a raiding band of Iroquois who were striking far south of their usual territory, of the South Carolina soldier Barnwell, who had gathered a force of more than a thousand, many of them Indians, to put down the uprising between the Neusioc and the Pamticoe Rivers.

"North of the Albemarle, I met a man who would teach our people, Kokom."

The old chief's eyes grew guarded. "Our people need no teaching. The wisdom of our grandfathers is ours."

"Our grandfathers did not live in a world filled with English and Swiss, with French and African and German. Do not make the mistake of believing all white men stupid in all things, my friend. Many are blind. Many leave their wits beside their soft bed when they arise, but do not underestimate their strength and cunning. A hunter who does not study the ways of his quarry will go hungry and cold."

Kokom appeared to ruminate for some time. Stormwalker waited. He knew the value of patience.

"This man you say you have found. Is he of our people?"

"His father was Yauta-wittapare. Red Moon."

Only a man who knew him well would have been aware of Kokom's surprise. "Yauta has been gone for many years."

"He was taken captive by the Coranine and sold in the high hills. He took a Cherokee woman there—I do not know her name. Tiree Kiro is their son. A part of each foot was cut off to prevent Red Moon from escaping, as is the way of the Coranine. When he died, his woman was taken by another man. Tiree Kiro was sold to a man from one of the great houses on the upper Albemarle who was known for treating his slaves, red and black, with great kindness. The boy was taught alongside the sons of the house. He dressed as one of them, and took his meals at his owner's table. He was given his freedom when his owner died."

"I have never heard of such a thing before." Kokom frowned.

"It is rare. Yet our people have taken in others. Gray Otter once took in a child called Kitappi."

"I will think on this matter," Kokom said after a long pause.

"I have told him he will be welcome here."

The old man said nothing, and soon Stormwalker took his leave.

It was three days before Stormwalker resumed his eastward journey. He had spoken to Kokom again of Tiree Kiro, who had promised to make his way south to Num Peree as quickly as he could, but travel was uncertain these days, and T'kiro, for all his learning, was no woodsman.

Surely someone would look after him until Stormwalker could return. For all he had lived in a great house and worn silks and white wigs on his head, Tiree Kiro, whose name meant Wolf, possessed no more than the knowledge in his head.

And his freedom, Stormwalker amended thoughtfully. That was worth more than all the riches in the world.

It was late by the time Stormwalker neared the mouth of the river. The wind was fitful. It would storm before morning, but he had been too restless to remain any longer. The small sticks that he would throw over the side from time to time, observing their angle in relation to the stern of his dugout, would keep his bearing true. By the mid of the following morning, he would reach the south shore of Croatoan, which he would follow in a northeasterly course to his father's village.

The rhythm was addictive. His back and his arms were strong, and it would be good to be free of land. Already he fancied he could smell the salt air before he had even cleared land.

Nighthawks laced the sky with their graceful dance. A heron croaked noisily, and from the nearby island came the deep voice of a frog.

The current met him head-on as he neared the mouth of the river, veering the narrow dugout toward the dark shadow that was Bad Medicine Island. Stormwalker welcomed the coming storm as he would have welcomed a worthy competitor. It had been many years since he had tested his strength and endurance against a storm.

Lifting his paddle blade, he paused.

And then he continued. It was nothing. The wind. Like most wise men, Stormwalker believed in spirits, yet he knew that over the years, storms would have washed the island clean of all bones, and likely of all spirits, as well. An island was intrinsically a good place, cleansing itself again and again with the purifying wash of the seas.

Yet even as he prepared to move on, it came again—a long, keening wail. The cry of a mating bobcat? There were no bobcats on the island, of that he was fairly certain. Besides, the cry had sounded more...human.

By the time Stormwalker eased his canoe in among a stand of cattails, the moon had slipped behind a fast-moving bank of clouds. Thunder muttered sullenly in the distance. He took only a moment to get his bearings, then waded ashore, moving silently toward the shadowy edge of a dense grove of trees.

This time there was no mistaking it. That long, wavering scream had issued from a human throat. It was followed by a series of whimpering noises that made his blood run cold. Moving soundlessly over the pale sandy shore, he followed the pitiful cries.

He was getting closer, but the cries were getting weaker. Stormwalker was no stranger to pain, but something out there was suffering more than mortal should be made to endure.

She was lying on her back when he found her, her knees drawn up against the ungainly swell of her belly. The keening sound was much weaker now, almost too weak to carry over the constant rumble of thunder and the wind rattling the reeds along the shore.

Stormwalker dropped to one knee beside the small figure. He could not see her face—clouds had covered the moon. But he knew. Just as he knew that there was little chance she would survive the night.

The wind had turned. Lightning flashed almost constantly. Soon the rains would come and they would be fierce, lashing mercilessly at the small figure lying exposed, her body already cold and her life spirit dangerously weak.

He stood and stared down at the still figure. Could she survive the trip back to his village? Lightning danced on the water, accompanied by a deafening clap of thunder. The sound had barely rattled off into the distance when she cried out in agony, and he knelt beside her and placed his hand on the writhing knot that was her belly.

How he wished his mother were here. This woman needed one of her own kind, for if she opened her eyes and saw him leaning over her, she might take fright. He could not quite forget that the last time she had seen him clad in only breechclout and armband, his hair in two braids with the beaded headband that held his feathers of rank, she had attacked him with a knife.

This time she had no such defense. In her great pain, her terror might be more than she could bear. He had seen wild creatures die of fear.

"*Ne reheshewau*, Little Sparrow," he murmured, smoothing her hair from her distorted face. "Do not be frightened, I will help you."

Lifting his face, he opened his heart to the Great Kishalamaquon and waited only a moment. The Voice That Speaks Silently came swiftly, leaving him in no doubt as to what he must do. He had not been the one to violate this woman, yet it was he who had been given the responsibility of caring for her now and helping her babe into the world.

This he would do. Kishalamaquon had sent him to her; so it would be.

As nearly as he could recall, there was a rude cabin not far from where they were. He had often passed close enough to

see the smoke from its fire when Edward Gray had come to
fish the river. Lifting her carefully, he carried her as swiftly
as he dared to its shelter.

Her only garment was a thin shift such as the English
women wore underneath their outer garment. It was wet and
cold, and though her skin was beginning to burn with fever, she shivered uncontrollably. Every two of his breaths,
her belly would draw up like a fist and she would cry out.

He gave thanks when they reached the cabin, praying he
would find candles there and herbs to ease her pain. It
quickly became obvious that she had lived here for some
time.

Since she had run away from him in town? He thought of
the ice storm that had followed and his face grew even more
grim.

Lowering her to the floor, Stormwalker felt in his pouch
for the wad of spunk he always carried. Within moments,
he had kindled a small fire. A quick search for dry wood
proved fruitless, and he broke up a crudely constructed chair
and fed the flames until the warmth reached out into the
small room. Then he began a search for something to ease
her agony.

There was nothing. No herbs, no spirits—scarcely any
food. Evidently she had not been able to gather food for
days, but in a basket covered with canvas he found a handful of acorns and a few ears of dried corn. Setting a battered kettle of water over the fire, he looked about for
something to grind the corn and was distracted by a piercing scream.

A low groan escaped his own throat. Her eyes were now
open wide. Had she recognized him? Did she even know he
was there? There was no way of knowing.

Remembering the second time he had seen her—remembering the look in her wide gray eyes when she had opened
them to see him kneeling over her, he found himself hoping
she had forgotten. If she remembered him at all, let it be as
John Walker. She had run from him once and he had let her
go, sensing that his presence would do more harm than

good. This time she could not run. Nor could he leave her. The babe must leave her body or both would perish.

Suddenly Stormwalker knew he could not allow that to happen.

As his eyes became accustomed to the dim light of the fire, he saw her bed. It was no more than a pallet of moss covered by a worn blanket. Lifting her, he cradled her momentarily in his arms, hoping his warmth would somehow bring her comfort. Naked except for his breechclout, he could feel the fire of her body against his, yet her hands were like ice as he lowered her to the rude pallet. In the flickering firelight, her face was as pale as the new moon.

The storm hurled its fury at the small cabin, driving rain through the cracks between the logs. He held her and whispered words that she would not have understood, even had she heard them.

He needed his mother's wisdom. *She* needed a woman's care!

Thinking of all the medicine he had learned from both his people and the English, Stormwalker cursed in a tongue this woman would have understood clearly. He had been concerned with fevers, not childbirth. The women of his people bore children easily and went about their business, often the same day.

What would old Soconme have done? What would his mother have done to ease this woman's pain, to force a child who seemed in no hurry to emerge from the safe warmth of her body?

How could he help this small creature whose strength was draining away with the dark fluid that seeped from between her pale thighs?

For the first time in many years, Stormwalker cursed his own ignorance. How could a man prepare himself for the future when the future was in the hands of the gods? Where was the order in such a world?

The scent of sweat, woodsmoke and blood filled his nostrils. If he could have pushed the wretched thing from her body to bring her peace, he would have done so.

Push it out? Push *where*?

"Ah, Little Sparrow," he groaned, "only tell me what to do and I will do it. Women are not built to endure the pain of battle. You were made by the Great Spirit to be soft and gentle for man's comfort. It is man who was given strength and daring—that is our lot, just as patience and endurance is yours. It is only together that we become complete, the daring and the gentle, the soft and the strong, the patient and the bold."

Speaking softly, he used his own tongue. She was beyond the reach of his words, yet Stormwalker found that he needed the comfort of saying them.

Never had he felt so weak and helpless. He was frightened by his own uncertainty, yet he could not let go—he could not walk away. "Why?" he cried out, the sound loud in the sudden stillness between thunderclaps. "This woman has harmed no one! Take the child, if you must, but let the woman live!"

As if roused by the sound of his voice, she moved against him, her fingers clutching at his arm. "Water," she breathed, so low he could scarcely hear her.

But when he would have left her side to grant her wish, she clutched his arm, her fingers biting into his flesh. "Don't leave me! Stay with me, please..." The sibilant sound was lost in a loud crack of thunder.

Helplessly, Stormwalker gathered her up into his arms so that she was sitting with her back supported by his chest. He reached around her to rub her belly, wincing when she groaned, cursing when she screamed. "Rest now," he whispered, knowing there would be no rest for either of them until this thing ended.

The low, animallike moan started deep in her throat. It was different from the other sounds. Stormwalker felt a cold chill break out along his flanks. Suddenly, she jerked in his arms, and it was all he could do to hold her. The back of her head pushed against his chest, and he clamped his thighs around the outside of hers, feeling her legs press outward.

"Open, then, but slowly. Do not fight so, Little Sparrow."

Her hand gripped his thigh. He felt her fingernails break through his skin, but he felt no pain. Even in the dim light, he could see the mound that protruded from her small frame bunch up and press downward, as if it were trying to empty itself of an unwanted burden.

He would have helped push it out if only he knew where to push.

"Push!" he grated. "Hard—*harder*! No more now. Breathe, *wista-yecca*, breathe!"

For an instant he thought she had died. She did not move. She did not breathe.

As if hearing his command, she suddenly gasped sharply. He felt a warm wetness flood the floor around them, but before he could discover the source, the whole process had begun again. This time he placed his hand daringly on the swollen mass, and when it tightened, he began a downward caressing movement.

Her groan ended in a sharp scream. A moment later, she stiffened and bucked against him. Stormwalker was in no position to see what had happened, but he knew that something had given way. Something had ended.

It was over. Laura felt unbearably weary, as if she could sleep forever. Somewhere a light kept flashing against her eyelids. Fire?

Lightning.

A clap of thunder sounded overhead, but she was far too exhausted to care. Let it storm, nothing could hurt her anymore. She was beyond pain, beyond even the sound of that deep, rasping voice that had been slicing through the rim of her consciousness for so long, making her do things she didn't want to do, making her push and breathe when all she wanted to do was close her eyes and drift away on the tide.

It was finally ended. She was free.

She slept.

Chapter Seven

After only a moment's consideration, Stormwalker knew what he must do. As to how to go about it, he had watched the birthing of various animals—this could not be too different.

Using the blade of his hunting knife, which he first heated in the small fire until it was searing hot, he separated mother from babe and laid the small wet bundle across her breast while he dealt with the other.

After that, it was the work of very few minutes to gather an armload of fresh moss, which was wet but better than her ruined bedding. After the moss had had time to dry out by the fire, he covered it with a scrap of canvas that hung from a rafter. The blanket he placed close to the fire to warm.

And then he commenced washing the tiny, squirming boy child, marveling at the small fists that flailed the air so furiously. Now and then he glanced down at the woman, who slept deeply, exhausted by her long ordeal, but then he would turn back, crooning nonsensically to the boy. He would be called Thunder, Stormwalker decided, for the storm that was just now receding outside and for his lusty cries.

"I knew your grandfather, young Thunder, did you know that? He was an honorable man. My people had no bad words to say of him, except that he planted corn again and again on the same land, which is a foolish thing to do. He would have learned in time. You would have known, and you could have taught him, for your—"

A soft moan drew his attention, and he turned to find the woman stirring restlessly. He touched her, and her skin was cool. That was good. Still, he could put it off no longer, for she was weak. If fever came to her, she would not be able to fight it off.

There were things to be done that no man should be called upon to do. All knew that a single drop of a woman's monthly blood would rob a warrior of his strength. Was this any different?

Yet there was no one else. If he turned away from her, she would die. Honor would not permit him to allow any woman to die if it be within his power to save her.

Stormwalker offered a brief prayer to the Spirits that governed such matters to overlook his interference in what was not man's work, understanding that he had been given no choice.

Even so, she might die. If she did, he would bury her with her people and offer a song of sadness for her journey, and then he would take the boy to Num Peree. His people would welcome another child, for the Hatorask were few. Little Thunder would not be held responsible for the sins of his father. With proper teaching, he would grow into a fine man.

But first there was much to be done.

Wrapping the boy in the warm blanket, Stormwalker squatted on his haunches and began easing the ruined bedding from beneath the sleeping woman. She mumbled but did not awaken as he supported her slight weight with one arm.

Using only his hands, for he had neither doeskin nor cloth, he bathed her with the warm water, from her face to her small dirty feet, paying particular care to those parts of her that had suffered most.

As he went about the task of cleansing her, Stormwalker deliberately severed his mind from what his hands were doing. He thought of the fine thick pelts he had brought down from the high hills. He thought of his parents on Croatoan, where he had been bound when her cries had reached his ears. He thought of the feast that had been given in his honor before he had left Num Peree and, reluctantly, of Kokom's last reminder that a young brave needed a woman to look after his needs and that his daughter, Kitappi, was plump, industrious and obedient.

Stormwalker uttered a sound of frustration. The woman stirred but did not awaken. Gently, his hands moved over her, cleansing and calming. He had learned long ago of the healing that could sometimes come through touch alone, if the heart willed it so. She was a wounded creature, his the hands chosen by the Great Spirit to heal her. Nothing more. If he allowed himself to think of the woman he had once held while she wept—the woman who had come to him night after night in his dreams—he would not have been able to perform the simplest tasks.

Think of the boy. Think of Little Thunder, who needs this woman to survive. Even now his cries grow weaker. He must suckle soon or he will perish!

Unfortunately, as far as Stormwalker could recall, there was not a single woman in the entire village of Num Peree who was newly with child. If he had to search much farther, the boy would starve.

Carefully he cleansed each finger of her right hand—a hand that was hard and calloused, not soft, as were the hands of Kitappi, from years of working deer brains into hides to render them supple.

Yet for all their hardness, these hands were shapely and small, with long, delicate fingers and small, pink nails. Surprisingly clean nails, he noted with relief, recalling the four crescent-shaped wounds in his right thigh.

"Soon, little warrior," he murmured as the boy wailed lustily. "From the sound of your voice, you will soon be able to outrun the swiftest among all your brothers."

Before too much time had passed, both mother and child were clean and dry, lying on a fresh bed of moss covered over with the woman's own bedding. Stormwalker would have much preferred a bed of soft fur, but the pelts he had saved for his father were in his canoe on the far side of the island.

Having tossed a handful of acorns onto the hearth earlier, when he'd thought to make a nourishing broth of them, he absently reached for one. Peeling away the hot skin with a thumbnail, he nibbled appreciatively on the rich yellow meat.

She would need food when she awakened. The babe would fare well enough, for he needed nothing that the woman could not provide, but the woman herself would need thick, rich broths. He had brought along a plentiful supply of food for his own use on the journey north to Croatoan, knowing that most of it would be given to the elders in the village who had no one to hunt for them.

A single glance was enough to tell him that the woman slept peacefully. The babe would come to no harm in the short time it took him to return to his canoe and guide it closer to the cabin. The rain had almost ceased and there was a sliver of a moon showing through the thinning clouds.

He would be back before either of them knew he was gone.

Laura pushed weakly at the weight on her chest. She couldn't breathe! Her lips were parched, her body ached in strange places and there was this awful tightness in her chest that made it hard to draw air into her lungs.

Restlessly, she turned over, heard a protesting squawk and felt a solid lump under her left shoulder.

And then it came back to her... The baby. Her Ned. She'd been splitting open and she'd run outside, trying to escape the awful pain, and then she'd tripped and fallen, and...

Easing onto her back again, she felt about in the darkness for the unfamiliar lump, but instead, her hand came in contact with a small warm bundle that squirmed at her touch. Smiling weakly, she rolled over and gathered it close to her body.

Ned. Her own sweet Ned had come early and he was fine, just fine—warm and alive and all her own.

Scraps of memory drifted through her mind, like tattered clouds after a storm. A voice? Why did she keep remembering a certain voice? And the feel of hands? Kind hands; with a gentle touch that had made her feel the way her mother's hands once had.

Yet it wasn't her mother's voice that echoed in her memory, but a deeper voice, speaking words she'd only dimly understood. Some of which she'd understood not at all.

She'd liked the sound of that voice and the feel of those hands. Where were they? She tried to call out, but her own voice refused to cooperate.

"Never mind," she whispered. "We don't need anyone else, sweeting. Mama will take care of you." Cradling the small warm body in her arms, Laura smiled in the darkness and slept.

When next she opened her eyes, the sun was shining through the cracks between the logs and a fresh, just-washed breeze from the open door was stirring her hair across her cheek. A coverlet of some sort had been tucked around her in spite of the heat and now she was wringing wet! Not only that, she felt as if someone had piled a heap of rocks on her chest—even her arms were cramped, as if she'd spent the whole morning toting sacks of grain.

And then she remembered. "Ned?" she crooned, a smile melting away the frown on her face. Poking her head up so that she could see her son for the first time, she struggled to sit up. Somehow, both she and her son had got themselves tangled up in the blanket, tighter than a nubbin in a cornshuck. And her blanket—it smelled like ...

Laura wrinkled her nose and sniffed again at the pungent, unfamiliar scent. It put her in mind of something she didn't want to remember—an animal smell, musky and thick. Like the bundles of pelts she had dragged into the storeroom at Packwood's.

Curiously, she fingered the edge of the thing that covered her, recognizing the softness of a well-tanned skin, such as those her father had traded for so that her mother could make him a pair of trousers and a coat.

For some reason she couldn't explain, the smoky wild smell of the leather brought on a creeping feeling of horror. She managed to unwrap a portion of the bundle she was clutching in her arms and then she stared down in stark disbelief. "Oh, no," she whispered. "Oh no, oh no, oh no!" This was not her Ned! This was no bright-haired English baby, but a dusky, black-haired, squint-eyed creature who bore no resemblance at all to the son she had dreamed of!

Just as a shadow blocked the sunshine that slanted into the small cabin, she sat up and thrust the imposter from her, not caring that it tumbled from the pallet onto the floor. "Get it away from me!" she cried, shuddering. "Where's my Ned? What have you done with my baby?"

The shadow moved away from the door, and Laura, scuttling as far away as she could manage with her legs still tangled in the soft, musky covering, stared at the small screaming thing as if it were a serpent. This was not her baby—it wasn't even English! Its skin was as dark as old copper, its hair as black as a crow, and even its head was all funny shaped—as if its face had been mashed flat from nose to crown.

"Get it away from me!" she screamed again, trembling all over.

Someone knelt down and gathered the screaming thing up off the dirt floor, and at the sound of that deep, oddly familiar murmur, a fresh chill swept over her. She suddenly felt as if she'd walked into an ice-covered river that had closed completely over her head.

"Hush, small sparrow. This is your son. He needs you."

"That's *not* my son, it's *not*! Do you think I wouldn't recognize my own baby?" For the first time, she lifted her gaze to the tall man who stood before her, naked but for a scrap of a leather apron. He was holding a skinned marsh rabbit by the ears, and there on his right arm, highlighted by a shaft of sunlight that streamed in through the doorway, was a jagged white scar.

For a moment she felt herself slipping away to a place where it was warm and safe, a place where there was no pain and no memories. She *wanted* to go, but something held her back. Reluctantly, she forced herself to look up into the face she would remember to her dying day. "I know you," she whispered. "There *is* no Ned—there never was a Ned.

Here—'' she gestured to the unhappy mite beside her
''—take your wretched brat and go, for he's no child of
mine.''

''Quiet, woman. You have not yet recovered your wits.''

''There's nothing wrong with my wits—'' Pressing herself against the wall, she watched him place the rabbit over
the coals and then turn to lift up the child. ''If you think I'm
going to touch it, *you're* the shatter-wit!'' Turning away
from his hard, wicked face, she forced herself to examine
the ugly, wriggling creature he held in one powerful arm.
Like the freshly skinned rabbit, it was all red and tiny, and
she wished he would remove it from her sight, but she lacked
the strength to take her knife to him again.

Defeated, she turned over onto her side and curled up into
a small miserable knot. But no matter how tightly she shut
her eyes, she couldn't block out the sight of the man who
had murdered her parents and nearly killed her, as well.

Perhaps it was all a nightmare. Perhaps she'd only
dreamed the pain and the storm and the voice that had
droned on and on.... After all, it wasn't even time yet.
Martha Packwood had said June, and it was only May.

Cautiously, she felt her belly, hoping to convince herself
that her own Ned was waiting inside her until it was safe to
come out.

Something had changed. She felt—different. Not flat, as
she used to be, but—different. Soft and oddly empty.

He'd only shifted inside her, she told herself a little wildly.
That was all it was. Even now he played games with her, the
way they would play games once he was old enough to come
out of hiding. That was it, she told herself desperately—he
was playing hide and go seek with her!

With that thought, she slipped back into the comforting
womb of sleep.

Stormwalker rocked Little Thunder absently as he stared
down at the sleeping woman. For all her fierceness, she
looked pathetically small and he could not find it in his heart
to condemn her. He had heard of such things before—now
he understood better. For a woman to undergo such pain,
it would be necessary for her to allow her mind to slip away.

He had simply not given her enough time. When next she awakened, her wits would have rejoined her body and she would accept her babe and suckle him, for already her breasts were beginning to swell.

Without shame, he studied the crumpled form in the thin, revealing shift. The belly that had so recently harbored this small, lusty boy was now soft, sagging away from the sharp bones of her hips. There was little flesh on her bones except for her woman's softness there and on her seat and the small, full breasts that were strangely pale and marked with a delicate tracery of blue veins.

Stormwalker had noted other details, yet he pretended to himself that he had not, for it was not seemly. He counted himself an honorable man, yet he had always been cursed with more curiosity than any among his friends. Before that day when he had come upon this woman injured and near death, he had never before seen the body of an English woman. His mother was modest, as became a married woman. Of course, he had seen many women of his own people, for there were always beautiful maidens in every village who thought it not to their discredit to lie with any man who pleased them before they chose one for their own. He modestly admitted to having pleased many.

The child stirred in his arms, and he turned his attention from the woman lying at his feet. "She did not mean those words, Little Thunder," he murmured to the child, who seemed to find some measure of comfort in his arms, for he had ceased his screaming. "You must allow her time. When next she opens her eyes, I will give her meat broth and yaupon tea, and then she will be ready to suckle you. You were not gentle on her, little warrior. A few harsh words are no more than your due."

But when next Laura opened her eyes, she was in no mood for broth and tea, much less for suckling a small dusky savage. The first thing she noticed was that someone had covered her again with the stinking buckskin, leaving only her shoulders bare.

The next thing she noticed was a pair of polished bronze legs altogether too close to her side. Before she could scramble away, the creature was squatting down beside her, trapping her between the hearth and his powerful thighs.

"Welcome to this morning, Laura Gray," the deep, half-remembered voice greeted her. "You have slept through another night."

Realizing that she'd been staring at that which was directly in front of her face—a flap of thin soft leather that fell between a pair of smooth, muscular thighs—she jerked her eyes away, only to find herself looking, instead, into the face of the man who had attacked her nearly nine months before. The same man who had come back for her in the root cellar, not content to have murdered her parents and done God knows what horrid things to her, after first bashing her in the head with a stone.

When she'd first seen him she'd thought she was dreaming, but the nightmare was real. This animal had known to the very day when she would be throwing off his foul get. Somehow, he'd managed to track her down and now he'd come for his half-breed bastard.

"Take him, then," she said in a fierce whisper. "He's yours. I want nothing of him, or of you."

"Little Thunder needs you," the golden savage said as simply as if he'd been commenting on the likelihood of rain.

She looked pointedly at the fine white scar on his right arm. "He doesn't need me. Find some bitch with pups to suckle him, for I'll not."

Blue eyes narrowed on her, causing her to shift uncomfortably.

Blue eyes? Since when had these heathens had blue eyes? Laura wondered fleetingly. But blue eyes or black—or yellow or purple, for that matter—he was a savage. Her pa had called them wild'uns, likening them to the wild creatures of the forest that could be tamed with patience and kindness, and for his own patience and kindness, they had killed him.

"Savage!" she said deliberately. "Take your brat and go, or next time, it won't be your arm I slit, but your throat."

Two days passed with neither Laura nor Stormwalker giving way. The stern faced man would enter silently, study her with those unnatural eyes of his, and then quietly make his demands.

Demands which she ignored.

"Eat this," he would say, thrusting a wooden bowl of mush at her.

She would cross her arms over her aching breasts and clamp her mouth shut, glaring at him from her place on the floor.

Or he would slip in and place the babe on her breast while she slept, thinking she would wake and accept him before she realized that he was not hers. As if she could suckle any creature, no matter how frail, who would grow up to be as vicious as his wretched sire.

She would deliberately roll onto her side, allowing the babe to slide off onto the edge of the pallet, where the poor mite would wail and sob and kick out with his skinny little legs....

The poor mite? What was she thinking of? That was no poor mite, but the son of a murderer! Desperately she sought to convince herself that he had not come from her body, his flesh a bond between the haughty savage and herself.

"You need to walk about," the man who called himself Stormwalker told her on the third day. "Our women do not lie about after bringing forth a child. It weakens the body."

"Leave my body out of this," she growled, knowing he was right, that she was growing weaker with each day of lying abed, and hating him for noticing.

It wasn't that she didn't eat. After the first day she'd discovered that she had only to wait until he'd offered her food and she'd refused it for him to slam his ignored offering down on the hearth and storm outside. She had no notion of where he went or what he did when he was gone, nor did she care. All that mattered was that his absence gave her time to crawl over to the hearth and gobble down a portion of whatever he had made, and then add enough water to the bowl so that he wouldn't notice when he came back inside.

She refused to let herself think about what the bowl contained. It could be rats or snakes or any number of disgusting creatures. She carefully avoided the bits of meat that floated in the thick broth, but whatever it was, it was tasty and filling, and it gave her strength to go outside long enough to relieve herself.

The babe was growing weaker. He lay on a corner of her own pallet, for she refused to touch him even to move him. He slept most of the time, waking to whimper now and again, and she hardened herself against giving in to the pair of devils. Let Stormwalker take the babe away and give it to one of his own kind.

Yet is was half her own, an unwanted voice whispered inside her.

Little Thunder. As if a son of hers would have such a heathen name.

The shaft of late-afternoon sunlight that spilled across the door suddenly disappeared, and Laura sensed Stormwalker's anger before he even spoke. He had stalked out earlier and not returned till now.

"The boy is dying. He needs milk."

"Take him to some other woman, then, for he'll have none of mine," she replied, deliberately making her voice as cold as possible. The poor little thing should not be made to suffer for the cruelty of a parent, but that was none of her doing. She herself had suffered under the hands of the same wicked savage. Her own parents had been viciously slaughtered by this hard-faced devil who begged her milk for his son.

Picking the child up, Stormwalker held him against his chest and continued to watch the woman, revealing nothing of his feelings. Only slowly did he become aware that the small head was bobbing against his masculine chest, rooting about as if in search of food.

To his great shame, he felt heat rise to his face. "You'll suckle the boy or I'll take the milk from your breast and feed him myself. He is your own son, woman! How can you avenge yourself through the death of your own son?"

"Then feed him yourself," she retorted. "You keep flaunting your poor flat breasts—surely they must be good for something."

This time, not even Stormwalker's innate stoicism could hide his shock. Blue eyes widened, making them look all the more remarkable set among such dark, angular features. *"Sehe, yica!"*

"Don't speak to me in that heathen tongue! If you've something to say, then say it flat out and leave me be!"

Quickly regaining control of his emotions, Stormwalker stared down his high-bridged nose at the small, defiant creature. A woman who rejected her own child? Such a thing could not be. The child had been born of hatred, yet he had been born of her body. Could neither of them see how greatly they needed one another?

In the beautifully precise English first taught him by his mother, he repeated, "Hush, woman. Do you understand my words now?"

She stared at him belligerently. Even now in her weakness, her hair dull and matted and her face pale as the new moon, she continued to defy him. And against all reason, he found himself drawn to the spirit of defiance that burned so brightly in her small body.

But it could not be allowed to continue. The bodice of her faded gray gown stretched tightly across her swollen breasts. Dark stains marked the nipples, and he was sorely tempted to remove the rag from her body and let the boy suck what milk he could from the soft cloth.

The gown had been hanging on a peg. Evidently it had grown too tight, and she'd taken to wearing only the loose white garment he had found her in. But when she'd glared at the fine buckskin he had spread over her as if it were unclean, he had snatched the thing off the wall and dropped it in her lap.

"Cover yourself," he had ordered, his rough voice hiding feelings he refused to acknowledge, even to himself.

At least he no longer dreamed of her. Between watching over them both, snaring fish and birds to make the broth, and trying to force it into a child who wanted none of it, he found little time to sleep.

Glaring down at her now, he allowed his anger to rise to the surface. "If ever two stubborn people needed each other more . . . !" he muttered under his breath.

She refused to look at him. Known widely for his even temper, Stormwalker fought down the urge to strike out at something. Few men and *no* woman had ever affected him this way! Did she not realize that it was beneath the dignity of any man to cook for a woman, to serve her, to wait on her, to wash her body when, by rights, she should be doing such things for him?

He was the son of a great chief, the grandson of a great chief! He had studied in the white man's schools—although never long in any one, for he could not abide the walls and the smell of so many unwashed bodies all around him.

He had humbled himself for this woman. Humility was foreign to his nature. Yet the ungrateful creature was too proud even to let him see that she ate what he provided!

Remembering all the unseemly services he had provided, Stormwalker growled in frustration. How was it that such a small, insignificant creature could drive him to such lengths?

For the boy's sake, he could not allow it to continue. If she would not willingly do her duty, then he would force her to do it. One way or another, she *would* accept this child!

Standing over her, he said, "I will leave you now, for I can no longer abide the stench of this place. When I return, I will bring water. You will wash Little Thunder and then yourself, and then you will feed him." He placed the child beside her, and she crossed her arms stubbornly over her aching wet breasts.

"And you will have your throat slit for your troubles and go straight to hell," she replied quite calmly. She underlined her words with a thrust of her small chin that made him want to lift her up and shake her.

Speaking slowly and with great emphasis, Stormwalker said, "Little Thunder is *your* son. Not mine. You will suckle him willingly or I will remove that ugly garment and hold the child to your breast until he drinks his fill. The choice I leave to you."

A long silence followed his words. Laura sensed that this time the savage truly meant what he said. She knew he'd been trying to feed the boy, for she'd waked to see him dribbling broth on a strip of her old shift and dangling it between those tiny dark lips.

She stared at his hands. They were long hands, the fingers straight and square-tipped, not at all the hands one would expect of a murderer. With a sudden quickening of her pulse, Laura knew she would die if ever he were to touch her again.

"Leave then," she said grudgingly.

His eyes narrowed suspiciously. "I do not trust you. I will stay."

"If you want me to feed your child, you will leave me alone!"

"If I leave you alone you may drown him, instead." Without moving, he seemed to loom closer. "I stay. Now bare yourself and take the babe in your arms."

Suddenly, Laura was uneasy. While it was one thing to dare the devil when one was too weak to care for the outcome, it was another thing altogether to test his strength when she herself was growing stronger each day—when she stood a chance of escaping him as long as she didn't anger him into murdering her first.

Reluctantly, she stared down at the baby he called Little Thunder. "I'll likely sicken and die from suckling him—it's unnatural," she muttered. Yet a voice inside her whispered as she drew the small bundle up against her breast that a child should not be held accountable for his parents. It was not poor Little Thunder's fault that his father was an animal—a murderer. A ravager of women.

Milk gushed from her breasts, and as if sensing what was to come, the child began to wave his tiny fists in the air—his little head, not nearly so misshapen as she had once thought, wobbled on the stemlike neck as he beat his tiny nose against her wet gown.

"Open your gown," came the orders from on high.

Ignoring the man who towered over her, his moccasined feet pressing into the edges of her bed, she sought to drag a corner of the quilt over her breast, to hide herself. "How can I do this if you're going to stand there looking at me?" she cried finally.

"There is nothing of you that I have not seen," he growled. "Nor that I wish to see again. Suckle your child, woman. I will leave you in peace."

Laura stared after the retreating back as she instinctively guided the small mouth to her nipple. Peace? She would never know peace again.

Chapter Eight

After a few days, Little Thunder began to fill his skin so that he looked less like a dried plum. He was a vigorous feeder, and once he discovered what it was all about, he cried to be suckled so often that Laura began to wonder if the lusty little creature had deliberately set about wearing her out.

No longer did she make any pretense of ignoring the food Stormwalker set before her. She had neither the time nor the energy to expend on foolish games. Besides, she seemed to be ravenous all the time now.

As if satisfied that she was doing her maternal duty, Stormwalker left her largely to her own devices. Each morning he brought in fresh water. He cooked as handily as any woman, although Laura was growing mightily tired of mush. And after setting her food before her, he would disappear again, returning much later with a fish, a cluster of spiny mussels or a few bird eggs.

All of which he invariably made into a thick, gray mush. If she complained, he told her it was nourishing. If she asked for a bit of salt to make it more palatable, he claimed to have none.

None he would share, more likely. She noticed that he ate none of the tasteless pap himself.

She could picture him off alone somewhere, sprawled comfortably in the shade of an oak while he feasted on succulent roast fish and all manner of tasty game. And while she knew she should be thankful that he provided for her at all, she was growing heartily sick of the monotonous fare!

Puzzled by the contradictions she found in his nature, Laura began to watch him more carefully. She had to admit that among all the wild'uns she'd ever seen, he was by far the most handsome. Even Coby Packwood, who was deemed to be right handsome, suffered by comparison, for whereas Coby's body was inclined to stoutness, Stormwalker was tall and lean and beautifully formed, with broad shoulders, a flat belly and hips even smaller than her own, for all his height. Instead of being stiff and dull from an accumulation of grease, sweat and grime, as was Coby's, his hair was as soft and lustrous as the wing of a blackbird.

He was clean. And that, too, was a puzzle, for she could have sworn he'd been rank as a polecat the day he'd attacked her.

Had he attacked her? Had he told her that he was not Little Thunder's father, or had she only dreamed it? He bore a scar on his arm, and she remembered using her knife . . .

Little Thunder is your *son, not mine,* he had said. She could never have dreamed his haughty look when he'd made that claim.

Then whose? If this man who had bullied her and saved her life, caring for her in ways so intimate she blushed to think of them—if he were not the one who had attacked her, then who was he? Why was he doing all this?

Perhaps all wild'uns changed with the moon. Perhaps it amused him to be kind for a while, and he would soon grow bored with it.

She would simply have to gather her strength as quickly as possible and watch for a chance to get away.

A discomfort that had been hardly noticeable at first increased gradually until, on the fourth day when Little Thunder woke and began crying to be fed, Laura found herself cringing.

Stormwalker, who had been blowing gently on the coals banked in one corner of the hearth, turned at the babe's cry in time to see the expression of dread cross her face.

His own face grew still as he waited to see what she would do. Did the boy's cries offend her ears? Surely no woman could reject a babe after having once suckled him at her breast. From his sleeping place outside, Stormwalker had even heard her crooning softly in the night when the boy was fretful. His heart had swelled with gladness, knowing that his patience had finally paid off—she had accepted her son.

Among his own people, babies were taught early not to cry. It was the duty of a mother to see that her child had nothing to cry over, but this one knew less than nothing about mothering. It had been Stormwalker who had led the way, while she had resisted at every turn. He had given her the bear oil that had been meant for his mother, to use on the boy's tender skin, but had she appreciated it?

He had showed her how to rub the oil into the boy's bottom and then pack it in a nest of moss before wrapping him in a tight bundle, and she'd accused him of treating the child as if he were an animal.

"Shall I tell you how an animal would cleanse her young?"

She'd pinched her mouth up into a disagreeable knot. "I reckon the moss will do well enough, since I haven't anything better to use, but I'm not about to grease him down with some vile Indian potion. For all I know, it could be poison."

"In which case," he'd replied smoothly, "I would have used it on your ugly white body to still your wicked tongue. Take it." He'd removed the wooden plug from the bottle and thrust it at her. "The oil will keep his skin soft and smooth. No matter what you think of me, I would never hurt the child."

"I'll do it because you're bigger and stronger and you'll likely remove my hair if I defy you, but I'm warning you, it will sicken me every time I have to hold him, because I can't *bear* that rank, greasy smell!"

"There *is* no smell! Unlike the rancid grease made from your cow's milk, which your people hold in such high esteem, the oil of a bear has no scent at all! When Little Thunder grows to manhood he will thank you for protect-

ing him from the cold and the torment of insects, as my
mother did her own son.''

"Huh!'' was all she'd been able to come up with, but
she'd dutifully poured a small amount of the clear oil in her
palm and massaged the small plump body until it had
gleamed like the nut of the chinquapin tree.

Stormwalker sighed inwardly. Through a mixture of
practice and the inherent reticence that was his nature, he
allowed no hint of his true feelings to show through.

So it had all been pretence on her part, the duplicity for
which so many of her people were known among his—the
ability to say one thing and do another, to profess affection
while harboring only rancor in their hearts.

Now, watching the array of expressions flicker across her
face, fear being the most easily recognizable, he said quietly, "You will feed your child, woman.''

"It won't hurt him to wait a bit.''

"If offends my ears to hear his protests.''

For one long moment the ensuing silence was broken only
by the fitful cries of the hungry babe as they stared at each
other. And then, to Stormwalker's consternation, Laura's
gray eyes suddenly shimmered with tears. Her hand moved
hesitantly toward her swollen breast, almost as if she would
protect herself.

From him? Surely not from her own child.

Suddenly he realized that she had not rejected the boy—
at least, not willingly. For some reason, she was afraid of her
own child.

"Let me help you, Laura Gray.'' Kneeling beside her, he
lifted the babe and began jouncing him gently in his arms.
"Tell me what troubles you and I will do my best to mend
it.''

Round black eyes stared up solemnly into his own. A tiny
chin, no bigger than the tip of his thumb, quivered once,
and then grew still.

"*Roocheha,* Little Thunder? *Roocheha, yenxauhe?*'' he
whispered.

Moved in spite of herself by something she only barely
understood, Laura took refuge in anger. He had no right to

speak to her son in that heathen tongue! The man could speak English near as well as she could, so why did he persist in this tormenting game?

With her aching breasts dampening, throbbing for relief, she gave up and began easing her bodice down over one sore and bleeding nipple. The sooner she commenced this miserable business, the sooner it would be over. Until next time.

For the sake of modesty, she tugged a portion of the buckskin over her breast and reached for the boy. "I warn you, stop teaching him words I don't understand or I'll—I'll... Oh, just give him to me!"

Turning, Stormwalker carefully lowered the child to her outstretched arms. But instead of leaving them, as he usually did, he stood his ground. For reasons he could not pretend to understand, she was once again reluctant to do her duty. "Perhaps I was comforting your son for having been born to a woman who has all the mothering instincts of a cowbird."

Laura glared at him. What would he know of mothering instincts? Savage one moment, suspiciously kind the next—if she lived to be a hundred, she would never understand the ways of the wild'uns.

Gasping softly, she braced herself to endure another painful assault on her tender flesh. Why didn't he leave? Did he enjoy watching her suffer? She bit her lip against crying out, hoping he could read the hatred in her eyes.

The heathen savage! Look at him, standing there in a thin scrap of leather that barely covered his privities, one elbow cupped in his hand, his chin resting on his other fist, as if he were lord of the manor. Suddenly, it struck her as ludicrous. It was such an English pose, one she'd often seen her father assume, that for a moment, as she marveled over his clever mimicry, she almost forgot the agony she was enduring.

"Don't you have something better to do than gawk?" she snapped.

"Gawk? What is 'gawk'?"

"Gawk—stare! To look at what doesn't concern you!"

But when he failed to rise to her baiting, she soon forgot his presence. Hunching her shoulders, she did her best to alleviate the discomfort, but it was no use. She was raw from the unaccustomed attention to a tender part of her body that was unused to such abuse.

"How can the bite of a babe bring pain when he has no teeth?"

Forgetting modesty for once, Laura lifted Little Thunder away from her breast. A spurt of milk shot across the pallet and dampened the toe of Stormwalker's moccasin. "I don't *know* how!" she cried, even as blood beaded on her distended nipple and mingled with her milk, "But believe me, it does!"

Almost before she realized what he was doing, Stormwalker had knelt and removed the babe from her arms. Ignoring his angry screams, Stormwalker laid the child aside and frowned at the evidence of the woman's injury. "Why did this thing happen? You look no different from all other women, save for the sickly color of your skin. Are not all women made for suckling children?"

"If you know so much about *all women*, you can answer your own question," Laura retorted, stung by the unflattering description of her looks as well as by another, less easily identifiable emotion. "You seem to know everything." If her own mother had been able to bear the pain of suckling her, she could do no less for her own child. "Get out! Go do whatever it is you have to do—I won't let your precious son starve."

Squatting before her, his arms crossed over his powerful thighs, Stormwalker shook his head. "Not my son—*yours*."

She hadn't dreamed it, then. But she hadn't done it alone. And Little Thunder looked more like this man than he did any of her family—except for the eyes.

She wasn't ready to trust the red man yet, not entirely. "For as long as he needs what I can give him, perhaps," she muttered, wincing as Stormwalker handed her the child and she put the babe to her breast. "Then no doubt you'll take him off into the wilderness and—and give him away or sell him, not even caring if I've grown fond of him." Gritting her teeth against the fresh assault, she tugged a corner of the buckskin over breast and baby alike.

In spite of all she could do to hold them back, tears brimmed her eyes and overflowed. Stormwalker stared first at her face and then at her breast, looking both puzzled and concerned.

Abruptly, he stood. "Wait. I can help." Without another word he left the cabin.

Laura stared after him, telling herself she wished he would keep on going—back to where he came from—and leave her in peace. Yet even as the thought formed in her mind, she wondered if it were entirely true.

Within minutes Stormwalker returned, bringing with him the fine white doeskin Kitappi had sent as a gift for his mother. With the tip of his blade, he slashed the velvet-soft skin into several pieces the size of his hand and then punched a small hole in the very center. "This will help," he said, and before Laura could know what he was about, he had bared her breast and laid the soft shield in place, working the nub of her nipple through the hole in the center with a deftness that left her gasping.

Her first instinct was to tear the strange thing off her body, but before she could move, he placed Little Thunder back in her arms, positioning the small face against her breast so that the questing mouth had no trouble finding what it sought.

It was much better. Not perfect, for there was still much discomfort, but at least it was bearable now. Laura knew she owed her thanks to this strange wild creature, but with the feel of his hands still burning her intimate flesh, she found it impossible even to look at him.

When she did, he had turned away. He was kneeling, his back to her as he cut the remaining doeskin into several pieces, poking a small hole in the center of each.

How could one man have so many different sides? she thought wonderingly. It was as though two men shared the same body, one a savage and one a gentle friend.

He had saved her life, of that she had no doubt. He had forced her to accept her own son. He had provided food and then cooked for her. Would the savage she had thought him to be have cared for her so patiently?

And now this. "I—that is, I'm grateful to you," she said, her voice so low as to be barely audible.

He heard, all right. She could see the sudden stillness of those hard, clever hands, see the quick lift of his proud head. She had finally managed to shock him, and that pleased her to no small degree. In the short time since he'd found her, she had suffered the loss of her independence, her modesty, her control over the smallest part of her own life. But if she could surprise him, then he was not quite so invulnerable as he would have her think.

"Use these each time you suckle the boy," Stormwalker said gruffly. "I will wash them and place them by the hearth. When they are dry, work them between your knuckles so that—"

"I *do* know how to soften leather," she snapped.

"Use the oil on your nipples," he went on as if she hadn't interrupted. "It will harden your skin until you grow accustomed to your task."

But Laura had had quite enough of being told what to do for a while. "I would rather not, thank you."

He shrugged. "Then I will wait until your flesh grows angry and swollen, and your stubborn mind burns with fever, and I will pour rum over your breasts."

"Try it and I'll lay open your other arm."

There was almost a quality of indulgence in the way he watched her. Like a hawk gliding lazily over the edge of the forest, enjoying the way his small prey darted this way and that to escape the shadow of his wings.

Laura felt it. In spite of the heat inside the cabin, she shivered. She would escape, all right. There was no way of knowing what he'd planned for her future. Perhaps he planned to sell her to a band of Indians, for she'd heard that white captives were prized by the heathens.

She would bide her time, regaining her strength and laying careful plans. Meanwhile, as distasteful as it was, she knew she must lull the big savage into thinking she was perfectly content to remain here forever, eating his tasteless mush, nursing his son—*someone's* son—and allowing him to treat her as if she were already his slave.

Chapter Nine

As late spring gave way to summer, Laura recovered the strength she had lost over the winter months, when she had been miserably pregnant and unable to provide more than the barest necessities for herself. If she'd had an elder brother, he could have shown her no more consideration than did Stormwalker.

Yet, there was nothing at all brotherly about the wary relationship that had sprung up between them.

At times Laura was certain that Stormwalker could have had nothing at all to do with the horror that had struck so suddenly that day last September—yet he had been there. He wore her scar to remind her, but try as she would, she could not remember clearly what had happened.

He was maddeningly stubborn. He was abrupt. He was inclined to be dictatorial, as if he were unaccustomed to having his word challenged. Yet she could find little of the savage in him, in spite of the fact that he went about clad in no more than moccasins and a scrap of leather barely big enough to preserve his modesty. And there was no denying that he had saved her life and the life of her son.

Too often for her own peace of mind, she found herself wondering about him—about his home, his life with his own people. Did he have a wife? Perhaps he had several, for she'd heard the Indians thought nothing of filling their lodges with as many wives as they could afford.

Imagining him lying with a woman, touching her in that special way her father had sometimes touched her mother, always brought on an uncomfortable feeling of restlessness, and she quickly dismissed the thought. As long as he restricted his choice to his own kind, he could lie with a hundred women as far as she was concerned. As he probably had, she thought with a sidelong glance at the tall, virile figure deftly skinning a muskrat outside the cabin.

At times she would gaze down at Little Thunder and wonder. Could the man who not only provided her food, but cooked it, too, possibly be the same man who had used her so brutally that day last fall?

Her head said it was possible, but her heart said emphatically *no*!

She examined the tiny features of her son again and again, but in spite of a similarity of coloring in skin and hair, she could see nothing of Stormwalker in the child's face.

Stormwalker. She was almost certain her father had mentioned a wild'un called Stormwalker...or had it been Stoneworker? She wished now that she had paid more attention.

As days passed, Laura felt an increasing need to understand this strange, silent man who had taken the place of both friend and family in her life. But trying to see into Stormwalker's heart and soul was like trying to see into the dense morning fog that sometimes came rolling up from the river in the early spring.

She would do better to try and understand herself. Was she the only one who was aware of the strange tension that seemed to spring up between them without warning? It was a feeling she'd never experienced before, something she was at a loss to explain. They would be talking of perfectly ordinary matters, such as whether a particular fish was better roasted, boiled or wrapped in leaves, buried in coals and baked, when suddenly he would rise and walk out without another word.

Or he would come in to find her feeding Little Thunder, something he'd watched her do countless times before he'd entrusted her with the task, and he would stare as if he had never seen either of them before. For reasons Laura was at a loss to explain, her face would suddenly catch fire. She would grow angry and snap at him, and he would mutter a few words in that heathen tongue of his and disappear for hours.

At least he no longer fed her that awful, tasteless pap, but allowed her all manner of fish and game, as well as a sort of bread that he made from ground corn and acorns. He claimed it was not near as tasty as that made by the women of his village, but to Laura, who was starved most all the time these days, the thin, crusty cakes were delicious.

"Tell me about your life with your own people," she said one evening when they had reduced a feast of roast squirrel to a neat pile of polished bones.

Hiding his surprise, Stormwalker considered his words carefully before replying. Never before had the woman evinced the least interest in him as a person. As a man. He had expected her to show some small curiosity about the evidence of his mixed heritage—to be disgusted by it, as were most of her people. But it was as if she were blind to anything so personal as the color of his eyes.

Had he come to her in the guise of John Walker, he had no doubt that she would have accepted him readily enough. She might even have remembered the day he had comforted her outside Packwood's Store, the day she had stood up for Kitappi, at such great expense to herself.

Stormwalker had not forgotten her bravery. Nor had he forgotten the way she had felt in his arms, so small, so fragile. Her sweet woman scent had remained in his nostrils long after she had disappeared—long enough to have haunted more than a few of his dreams.

Did she remember? Had she even been aware of him that day, other than as something to lean on for a moment while she recovered her composure? He knew she still remembered Three Turtle's attack, for Little Thunder was a constant reminder. Did she also remember the man who had tried to help her? The man who had buried her parents to spare her having to see their mutilation? The man who, when he would have taken her away, she had struck with her knife?

The woman had suffered much. It would take time to heal.

"Should I not have asked?"

Her hesitant voice reminded him that her question about his life with his own people had gone too long unanswered. "Much the same as your own. We are little different from any other people—some among us being lazy, some industrious, some wise and some foolish."

"You—you keep to yourselves, though," she prompted.

"Not at all times. We trade with your people, as they trade with ours. I have friends among your people." He was about to say that her father had been among them, when she leaned forward, her eyes brilliant in her small face.

"Then why do you murder us?"

Sending a fleeting prayer to the Great Spirit for wisdom in the choice of his words, Stormwalker tried to explain the fears and quite natural resentment of his people toward hers.

"Since the time before the beginning, Laura Gray, my people have lived on these lands. We planted corn and hunted game, and then moved on before we had angered the animals and scarred the land. At times we fought, for it is the way of men to fight, but we also feasted and played together."

He wondered how he could make her understand, why he should even try. Yet try he must, for his whole life had been directed toward forming a better understanding between the two great people whose blood flowed in his veins. "Your people came to our land and began to clear the forest. They made fences and told us we could no longer follow the game because the land now belonged to them."

"But there's so much land—how could you begrudge my father enough to grow corn to feed his family?"

Ignoring her interruption, he went on. "They fought us with weapons we did not understand, with guns and fevers and laws that were made by foolish men and written in words that change, depending on the color of a man's skin."

"My father harmed no one—he liked the wild'uns."

Stormwalker was amused to see the color rise to her cheeks. Poor little one, did she truly not understand the foolish arrogance of her words? "Your father is but one among many, Laura. Did the white man trade the Great Spirit a handful of beads for the land? Did he say, Great Kishalamaquon, I will give you three pieces of the gold, which I dug from your belly, and in exchange, you will give me all of yourself?"

"That's ridiculous—the king—"

"Whose king?" Stormwalker interrupted quietly.

"Why—I reckon it was Charles, but now George—"

"Did these kings of yours make the earth that they can give it to a chosen few?"

"You don't understand," she cried, shaking her head so that her hair caught the glitter of firelight.

He understood better than she realized, for he had lived among her people in his travels, his schooling. But somehow, he had to make *her* understand. He did not know why it was so important—he only knew it was.

"Many of my people are frightened, Laura. There are those who hate the white man for forbidding us to hunt near their plantations, for spreading their diseases and their vices among a people who are too weak to resist." No hint of feeling could be discerned from his austere features as he picked up one of the small bones and began idly working it into a fish hook with his knife. After a moment he lifted his eyes and said quietly, "If hatred can be justified, then there are some, such as the man who attacked your family, whose hatred is just. Three Turtle lost his young sister and his mother when a white trapper came upon the child at play. Three Turtle was once a man of honor, Laura Gray. He was once my friend. Now he has become little better than an animal."

"An animal who preys on innocent people." Laura shivered in spite of the warm night air. Their eyes met and held, and Stormwalker watched with pity and understanding the feelings that flickered across her face. He had come to know her well in the weeks he had remained on Bad Medicine Island. For all her stubbornness and foolish bravery, there was neither guile nor wickedness in her heart.

Gathering up the pile of bones, he rose in one fluid movement. "I will leave you now," he said. It was as close as he had come to bidding her good-night, for all too often their days ended with an exchange of sharp words.

By now, Stormwalker knew her habits well. Each day, at that special time of quietness just before the sun slipped beneath the earth, Laura went to the small pond to wash herself and her few garments. Each day, he found something to do that allowed him to remain close enough to hear if she cried out, yet far enough away to preserve the modesty that was so precious to her.

Which seemed foolish in the extreme, considering the fact that he had brought her son into the world and cared for her most intimate needs afterward because she had no one else.

Still, he would not risk offending her, much less frightening her. He knew well that she did not yet trust him completely. It was in the way she watched him, as if wondering when he would leap on her with his knife and take her scalp.

If the truth were known, he had far more reason to be wary of her than she of him. He had never laid a hand on her in anger, even though he still wore the mark of that rusty blade she kept beside her even now. Surely she must realize that all men were not like Three Turtle. Or even the younger Packwood.

Stormwalker suspected that he could have won her over much more easily by telling her of his own mother, whose skin, hair and eyes were as pale as her own, yet he could not bring himself to do so—not yet. For reasons he could not explain, it was important to him that she accept him as the man he was—Hatorask by blood, by choice and by inclination, despite his English mother.

It could have been the storm that brought on the dreams, the nightmare. It was the rains that had brought Stormwalker inside to sleep under the leaky cabin roof.

Laura had been asleep for several hours, Little Thunder having long since filled his belly and fallen into a sound slumber. At first the images that formed in her unguarded mind were shadows, the voices hollow, as if muffled by fog.

James Burrus's cry was still echoing on the early morning air
when Laura, who had turned back to fetch her boots, only
to have them float out of her grasp, was running barefooted after her parents, her arms flailing, her breath coming in great gasps. No matter how hard she ran, she could
not seem to move above a crawl. And then, just as she was
about to call out to her parents to wait for her, a long bronze
arm snaked out from the roots of a tree and grabbed her
ankle, throwing her to the ground. In silent horror she felt
a great wicked taproot reach out to wrap around her throat,
choking off her air, and she tried to scream. "Ma! Pa! Oh,
Pa, please—"

Stormwalker opened his eyes in the darkness. Instinctively he remained still, waiting for the sound that had
awakened him to come again. And then he heard it—the
unintelligible whimpers, the groans. A slow prickling feeling moved from his brow to the back of his neck, as if every
hair were standing away from his scalp. If a scream could be
whispered, then that was what he had heard.

She was fighting. While the boy slept peacefully beside
her, Laura was fighting as if her very life depended on it,
and Stormwalker had no doubt as to the identity of her un-
seen enemy.

Moving silently, he lifted the babe and placed him out of
harm's reach, and then he knelt over the woman, stroking
her shoulders with a touch that was both calming and
gentle—a touch that could in no way become a part of her
dream world.

He whispered her name. "Laura. Open your eyes, Laura
Gray. It is but a dream. You are safe, all is safe. Open you
eyes now, for no one will harm you. You are safe, Little
Sparrow, safe . . . safe. . . ."

Gradually she grew still. The feeble sounds quieted, but
her skin was cold as the heart of winter. With his warm
hands, he began to chafe her bare arms, his fingers trailing
down to her own small hands, grown soft these past few
weeks, and then up again, to her throat, where a pulse beat
like the wings of a frightened bird.

With infinite patience, he stroked each finger, forcing heat to flow through her frail body once more. He leaned over and breathed the warmth of his own body onto her throat, so that it would carry downward to her heart.

Warmed by his moist breath, the clean woman scent of her body drifted upward, causing his nostrils to flare. For one brief moment, Stormwalker was shaken by an urge so powerful, yet so completely unthinkable by any conceivable standard, that he groaned softly.

Slowly, he began to edge away, taking care not to awaken her. Reaching for Little Thunder, he placed him close beside his mother and stood up, taking only a moment to gaze down at them both.

His eyes well adjusted to the feeble light from the banked coals, Stormwalker had no trouble seeing the pale form of the woman and the much darker shape of her son. He sighed. There was no way he could remain with them much longer. The woman was rapidly becoming a threat to him. He had a duty to his own people that was more important than his own desires.

She had recovered from childbirth. He was no longer needed here, he told himself, knowing that it was only an excuse to keep from facing the fact that he wanted her.

That he wanted them both—the white-skinned woman whose blood would further weaken that of his people at a time when they most needed strength. And the son of his old friend.

Silently, Stormwalker left the cabin. There were worse fates than sleeping under a hard summer rain. In his present condition, it could even be considered a blessing.

The sun was shining with a freshly washed brilliance when Laura opened her eyes. Little Thunder was hungry and unwilling to wait another moment, for he'd slept far longer than usual through the night.

"Oh, so you like thunderstorms, do you?" Laura teased. "Sleep through a stormy night with never a squeak, hmm? No wonder Stormwalker called you Little Thunder—his own mother must have had her hands full when he was your age to have named him as she did. At least you're not wandering about yet." Without taking time to wash and change him, she lifted him to her breast, where he latched on and began to suckle greedily. "Little Leech is more like it," she murmured, stroking the silky black hair that seemed to grow longer and thicker each day. She'd thought just lately that she was beginning to see something of her father in his nose and chin, though both features were so tiny as to be laughable.

Leaning back, Laura could almost enjoy the familiar lassitude brought on by sufficient food and little to do but sleep and eat and care for her son. Sooner or later she was going to have to take charge of her life again, but of course, with Stormwalker lording it over them both, there was small chance of succeeding. Better to save her strength for when he tired of playing nurse and nanny and went back to whatever it was an Indian brave did—running around the forest hunting, squatting around fires with his friends—drinking rum until every last one of them toppled over like a felled tree.

Not that she could picture Stormwalker falling under the spell of rum. He was far too dignified, too stern. If he drank at all, he would dare the stuff to addle his wits, and rum would come out the loser.

She smiled at the thought of seeing her solemn keeper staggering about and spouting all manner of nonsense the way both the Packwood men and even her own Pa did on occasion.

As the sun climbed higher in a cloudless sky, the heat inside the small room became intolerable. Laura drank the broth of wild leeks and spiny mussels that Stormwalker had brought inside just as she finished oiling Little Thunder's squirming body and replacing the soiled moss with clean.

It was time she started walking more. So far she had hardly ventured out of sight of the cabin.

Taking time to splash off her face and hands in the nearby pond, she settled the boy comfortably on her hip and set out along the faint trail that led around to the other side of the island, the side that faced the mainland. She could walk completely around the island in far less than an hour, even allowing for circling the marshy places and clambering over the trees that had died of old age or been blown over by storm winds in years past.

"Those strange creatures flying just above the water are called pelicans, Thunder," she pointed out. And several minutes later, when she paused to rest in a shady oak grove, she dutifully pointed out the tiny, green-scummed pond to her sleeping son. "The water's sweet enough I reckon, but I'd be scared to drink it, it's so black from all the oak trees. Your grandpa called it the black pond—claims he used to drop a hide in there for no more'n half a day, and it'd be tanned hard enough to make door hinges without him having to do another thing to it. But you know Pa—he was a wicked one for yarning."

It was not until she reached the far side of the island, where the mainland lay like a hazy green blur upon the horizon, that she saw Stormwalker.

"You startled me!" she accused.

"I did nothing."

"Well, how was I to know you'd be hiding out here in the bushes this way? Or have you been following me all along?"

"I have no need to follow you."

Dimly, Laura was aware that she was being unfair. Stormwalker had done nothing to frighten her; he had merely been standing at the edge of the woods, staring out across the water. As if he could see the scattered ruins of all the farms that dotted the rich low land.

"Have you seen any boats?" she asked, unaware of the wistful note that crept into her voice.

"Three," Stormwalker replied, and without asking permission, he lifted Little Thunder from Laura and held him easily in the crook of one powerful arm. Laura tried to resent it, but the truth was, the boy was growing heavier each day and it had been a long time since she had lugged around heavy bundles of pelts or helped pry stubborn stumps from the hard ground. Her arms had grown weak.

"Fishing boats?"

"Only one carried canvas. The other two were from the village of Secotan."

"Indians," she murmured with a small shudder and then bit her lip in chagrin. After all he had done for her, she owed him politeness, at least.

"We are not Indians, Laura Gray. We are called *Unqua* by some, *Nuppin* by others. My people refer to our brothers as *Yauh-he*. What you call boats, we call *watt*." He shrugged, a gesture that struck her as peculiarly English. "Call us what you will, I do not care."

He fell silent, and Laura could think of nothing more to say. She could have asked if any of his brothers, as he called them, were likely to visit the island, except that he had already explained that most of them were far too superstitious to risk incurring the wrath of an angry spirit that might have survived the floods that had washed over the island since those poor mortals had been banished there to die.

Most of them, but not all, she thought, idly toying with a cluster of small green acorns. For instance, Stormwalker had not been frightened off by the thought of a stray ghost.

Tossing the acorns aside, she was about to reach out for her baby when Stormwalker took a deep breath and said, "I will be leaving at first light tomorrow."

Laura was stunned. How many times had she willed him to leave, hated him with every beat of her heart when she'd thought he'd been the one who had murdered her parents and raped her—and even after she had learned the truth, she had chaffed at his constant bossiness, the irritating way he had of always knowing what was best for her and seeing that she did it.

But *leaving*?

"Leaving?" she repeated, her large gray eyes widening expressively as she stared at the tall, handsome man she had come to depend on over the past few weeks.

He nodded briefly. "I have been gone too long. My people will wonder if I have forgotten them."

"I suppose," she said, more dejected than she would ever have believed possible. "You have family—friends. Goodness knows, I certainly don't need you any longer, but I thank you for all your help. That is, for the food and the—uh . . . other. But I'm fine now, just as strong as an ox, and Little Thunder—I'm thinking of naming him Edward, did I tell you? Once I get back to town, I thought I'd call him after my father, which is what I'd planned all along, only—''

Stormwalker cut into the flow of words, wanting to take her in his arms and not daring to touch her. ''Edward. It is a good name.''

Mutely, she stared at him, her lips pinched tightly as if to prevent another awkward rush of words. He wanted to tell her he would be back before nightfall, but he did not know if she would be pleased or angry.

Instead, he said only, ''There were two fat fish in the weir. They will be best roasted.''

Laura's head lifted immediately. ''I believe I will boil them.'' She reached out and removed her son from his arms, angry with herself for talking too much, for not wanting him to go—for caring at all.

''Roasted would be better,'' he said with a suspicion of a smile.

''I prefer them boiled.'' As if she hadn't caught her own fish before he ever came along. Caught them, cleaned them and cooked them, too, as well as birds, squirrels, shellfish and even a possum, although that had been too fat for her taste. ''I do appreciate all you've done,'' she said with a lightness that cost her dearly. ''As it happens, I'll be leaving soon, myself. I have so many friends—I thought I might visit at Packwood's Crossing for a spell and then go up to Bath Towne.''

Without moving, Stormwalker seemed to come closer until he was looming over her. ''You will stay. It is not safe for you to journey so far alone.''

''I'll not be alone. Little Thunder will be with me.''

He didn't bother to reply. He didn't have to. His eyes said it all, those strange blue eyes that were so completely alien in a face that was totally Indian. Or *Yauh-he* or whatever it was he'd called himself.

Suddenly Laura felt unbearably vulnerable. Not because he was leaving her, but because he was looking at her. As if he were threatening her somehow. Yet all he'd said was that he was going and that she was to stay. Where was the threat in that? Once he had gone, she would be free to do as she pleased, and it would please her mightily to be shed of the arrogant creature who barked orders at her all day long. It was either "wash now" or "eat this!" "Sleep now" or "drink this."

Why, he had even ordered her not to go into a certain thicket to relieve herself because he had found a nest of young cottonmouths nearby.

"The baby's getting hungry again," she muttered sullenly. "I'd best go back."

She turned to continue on the way she'd been headed, but he touched her arm and shook his head. "Go back the way you came."

"What difference does it make? I've come halfway—it won't take any longer to go on around the island."

But Stormwalker was quietly adamant. "Go back the way you came."

Laura started to protest again, but thought better of it. If she angered him now, he might decide not to leave tomorrow. And she had already made up her mind. The minute he was out of sight, she would make her own escape. It was past time she got on with making a place for herself and her baby among her own people. If they remained here much longer, Little Thunder would grow up as wild as an Indian.

Chapter Ten

The children saw him first. Their cries of delight alerted the small group of women who were gathering groundnuts outside the palisaded village. Kitappi broke away, tossing aside her basket, and ran to meet him.

"Stormwalker, I thought you would never return! Is your mother well? Did you bring me a gift? Will you speak to my father for me?" And then, with hardly a breath in between, she snatched up his hand and tugged him toward the village, taking three dancing steps to his one. "Oh, I am so happy to see you! I have so much to tell you."

"To answer your questions, I have not seen my mother, so I do not know if she is well. I brought you no gift, and yes, rattle tongue, I have every hope of speaking to your father if you will release me before I grow too weak with hunger. I am happy to see you, too."

Kitappi's bright eyes sparkled with determination as she said, "Why must you think of your belly while my whole life is passing by with nothing to show for it? You may eat first if you must, but then you can tell him this for me—say that Three Turtle is less than the stench of a dead fish, but that there is another man who is worthy to become his son."

Stormwalker's features, usually so stern, had gradually relaxed into a broad grin as he enjoyed her dancing steps and her excited chatter. Since the day Gray Otter had rescued her from certain death, Kitappi had been outrageously indulged by all who knew her, for who could resist such a disarming bundle of mischief and virtue? Not long ago

Stormwalker had even entertained the possibility of taking her for his first wife, but now...

He chose his words carefully, not wanting to hurt his beloved little friend by rejecting her improper offer too quickly. "Think carefully before you burden yourself with the care of an ill-tempered man. He would work you until you grew into a withered old woman."

"Ah, but there are ways of sweetening even the nastiest temper, if a woman is wise and willing."

"Do you claim to be wise, little cat?"

She grinned up at him, clasping his hand between both of hers. "Wise enough to know how to make a man content with his lot."

By pretending an itch that needed scratching, Stormwalker managed to ease his hand away. She was comely, he told himself—for all her playful ways, she was a hard worker. She would make him a fine and faithful wife. If his loins did not quicken at the thought of taking her to his lodge, it was only because he was tired.

"Perhaps in a year or two..."

Kitappi pretended to pout. "In a year or two, I will be an old woman."

"You are little more than a baby."

"Hooo! Much you know about it!" she taunted. "I have been a woman for three years. Even my father is afraid I will wither before I bear fruit."

"Yes, but—"

"And Tiree Kiro is so very—"

"Tiree Kiro?" Stormwalker's first feeling was one of immense relief. And then it hit him. "*Tiree Kiro! He is here?* Where? Why did you not tell me? How long ago did he arrive? Has he been made welcome?"

Kitappi came to a dead halt. Hands on her hips, she confronted the man who stood a good three heads taller than she. "Now who's the rattle tongue?"

"Please, Kippi!" In his distress, Stormwalker lapsed into the use of an old pet name for the child who had slept upon him, wet upon him and generally submitted him to all manner of indignities over the years. "This man is my good friend—I would know these things."

"If he is your good friend, why did you never bring him here before?"

"My reasons were sound. When did he first arrive?"

Resuming her course, Kitappi said, "Five suns after you left us. He walked into our village unarmed and spoke your name. Old Cotchee could not understand what he was saying. No one could."

"His father spoke our tongue, but his father died many years ago. T'kiro speaks a mixture of Hatorask and Cherokee, but he speaks English quite well."

"I know. Cotchee took him to my father, and they spoke together in the white man's language. Did you know that T'kiro speaks even better than you?" She glanced at him quickly, as if to see the effect of her words. When he failed to react, she went on. "They talked a long, long, *long* time! I grew impatient."

Stormwalker could well imagine her feelings. Kitappi had been known since childhood for her curiosity, and if one thing outweighed even that, it was her lack of patience. "Has Tiree Kiro told you why he is here?"

"To find a wife?" She looked at him hopefully and Stormwalker searched for a tactful way to let her know that his young friend had neither the time nor the wealth to acquire a wife, and certainly not a wife who was the daughter of a chief.

But before he could find the proper words, they were met by several of his friends, who walked with them to the door of Kokom's lodge, permitting no more to be said on the subject.

Barely restraining his own impatience, Stormwalker waited through the ritual greeting, the smoking of pipes and the offering of thanksgiving for his safe return. He explained to Kokom as briefly as possible that he had not gone to Croatoan, as planned, but had remained on one of the many islands that dotted the sounds and rivers to assist a woman and her child, who were alone and greatly in need of help.

"The woman would have died, her son with her," he said, and drew deeply on his pipe to allow him time to consider how much to tell his old friend.

"Did you not fear her illness yourself?"

Stormwalker choked and pretended that the cause of his distress was the strong tobacco. Recovering, he said, "You need have no fear that I have brought illness among our people."

"She is an English woman," Kokom said flatly.

"You see beyond my words. I could not leave her, Kokom. Her family had been taken from her by one of our brothers."

Kokom grunted. "The work of Hancock," he said, and spat unerringly through the open door of the cypress bark lodge.

"This man did not need Hancock's words. His hatred of the English runs deep and hot."

Stormwalker knew that the relationship between the Mattamuskeet and the Hatorask was delicately balanced. Three Turtle had sought to gain the upper hand over the small divided band of Hatorask by wedding Kitappi. The second offer was yet to be made; the ritual must be followed. The offer must be made and it must be considered by the elders before being rejected, for to do otherwise would bring dishonor to both the Hatorask and the Mattamuskeet.

With so much to be discussed, Stormwalker found it difficult to leave the company of the old chief. Yet he had hoped to return to the island by nightfall. In such times as these, it was not wise to leave a woman and a child unprotected. "Kitappi has told me of your visitor. I spoke to you about Tiree Kiro when last we met. He is a good man."

"How can he teach our people when they cannot understand his words?"

"He has not heard our tongue spoken for many years— since Yauta died. He will learn quickly. It will be good for our runners to learn the Cherokee tongue as long as we trade in the high hills."

"Paugh! Our yaupon speaks the language. They would not cheat us, for they value their black draught too highly."

Of the yaupon tea, which grew in abundance along the east coast but not at all farther west, Stormwalker said, "Others trade with the Cherokee, as well. They can provide what we will not."

"We will see. The boy is small."

"He is a man, not a boy. He has survived more than you know."

"Our people do not want to learn the ways of the English. Even those among us who have always lived in peace with the white men grow weary of their ways. They breed too quickly. Each tide brings great ships from across the sea bearing more of their kind. They would force us from our lands."

"To live in the world of the cottonmouth, one must learn their ways. To trap the mink, one must learn the habits of the mink."

"You would have us learn to live like the white man! Paugh! You speak like your father!"

Stormwalker's straight back seemed to grow straighter still, but his voice remained even. "My father did not bring the English to our shores. It is not within his power, or the power of any man, to send them away. Those who do not learn to live beside these people will perish."

"I am too old to torment my feet with the hard moccasins of the English," Kokom grumbled. "I will not cramp my spirit by forcing it to abide behind walls that are behind fences that are behind palisades. It wearies me to speak of such things."

Pointing out that Num Peree was made up of walled lodges behind a palisade of pointed logs, Stormwalker permitted himself a chuckle. "Did my mother so change the ways of my father?"

Kokom himself had to laugh at this, for both men knew that Bridget Abbott would not change her comfortable doeskin shift and her beaver moccasins for the miserable constricting garments worn by the English women. Nor would she dream of giving up her clean, snug *ouke*, built fresh each season upon the sands of Croatoan, for the finest house in all of Bath Towne.

"I would speak to my friend T'kiro, and then I must leave you. The woman and child are alone and in need of my protection."

Kokom made no attempt to disguise his curiosity. "Will you bring this woman and her child to your lodge, son of Kinnahauk?" It was less a question than a subtle reminder of the complex reasons why it would be impossible for Stormwalker to consider making such an alliance.

"She wishes to return to her own people." The two men studied each other, Kokom recognizing the evasion, but knowing his curiosity would not be satisfied with further questions.

Stormwalker understood that the subject of the woman was closed. He nodded imperceptibly. "I saw three *watt* yesterday. They bore the Coranine mark. Each one carried ten fighting men."

"They were painted?"

"They were painted. Their hair had been dressed with the blood root." It was clearly a war party. No man, with the exception of John Walker, colored his hair red unless he was bound for battle.

"So the raids continue," Kokom said, his shoulders slumping as if under a heavy burden. "If I were a younger man, I would move my people to a new place. I am too old. My bones will no longer carry me as they did in my youth. Have you thought more about taking my daughter as your wife, Stormwalker? You would be a good leader. Your father would be pleased."

"My father may have need of me on Croatoan. My sister Anne has three sons, but her husband is a white man. I do not think they will be accepted by our people."

"It is time our people were reunited under one leader."

"Where? Those on Croatoan will not leave the island. Your people in Num Peree will not want to leave the rich land, where game abound and corn grows well."

Staring out at the peaceful scene, at the orderly rows of lodges, the playing children and the women calmly going about their duties while the old ones sat in the shade and talked of heroic deeds of the past, Stormwalker felt as if he were being torn into many pieces. It was not a feeling he enjoyed, nor did it help his temper, which had been growing more uncertain since the troubles began and never more than during his stay on Bad Medicine Island.

"I will think on your words, Kokom, but the time has not yet come. We are at peace here. The corn grows well, there is still game to be hunted and the herring were so plentiful in the planting moon that they walked on the banks of the rivers."

"Gray Otter can never return. Soon her spirit will be free, for she has suffered long. I would ride the shore once more with my old friend, Kinnahauk. Here, we are surrounded by warring Tuscarora and English, who want none of us. There is no more peace."

"Croatoan has changed, my friend. There are now fences. There are English. They are not yet our enemies, yet the island is no longer as it was."

"Think on my words, son of my old friend."

"I will think on your words," Stormwalker promised. How could he not? His loyalty lay with his own people, for his sister Anne, who was half white, as he was, had married Jedd Rawson. By the old laws, her husband would be chief, but he had no great love for the Hatorask, save for his wife. Would the Hatorask accept her sons as chief? They were more English than Hatorask.

Or would they look to Stormwalker for leadership, as was the case when there were no daughters to chose a proper leader?

The shadows had already swallowed up the distant shore by the time Stormwalker neared Bad Medicine Island. He would have spoken longer to Tiree Kiro, for there was much to be decided, but he had felt a growing uneasiness as the day wore on.

Now his paddle sent the light craft skimming over the surface of the water, driving it high up onto the shore. He leaped out and gathered up the bundles he had brought back with him, wishing he had thought to bring his Little Sparrow a fine doeskin gown and a pair of soft moccasins to protect her small feet.

He had brought only food. That much he had promised her, but a gown would be different—it would be a gift.

It was beneath his dignity to call out as he strode toward the cabin. Even so, he had expected her to come forth to meet him, for he had taken no pains to hide his coming.

He would have to teach her to be more cautious, for others might venture onto the island, even as he had. The old spells were no longer quite so powerful since the coming of so many white men. It was all changing—their beliefs, their language, their habits—their very way of life. Not even the gods were powerful enough to stem the tides of time.

"Woman, I have returned," he announced quietly as he pushed open the door.

There was no response. Even before he searched, he knew she was not there. There was nothing of her there—nothing of Little Thunder. Only the bed of moss and the buckskin that covered it.

Lowering his burden to the dirt floor, Stormwalker looked for some sign of distress. Finding none, he knew a small measure of relief and he told himself she had merely wandered too far, grown tired and stopped to rest. Just yesterday she had wanted to walk around the island and he'd stopped her.

He had stopped her because he had not wanted her to pass by the place where she kept her boat and know that he had hidden it from her sight. Now he wished he had broken it! Because it had gone against his nature to waste a potentially useful craft, even such a clumsy one as those fashioned by the white fishermen, he had merely removed it from where she had left it and hidden it in a stand of reeds.

If she had found it—

Or someone else had found it and gone in search of the owner...

Before the thought was completely formed, Stormwalker was running silently along the shore.

* * *

Laura waved tiredly at the swarm of midges that clouded the air about her head. There was no wind at all. What little there had been during the day had dropped off as the sun had begun to settle.

Back aching from the unaccustomed exertion, she bent to the task of emptying her boat of all the rainwater it had collected over a period of a month or more. It had taken her almost half a day to find it, for it had been well hidden. At first she'd thought it must have drifted off with the tide. There had been several squall shifts that had filled the low-lying marshes with water.

If it hadn't been for the blue heron that had taken alarm and lifted off just as she passed the thicket of reeds for the third time, she would likely have missed the boat completely, but she had looked at the heron and caught a glimpse of pale weathered wood, well hidden from both shore and water.

She had sworn long and loud at the arrogance that had prompted Stormwalker to move her boat from where she had left it. *Her* boat—not his!

It had been more than half full of water, which had meant further delay. Not only that, Little Thunder had decided he didn't like being left up on the bank in the rough hammock she'd fashioned from a buckskin and a length of fishing twine. Nothing would do but that she suckle him until he grew drowsy, and so she'd suckled and bailed, suckled and bailed, and now the sun was sinking. She would have to set out in the darkness, and she was frightened.

No, she was *not* frightened; she was furious! With Stormwalker, because it was all his fault!

Sweat dripped into her eyes, scalding them with salt. She tried an experimental scream, soft enough not to wake her sleeping son, and found there was little comfort in it. What she wanted to do was yell her head off. What she wanted to do was strike out at something and feel her fist connect with solid flesh.

Stormwalker's flesh. Because suddenly it seemed that everything that had happened to her was his fault. The day she had first laid eyes on him, her whole world had fallen apart, and since then nothing had gone right, and it was probably his doing—some way or other. At the moment she was too tired and too angry to try to reason it all out.

How he had gulled her into accepting his presence here she would never know, for every ill that had ever befallen her, and the list grew daily, could be laid at his doorstep.

The damned naked heathen didn't even *own* a doorstep! As far as she could tell, his earthly possessions consisted of a murderous looking knife, a bow and a quiver full of arrows—which he never brought into the cabin, but collected only when he set out to hunt—and that ugly old hollow log he called a boat.

She sighed, waved away another swarm of midges, mopped the sweat off her forehead with a salty forearm and then screamed at the top of her voice as something—someone—moved out of the shadows. "*Sehe, yica!* Would you startle the birds from their nests?"

Not a stone's throw from where she crouched in the slippery wet boat, Stormwalker stood holding her son in his arms. "Don't say things I can't understand! How long have you been here? You have no right to sneak around and scare a body out of her wits!"

"I said, be quiet, woman. Now you understand. I have been here long enough to know that a war party could have come upon you and stolen your son and you would have seen nothing, heard nothing, known nothing until your head was split like an overripe melon."

While Laura was still searching for words to defend herself against the unjust charge, he knelt and placed Little Thunder back on the buckskin and whispered something in the tiny ear.

And then he strode directly toward where she still crouched in the bottom of the boat, the gourd she'd been using to bail with dangling from her nerveless fingertips.

"You stay away from me," she ordered, not liking the purposeful look on his lean face.

He continued to wade through the reeds, heedless of the mussel shells and the sharp roots that had cut her own feet and the possibility of snakes that had haunted her ever since she had discovered the swampy hiding place.

"I am tired, woman. I have had nothing to eat all day. I have gone far and accomplished little, and I am in great need of a bath to cool my temper and cleanse my body."

"Then eat and wash, but stay away from me." Laura began to edge toward the stern of the boat, but her knees slipped on the green slime that had formed on the plank bottom and she fell flat, striking her shoulder on a brace.

"But not even my need is as great as yours, woman. The sight of you offends my eyes. The stench of you offends my nostrils. You will wash yourself, and then you will prepare the food I have brought. After I have taken my fill, if there is anything left, you may have it."

By that time he had reached the boat. Laura managed to get out five words before his hands clamped onto her waist. "I am *not* your bloody—" Squaw, she was about to say, knowing full well how all Indians hated the term her people had given their women.

And then she was in his arms, held tightly enough so that her struggles only served to demonstrate her own helplessness. In less than the time it had taken to lift her from the boat, Stormwalker had reached water that was deep enough for his purpose. Lifting her high, he tossed her as far out as he could.

Laura came up gasping. She floundered around, trying to stay afloat until she could touch the bottom, but her legs were not long enough and her wet gown tangled around her, pulling her down.

Clear cool water closed over her head and she kicked out wildly, struggling to reach the surface again. One of her feet came into contact with something hard and slippery, something that gave her the boost she needed, and she gasped as she felt her face break above the water.

Stormwalker was only inches away, his face oddly contorted. She felt herself sinking again, and she grabbed for him.

At first she thought he was going to push her away, let her drown. After all, why else would he have thrown her out into water that was clearly over her head? damn you! You—'' She went under and bobb face again. "You're just like all the other— hank of wet hair away from her eyes, she flapp in an effort to stay afloat. "The other damned sa even if you hold me under until I sink like a rock, ll come back and haunt you, you just see if I don't!''

Blue eyes widened comically. "You kick me in the *nimmia yopoonitsa*, and you accuse me of trying to kill you? Woman, the moon spirit has stolen your wits!''

"I warned you not to speak that heathen tongue to me! If you have something to say, then say it right out so that I can understand you!''

"The nut box. You kicked me there. A woman who does such a thing to any man deserves to—''

"*Nut* box! It's you who's lost your wits!''

Stormwalker grabbed one of the hands with which she had been clinging to his shoulders and carried it beneath the surface of the water. Laura felt something soft and recognized the feel of wet buckskin. At first she didn't recognize what lay beneath it, for the shape was curious and complex and seemed to change even as her palm was pressed against it. What had been small and soft was rapidly becoming large and hard.

Realization came slowly, then all at once. Laura gasped, half filling her lungs with water. She struggled to remove her hand, but he held her there, and when she cast him a pleading look, she was terrified by the narrow glitter in his eyes.

She was coughing, trying to clear her lungs, and when Stormwalker finally released her hand, his breathing not much better than hers, she shoved herself away and went under immediately.

He lifted her head above the water, and she was forced to hang on to him, for with her heavy gown pulling her under, it was either that or drown. Holding her against him, Stormwalker turned toward the shore, and Laura, the last of her small store of strength now completely gone, lay her head on his chest and allowed him to carry her.

⊃ e managed two steps after he released her before collapsing onto the hard-packed sand some few yards away from the reed bed. Rolling over onto her stomach, she cradled her burning cheek on her arms and closed her eyes, still breathing hard. Her limbs felt heavy as logs, and she wished she could simply sleep and sleep and wake up a hundred years from now and find herself back on the farm with Ma and Pa, clearing and planting and walking proudly through the neat rows of corn and pun'kins and beans and tobacco.

She sensed his presence beside her before he spoke. One more thing she hated about him—the way he had of sneaking around, silent as a shadow, and catching a body unaware! "Go away," she mumbled.

"Your gown is broken."

It had split across the shoulders soon after she had begun bailing, fibers weakened by years of wear and the fierce summer sun. "Gowns don't break, they tear," she muttered sullenly, and then wondered why she wasted her breath. What difference did it make? What difference did it make that soon she would be forced to go around in less than even this naked savage wore—unless she fashioned herself a gown like her friend Kitappi had worn from the buckskin that had served to cover her bedding.

"When you are rested, we will go."

"I'd just as leave stay where I am."

"You are not *rockcumme*, Little Sparrow, only *roocheha*. Come, we will go."

"I warned you, Stormwalker—"

He interrupted smoothly. "I have learned your tongue well, woman. Will you not learn mine, or are the wits of the English people less nimble than those of the Hatorask?"

"My wits are sharp and my knife is sharper still, as you know to your sorrow." Her face was still turned away from where he knelt beside her. The sky had grown almost dark now, and in her wet gown, she was chilled. A warm fire and a bite to eat would be welcome, but she would die before she would admit it.

It was the sound of his laughter that undid her. Slowly, she sat up, making no effort to brush away the sand that stuck to her skin and the front of her gown. "I suppose I may as well. If I refuse, you'll drag me there by the hair on my head," she muttered.

Stormwalker stood and held out a hand to assist her. She ignored it and made a clumsy business of getting to her feet, her heavy, sandy skirts seeming to weigh more than she could lift. "I doubt I'll be able to walk, after you did your best to drown me."

"I'll not find it much easier, after you did your best to castrate me."

"To *what*?" she shrieked, spinning around and almost losing her balance.

"You mean it was not deliberate?" The sound of innocence in his voice was almost too great to be real.

"You know it wasn't, and furthermore, I do wish you would not say such things."

"What things do you not wish me to say?"

"That I—that you—that word!"

"Which word?"

"You know very well which word, you—you bloody ignorant savage!" He was toying with her the way a cat toyed with a mouse. The way a hawk circled lazily over a sparrow, knowing it was no match for his great wings and sharp talons.

The light of the devil glinted in his eyes as he watched her clumsy progress across the soft, dusty sand. She had gone no more than three steps when Stormwalker reached out and spun her about so that she collided with his hard body.

"Woman, your tongue is as vicious as your kick. I grow weary of your scolding, for I have done nothing to deserve it. You will learn to be more respectful."

"Of *you*?" she crowed disbelievingly. "A naked heathen who tried to drown me? I would sooner curtsey to a far-rowing sow."

Stormwalker's smile was not a pleasant thing to see. Laura felt goose bumps rise along her arms, but she stood her ground. This had not been a good day. Nothing had gone right, and she had a sinking feeling that things were going to get worse.

Chapter Eleven

Before they had covered half the distance to the cabin, Laura, clutching her ragged blanket, was once again gasping for breath. Stormwalker had bundled Little Thunder into the buckskin and slung it over one shoulder, where the babe bobbed along contentedly. With the rock-hard knuckles of his right hand, Stormwalker prodded Laura along before him, poking her between the shoulder blades if she didn't walk quickly enough to suit him.

Laura was all but running, stumbling every few steps as they neared the eroded place where the roots of long-dead trees lay exposed on the sand. Now she felt his hand on the bare skin of her back again and bit back a cry. She was furious with him for—for everything! But even more furious with herself for being so terribly, constantly aware of him.

When she had thought he had left for good, she had told herself she was glad and forced herself to believe it. But when he had come back, her heart had flopped over in her breast like a fresh-caught shad. For a single instant she had wanted to hurl herself into his arms.

Instead, she had somehow managed to make a complete fool of herself.

"I can't go any faster, damn you!" she panted.

He said nothing. He had not spoken a single word since he had collected her baby, snatched up her blanket and thrown it at her, and pointed her in the direction of the cabin. Since then he had chivied her every step of the way until she was fit to drop.

It was almost totally dark inside the cabin. Laura stopped dead in her tracks, too spent to move a step farther. Her ears strained to hear what he was doing, but his moccasined feet made no sound as he crossed the earthen floor. She sensed when he lowered Little Thunder down onto the buckskin, which was all that remained of their bedding. Wholeheartedly, she willed him to run into a wall, to trip and fall flat on his insufferably proud face.

No such luck. The red devil could see as well in the dark as he could in the broad of day.

Laura slipped back out through the door, hardly knowing what she was doing—only knowing she couldn't bear to be shut up in that cabin with him a moment longer. He affected her like no other man she had ever known. It was as if there were three Stormwalkers living inside one skin. One she feared, one she had gradually come to trust and one she . . .

Still standing there, she was trying to accustom her eyes to the dim starlight when Stormwalker emerged and came to stand before her. He didn't speak. He didn't touch her.

And after all their exertions, he wasn't even breathing hard, which irritated her all the more.

Laura was ready to collapse. She had been going at a dead run all day, first in search of her boat, which had taken forever to find, and then in search of something to bail it out. The gourd she had finally found had been back by the cabin, beside the fresh pond, and, of course, she'd had to carry Little Thunder with her every step of the way. She could hardly leave him on one side of the island while she ran back and forth to the other.

With a contrariness that had driven her to distraction, he had insisted on nursing far more often than usual, as if sensing her uneasiness and seeking the only security he knew. She might have been tempted to let him cry, but after hearing of the three canoes that had passed close by only the day before, she had been afraid of attracting unwelcome attention.

By working until her arms were fit to fall off, she had nearly finished bailing the boat. She would have set out, no matter how late the hour, for she had been determined not to lose the opportunity, but then Stormwalker had returned and tried to drown her.

Why? He had seemed so friendly these past few weeks. He had saved her life and nursed her back to health. They had begun to talk, and lately they had even laughed together a few times.

Why would he suddenly turn against her?

Stormwalker could have told her if he had been in the habit of explaining his actions to anyone, but he was not. And certainly not to a woman—a white woman, at that.

He might have explained the devastating sense of loss that had come over him when he had thought her gone. He might even have explained the feeling of happiness when he had found her again. But how could he explain his anger that she should try to leave him?

Or the guilt he felt for not wanting her to go—ever.

Laura tensed as he came to stand beside her. She could feel the heat of his body, could smell the familiar mixture of woodsmoke and leather and herbs—and some faint, intriguing scent that was all his own.

Confused by her own turbulent emotions, she stepped back and her heel caught in a tangle of briar runners. She would have fallen had not two strong hands reached out in the darkness to catch her. Imprisoned in a cage of hard flesh, she suddenly felt the last vestige of resistance seep away on the still night air.

"I would not harm you, Little Sparrow."

It was as if the words, spoken softly in that deep, familiar voice, shattered the control she had clung to for so long. Unable to stop the tears, she felt her cheeks grow wet. Her throat ached with hopelessness, with frustration and with a grief too long denied.

When Stormwalker pressed her head against his chest with one of his large hands and held it there, smoothing her hair away from her wet cheeks, she gave up and began to cry.

"*Mothai*, Little Sparrow, my shoulders are strong. You are safe...safe...safe now."

She cried until she had emptied herself of tears, completely unaware that her arms were wrapped tightly around Stormwalker's waist, her damp face burrowed against his warm chest. He was comfort—that was all she knew. A solid, reassuring wall of warm comfort that she desperately needed.

Now and then he spoke again in the low, deep murmur that rolled over her head without actually piercing her consciousness. His hand stroked her back in slow, soothing circles, and after a while, she lifted her head, drew in a deep, shuddering breath and tried to step away from his arms.

"I'm sorry," she whispered, and then wished she hadn't. She owed him no apologies, for he was the cause of too many of her troubles.

Only gradually did she become aware that her hiccups and occasional sniffles were not the only sounds to be heard in the still darkness. From inside the cabin, Little Thunder had begun to fret, letting her know that it had been hours since he had last filled his belly.

Stormwalker's arms fell away, and she stood awkwardly before him. She was ashamed of her weakness, of letting herself be held that way, and embarrassed because she had liked it so very much. If the truth were known, she would like nothing more than to burrow back into the same warm shelter and forget about Packwood's Crossing and Bath Towne and the fact that life consisted of more than just three people and one small island.

Little Thunder stopped whimpering and began to cry in earnest, and she took another step back and forced herself to turn away, grateful for the excuse. "I—Little Thunder—" she murmured, and then she called out, "I'm coming, sweetings."

Without looking back, she hurried into the cabin. She didn't want to think about Stormwalker, about the way she had clung to him, as if she had every right—as if he were an ordinary man.

Yet even as she lifted Little Thunder up and began to unfasten her bodice, she could not put it from her mind. It had felt so right, so familiar. As if she had once sought refuge in those same arms, wept her heart out against that same hard, warm chest.

And heard the same whispered words—words that had somehow found a secret place in her heart and lingered there.

Which was crazy, of course, because she would never have dreamed of doing such a thing with any stranger, much less a wild'un.

More than an hour had passed by the time Little Thunder was ready to sleep again. He had drained both her breasts and would have taken more, she suspected. Evidently, he had thrived on the day's excursion. She had brought up his wind and then watched as he kicked and gurgled, waving his tiny perfect fists in the air.

In the meantime, Stormwalker had come inside and built up a small fire on the hearth, which tempered the night chill and enabled her to see a bit. Laura still wasn't sure if she'd been glad or sorry when he had turned and walked out without a word.

While Little Thunder slept quietly, she took the opportunity to brush the sand from her scalp with her fingertips and braid her hair, tangles and all. There was nothing she could do about her gown, which made it all the more imperative that she get away before much longer.

She knew from painful experience how it felt to face a whole town wrapped in a few tattered rags and little else. It would be doubly awkward this time, for she would be carrying a dark-skinned, sooty-haired babe packed in moss and buckskin.

And no matter how kind and generous Stormwalker had been—and he had, in his own infuriating way—she knew this was something she would have to do alone. His presence at her side would only give rise to more questions. Questions she was not yet ready to answer.

Laura was preparing to settle down for the night when Stormwalker appeared in the open doorway again. Her heart beating only a little faster, she bade him a quiet goodnight.

"Come outside, Laura."

"I'm tired. It's been an exhausting day."

"I would offer to carry you, but I still have not recovered from your attack on my—"

Furious with him for reminding her of that embarrassing episode, she said through clenched teeth, "Would you *hush*?"

"—*nimmia yopoonitsa,*" he finished drolly.

"If I thought I could get away with it, I would have whacked off your precious *nimmia yopoonitsa* and fed it to the turtles!"

Little Thunder stirred in his sleep, and Laura murmured soothingly to him, still glaring at the tall, shadowy figure that filled the doorway.

"You are quick with a blade, Little Sparrow, and even quicker with your tongue." Laughter lurked just beneath his deep voice, and impatiently, Laura scrambled to her feet and stood before him, hands planted militantly on her hips.

"All right, all right—just get out before you wake my son! I'm the one who'll have to settle him again if you get him all riled up."

The rude hut stood in a small clearing surrounded by white sand that reflected the starlight. On all sides the dense black forest closed in, offering protection from the harsh winter winds. A tangle of wild vines spilled into the clearing, and to the right, a bright glint revealed the presence of the fresh pond. The small island seemed boundless and mysterious at night, and Laura was suddenly uneasy.

The raucous call of a night heron broke through the nightly chorus of tree frogs. As if it were a signal, two bullfrogs began a well-rehearsed duet. Her island was both beautiful and peaceful, Laura told herself. It had sheltered her well when she needed shelter. She had nothing to fear.

So why was she trembling?

"You have not eaten," Stormwalker said as calmly as if he had not practically forced her to come outside with him.

"Is *that* all you wanted to say? My belly already reminded me, thank you, and since there's nothing I can do about it now, I'm going to sleep and forget it." She turned to go.

"Stay."

She knew better than to try and outrun him. He would just snatch her back, and she didn't think her nerves could bear it if he touched her again. "I have no intention of standing out here in all these mosquitoes until you think of something worth saying." She crossed her arms under her full breasts, cool in spite of the midsummer heat.

"I did not take time to eat before I left here, nor while I was gone."

"Good. Perhaps you'll starve before morning." With a grim smile she edged two steps back toward the cabin before turning her back on him.

Stormwalker grunted a rough word that would have been a curse in any language. Catching her by the elbow, he spun her around, and this time when she slammed into his body there was nothing even faintly comforting in his strength.

"Waurraupa wunneau!" he growled, his sweet breath warm on her face. His eyes seemed to glow in the light of the rising moon.

"D-don't speak to me in th-that heathen tongue!"

"Are you not a crab? A scrawny white crab? Even with her claws removed, the crab will inflict pain to anyone who tries to hold her tightly. She is all sharpness and hard shell, Laura Gray, but once her outer shell is crushed—" His voice took on a quality that was even more frightening than his anger "—she is sweet and tender inside. Are you sweet and tender inside, Laura Gray?" The fingers that had bit into her flesh with painful force had grown gentle. Now they moved slowly over her upper arms, stroking, soothing, casting a spell that she could see as clearly as she could see the rising moon, but was helpless to resist.

"What do you want from me?" she cried despairingly.

She heard the soft catch of his breath as he opened his mouth to speak. At first no words emerged, and then he said quietly, "I do not know. I do not know."

Nothing he could have said would have had such a profound effect on her. She had known him a month—more like a year if you counted the first time she had ever laid eyes on him. And one thing she could say with certainty— Stormwalker was a man who knew his own mind. Since coming to know him on the island, she had been forced to admit that along with his more irritating ones, he possessed many admirable qualities. Intelligence, for one. Kindness in no small measure and determination.

She knew, too, that he was a proud man, one who did not easily admit to weakness. And for him to admit that he didn't know something must be almost as difficult as—

As for her to admit that she was growing dangerously fond of him.

"Come, we will eat now," he said abruptly.

Relieved and disappointed at once, she said, "There's no food. What little bread we had is still down by the boat."

"I have brought smoked fish. I have brought dried venison. I have brought cakes made of *cose* and *yonne*."

"Cakes made of what?" Cakes made of anything suddenly sounded like heaven.

"Cose. Yonne," he repeated, knowing full well she had no notion of what they were. He could be offering her cakes made of snake tails and fish guts and she wouldn't know the difference until she'd tasted them.

"Do you want to know what it is, Laura Gray?"

She was sorely tempted to tell him what he could do with his cakes, but she was starving. The mere thought of food had set her belly to grinding until she thought she would faint. "Hmm," she admitted grudgingly.

"What word do you wish me to explain, Laura? Cakes? They are—"

"I *know* what cakes are!"

"What word, then?"

"You know what word—there were two of them."

"Which two?"

He was openly teasing her now, leading her on. And like a fool, she let herself be led. *"Cose! Yonne!* What do they mean?"

"Ahh, *cose*. It is only what you call corn that has been parched and ground until it is soft enough to work."

Not fish guts, then. "And the other word," she reminded him grimly.

"What other word? Parched? It means—"

"Not parched, you stubborn heathen! *Yonne!* What does it mean?"

"*Yonne* is only the fruit you call peach."

Leaning forward, Laura grabbed his arms. "You have peach cakes? Where? Why didn't you tell me?" It seemed like a lifetime since she'd had anything near so wonderful! She could remember her mother's peach dumplings, running with honey—ahh, she would die for just one taste.

Stormwalker chuckled under his breath. A few crumbs and he had the little sparrow eating from his hand once more. "You see—it is not so difficult, is it?" he teased.

"Stormwalker, please! The cakes?" And then, more tentatively, "What's not so difficult?"

"Speaking my filthy heathen tongue. Already you have learned much this day. First *nimmia yopoonitsa*, and now *cose* and *yonne*."

Even in the darkness she could see the white gleam of his smile, and it was all she could do not to answer it. The man had witched her good and proper. There was no other possible explanation.

Stormwalker spread the blanket she had dropped when he'd hurried her back to the cabin. He urged her down, and without another word he disappeared back inside the cabin.

It would kill him to tell her where he was going, Laura thought, irritated all over again by his arrogance but, oddly enough, no longer truly angry. And certainly not afraid.

He was back before she could think of following. Her eyes, now accustomed to the thin light, saw the small bundle he carried in one hand. Easing down beside her on the blanket, he began untying the packet of food, while her belly rumbled like a thunderstorm.

The feast spread between them on the thin, patched wool, Laura practically fell upon the cakes. She had gobbled down two before she remembered herself sufficiently to sit up and take a deep breath. "They're a bit tart for my taste," she said, as if a haughty tone could make up for her ravenous behavior a moment before. "However, they're quite acceptable."

Again she saw the flash of his grin, but other than that, he made no comment. After her brief attempt at restraint, Laura gave in. If the cakes had been delicious, the smell of smoked fish and venison that had been heavily spiced and dried slowly in the sun was totally irresistible. She reached for a chunk of the black-crusted white flesh that flaked apart in her hands.

"Mmm, this is wonderful," she said with her mouth full. Mosquitoes swarmed about her head and she swatted them away absently, too intent on eating her fill of this glorious feast to worry about a few itchy bites. After the recent rains, the pests had been worse than ever.

"Your mother should have prepared your skin with bear oil when you were young, then you would not feel the bite of insects nor the heat nor the cold."

Tearing off a bite of venison with her teeth, Laura chewed a moment before answering. "All right, so I was wrong about that. It doesn't stink, it's not sticky and it's done a wonder of good for the rash on Little Thunder's bottom, but you can't make me believe it can do all that."

Instead of replying, Stormwalker rose and went to the pond. He scooped sand and rubbed it on his hands and his mouth, then rinsed them with water before drinking his fill.

Then he returned to stand over her. "Do not eat any more now or you will sicken."

"But I've only just started."

"It will keep. You are no longer hungry."

It was true. She had crammed in more food than she usually ate in two days' time, and who knew what the next few days would bring. Now that she had found where he'd hidden her boat and bailed it out, she might even slip away while he was out fishing. There were other islands where she could hide until he gave up searching, and then she would be free to go back to her own people.

But did she really want to leave?

Of course she did, she told herself quickly. She could hardly spend the rest of her life living like this—like a squaw.

Stormwalker sat down again, and she avoided looking at him, feeling oddly guilty at the thought of deluding the man who had done so much for her, even though he could still irritate her beyond all reason.

In the dim light, she could barely make out the soft gleam of his hair, the high planes of his cheekbones and the proud arch of his nose. His knees were drawn up before him, and he clasped them with his arms. A copper bracelet gleamed softly on his upper arm. It was so much a part of him that she had never wondered about it before.

"Why do you always wear that band about your arm?" she asked now.

"It is a mark of my rank."

Her brows lifted in surprise. "Your rank? You're a chief?"

"No. I am only the son of a chief *werrowance*, the kinsman of a lesser chief. Even so, I have a duty to my people, which I have neglected far too long."

"Because of me, you mean."

"Because of you. Because of your son. Because of what one of my people did to you and to your mother and to your father, who was my friend."

They had been friends. And this same friend had likely been the one to bury her parents and then try to help her. She had thought he was attacking her and had wounded him twice.

Once more Laura realized that she owed this man more than she had ever owed another living soul—far more than she owed the Packwoods. She felt ashamed of all the bad things she had once thought of him—and still did, more often than not.

"Tell me about that day, Stormwalker. I can't remember much that happened."

After a long moment in which she feared he would ignore her request, he said quietly, "It is a kindness of the mind, Laura. It can do no good to remember now."

"But how can I forget? They were my parents—they were all I had, all I loved."

"Now you have Little Thunder. You must look to the future, not the past."

What future, she wanted to ask him. *What possible future can a lone woman have when her child was conceived in shame and horror, not in love?*

With all her heart she wished she had the courage to ask him that question. What future could there be for a boy who was part white and part Indian? Stormwalker was a mixed-blood. He was accepted by his own people, and even by a few of hers, but he was the son of a chief, a magnificent and an educated man.

What chance would the son of a murdering savage have?

Chapter Twelve

Not until his lungs were fit to burst did Three Turtle allow himself to rise to the surface. This time he had gone twice the length of three war canoes without air. Surely not even Stormwalker could have gone so far without rising to the surface for air. In his mind he could hear the cheers of his people, hear the songs they would sing of his prowess, so that their sons and the sons of their sons would know who was the swiftest, the strongest, the most cunning of all men.

Flinging back his long black hair, the Mattamuskeet brave sent a shower of sparkling drops out across the vines that spilled over the banks of the river. Midsummer heat shimmered in the air, making the distant shore seem to float above the surface of the water.

Three Turtle was restless. Visions had lately plagued his sleep, visions of two youths, bows drawn, eyes on the same small doe. In his night visions, Three Turtle always sent his arrow flying first, yet it was always Stormwalker's arrow he found when he went to claim his prize.

Thus it had always been. The eldest by more than half a year, Three Turtle had once been the better tracker, the swifter runner, the most deadly hunter, yet by the time they had reached early manhood, Stormwalker had somehow managed to trick them all into believing he was the better man.

Hatred had slowly replaced their early friendship. Three Turtle told himself that he would gladly have taken second place to any one of his true brothers, but to be defeated by a half-blood was too great a shame to be borne.

As the hot sun caressed his tawny skin, the young brave breathed deeply of the rich forest scents—the gum and holly, the resinous pine and sweet smelling myrtle. From downriver came the cry of a gull, and Three Turtle's sharp eyes searched for the soaring white shape, following as it swooped down over a clearing on the north bank.

Even the gulls, he thought bitterly, had accepted the white invader, gleaning his fields, following his fishing boats. The red-tailed hawk waited at the edge of their broad grain fields, ready to pounce on the small game that fed there. Soon there would be no more game. With their words-made-by-marking-on-the-skin-of-a-goat, the English would have claimed all the land, clearing it and filling it with fences and small airless lodges in the name of their own chief. Even the four Wind Gods were on their side. At times the rivers were so filled with their great winged canoes that a man could not travel safely in a dugout without danger of being overrun.

Three Turtle was tired. Since the last raid, he had worn the blood of his enemies as a badge of courage, their stinking scalps dangling from a strip of hide about his waist. Now it was good to be free of the stench of battle.

The Mattamuskeet brave took great pride in his trophies, for they were symbols of his courage. They were symbols of revenge against those who had taken the lives of his sister, Makes Wind, and his mother, Six Toes. But when the sun beat down upon them, the stench of even the finest trophy became an abomination in his nostrils. Now that this last long raid was ended, he was glad to be free of the smell.

For the first time since he had climbed out of the river, he began to look around. He knew this place. The osprey's nest with the dangling snakeskin that had somehow weathered the cold winds. He had seen that before. And the dead cypress leaning out over the water.

Memories began to drift back, like broken patches of fog. Was not this the place where he had come upon the two old ones running toward the river? And the other one, the yellow-haired woman who had come after them. Were not these the very woods where he had thrown her down and—

Feeling his manhood begin to stir, he tried to shift his thoughts. Unless he doubled back to Num Peree and captured Kitappi, taking her into the woods, there was small chance of finding an outlet for such feelings. He was too weary to seek out another woman.

The rum he had drunk earlier had been enough to heat his blood, yet not enough to numb his senses. Halfheartedly he had vowed once more to turn away from the white man's poison, knowing that such a vow was no more real than yesterday's shadows. As a young brave, he had fasted before each battle. He had made sacrifices to the Great Spirit. But neither fasting nor sacrifices had prevented the white tide from flooding his land.

Now he no longer sought visions. He no longer fasted. He no longer made sacrifices to the gods. He had found another source of courage, one that lent him strength in the face of great danger, that enabled him to forget when the pain grew too great to bear.

Rum. It was more powerful than the bravest white soldier, more cunning and more deadly. This he knew, yet he was helpless to fight against it. The morning when he had come upon this place, he had been alone, his companions having already fallen into a drunken stupor. Three Turtle had been drunk, as well—not only with rum, but with visions of the glory that would one day be his. He had taken the two old ones first, his arrows finding their mark even though he had not been able to stand without leaning against a tree.

The yellow-haired woman had taken him by surprise. She'd come running past, and he'd leaned away from his tree, catching her about the throat. They had fallen to the ground together, and he'd managed to crawl deeper into the woods, dragging her struggling form with him.

One blow from his tomahawk had quickly put an end to her screams. He had prided himself that he'd had the presence of mind to use the flat side, for such long, yellow hair would have been his proudest trophy, brushing against his bare leg with each step he took, reminding him all over again of his prowess as a great warrior.

After days of killing, burning and drinking, he had been hot and ready at the first scent of her woman's flesh. Jerking off his breechclout, he had mounted her. She had been unused, and the ride had been over almost before it began. He had spilled his seed and then collapsed onto her soft white breasts.

Now she was gone, her bones picked clean and scattered by the wolves. Three Turtle knew a feeling of pride to see that the scars left by the white intruders were fading. Fields were grown over. Vines had all but covered the small heap of charred rubble that had once been the lodge of the old man and his women. Only the chimney still stood, and that was beginning to crumble. Soon there would be nothing left to show that an English dog had once pissed on these trees.

Now he wished he had taken the yellow-hair's scalp instead of mounting her. Had not the rum heated his blood to the boiling, he would have had something more to show for his troubles than a shameful memory of spilling his seed into an unworthy vessel.

If he had not been far gone with rum, he might even have let her live. As his captive, he could have used her again and again before selling her at a great price to one of the western people, who did not often see yellow hair and pale skin.

No. He had acted honorably, treating her as the white trapper had treated his little sister when he had come upon her bathing in the river. He had shown the yellow-hair the same mercy the white dog had showed his mother when she had heard the cries of her ten-year-old daughter and gone alone into the woods to find her.

Three Turtle, a youth of twelve winters then, had been out hunting with the other men, his father having recently died of a weeping fever. They had come upon the lifeless bodies of Makes Wind and Six Toes on their way back to the village.

Knowing what he must one day do, he had waited impatiently to gain the strength of manhood, learning as he grew to run faster than the swiftest catamount, to swim better than the fish in the rivers. He had learned to send his arrows straighter and his knife more surely than any other man, red or white.

Again and again he had tested his strength at the feasts of harvest, the feasts of peace, the festivals where many different peoples met to dance, to sing of great deeds, to exchange gifts and trade goods and to find wives. For at all these gatherings there had been tests of strength, skill and endurance among the young braves. Three Turtle, with a deadly purpose in mind, had bested them all.

All save one.

Now hatred burned like raw whiskey in his gut. Sometimes the hatred grew so large he could not see beyond it. His own sister had been dead these many years, but the sister of Stormwalker still lived. For that, he hated the man who had once been his friend.

Stormwalker's sister had taken a white man for her husband. For that, he hated her!

His own mother was dead, but the mother of Stormwalker still lived. She was an English witch, and he would have killed her if he had not feared her magic.

Now his hatred focused on Stormwalker, who walked freely among red and white, telling each of the goodness of the other. Walked with an arrogance that fed the fires of that hatred.

Three Turtle knew just how much goodness could be found in the heart of a white man. It was no more than a single grain of sand, to be washed away by the weakest tide, blown by the least wind.

One day there would be no more English in their land. Hancock had said it, and Hancock was the greatest of all chiefs, greater than Kinnahauk of the Hatorask, with his yellow eyes and his white woman.

But one day even Hancock must die. When that time came, all the people would know how Three Turtle had proved himself in battle. When a new leader was chosen among the Tuscarora, all would remember that it was Three Turtle of the Mattamuskeet People who had fought hardest to rid the land of the white dogs.

Kitappi would be his first wife. He had vowed to have her after learning that Kokom and Gray Otter wished to offer her to Stormwalker. Thus, when the old chief died, he, Three Turtle, would be ruler over the Hatorask, who were not even of the Tuscarora.

He would choose his second wife from among one of the villages north of the Albemarle, thus becoming leader of the mightiest nation among all The People.

With a heavy sigh that dredged the depths of all sorrows, old and new, Three Turtle picked up the two bands of filthy buckskin, one broad, one narrow, and dressed himself. Headband once more in place, he stood on the bank of the river near what had once been Edward Gray's plantation and stared unseeingly out across the shimmering heat waves.

A blue-tailed lizard mounted one of his feet, paused to look around, and then scurried away. Three Turtle never even blinked. He was not a tall man, yet he was well favored, his features strong and his carriage erect. Eyes half closed against the lowering sun, he was deep in thought when a sense of awareness caused him to stiffen. Without hesitation, he eased behind the broad trunk of an ancient cypress tree and waited.

It had been voices he'd heard. Two people, one chattering like a squirrel, the other putting in an occasional word.

Had his thoughts summoned them up?

Not daring to move—hardly daring to breathe—Three Turtle carefully avoided staring directly at the man and woman approaching from the far side of the clearing. All but the least among animals could sense the eyes of a predator upon him, and at this moment Three Turtle was every inch the predator.

Here was the chance he had awaited. He could send his arrow into Stormwalker's heart and have Kitappi before they even knew he was near. Rolling Stormwalker's body into the river, to be taken by the outgoing tide, he could carry Kitappi off and hide her where no one would find her. Who would think of searching Bad Medicine Island? All men feared the spirits of the dead. Three Turtle alone among men knew no fear of those spirits, for as a child he had gone often to the island, seeking the spirit of his father.

A rare smile spread over his strong features as he considered his plan. He would go to Kokom and tell him that he would have to agree to the marriage and lower his bride price, for if he did not, he would never see his daughter alive.

Yet something stayed Three Turtle's hand. Instead of drawing his bow, he watched as Stormwalker uncovered a canoe that had been cleverly concealed under a fall of fox grapes. How could he have missed seeing it?

No, he thought bitterly as he watched the two people—one he hated, one he coveted—head for the middle of the river where the tidal current carried them swiftly downriver. The time was not yet right. He was weary from many days of raiding, and Stormwalker was a cunning foe. For the sake of his own honor, Three Turtle knew that when they finally met in battle, it must be as equals. Only then could he know the joy of watching the life-spirit fade from Stormwalker's blue eyes as his blood flowed into the earth.

Let them go. Stormwalker could only be taking her to Croatoan to visit with his people. They would soon return, for with Gray Otter growing weaker each day from the wasting disease, Kitappi would not stay away long. That old fool, Kokom, would not allow it.

Laura was bathing Little Thunder near the freshwater pond when she saw Stormwalker appear on the path that led up from the shore. He had been gone three days and she had missed him sorely, but this time she had believed him when he had told her he would return.

Her heart seemed to swell inside her, and with one hand holding the wriggling infant across her knees, she watched him approach, unable to contain the joyous smile that spread over her face. Three days? It had seemed more like three weeks!

His black hair gleamed in the sunlight, while the same sun turned his smooth skin to bronze. How tall he was—how lean, yet how very strong. She had never thought about men's bodies before meeting Stormwalker.

Embarrassed at her own thoughts, she said, "I wasn't certain when you were coming back. I didn't—that is, I wasn't—" Her gown was still damp where she had lolled about in the shallows earlier, but at least she was clean. She had crushed honeysuckle and wax-berry leaves and rubbed them on her arms and her throat. Not because they smelled so sweet, she told herself, but only because she thought it might offer some protection against the mosquitoes.

"I have brought you a surprise."

At the sound of his deep, measured voice, her swollen heart flopped over in her chest. It was unseemly for a woman to harbor such thoughts about one of the wild'uns, no matter how kind and helpful he was, but try as she would, she couldn't seem to put them from her mind.

"A surprise?" she asked a little breathlessly.

Sunlight glinted on the copper band he wore, and she stared at his arm. And then her gaze moved up to his muscular shoulder, gleaming like polished wood in the sunlight, and then strayed downward over his chest. It was several moments before she realized that she was staring at the flat bronze disk of his nipple, and when she did, she ducked her head, furious with herself—and with him—for the feelings of confusion that suddenly overcame her.

"I hope it's a kettle," she muttered, turning Little Thunder over onto his belly when he began to fret at being ignored. Distractedly, she patted his plump bottom as he bobbed his dark head in an effort to hold it upright.

"Ooooh, what a beautiful baby!" cried a familiar voice.

Startled, Laura looked up again to see Kitappi dart from behind a tree and run toward her. "Kitappi, where did you...?"

"I am so pleased to see you again, Laura Gray. Many times I wondered where you had gone and if you were well. Oh." Kitappi stopped several yards away, the fringe on her pale doeskin shift swaying. "But you wanted a kettle. Would it please you if I went back to my father's lodge and sent back my mother's finest iron kettle in my place?"

"I didn't mean— Kitappi, I'm so glad to see you! How did you—"

Never one to stand on ceremony, the younger girl approached, an engaging mixture of shyness and curiosity in her manner.

"This is your surprise, Laura," said Stormwalker. "I have brought your friend from Packwood's for a small visit." Kneeling beside the two women, he lifted Little Thunder from Laura's lap without asking permission, grinning broadly as a tiny fist connected with the side of his high-bridged nose. "Ho there, little *yauh-he*, you are growing much too quickly. Soon you will be taking my bow to hunt the *yauta* so that you may wear his *soppe* in your headband."

It was Kitappi who removed the baby from Stormwalker's arms, nuzzling his fat neck. "Do not listen to this foolish one, little honey blossom. First you must learn to wear something besides moss to catch your droppings, and then we can worry about making you a headband and finding a feather for it. Laura, does he eat well? How old is he? Where did you find him? What happened to your own—"

And then her eyes grew round with realization as she looked from Laura's flat belly to Little Thunder and back again.

By the time they had feasted on the roast turkey and tubers Kitappi had brought, Laura's throat was aching from all the unaccustomed talk. Kitappi had insisted on hearing the whole story of how Laura came to be on the island and how Little Thunder had come into being, and this time the telling of it had not been quite so painful. Almost a year had passed. She still mourned her parents, yet they could not be helped by her grief. Her father would be the first to advise her to spend whatever time she had left wisely and well, for time was short and life was exceedingly hard.

Her ears were tired, as well, for Kitappi was not one to endure silence. She insisted on relating all the village gossip, most of which passed right over Laura's head, for she knew none of the people and found the names confusing, and besides, her mind was busy with thoughts of her own.

She had learned that Kitappi's mother had been growing weaker for some time and that Kitappi was doing more and more of her chores, as was fitting. "My father sent me away with Stormwalker, pretending that it was so that I could rest from taking care of my mother, but I think he had another reason in the back of his mind. My father may be the greatest of all chiefs, but he can also be as devious as the killdeer, who pretends one thing to accomplish another."

Laura murmured a response she hoped was suitably sympathetic, but her mind was filled with questions as to the chief's true purpose. Was he giving Stormwalker and Kitappi the opportunity to be alone together to further a match between them? Or was the trip Stormwalker's idea? Or Kitappi's?

Laura had taken to the young Indian girl the first time she ever met her at Packwood's. They had managed a few minutes to visit each time Kitappi had come into the store. Odd that she had never noticed her dusky beauty until now.

Suddenly, Laura became aware of her own pale hair, dull from lack of a brush and from lack of soap. Her arms had grown darker from the sun, and for all she knew, her face could be covered with freckles. With no looking glass, how could she tell?

She did know that her breasts were far too full and her belly was still soft and rounded. Would it remain that way? Would it grow larger?

Oh, how she wished her mother were there to answer the countless questions that only a wife and mother could answer!

When Little Thunder cried to be fed before being put down for the night, Kitappi insisted on singing him a song. Partly amused and partly dismayed, Laura listened as her friend launched into a bloodcurdling ballad about a mouse who stole grain from the village storehouse, the owl who pounced on the unwary creature and the hunter who sent an arrow all the way around the sun to pierce the owl's breast, making his white feathers fall to earth as snow.

"Where on earth did you hear that song?" Laura asked as she covered the sleeping infant with a light spread.

"My mother sang it to me—I think." Kitappi frowned. "One of my mothers must have. Among our people, the children have many parents, for they are our most precious possession. They are our future." Never still for very long, she squirmed and then she sighed. "Father says it is important that our children be taught the way of their grandfathers, for soon there will be no old ones left to remember. Soon the white ma—"

She broke off in consternation, and Laura, gathering up the used moss to put outside, knew a moment's pity for the people who were having to adjust to ways not their own. It must be difficult.

On the other hand, she had adjusted well enough, after the first awful weeks. She had learned not to question what was in the tasty stews Stormwalker had prepared to help her regain her strength. He, on the other hand, had condescended to take his meals with her, after carefully making it known that this was not the normal way of things in his village, where the men were taken care of first and the women saw to their own comfort only afterward.

That night Stormwalker had taken his supper outside, claiming the cabin was too small. He had mentioned gathering moss for a bed for Kitappi, but had failed to say whether it would be inside with Laura and Little Thunder, or outside under the stars with him.

Now Laura wondered if she would get any sleep at all with the restless, talkative girl on a pallet beside her own.

On the other hand, how much sleep would she get with the pair of them lying out in the darkness, whispering, doing other things . . . ?

Doing *what* things? whispered an unwelcome inner voice. Well, whatever they did, it was no concern of hers! Stormwalker had said himself that he'd brought Kitappi to the island for Laura's pleasure.

Or was it for his own? came the same taunting inner voice.

"Do you need to go out to the necessary?" she asked brusquely. And then, relenting, "It's only a clear place surrounded by bushes, but the sand's white, so you can see any snakes even in the dark. I could show you."

"You go if you wish to. I would rather stay with the baby. Will he waken and cry if I place my hand on his bottom while he sleeps? He is so warm, so sweet. You are so lucky to have him, Laura."

After assuring her friend that Little Thunder slept like the dead once his belly was filled, Laura slipped outside, not needing to relieve herself so much as to see what Stormwalker was doing. If he was spreading two pallets side by side, she would bid him the night and leave without saying a word.

What could she have possibly said? That while she appreciated his "gift," she preferred having him all to herself? That was too foolish to dwell on. She would say simply that she had missed him the three days he had been gone, but she had got along just fine without him, and if he and Kitappi wanted to—

"It is time you were sleeping, woman," the deep, familiar voice said quietly, startlingly close behind her.

"Oh! I was—that is, you shouldn't— Stormwalker, how long have you known Kitappi?"

"Since she was hardly older than Little Thunder." He sounded amused, as if remembering all the years they'd shared.

"You must be good friends." And before he could comment on that observation, she rushed on, wishing she had the good sense to let the matter alone instead of worrying at it like a sore tooth. "Well, I can understand that. She's sweet and funny and kind, and—well, of course, she's really beautiful, too. When I worked at Packwood's, I used to look forward to the days when she would come to town. She could make me laugh over nothing at all."

Looking back, Laura remembered how precious those few brief visits had been. She had hardly smiled in those days. Laughter had been as rare as gold.

As her eyes adjusted to the night brightness, she saw him move closer, and then she felt the warm clasp of his hand on her shoulder. "Thank you for your gift," she said breathlessly, wondering if the burning touch of his hand would be visible on her skin in the light.

"Next time I go, I will bring you a kettle." There was a teasing note in his voice. There had been a time when she, like most of her kind, would have sworn the Indians had no sense of humor.

"See that you do."

"Do not be too demanding, little squaw. That is the word your people use for the women of my people, is it not?"

"Demanding?" Laura asked, all innocence.

His fingers tightened on her shoulder, and she could feel the moist heat of his breath. Somehow, he had moved to stand much closer to her—perhaps in order to see her in the dim light. "You know which word I meant," he said deeply.

From inside the cabin Laura could hear Kitappi's soft voice singing another song to Little Thunder. Ignoring it to steal this moment for herself, she swayed closer, lifting her chin in a gesture that was half dare, half defiance. "How could I know? You have so many words for everything. What do you call your own women?"

"*Yicau. Yecauau.*"

She broke in triumphantly. "There! See? Our only word for woman is woman."

"Not so," teased Stormwalker in a voice that was little more than a whisper. "There is wife, lady, crone, girl, maiden—shall I go on?"

They were standing so close that she could feel the heat of his body. Each shallow breath she drew filled her senses with the intoxicating smell of woodsmoke, leather and herbs, the musky, masculine blend that was uniquely his own. "They—they're not the same. A crone is an old woman, while a maiden is— And a lady..."

"Among my people, when a woman grows old, she is called *yicau*. When a woman marries, she is called *yecauau*. Her children call her by yet another word, while a lover has many words for the woman he would take to his lodge. Which of these would you like me to teach you?''

Laura could not have spoken if her life had depended on it.

''You are no longer quite so demanding, Laura Gray. Why is that? Are you learning to be a proper squaw?''

It was the gleam of his broad smile that proved her undoing. Laura made a low sound of frustration, and Stormwalker laughed aloud, bringing her against his hard body. Clasped in his arms, she could feel the laughter inside him. It was not only his proud, handsome features, but his strength, his gentleness, the lure of his fascinating mind that had set the trap that drew her ever closer, holding her with a power that was almost frightening.

Stiffening, she tried to draw away. ''I only came out to— that is, I must—''

''I will not tease you any longer, Little Sparrow. Send Kitappi out to me when you go inside.''

And then he kissed her. It was no more than the briefest brush of his mouth against her brow, yet long after Laura lay abed that night, staring up at the chinks of moonlight that filtered through the cabin roof, she could feel the soft pressure of his lips. Firm, gentle, dry, she feared they had branded her for all time.

Chapter Thirteen

Even though Kitappi slept inside the cabin each night, Laura could not help but be aware that she spent much of her waking hours with Stormwalker. Often she would come upon the two of them talking together, a beseeching look on Kitappi's face, as if she wanted something from him. As if she were pleading with him.

For what? What more could she possibly want? She had a father and a mother who loved her above all, if what Stormwalker had told her was true. She had half the young men in their village, and the other villages besides, falling over their feet in an effort to gain her attention. She spoke of it as if it were no more than any young woman of marriageable age could expect, but Laura knew otherwise. She, too, was of marriageable age, yet only Coby Packwood had offered for her. And even he had changed his mind.

The Harker twins, an impish pair with more freckles than sense, had once asked if she would consider being wife to both of them, but as they'd been only fourteen at the time, she had discounted it.

If Kitappi could be believed, Edward Gray had gone about the task of finding her a husband all wrong. Kokom had named an outrageous bride price for his daughter, and he'd found suitors thick as flies about his door. "Do you mean to tell me that among your people, the men actually *buy* their wives?" Laura had asked when they'd lain abed that first night after Kitappi had come inside from talking with Stormwalker. Laura had wanted to close her eyes and dwell on all the strange new feelings that had afflicted her of late, but Kitappi had whispered and giggled until it was impossible to think.

"A woman is a valuable thing, Laura Gray. Without daughters, who will take care of old fathers and mothers? Who will feed them and clothe them and restore the bark on their lodges when it dries and breaks away? Who will poultice them when the winter cold brings on fevers of the chest and makes old bones grow large and crooked? A daughter is a valuable thing. My father will take no less than one goat that gives milk, five horses, five bags of salt, five bearskin robes, a new musket and a large looking glass for my bride price, for I am a good worker and I never sicken."

Laura thought of the custom of dowry among her own kind. It was as though a father were all too anxious to be rid of his daughter, to have to pay some poor man to take her off his hands.

Her own dowry would have been small enough—two sturdy woolen blankets, a good kettle, an elderly ox and the wheel and loom her mother had kept even after she had begun buying her cloth from Packwood's Store.

Perhaps that was why Coby's ardor had cooled so quickly. Come to think of it, he had always seemed to be wearing his best shirt on the day when Margaret Small came in with her parents to trade at the store. The Smalls had the largest holding on the river, with a fine brick house and slaves to work the cotton fields. Come summer, Mr. Small would load his whole family into his shallop, along with enough servants to see to their comfort, and head for his lodge on Ocracoke.

In the dark cabin, Kitappi sighed. "Perhaps my father asks too much for my bride price. Some cannot pay such a price, even for a first wife who is daughter to a chief. Perhaps I will grow old and ugly before any man can gather so much wealth."

A first wife. Laura knew she would never be able to abide such an arrangement—but then, she would never be asked to. "Have you set your heart on a special one yet?" The moment the question was asked, she knew she didn't really want to hear the answer.

"My heart is set, but it makes no difference. It is my father who must decide. He tells Stormwalker that soon I will be too old to bear sons, but when I told him of my choice, he said I was young yet, that my mother needed me, that no man would keep me for a wife until I learned to behave with proper respect."

"Mmm," Laura commented drowsily. She had no doubt that Kokom knew his daughter better than she knew herself. Hardworking she may be, but from what Laura had heard, Kitappi had her entire village wrapped around her little finger. She was a flirt and a tease, albeit a charming one.

"That is why he sent me away, you know. He thinks to distract my heart."

Laura wondered sleepily why Kokom would go to the trouble of throwing Kitappi and Stormwalker together when he was not yet ready to let them wed. More strange heathen customs. Tomorrow, when she wasn't so sleepy, she might try to learn more about their ways.

Then again, she might not. "Mmm-hmm. Little Thunder wakes all during the night. Best close my eyes while I can."

Throughout the following day, Kitappi insisted on taking over the care of Little Thunder. Stormwalker set out at daybreak after fish, for in the heat of summer they were not so easy to find. The sun had just climbed above a low cloud bank when he returned with his catch, and while Laura cleaned them, marveling over the plump roe, he joined Kitappi as she played with Little Thunder.

Laura's gaze lingered on the two dark heads, their glistening black hair similarly bound as they bent over the dusky, dark-haired baby. It occurred to her that her infant son looked far more like both Stormwalker and Kitappi than he did his own mother. For all the ease and affection that passed between them, they might easily have been husband, wife and son.

With a feeling of sadness that baffled her, she went inside to change the bedding in the cabin, while Kitappi, with Little Thunder on her hip, watched Stormwalker fashion a board for carrying him on her back. By the time Laura ventured outside again, he had finished the cradle board, and Kitappi had set him yet another task. Claiming that the cabin was too hot and the sun too strong for Laura's delicate English constitution, Kitappi had talked him into contriving an open shelter in a place near the highest part of the island, where the rare summer breeze could usually be found.

Laura tried to feel grateful. Actually, she looked forward to having a place out of the sun to spend her days, but perversely she wished it had been Stormwalker's idea and not Kitappi's.

All morning she watched while he set poles and gathered bundles of rushes under Kitappi's teasing guidance. The two of them laughed and joked together as if they had been doing it all their lives.

As they probably had, Laura told herself glumly. With the cabin tidied and two fat fish slowly roasting over a bed of coals, she was at odds with herself. Most days she could content herself with counting her baby's fingers and toes and teasing a smile from his tiny lips, but Kitappi had taken over his care between feedings, making Laura feel restless, useless and oddly resentful.

Furiously, she sanded the one battered kettle she possessed and wished she had more. She was in a mood to scrub and scour, but there was little satisfaction to be gained in a dirt-floored, one-room cabin.

She simply wasn't used to being idle. At home, there had always been work to be done.

After feeding Little Thunder again, she left him sleeping on his new board and set out for the southern tip of the island, basket over her arm. It was early yet for the bramble berries to be ripe, but she felt a powerful need to get away. For reasons she didn't care to dwell on, the sight of Stormwalker and Kitappi together was beginning to make her throat ache. Perhaps she was coming down with a summer complaint.

There were berries aplenty, most of them green as grass. A few had turned red, fewer still were black. These Laura ate, taking pleasure in her own selfishness, although they were not all that good.

She returned with the empty basket over her arm just as Stormwalker left to check the weir he had set on the inland side of the island. The sun was almost gone by the time he returned, bearing three more fish, which he hooked by the gills over the coals to smoke slowly.

"The fish know I do not like to hunt them where I might be seen from shore," he said. "They gathered there, thinking themselves safe."

"Paugh! You worry too much over nothing," Kitappi dismissed. "The fighting has died down. All the white-eyes are cowering in the garrison at Bath Towne like— Ooooo." She covered her lips with her hand. "I am sorry, Laura. My tongue sometimes runs away from me."

"Just so it's ended, I don't care who cowers where."

"Will you go to the garrison when you leave this place?" Kitappi asked, her voice filled with concern.

Laura hesitated. Did she dare go back to Packwood's Crossing? She had a fair notion of the welcome Little Thunder would receive from the likes of George and Coby Packwood. Making some noncommittal reply, she got on with preparing the evening meal.

The three of them shared the two roasted fish, sitting cross-legged on the ground out under the fine new shelter Stormwalker had built. "This is our last night together," Kitappi said, reaching out to touch Little Thunder, who lay kicking and chortling on a pallet beside her.

Laura tried hard to hide her dismay. Kitappi could not go alone. Stormwalker would be leaving with her. This time, he might not return.

She didn't want to think about it. It was one thing for *her* to decide to leave. It was another thing altogether for Stormwalker to go away and leave her here all alone. And for the life of her, she didn't know why.

"Stormwalker will want to leave before the sun even awakes," Kitappi grumbled. "He never sleeps, you know." She leaned closer to Laura and whispered loudly, "He thinks no one knows, but I have heard that his true father is a raccoon and his mother is a possum. At night he sprouts wings like an owl and hunts unwary mice in the white man's corn fields." Grinning broadly at her own jest, Kitappi licked her gleaming fingers and cut her eyes at the stern-faced man beside her.

"Must you go back so soon?"

"We go to Stormwalker's home on Croatoan," the Indian girl corrected. "My father lets me visit there each summer, for I love the sandbanks. The water is salty and never hot like it is here in the summer, and the wind blows cool, even when the sun burns the skin. Stormwalker always takes me home with him in the hot months, don't you, *Yenxhaue*?"

Lying back on one elbow, Stormwalker allowed his gaze to move from one to the other of the two women. Observing the stricken look on Laura's small face, he smiled inwardly. She would be wondering at the meaning of the word, as she always did. He thought perhaps he would not tell her it meant only "brother."

Not yet, at least.

The evening passed far too quickly. Laura was torn between wanting to be rid of her friend and wanting to confide in her. Although just what she could say, she had no idea. Kitappi was even less experienced than she was and would have no way of advising her on what to do when Little Thunder fell asleep at her breast and failed to empty them, causing them to ache abominably.

How could Kitappi know if it were natural or not for a woman's monthly flows to hold back after giving birth to a babe? Her mother had once given birth to her, yet she had still endured the monthly discomfort and bother.

Even more worrying, was it natural for her to feel those strange, prickly sensations between her thighs and in her breast whenever Stormwalker happened on her while she was nursing?

Face warming at the thought, Laura knew she could never confide to a living soul the dream she had had the night before, after Stormwalker had kissed her.

Never one to skirt the truth, she had already admitted to herself that she was jealous. It shamed her greatly, for it was beyond all that was reasonable. She was an Englishwoman, for goodness sake, born in the Virginia colony of good Devon stock. She had no more business thinking such unnatural thoughts about a wild'un than a bee did making up to a butterfly.

The wind whispered softly through the rush roof of her new shelter as Laura wrapped her arms about her updrawn legs and stared into the darkly glowing coals. What was happening to her? She desperately needed someone of her own kind to talk to. Martha Packwood would have likely known the answers, but her menfolk had made it difficult, if not impossible, for Laura to go back to Packwood's Crossing.

Knowing she must look to herself for answers, Laura tried to tell herself that it was merely Stormwalker's unexpected gentleness that had tricked her into thinking of him as an ordinary man. He was still a wild'un. Half wild, at any rate, which made him even more of a puzzle. Teasing one moment, overbearing the next—gentle and arrogant by turns... A body never knew what to expect.

As for the strange fanciful feelings that had plagued her recently, they were likely brought on by all that had happened to her, from the loss of her parents to the birth of her son. Little Thunder had changed not only her life but her mind and body, as well. Never again could she go back to being the carefree girl who had swung herself up onto the end of a sapling to help her father pry a stubborn stump out of the ground one evening in late September.

"Go with us," Kitappi pleaded for the third time. She had first suggested it while they lay abed the night before, again while they were squatting behind the bushes in the chill before dawn. "You'll like Bridget," she said now as they prepared to leave. "She's as English as you are, for all she dresses and speaks as we do."

Laura stole a glance at Stormwalker as soon as they emerged. What was he thinking? Did he want her to go with them? Or did he want to be alone with Kitappi?

"The journey will probably take too long," she said, meaning *tell me that you want me to go with you.*

"With the wind at our backs, we will reach my father's village before the moon rises on the second day," Stormwalker said.

There was nothing in his voice to indicate his feelings. Perhaps he had none. On a more practical level, Laura knew that with two extra passengers, the canoe would be crowded. "I have no notion of how Little Thunder would take to such a journey. Perhaps I'd do better to stay here." She even managed a smile. "Now that I have such a fine sunshade, I'll likely spend all my time there while you're baking under the hot sun."

No one argued. While Kitappi scooped up the baby for one last cuddle, Stormwalker made swift work of loading provisions into the dugout. There were skins filled with water, smoked fish wrapped in dried leaves and something he had brought from home that was brown and thick with seeds embedded in it, which Laura thought best not to inquire about.

"Take the baby to the cabin, Kitappi," Stormwalker ordered quietly when the canoe was readied. "I would have a word with Laura."

His tone left no room for argument, not even from Kitappi, who, as Laura had recently discovered, was inclined to be willful. When she had gone, the baby over her shoulder and her fringes swinging impudently, Stormwalker turned to Laura.

"You will fare well until I return?"

"Of course I will fare well," she snapped. "I fared well enough before you came, and I'll fare just as well after you're gone!"

Ignoring her anger, which had risen like a summer squall and which they both knew was unwarranted, he went on to say, "The island should be a safe place, for most are afraid to come near. Even so, you will not go on the inland side until I return. Stay near the cabin. If anyone approaches, slip out the back and go up onto the roof. You will leave no tracks, and you cannot easily be seen if you lie flat. Little Thunder has not yet been taught to remain quiet on command, so you will either cover his mouth with your hand or give him your breast."

Laura was stunned. "You have no right to—"

"I take those rights I wish," Stormwalker said calmly.

"You'll not take them from me! I intend to go where I wish and do what I wish, and if someone does come to the island and finds me here, likely it will only be a fisherman, since they're hardly likely to be frightened off by some foolish heathen superstition!"

"Do you wish to be found, Laura Gray?"

"Of course I wish to be found! I can hardly spend the rest of my life grubbing for mussels and roots like a naked savage! I'm tired of living this way, of—of eating unsalted fish with my fingers!"

Anger and an inexplicable urge to cry had driven her to such reckless, hurtful lengths. Laura knew she should apologize, but the words simply would not come. Instead she turned away, jammed her fists against her mouth and willed her anger to subside.

Why did she hurt so? What was wrong with her?

For one long moment Stormwalker stared at the slight figure in the torn and faded gown. His own heart was filled with an uncomfortable mixture of rage, confusion and tenderness. It was the tenderness he feared most, for it could not be allowed to grow.

Yet he could not leave her this way. Setting aside all the wisdom he had gained in his six and twenty years, he reached for her, turning her as he drew her into his arms. "Do not shed tears, Little Sparrow. I cannot bear to see you weep, for your tears pierce my heart so that I bleed inside."

She sniffled noisily and tried to stem the flood, but it was no use. It had been building for too long. "D-don't say such things to me, Stormwalker. I don't like it."

With her head burrowing under his chin and her warm, soft body pressed tightly against his own, Stormwalker wondered how much truth was in her words. She was too small to contain such a large anger. He had not meant to provoke her, speaking as he always did, for her own good.

With a patience he was far from feeling, Stormwalker tried once more to explain the wisdom of his advice. "Not all your fishermen are to be trusted, Laura."

"Oh, and all wild'uns are kindness itself, I suppose!" Held fast about her waist, she drew back and glared at him indignantly, her anger only increasing when she saw the familiar teasing smile on his lips.

"Only the blue-eyed ones, I'm afraid. Until heads cool and reason can prevail."

"My head is perfectly cool and—"

One large hand lifted to the back of her head, as if to test the veracity of her words. Still holding her, he bent closer. Her eyes were wide and glaring when first she felt the touch of his mouth on hers. Moments later they fluttered closed.

The kiss was a mistake, this much Stormwalker knew the moment he tasted the fruity sweetness of her lips. Yesterday, when she had come back with the empty basket over her arms, her lips had been stained with the juice of ripe berries and he had suffered the agony of wanting to know their wild sweetness from her tongue.

Now he traced the curve of her full lower lip with the tip of his tongue and felt her shudder in his arms. Her mouth remained closed, and he teased at the line between her lips, one hand holding her head still for his attentions, the other holding her tightly against his body.

By all the gods of all men, he wanted her! He wanted the soft womanly fullness of her breasts, wanted to suckle the milk as greedily as did her babe. His manflesh stirred between his thighs, straining the soft hide of his breechclout as it searched instinctively for the cleft of her womanhood.

A groan arose from deep in his throat as he felt her begin to respond. It was too late—he was leaving! It was too soon, for he did not know if she had yet healed from the ordeal of giving birth.

An involuntary image rose before his eyes of her small body, swollen with child and twisting in agony on the white sand. Desperately, he tried to shut it out. He had known this woman as no man among his people had ever known a woman, for such things were forbidden!

And even then he had lusted after her.

Laura's hands tightened on the sleek flesh above Stormwalker's knife belt. Her senses were drunk with the taste of his mouth, the feel of his arms around her and that hard ridge that was pressing into her belly. Her face buried in the curve of his throat, she drew a deep breath that was laced with his intoxicating scent—woodsmoke, leather and an exciting musky quality that made her knees feel incredibly weak.

"Please—you mustn't," she whispered, still clutching him to her.

Above her head, Stormwalker smiled grimly. *No, Little Sparrow, I must not, yet how can I fight against my own heart? Such a foe is more cunning than an army, mightier than the fiercest storm. I am of the Hatorask. For the sake of my people, who grow fewer with each passing year, I must have sons and daughters of my father's blood, not sons with pale skin and yellow hair.*

"You are not of my people, Little Sparrow," he whispered in his own tongue. "I must return you to your own kind, yet I cannot let you go."

Chapter Fourteen

My smoke has not yet gone up, my son. Come. Sit with me in the shade, for the day grows warm.''

Stormwalker was not deceived. While Kinnahauk would never say so, he preferred the quiet sounds of the forest and the nearby lapping waters to the sound of clacking female tongues. Now well past his fiftieth year, the old chief often sought solitude when he could not have the company of his Bridget alone.

As the two men walked toward the shelter of a spreading live oak tree, Stormwalker was heartened to note that his father stood as tall and straight as ever, his hair as thick and dark as a man half his years. His face was lined but still handsome, the spark of keen intelligence that lit his golden eyes as strong as ever.

"When I was a youth, you were ancient, my father," Stormwalker observed with the same note of dry humor that could often be heard in Kinnahauk's voice. "Now that I am a man, you have grown younger."

Kinnahauk's smile held both sadness and acceptance. He is young, so very young, he thought. He will walk paths my feet have never trod. He will drink from streams my eyes have never beheld. "I am old enough to hear my name on the wind," he said. "You will go far, my son. My wings will shadow your path." Seated, he drew deeply on his pipe and passed it to his son. "Kitappi grows to womanhood. When will you take her to your lodge?"

From the fire near the small circle of lodges, woodsmoke drifted lazily across the clearing to mingle with the scent of tobacco. The only sound was the laughter and gossip of the women at their work and the chittering of a flock of small yellow-green birds.

Stormwalker drew deeply on the blackened clay pipe and passed it back to his father. "There is time," he said.

"When I was but a child, time stretched before me like the waters of the Great Sea. When I came to be a young man, I did not think of time. Now I am grown old. Time trails behind me like a robe of many colored feathers. I must look over my shoulder to see where my time has gone. Only the children of my children lie before me. I would know them before my spirit takes wing."

Stormwalker glanced quickly at the man beside him, searching for any sign of faltering health. He found none. As usual, the wily old chief sought to gain his own ends by shaping the feelings of those around him. As his physical prowess ebbed, he grew ever more adept at such games.

"Anne White Swan has given you three grandsons," Stormwalker said dryly. "Three should please any man, even so great a chief."

"She has given me four, for another was born to her three days ago. Four should be enough to please any man, yet I find I am grown greedy with the passing years." The sun glinted off the worn copper band on the old man's arm. There was a similar band on the arm of his son. On each was a hammered design that spoke of rank, of proud deeds done and vows made that were yet to be fulfilled. The design of Kinnahauk's band had been altered many times as the list of his proud deeds mounted, and one by one, the vows made were fulfilled.

"Is my sister well?"

"She is well. Your mother is with her."

"Four grandsons," Stormwalker mused. "I do not know them well, these kinsmen of mine, save the one called Cabel."

"They do not wish to know of their mother's people. It is only Cabel who knows the inside of my lodge. He has smoked my pipe. He alone of my daughter's children will know the deep sorrow of being caught between two worlds, a part of neither, for his spirit was not shaped by the same hand that shaped the spirits of his brothers."

Stormwalker's eyes took on a rare bleakness. He, too, knew the feeling of being half one thing half another, with wholeness denied him forever.

As if sensing his thoughts, Kinnahauk said, "The blood of two great people flows through your body, my son. This is an honorable thing."

The bleakness faded and Stormwalker said, "You have ripened, father. I have heard how you fought against the love you felt for my mother because her skin was white. You did not think Jedd Rawson was honorable when he asked to join with my sister. If I remember—"

"That was in the past," Kinnahauk interrupted. "A wise man learns from his mistakes. I have learned there is honor among all people. Each must prove himself in his own way."

Having gained a fair amount of wisdom himself, Stormwalker deemed it time to direct their words into another channel. "The new babe—have you seen him?"

"I have seen him."

"Four grandsons. I know of no other chief who can boast of so much wealth," Stormwalker said with a teasing grin.

"White-eyed grandsons!" the older man snorted. "If my own son refuses to do his duty and take a woman to his lodge, where will I find grandsons whose hair is not red or yellow and whose eyes are the color of a ripe acorn?"

It was entirely like the old man, thought Stormwalker, to have forgotten that he had taken as his own wife a woman who was as fair and as English as the man his daughter had wed. At times he found this amusing, at times exasperating. "The one called Cabel has hair as dark as yours or mine, father. His eyes are like the eyes of the red-tailed hawk, as are yours."

"Paugh! My grandsons have white man's names and white man's skins. They live in a white man's lodge and not one save the boy, Cabel, knows the way to my village!"

"They know, my father. It is not easy when one is young. Tell me of the new babe. A boy, you say? What do they call him?"

"*I,*" said Kinnahauk proudly, stressing the word, "have called him *Welka*, for the sound he makes is like a small hungry duck. His *father* has given him the name of Isaac."

"Perhaps he will find his own name when he is of age."

"He will not. Welka's blood is that of the *Wintsohore*— the English. Just as a woman leaves her father's lodge to go with her husband, her sons will accept their father's ways, not those of their mother's people."

"As my mother left her people and accepted your own," Stormwalker reminded his father gently. "And Cabel? I have hunted with him as a young man. He does not hunt like a white-eye."

"For a white-eye, he is a good man. I have given him the name of One Who Sees Beyond the Night."

Stormwalker looked at his father curiously. He had not known the old man was so close to any of his grandsons. "Have you told him?"

"I do not need to tell him. It is so."

On the second day of his visit, Stormwalker went to the white man's village to see his sister. His friend and kinsman Cabel was at sea, but he spoke briefly with Jedd Rawson. He was an honorable man. He had been good to Anne, but Stormwalker could not help but wish his sister had married one of her own kind. One day their people would need a new leader.

He spoke to her of this.

"Do you expect me to send my sons to King's Point to live? How else could they learn all that must be learned? Who could live up to Father? You?"

Their father, Kinnahauk, had been the son of a great chief, and their mother had been the daughter of another. Among the people of the sandbanks, Kinnahauk's power had been unrivaled. "I have no wish to be chief," Stormwalker said. "For years I have traveled and learned so that

I could teach our people to live in a changing world. This must be done, Anne, if we are to survive.''

"I had a vision the night before Isaac was born. It was strange, Storm—I do not understand what it meant."

"Father calls your newest son Welka, did you know that?"

"Ha! He is more like the *rummiseau* than the duck, for I swear he bleats like the goat the midwife had sent over from New Berne. But my vision, *yenxhaue*—I saw a red wolf—a male who was surrounded by pups, and the pups grew larger and threw more pups, yet they did not leave. All remained with the old male, which is passing strange, you must admit."

Stormwalker stayed for another half hour. He dutifully admired young Welka, who was also called Isaac, thinking him not half so handsome as Little Thunder, but far too polite to say so. As for Anne's vision, he could make nothing of it, but then, women were not supposed to have visions. Not even the daughters of chiefs.

The next day, he prepared to leave. His mother, who had been staying with Anne, returned to their village, where she was immediately set upon by Kitappi, who embraced her, complimented her effusively and then commenced to plead with her to intercede with Kokom.

"My father thinks highly of you. He says you are the wisest of all women. He says you were his good friend before he was banished."

"Oh, hush, child! Kokom was never banished!" She smiled over the head of the eager girl at her son, who was watching the two women indulgently. Had ever a woman had such a fine son? He had Kinnahauk's strong male beauty and her own mother's eyes.

"Brid-get," Kitappi pleaded, sensing the older woman's attention had strayed. *"Please?"*

"What? Oh—Kokom. Dearling, your father is a chief, almost as great as Kinnahauk." Which was hardly true, and Bridget would never have said as much in Kinnahauk's hearing, but the child didn't need to hear that. "I'm sure he wants only what will make you happy."

"Happy! He has set his mind that I will marry the man of his choice, and I cannot *bear* it!"

"Come, then, tell me about it and I will see what can be done." Bridget slipped off her moccasins and eased her stiff body down onto her unrolled bedding. It was good to be home! Her daughter's house reeked of too many leather boots and unwashed napkins. Moccasins and moss were better. "I thought surely Kokom had agreed that you and Stormwalker—"

"Oh, you do not understand," Kitappi wailed. Stormwalker had quietly slipped away, and now Kitappi dropped the flap over the door so that they would not be disturbed.

"What reason does your father give? He has only the greatest respect for my son, this I know. Both he and your mother have said more than once that they would welcome a union between our children. Perhaps you have misunderstood your father's wishes."

"Stormwalker? Oh, but surely you do not think—" Kitappi bit her lip, her dark eyes distraught. Faint traces of dried salt showed on her cheeks from an earlier frolic in the water, making her seem even younger than usual, though she was nearing her seventeenth year.

"I do not think what, Kippi?" Bridget prodded gently, using a pet name bestowed upon the girl by her doting father.

"That I— That we— Bridget, I love your son as if he were my own brother, but . . ."

"Oh-*ho*! So *that* is the way of it." Poor Stormwalker. Kitappi was a fetching little bit of mischief, as pretty as a newborn fawn. In time, she would make him a good wife, but Stormwalker needed a woman in his lodge now, for it was time he ceased his endless wandering. There was only so much to be learned from even the wisest of men.

Besides, in these troubled times, he could be in grave danger. There were those among both sides who called him a troublemaker and who despised him for insisting that the young Indians learn of the white man's ways, and others who hated him for his mixed blood. Although she seldom left the island any more, Bridget was well aware of these things.

"What would you have me do, child?"

"Visit my father! Talk to him! Make him understand that I will be *miserable* if I cannot have Tiree Kiro. Just because he has no wealth, my father turns against him, yet T'kiro is wiser than any man I have ever known. He is so beautiful, so gentle, so very—so..."

"You care for this man?" Bridget asked gently, hiding her amusement. Poor Kitappi. Kokom she could have twisted about her little finger, but Gray Otter was another matter. As ill as she was, if Gray Otter had set her mind on having Stormwalker for her daughter's husband, for whatever reasons, changing her mind would be about as easy as directing the tide to reverse itself.

Although, Bridget mused, even the tide could be turned if one willed it so at the proper moment. It was merely a matter of timing. "I will send word to your father that Kinnahauk wishes to see him," she said.

"Does he?" The look of bright expectancy on the young girl's face sent a pang through Bridget's tender heart. Young love was so precious. And so very fragile, as she remembered well. At times even now, when she lay in Kinnahauk's arms, she could remember the way she had felt that first time....

"He will when I have spoken to him," she said, smiling serenely. "Go now. Visit old Sits There, for she cannot move about freely these days. She will welcome a bit of company. Give her all the news from your village, and later I will visit her so that she can relate it all to me. That way, her pleasure will double."

Laura had kept herself busy since Stormwalker had set out three days before. She told herself it was not jealousy she felt, but loneliness, yet it was a far different sort of loneliness than that she had felt while living alone on the island all those months before Little Thunder was born.

The sun beat down relentlessly. She knew she had been wise to remain there instead of setting out across the Pam-

ticoe Sound in an open boat. She might have managed to
shade her son, but she would have been burnt to a crisp and
probably been sick besides. The longest sea journey she had
ever taken had been half a day's sail down the York River
to visit a family who had come over from Devon on the
same ship with her mother.

Dipping a scrap of canvas into the pond, Laura draped it
over the skin of fresh water that hung just inside the cabin
door to keep it cool. She wished she could drape a wet cloth
over her own body as well, for it was sweltering hot!

Little Thunder whimpered fretfully from his mat under
the shelter Stormwalker had built before he left. She only
hoped the bear oil was doing what Stormwalker had claimed
it would do, for the flies were bad whenever the wind
dropped. Today there was no wind at all.

How tempting the river looked, calm as a looking glass,
the cloudless sky reflected on its still surface. She would love
to sit on the bottom with only her head above water until her
fingers and toes wrinkled like pale, dried grapes.

She could dribble water over Little Thunder's belly, which
would cool him down enough. Perhaps she could dip her
gown into the pond and then put it on again. Or make herself a kettle of yaupon tea, which would cause her to sweat
profusely and have much the same effect.

Of course! She had often wondered why all women insisted on drinking hot tea even in the height of summer. As
a child, she had never understood why her mother wouldn't
simply jump into the river and cool off the way she and her
father had.

"It's uncivilized! Your father oughten never to allow it."
Turning to her husband, Mary Gray would say, "It was all
those years you spent here trapping and a-doing before me
and Laurie came down from Virginia to join you. If you had
your way, Ned Gray, your daughter would grow up to be
just like those wild'uns you're always a-going on about!"

"Don't fash yourself, wife. Laurie's only a little thing.
She'll grow up soon enough. First thing you know, she'll be
a-wearing enough petticoats to strangle a goat, come sum-

mer or winter. Let the child enjoy what little freedom she has left.''

And enjoy it she had. Still would, except for the fact that Stormwalker had warned her to stay clear of the shore in case she was seen by a passing boat. Not that she had made up her mind to obey him. However, defiance took a lot of energy, and today it was just too hot. Instead, she would stir up the breakfast coals and brew herself a nice cup of tea and take it out here in the shade until time for Little Thunder to wake for his next meal.

Fearing snakes, although it would be the bold snake who would dare cross the blistering sand on a day like this, Laura scooped up the drowsing baby and carried him into the cabin with her. It was almost pitch dark inside after the blinding brilliance of the midday sun, and he lay contentedly enough on his pallet in the corner while she raked the ashes off the glowing coals and filled the kettle, setting it to boil.

Laura was standing on tiptoe, leaning forward to reach the box of parched yaupon leaves down from the ledge above the fireplace when she felt a prickling sensation on the back of her neck. Off balance, she hung there, listening. Dozens of possibilities rushed through her mind—a snake had come into the cabin seeking coolness and shade, or an animal, though there were no dangerous ones on the island.

The breath she'd been holding began to crush her chest and she let it out in a noisy gust. Stormwalker—he had come back! And he'd thought to sneak up on her just to teach her a lesson, but she'd heard him. It would serve him right if she—

Suddenly, there was no light inside. The door dragged— it could hardly have been shut so quickly, which meant that someone had entered the cabin.

Tea or no tea, Laura was sweating heavily when she came down off her tiptoes. Clutching the uneven stones of the hearth, she turned toward the door. The shadowy figure in the doorway was much too short, too broad.

''Who are you? What do you—''

He was beside her before she could finish, one hand touching her hair, the other on her throat. Laura's nostrils flared as she caught the scent of something horribly familiar...something that sent her into a blind panic.

Wrenching away, she flattened herself against the wall farthest from where Little Thunder lay sleeping. If she could just work her way around to the door and get out, he would follow her.

Oh, God, if he found her baby—

There was not the slightest doubt in her mind that this man was dangerous. Laura didn't know how she knew, she only knew. Stormwalker had said to go up on the roof...but that was only if she spotted someone coming before she was seen. This animal would just follow her there.

The knife! Where had she put it the last time she'd used it? Oh, God, it was still out under the shelter, where she'd been cutting strips of hide to fashion tiny breechclouts for her son.

"Cheeth ware-occa, unta-ha!"

"Get out! My husband will kill you if you don't go now!"

"Entequos warko," the savage grunted.

Laura pressed herself against the rough log wall, prying frantically with her fingers at a splinter of wood. If she could only break it free, it would serve as a weapon. She would have to go for his throat, for it would break against his chest. "Stop babbling that gibberish to me! Get out of my house!"

The man rattled off a string of guttural sounds that were nothing at all like the clipped words that first Stormwalker and then Kitappi had tried to teach her. Desperate to draw his attention away from her baby, she cried, "Tell me what you want! How can I understand you if you insist on speaking that heathen tongue?"

"Cheeth ware-occa, unta-ha. White bitch go with me. I am know to talk white-dog words. White dog not know to talk my words. Huh! You come now!"

She would go readily, just to get him out of the cabin, if only she thought Stormwalker would return. But even if he did, Little Thunder could perish of starvation—or worse.

How could she go off and leave her son alone on an island when no one, save Stormwalker and Kitappi, even knew of his existence? By now they could be so caught up in each other that the sun could fall from the sky and they would hardly notice.

"You come now, English woman dog!" the savage roared, and Laura's eyes darted to the place where Little Thunder slept.

Shhhh. Please sleep until I can get rid of this wretched creature, my sweetling. Please!

As she edged toward the door, her skirt snagged on the rough hearth, holding her back, and she jerked at it ruthlessly, hearing it tear.

As if the sound of tearing cloth had suddenly enraged him, the savage reached out to grab her. One hand struck her in the face, the other one raked across her breast before closing cruelly on her upper arm. Laura cried out, and he clamped his hand harshly over her mouth. He turned her so that her back was against his sweaty chest, and she tried to twist away. She had to get outside! No matter what happened to her, she had to lead him away from her baby! Those few months at Packwood's, she had heard whispered horrible tales of how the savages had treated newborn babies—the very thought was enough to bring the taste of gall to her throat.

Thrusting one of his knees behind her legs, the Indian threw her to the floor and fell upon her. Laura hardly noticed his crushing weight, for she had struck her head against the hearth when she fell.

"No—not here! No, please don't— Humph!" The air was driven from her lungs once more as he lifted her shoulders and slammed her down again. She could feel his hands tearing at her breasts, which were suddenly full and aching, and as if the child could sense her milk, Little Thunder whimpered once and then let out a lusty cry.

Oh, dear God, no. While the animal on top of her was momentarily distracted, Laura managed to work her left hand free. She shoved at his shoulder, her hand slipping on the repulsive coating of sweat and rancid grease that covered his body.

"*Woccanooknee?* You have child?"

"He's sick! Fever! An awful fever, with great, weeping sores and—and foul dribblings, and—"

In the dim glow from the low fire, she could see the wolfish smile spread over his dark face. He knew she was lying! Terror driven, she lunged, throwing him off-balance. Acting purely on instinct, she grabbed at the first thing that came to hand—the kettle. Even before the pain could register on her own palm, she had dashed its boiling contents into the face of her tormentor.

His screech of pain was all she needed. Yanking her skirt out from under his knees, she stumbled across the small room, snatched up her son and fled.

If only she'd killed him! That was too much to hope for, she told herself as she ran as hard as she could for her boat. But if she had hurt him bad enough so that he couldn't follow...

She might even have blinded him, which would mean that she was safe once she got her boat out into the water. Pray God it hadn't filled again—they'd had little enough rain lately, and the sun had been hot enough to dry the boards.

Oh, God, she thought desperately as she raced across the burning sand, her baby clutched tightly against her throbbing breasts. What if the tide was out too far, leaving the boat high and dry on its muddy bed of rushes? What if it had dried out so much there were great cracks between the boards, causing it to sink as soon as she got out into deep water?

There was no time to worry about such things now. She could hear someone crashing through the bushes—he had taken the shortcut through the woods!

Putting on a burst of speed, Laura ignored Little Thunder's loud cries. She only prayed he would still be alive to cry tomorrow.

Chapter Fifteen

One eye useless, Three Turtle blundered through the woods, following the rasping sound of the woman's breathing. One whole side of his face, including his ear and part of his throat, stung as if he'd been attacked by a swarm of bees.

He would kill her. He would chop her miserable white pup into small pieces before her miserable white eyes, and then he would kill her. This he would do very slowly, so that before she died, she would know that no *nickreroruh* bitch could defy Three Turtle of the Mattamuskeet and live.

Seeing her stumble on a fallen log and nearly fall, Three Turtle used the few lost moments to cut into the woods and get ahead of her. He knew where she was going. He had seen the white man's canoe she had hidden in the reeds, for he had chosen the same stand of reeds to hide his own dugout.

He cursed as branches whipped the tender skin of his burned face. Cursing and rum were the only good things the white man had brought to his people. He used both, but would have done without either if he could have made the sun turn around and go backward on its path to the time when the lands belonged to all the People and men fought with honor, killing their enemies with spears and arrows instead of muskets, fences and diseases.

Now it was too late. The game was gone, frightened away by the stench of the white-eye towns and the thunder of their weapons. His mother was no more. His sister was no more. Kitappi . . .

Where was his woman? Where was Stormwalker? Why
had he found only the yellow-hair and her stinking pup instead of the woman he sought?

Frowning, Three Turtle crouched in the rushes, his mind
in turmoil as he waited for the woman to complete her
stumbling journey around the edge of the woods he had cut
directly through. He could remember clearly that the sun
had risen three times since he had watched Stormwalker and
Kitappi enter the clearing where he had been hunting the
rabbits that still came in search of the old man's corn. He
had drawn his bow, aiming his arrow at Stormwalker's
throat, but then he had lowered it. He did not know why. He
hated the man he had once called friend. Why had he not
killed him then?

Instead, he had watched them climb into Stormwalker's
canoe and head downriver. Thinking they would go beyond the island to the mouth of the river, and then on to
Croatoan, he had stared after them, cursing himself for not
killing the man and taking the woman when he had the
chance.

But instead of going on beyond, they had come ashore on
this cursed island.

Since that day he had waited for them to return. He had
watched constantly for three days and three nights, except
for a brief time when he had gone into the woods to take
food. That had been yesterday, just as the sun had reached
above the waters. He was gone but a short while, only long
enough to take two rabbits, which had been exceedingly
poor, to skin them and roast them and fill his belly, for he
had not eaten in all the time he had been watching.

They could not have left the island! Yet they were not
there.

He cursed again as small black biting flies settled on his
tender burned flesh. He had reached the boat in time to hide
himself. Now he began to smile as he thought of how she
would scream when she saw him there.

The cruel smile faltered as he stared at her long yellow
hair. He had seen such hair but once before, when he had

killed the two old ones and used their daughter before killing her, too.

Or had he killed her first? His memory often played tricks on him. Sometimes his little sister came to him and whispered of things he had forgotten, games they had played as children, songs they had sung. There had been one they had sung often, about a white otter swimming in the river, how far would it go, how far would it go?

How far will you swim, white otter, to save your wretched life? Three Turtle asked silently. Then he began to sing. *"Ware-occa chaunok, warko ahunt wakena, untateawa unta, untateawa unta?"*

Laura's head snapped up at the sound of the tuneless guttural chant. Clutching Little Thunder so tightly he began to protest, she dug her heels into the sand at the edge of the marshy bed of reeds.

Three Turtle rose up before her. "You go me," he grunted.

"You go to the devil!" Sliding one foot carefully behind the other, she gauged her chances of reaching the woods before he could wade through the reeds and catch her. If only she could just reach the woods, there was a hollow tree—

His right eye was swollen shut from the boiling water. A handful of sand might close his other one, at least long enough for her to get a head start.

The sun beat down relentlessly from directly overhead. Light-headed, Laura knew it was only pride that kept her from giving in to the terror that threatened to strangle her. Swaying on her feet, she stared unwaveringly into a single small eye that was black as deepest sin, ignoring the swarm of biting flies.

The savage's skin had been greased with something much heavier than the light, sweet oil Stormwalker used, that he had insisted she used on her baby. The wretched creature stunk! She could smell him from where she stood, and in spite of the unendurable heat, something about his rank odor sent a chill up her spine.

She stared at him, trying hard to remember—wanting only to forget. She had never seen him before, she was almost certain of that. She would have remembered his prodigious strength, which was magnified by the glistening of sunlight on his flexing muscles . . . wouldn't she?

And then, with a cold, dread certainty, she knew. This was the man who had killed her parents. The same man who had raped her and left her for dead.

Which meant that this wicked savage was the father of—

A low moan escaped her, and she took a faltering step backward, tripped on the torn hem of her gown and sat down hard.

He was on her instantly. Snatching Little Thunder from her arms, he threw him aside and then grabbed up a fistful of her hair, his teeth bared in a smile so frightful she felt the breath freeze in her lungs.

It was her son's cry of outrage that brought her back to her senses. The stinking heathen was actually unsheathing his knife when Laura managed to scrape up a handful of sand. With no thought other than to escape immediate death, she hurled the sand into his face at close range. Kneeling astride her, he reared up, howling in rage, and she acted on impulse, driving her knee as hard as she could into the only available target.

In agony, Three Turtle rolled off onto the ground, clutching his groin. He heard her run to the babe and then toward the woods, but he could make no move to stop her. Blood rushed to his head, causing it to pound alarmingly. He ripped off his headband, which suddenly seemed unbearable, and flung it aside.

She would pay for this. They were alone on this island, and he would track her down and see that she died very slowly and very painfully, so that with every dying scream, she would remember.

He would kill the pup first while she looked on. Or perhaps he would take her hair and then he would sell her miserable whelp.

That was what he would do! He would torture the woman and take her scalp very carefully, so that she would still live, and then he would sell the child as a slave to the Coranine, who were known for their vicious treatment of slaves and captives.

As his pain slowly began to ebb, Three Turtle wondered who the woman was and what she was doing alone on the island where he had hoped to find Stormwalker and Kitappi. He had meant to kill Stormwalker and take Kitappi to his own village. Instead, he had found the useless *wareocca* bitch and her sniveling pup.

Who were they? Why were they there? Who had brought them to this place that was feared by all except those who, like him, were wise enough to use fear for their own purpose?

The answer was plain. The woman was Stormwalker's captive. He had stolen her or bought her, either for his own pleasure or as a gift to Kitappi. The babe could be his, for it was dark and lacked the yellow hair of its mother.

Staggering to his feet, Three Turtle waded out into the water, wincing as it rose to his tender crotch. He wet his face, cooling the pain of his burns and washing away the sand. He would show them all that he was the better man. He had not gone to the white man's schools, as Stormwalker had done. He had not walked in the lodges of their chiefs nor worn their ugly clothing nor sat on a platform and taken his food from a higher platform, eating it with a pronged metal stick.

He, Three Turtle, was the greater man. This he would prove by stealing Stormwalker's slave, using her to lure his foe into following. After killing Stormwalker, he would sell the woman and her babe for enough to buy Kitappi and a second wife, as well.

First he must get the yellow-hair away from the island, for Stormwalker would know this place well. To fight an enemy on his home ground was to risk losing, for the enemy had the greater advantage.

This time Three Turtle would have the advantage. He would take the woman to the place where he had waited for three days before going after Stormwalker and Kitappi. He would leave a trail. Then he would wait for Stormwalker to follow. No man would accept the loss of a valuable slave. He would come.

As Three Turtle waded ashore and cast about for the small footprints that led into the woods, he considered another possibility. After allowing enough time to pass so that all knew of Stormwalker's death, he could take the whelp to old Kinnahauk and tell him it came from Stormwalker's seed. Who could say it was not so? If the old fool believed him, he would intercede with Kokom. Then Three Turtle could trade the pup for Kitappi and save the bride price to buy himself a comely second wife much sooner than he had expected.

Laura's milk refused to come down. Her gown was stiff from the dried stuff, for it was long past time for Little Thunder to nurse, yet now that she had the time, nothing came. Could it be because she was terrified that at any moment the savage would burst in upon them and split their heads open with that wicked weapon he kept strapped to his waist alongside his knife?

Little Thunder whimpered, and she shushed him, stroking his downy head. With the sour taste of fear in her mouth, she kissed his crown, stroking the dark fuzz that grew there with her lips.

"Bye-lo, my bab-y, bye-lo, my ba-a-by," she sang in a low monotone. Despite the sweltering heat in the great hollow tree where they crouched, she felt cold. Little Thunder's small body burned in her arms and she welcomed the warmth. A few hours before she had been wondering how to keep cool, and now she was wondering if she would ever be warm again.

It was this awful fear, of course. She knew that, but it didn't help. The fear was too real. She had dived into the tree without even looking first to see if it were inhabited. A raccoon sleeping through the day could have inflicted a nasty bite, but she hadn't even given it a thought. There were snakes aplenty on the island, and they always sought the cooler places in the heat of day, coming out at night to hunt mice and small birds.

Her need was greater than theirs, Laura told herself, shuddering at the smell of rotted wood and other less easily identifiable things.

"Bye-lo, my bab-y, bye-lo— Here, sweetling, chew on Mama's breast, for it will keep you quiet. My ba-a-by, bye-lo, my bab-y, Papa's gone away."

Oh, God, if only Papa would *go away. Go away and leave us alone, for I cannot bear the thought of that animal—*

"No, dearling, that creature has nothing to do with you. Stormwalker brought you into the world, my love. He's your real papa."

She had no conception of time. It was dark in the woods, for a canopy of vines, seeking light, covered the treetops. Now and then an occasional scratching sound could be heard, but today, even the birds remained silent.

She must have dozed. At first she had held herself stiffly, taking great care not to touch the rough walls of the rotted trunk, for there was no telling how many animals had taken shelter there. Nor how many vermin were waiting for a warm-blooded creature to feast upon.

Slowly, her muscles relaxed and her head fell back. The babe lay across her lap, held securely by her crossed legs, which were tucked up close to her body in the cramped space.

It all happened at once. Something latched on to her ankle, dragging her right leg out through the opening. Her left knee and both elbows caught on the rough bark, for the opening was wider at the bottom, tapering to a point a few feet above the ground. Waking suddenly, Laura screamed just as Little Thunder howled. Then both her ankles were captured and she was dragged out on her back, the baby falling off her belly, half in and half out of the hollow.

There was no time to fight back, no time even to pray. The savage struck her on the jaw, causing her head to snap back. Bright lights danced briefly before the darkness closed in around her, and the next thing she knew, she was being tossed into a dugout and Little Thunder was thrown in after her.

* * *

Even before she opened her eyes, Laura knew she was home. The familiar smell of clean bedding, savory meats and drying fruits had long since been replaced by the acrid smell of smoke. Now even that had been replaced by the earthy smell of the leaves that had fallen into the crevices and rotted there, of the vines that had all but covered the part of the hearth that was still intact and the finger of broken chimney still standing.

A small shelter of sorts had been formed when the chimney had collapsed into the root cellar. It was now half filled with debris from the fire. It was there that Three Turtle had chosen to hide Laura and Little Thunder.

She knew his name. He had told her, as if it were a thing to be proud of. Not only had she recognized the name, but her deepest instinct had recognized the man as the animal who had raped her and left her to die.

Was there a chance that he had forgotten? That he no longer recognized her? If that were so, then she dare not let him know, because if he even suspected that Little Thunder was his son, he would steal her baby and she would never see him again.

There had been time to think after they had left the island. Lying in the bottom of the dugout, bound hand and foot, Laura had realized that she could not count on Stormwalker to come after them. For all she knew, he could have decided to stay on Croatoan with Kitappi. Perhaps he had married her by now.

But even if he did return to the island, he would think she had gone of her own free will, for Three Turtle had towed her boat out into the deepest part of the river and knocked a hole in the bottom with his hatchet. With a knowing grin on his broad face, he had forced her to watch it sink.

The man was vicious. He had the cunning of a weasel and no patience at all. When Little Thunder had begun to cry soon after they'd left the island, he had picked him up with one hand and thrown him into Laura's lap, ordering her to make the child stop.

"He's hungry," she said, trying to soothe the baby with her bound hands.

"He eat."

"How can he eat? I can't nurse him when I'm trussed up this way! Untie me, you filthy devil!"

That was when she had learned to curb her temper, no matter how great the provocation. Moving as swiftly as a striking snake, the man had struck her. When next she'd opened her eyes, she had been sprawled in the bottom of the canoe, her bodice slashed open, with the baby lying across her breast.

"He eat," Three Turtle had muttered, and indeed, the babe had managed to help himself, dribbling milk that had run down under her arms and dried to a sticky crust.

"Please unbind me so that I can hold him," she'd pleaded, but before he could answer one way or another, she had felt the canoe scrape the bank.

Today was the fourth day of her captivity. Or was it the third? Or the fifth?

The wretched beast had refused her anything to drink save the broth he had made from fat white grubs and God knows what other kinds of vermin. Laura had looked at the greasy, gray stuff and retched. There was no way she could force such a vile concoction down her throat, even if she were starving.

As well she might. Her milk had held up well enough for the first two days, although she felt as if she were drying up like a corn husk in the August sun.

But it wasn't August, it was July—or was it still June?

Ah, how could she know? How could she know anything in this wretched heat, with the flies and the mosquitoes and the big red ants that bit in places she couldn't even reach, all trussed up like a wild turkey ready for the spit, with the river lapping the bank nearby and she dying for want of a drop of water?

It was a wonder she even knew her own name.

Hours passed. Or perhaps days. Laura no longer had any conception of time, for it had lost all meaning. She lay as comfortably as she could on the flattened pile of leaves in a corner of the ruined fireplace, staring up into a pale, cloudless sky. Tendrils of Virginia creeper waved listlessly from the top of the broken chimney, and she gazed, half mesmerized, at one of the dainty five-leaf clusters. Already it showed a tinge of red. Soon it would be a fiery scarlet. Where would she be then? Where would her baby be?

Where was Stormwalker?

"You eat. You not worth much dead." Three Turtle appeared beside her with no warning. He moved as silently as a shadow. She glanced at the misshapen bowl he held out to her. Another of his foul-smelling broths. But no matter how loathsome it smelled and tasted, at least it was wet.

Laura was almost tempted. She sighed.

"You not eat, kill boy."

It took almost more strength than she possessed to sit up, but for the sake of her son, she knew she could no longer defy him. It wasn't the first time he had threatened to kill Little Thunder. If the child so much as whimpered, Three Turtle would glare at her and make some terrible threat.

He was unpredictable and increasingly irritable. At times she wondered if he weren't a bit mad. He talked to himself more and more often lately—it had to be to himself, for he knew she couldn't understand his heathen gibberish.

She managed three swallows of the vile broth, spitting out a fourth. Three Turtle snatched the bowl from her hand and hit her hard across the face.

With the little strength lent her by the foul liquid she had swallowed, Laura turned her back, lay down on her side and drew her baby close to her body. He needed bathing. They both did. Three Turtle had untied her feet long enough for her to go into the woods and relieve herself, knowing she would not try to escape as long as he had her son, but he refused to allow her near the river.

Again and again the same question tormented her. What was she to do? What was he waiting for? Why were they staying here? Had he brought her here to remind her?

God, as if she needed reminding! Would that she could ever forget!

Knowing the horrible things of which he was capable, she could only wonder, the same questions circling endlessly until she fell into a restless sleep.

It was cooler when next she opened her eyes. Cooler and darker, the clearing filled with that lovely lavender color she used to love so much.

From somewhere near her left hip came a small rustling sound. Leaves stirring among the rocks? She was too tired to lift her head. A mouse, perhaps. She had never eaten mouse, but she had heard the meat was little different from that of a baby rabbit.

And then every nerve in her body came alive. The noise was no longer a rustle, but a rattle. It was louder now, and it came from somewhere in the shadows beside her right shoulder. Near her head, her throat.

Thank God Little Thunder was on her other side!

Frantically, she willed herself to ease away from the sound, but her limbs refused to obey her will. Then even her will flickered and went out, like a guttering candle. Dear God, to end like this, all black and swollen, her skin split open and oozing of poison—

She jumped at the startling sound of rock striking rock. A scream pierced her terror. Her scream. Leaping clumsily to her feet, Laura promptly fell in a heap, adding more bruises to those she collected daily, either through her own clumsiness or Three Turtle's cruelty.

"What—where—"

"*Us-quauh-ne.* We eat." Three Turtle pointed to the dead rattlesnake and then picked it up by the tail.

"*You* squanee, *you* eat," Laura corrected. Shuddering, she scrambled to her knees and hopped to where Little Thunder lay howling. She scooped him awkwardly into her arms, cursing her bound hands. At least they had stopped aching. Now they were only numb and swollen.

That night Laura insisted on sleeping outside on the ground. Better the dampness of dew and the chill that came before morning than another encounter with a snake. With all her other worries, she had stupidly forgotten the way the snakes had always crawled onto the projecting rocks of the chimney after the sun went down, seeking the stored heat.

Now she sat by the fire, Little Thunder cradled on her lap, having finished his own meager supper. Tonight she had not even been offered food. She desperately needed a sup of water, but that was the one thing her captor denied her. It was as if he knew that she could do without food far longer than she could do without water, especially when she was nursing. She had all but stopped sweating, and that alarmed her. Little Thunder's skin felt too dry to touch, as well.

The fire had burned down to a bed of glowing coals when Three Turtle suddenly appeared out of the darkness. From his hand dangled the body of the snake he had killed, it's head neatly severed by the blow from his tomahawk. He pointed proudly to the cluster of rattles, which he now wore on a thong about his neck, and then tossed the loathsome thing onto the coals.

Then he turned to her. Pointing into the fire, he muttered, *"Us-quauh-ne."*

Laura recognized the sound. She didn't know the meaning of it, but she knew she had heard it before. Lips clamped stubbornly together, she stared up back into his one good eye, defying him in the only way left to her.

With a grunt of irritation, Three Turtle whipped out his knife and flipped the snake over on the coals. Hearing the sizzling sound as its juices oozed and spurted, Laura gagged. Still, she refused to look away. All she had left was her pride and her son. She would hang on to her pride as long as she could, for when that went, she would have no other weapon with which to protect her son.

Again her captor muttered the word, drawing a wriggling line on the ground with the tip of his knife. When she continued to ignore him, he jabbed at the snake, which spurted a stream of juice that struck her bare arm.

She screamed. He laughed, as if it were the greatest joke in all the world. "Laugh, you ugly bastard," she swore. "One day I'll find a way to repay all I owe you. When that day comes, it will be *your* skin bursting in the fire and *I'll* be the one to laugh!"

But even pride requires sustenance. By the time the moon rose, Laura was sucking a bit of rattlesnake away from the bone. And while she would never admit it to a living soul, the meat was as sweet as any bullfrog leg she had ever tasted.

Not that she would have touched the evil thing if it hadn't been for Three Turtle's knife at her throat. Even then she had balked, but when his gaze had turned to where Little Thunder had lay sleeping, she had snatched the greasy, blackened chunk of meat from his filthy hand and put it to her lips.

Once she'd learned to slough off the skin, it was delicious. The fact that she was starved might have helped. That and the fact that Three Turtle promised her water when she had done.

He was as good as his word, bringing her the small bowl filled with water from the river. The fact that the bowl had not been washed, to her knowledge, had not decreased her enjoyment one whit.

"More?" she had pleaded.

"No more. You feed boy. Make big. Make good slave."

Her spirits plummeted. For a little while she had hoped her captor was weakening. If he fed her, surely he would soon unbind her hands. And if he did that, she could free her feet, and then the minute his back was turned she could escape, even if she had to run all the way to Packwood's Crossing. Surely someone there would help her. For the sake of her parents, if not herself, even George and Coby would not turn her away this time.

Listlessly, she roused Little Thunder and put him to her breast. He was half asleep, but he suckled for a while. She held him there until Three Turtle turned and left, her eyes following him to the place where he slept, halfway between the river and the place where the cabin had once stood. There were three ruined corn ricks there, which made a shelter of sorts. He was soon lost in the shadows and though Laura couldn't see him, she could feel his eyes on her.

Didn't the devil ever sleep?

Despite the rising sun, she was not even awake the next morning when suddenly Three Turtle was at her side.

Grabbing her by the hair, he forced her to sit up, but before she could question him, he whipped out a strip of rawhide and bound it around her jaw, covering her mouth and a part of her nose. At the last moment, he ran a filthy thumb down the bridge of her nose, shoving the leather down until it cleared her nostrils.

At least he was not ready for her to die yet. Frantically, she stared at him over her gag. Was he going to torture her now? Was this his way of stilling her screams?

Desperate, she twisted her head in an effort to free her mouth. She lifted her hands and fumbled with the thing, but it was too tight and her hands were all but useless.

"Mfffghhhh," she mumbled, rising onto her knees and twisting awkwardly about to glare at him. As frightening as this latest outrage was, it was the smile on his face that made her break out in a cold sweat.

Dear God, he's going to kill me now, she thought. And I won't even be able to cry out.

But to her amazement, Three Turtle turned and slipped away into the woods. She stared after him, wondering if he meant to go off and leave her there to starve. But instead of setting off deeper into the woods, he dropped to his knees and crawled behind a thicket of bramble berries. A moment later she saw him slide into the shelter of the tumbled corn ricks.

It was only then that she became aware of a movement near the shore. Narrowing her eyes against the glitter of sunlight on the river, she would have gasped if her mouth had not been so tightly bound.

Another canoe had just rounded the point, the man in it bent over to drive his dugout those last few feet onto the riverbank. Laura's heart leaped painfully. It looked almost like— Could it possibly be . . . ?

Not until he stood did she know for sure because he was painted, his face wearing bands of soot black and blood-root red. On his chest were stripes of the same colors.

But it was Stormwalker. A Stormwalker she hardly recognized.

Chapter Sixteen

The trail had been too easy. First he had come upon the headband with the notched and blood-tipped feathers, then the marks made by the dugout as it left the bank. One man had come ashore in the dugout; two men or a man, a woman and a child, had left in it. Laura's boat was missing, as well, but it had been taken in tow by Three Turtle's canoe. There had been a short end of twisted rope of the kind that would be used for such a purpose left where it would be found, one end frayed, the other freshly cut.

Three Turtle had taken Laura and the boy, hoping to lure Stormwalker into coming after them.

Which he had done. What choice did he have, Stormwalker asked himself. Only the knowledge that the man who had once been his friend wished him to follow gave him hope that he would find Laura and Little Thunder alive. For all that Three Turtle's mind had been twisted by hatred, he was not stupid enough to destroy a thing of value. Laura and her son had value, even to a man who despised them.

Stormwalker had made no attempt to hide his coming, knowing he would be watched from the moment he left the island. Now he stood on the bank of the river near the place where his friend Edward Gray had once lived. It was but another twist of the knife that the Mattamuskeet brave had brought Laura here, to the place where he had murdered her parents and raped her, leaving her to die.

And then Stormwalker saw her. A black rage flooded his heart at the sight of Laura bound hand and foot, a strip of filthy hide shutting off her air. Her gown was in shreds, and even from here he could see her bruises. Thank God she still moved!

Rage drove all caution from his usually cool and deliberate mind. He took off at a hard lope, intent only on freeing her before she perished for lack of air. Halfway there, he called out to her. "Laura, open your eyes!" She *must* live. He would not let her die!

Covering the last short distance in the time it would have taken an arrow to fly, Stormwalker fell to his knees beside her. She stared at him wildly, her eyes wet with tears, as though she did not believe he had come for her.

He pressed her tightly against him, eyes shut against the pain of her wounds. *Laura, beloved Little Sparrow, why did I not keep you safe inside my heart?*

But aloud, he said only, "Where is the boy?"

The scent of danger was all around them. Keeping the river at his back, he swept the clearing with narrowed flame-blue eyes, from the vine-covered chimney on his left, to the burned shed beyond, to the low mounds of ruined corn at his far right. The fields were grown over with weeds that could have hidden many men, but it was on the shadowy forest beyond that his gaze lingered longest.

A mewing sound from the woman in his arms caught his ear, and he cursed himself for letting her suffer one moment longer than necessary. Fingers clumsy with haste, he untied the binding around her face and then took the tip of his knife to the cord that bound her wrists. She cried out when those were free, falling against him in agony as blood rushed into her swollen hands.

"You came back, you came back," she whispered over and over.

Even as he held her close against him, Stormwalker was aware of a bone-deep chill that had nothing to do with the warm, restless currents of air that stirred all around them. As a sudden scurry of wind whipped through the clearing to twist branches and flatten the tall wild grasses, his eyes moved constantly, seeking a glimpse of the mad dog who had done this wicked thing.

"Where is the boy? Has he been harmed?"

"I don't know! I don't know! You've got to find him, quickly!"

At that moment, two things happened. A fast-moving cloud covered the sun and Little Thunder cried out, the sound seeming to come from somewhere near the tumbled corn ricks. Touching Laura's face reassuringly, Stormwalker stood and looked intently in that direction. The corn, which had already been ricked but not yet covered, had been ruined by rain the day Ned Gray had been killed. After that it had been quickly scattered by animals. Now, overgrown with all manner of weeds, it formed a barrier just high enough for a man—or a babe—to hide behind.

The cry came again, a thin, hungry wail. Stormwalker felt his tension grow until he could scarcely draw breath. Three Turtle had baited his trap well. The woman had drawn him thus far, the child would do the rest. Knowing this, he still could not save himself.

"Please—you must help him," Laura cried. Clutching his legs, she pulled herself to her feet.

"First I will free you so that—"

"No! Hurry, hurry—please, I beg you!"

He had been about to say that he would free her so that if he failed to return, she would at least have a chance, but she was weeping, pleading and pushing against him all at once.

"I cannot leave you this way!" he growled. Gripping the arm that had been pushing him toward the corn ricks, he quickly cut through the strip of leather that bound her feet. Before it had even fallen to the ground, he was running toward the place where he had last heard the child.

"Hurry, hurry!" she screamed after him, while before him, the boy cried out sharply once more and then settled into a pitiful wailing.

It is your own son you torment, offal of a carrion eater! Has she told you that?

Stormwalker never even saw the blow that felled him. Laura had seen it. A moment too late, she screamed after him to look to his left, but all his attention had been on the child lying naked on the ground, red ants, drawn by the stench of urine, crawling on his small body.

Horrified, Laura had seen Three Turtle throw off a covering of leaves and rise up from the sunken place in the ground where they had buried the carcass of a cow that had washed downriver two years before. Just as his tomahawk left his hand, she had screamed, but her warning had come too late.

Stormwalker was dead. She had killed him as surely as if she had thrown the wicked stone hatchet herself.

"Oh, God," she moaned, crawling forward. Ironically, she had fallen the instant her feet had been freed, for they refused to support her. "Oh, God, my baby—my love," she whispered, her eyes pale circles of glistening gray in her filthy bruised face.

And then Three Turtle turned to her. He was smiling as he lifted up her son, and with no more than a glance at his fallen enemy, he strolled across the clearing to where she was struggling to reach them and dropped him into her arms. "*Utserosta* hungry. You make eat."

"Have you killed him? Is he dead? Won't you *please* let me go to him?" With Little Thunder crushed tightly to her breast, all her thoughts were on Stormwalker, who had not moved since he had crumpled to the ground.

"Paugh! That one not dead. He die more slow. *Utserosta* eat. He got ants." With that, he turned and stalked off, leaving Laura staring after him in openmouthed confusion. By now, his inflamed right eye had crusted over, but all the other signs of his scalding had faded. With all her heart she willed him to fall dead of infection that very instant.

Hotserosta eats ants? What on earth did that mean?

Before she could puzzle it out, Little Thunder let out a yelp that brought her heart to her throat. And then she felt the wretched things on her arms—they were everywhere! Red ants!

Muttering frantic, soothing noises, she brushed them off, turning him on her lap to examine his backside, which was already marred by several red welts.

Her hands still ached abominably, but at least she could use them. Clutching Little Thunder under one arm, she began hobbling toward where Stormwalker had fallen.

Only he was no longer there!

Very quickly, the sky seemed to have grown ominously dark. A hot, damp wind rustled through the trees, causing the leaves to show their pale undersides. Had there been thunder? She wouldn't have heard. Lightning could have struck her and she wouldn't have noticed.

Where was Stormwalker?

The wind fell as swiftly as it had risen and in the silence, she heard a sound that caused her to whirl about. Three Turtle was behind her and—oh, God, he was dragging Stormwalker's body toward a tree!

"No!" she screamed. "Stop that! You mustn't hurt him, please—I'll do anything you say, only leave him alone!"

She might as well not have spoken. Horrified, she watched as Three Turtle, his eyes gleaming feverishly, knelt and whipped a length of rawhide around his victim's wrists.

"Dear God, the man is dead! What are you trying to do?" She hobbled forward, intent on stopping the wicked desecration before it went any further. Too late, she saw the grinning savage rise, pass a thick vine between the lashings on Stormwalker's wrists and haul him upright, suspending him from the crotch of the tree.

Sometime during the awful proceedings, solid sheets of warm, driving rain had begun to blow across the clearing, flattening her ruined gown against her body. "Oh no, oh no, oh no," she crooned tonelessly. She saw Three Turtle drop to his knees once more. By the time he stood again she was close enough to see that Stormwalker's feet had been lashed to the tree.

Did that mean he was truly not dead yet? Surely there would be no reason to tie a dead man to a tree, unless... Stormwalker still lived! That evil creature had said as much, but she hadn't dared believe him.

Then why...?

And then she knew. Torture! He was going to torture Stormwalker until he was truly dead, and she could do nothing to save him!

At the very moment Three Turtle unsheathed his knife, Laura carefully laid her baby on the wet ground, taking care that he was on a small hummock of weeds that would keep his head clear of the puddles that were already beginning to form.

With deadly purpose she began to run, her swollen feet clumsy in the slick and sticky mud. More than once she stumbled, but she kept on going, mouthing a silent prayer as she went.

She almost made it. She was so close she could see the drops of blood bead the smooth surface of Stormwalker's broad chest behind the tip of Three Turtle's knife. A perfect cross. Not deep, but deep enough to bleed freely.

The rain was blowing almost horizontally across the clearing by now, and Laura, half blinded by rain and by her own blowing hair, flew the last few steps. Just as she saw Three Turtle draw back his weapon, taking dead aim at the place where the two slashes touched, she screamed and hurled herself at his back.

Startled, he spun around just as the force of the blow knocked the knife from his hand. It fell point downward on top of her right foot, but Laura felt nothing at all. All her attention was focused on the man hanging suspended from the tree as the blade sliced neatly through her foot to the sole.

It was Three Turtle's scream that drew Stormwalker up from the painful depths in which he had been sinking. He opened his eyes in time to see the other man draw back his tomahawk.

Stormwalker opened his mouth, but no sound emerged. And then, from a source outside his own body came the strength to break free. With a blood-chilling roar, he lunged. The vine went flying as he brought his arms, still bound, down on the back of Three Turtle's neck.

The blow alone would have killed an ordinary man, but Three Turtle was no ordinary man. Like a felled ox, he sank slowly to his knees. But before either of the other two could move, he was up again. Snatching Laura by the hair, he dragged her some distance away, out of the reach of Stormwalker, who was lying prone, his feet still bound to the tree.

All around them, the wind howled, twisting limbs into tortuous shapes. Trees bent to sweep the ground. Some snapped off, others toppled, root and all, with a terrible sort of majesty. Never taking his eyes from Three Turtle, Stormwalker dragged himself up until he was standing. Holding on to the sapling to steady himself, he began to speak rapidly in his own tongue.

Even had she been able to understand, it would have made no difference to Laura, for at that moment, with blood from her injured foot flowing freely to mingle with the rain, she sank into a dead faint, sliding clean through the circle of Three Turtle's arms.

His expression one of almost comical confusion, Three Turtle gazed first at the woman now lying at his feet, and then his old foe. His knife had fallen away from Laura's foot and he picked it up. He had not wanted the woman dead. She was far more valuable alive. Even so, he still had Stormwalker and the boy.

A cruel smile split his face as he considered his once-proud enemy, now hobbled like a dog to the tree. "Who has won this coup, my old friend? Who has won this race? Who is the better man?"

"Kill me now, but spare the woman and boy. He is your son, Three Turtle."

"Paugh! You think the spirit of *cossarunta* live inside my head?"

Stormwalker bit back the words he would have uttered. The man was truly *cossarunta*—mad. But it would only madden him more to be told so.

"The boy is yours!" screamed Three Turtle. "The white female dog was yours! I have killed her. I will sell your son to the fiercest warrior at Raruta, where he will learn to hate the white-eye. One day he will cut open all white bellies and fill them with burning coals. He will split all white women in two parts and feed them to the wolves. He will spit on the name of the *ware-occa cheeth* who whelped him. If he lives.''

Not by a single sign did Stormwalker show how those words had affected him. All knew that the Coree at Raruta were feared by both red and white man alike for their cruelty. To one of mixed blood, as both Stormwalker and Little Thunder were, it was a particularly fiendish threat.

Putting aside all thought of revenge for the moment, Stormwalker concentrated on freeing himself so that he could protect the woman and child. The wet rawhide that bound his feet to the gum tree was already loosening, but he feared he could not free himself in time. He must rely on his wits.

''Would you fight me now, Three Turtle? I am ready.''

''You have no weapon.''

''My hands.'' Against a knife and tomahawk they would be useless, unless he could somehow outwit his old foe.

The trouble was, Stormwalker and Three Turtle had fought together too many times. They were too well matched.

Stormwalker's concentration broke for a single instant as he looked down at Laura. She lay as still as death, rain beating down on her to wash her blood onto the ground beside her. She was bleeding badly, but she still lived. He could see the faint lift of her breast each time she drew air into her lungs.

But for how long? The bleeding must be stopped, for already she was so pale her bruises stood out like black shadows.

He turned back to Three Turtle, who was watching him with a knowing smile. His right eye was swollen shut, as if it had been injured, but his left one glittered with the fire of madness. ''Well?'' Stormwalker asked quietly, ''Will you cast aside all honor and fight an unarmed warrior?''

''No man know how you die,'' Three Turtle countered.

''You would know, my old enemy.'' The balance shifted subtly from one to the other and back again. Like two male dogs coming together unexpectedly, both men were aware of this.

Three Turtle's fingers began to curl and uncurl. His left eye, his good one, narrowed in thought. *He has no way of knowing that the yellow-hair has half blinded me. Let him think it is honor that spares his life if it pleases him. Three Turtle's honor will be satisfied when every white-eye and every half-blood is dead!*

Aloud, he said, "I kill your female dog. You see her die and do nothing to save her." He smiled, and the smile held a terrible kind of innocence. "One day I kill you, my friend. For now I let you live. Know this. I have your son. Know this. The yellow-hair felt my blade. She die. Soon you die. Soon all white dog die."

"The boy! You will not harm him. He is your son, Three Turtle."

The Mattamuskeet spat in the direction of Stormwalker's feet, but the gesture was ruined by the rain. "Half-blood. Maybe I sell, maybe I kill." His smile still in place, Three Turtle turned away, stepping over the woman with little more than a glance. She was ugly, even her hair not worth the taking now, for it was caked with mud. He hated her. For ruining his eye. For crushing his manhood. For not being Kitappi. He hated her for being white, for having belonged to his enemy, for having borne him a son. If she were not already dead, he would have killed her now.

As the rain beat against him, cooling the fire that burned inside his body, Three Turtle strode across to where the boy lay crying weakly in the rain. Lifting him by one leg, he slung him under his arm and set out at a lope toward the swollen river that was already overflowing its banks.

From somewhere nearby, a tree snapped off, the sound like musket fire. Laura opened her eyes. She couldn't move, she couldn't see—everything was cold and gray. Dear God, she was blind! She was freezing to death!

"Li'l Thun'er," she whispered. "Whereareyou?" As the last slurred words left her lips, she closed her eyes again. Nor did she open them, not even at the sound of Stormwalker's swearing. Not even as two trembling hands lifted

her carefully from the ground. Barely conscious, she could
only turn toward the warmth.

The shelter had once housed oxen. It had stood empty
since the first raids. Stormwalker knew he could go no farther, for the storm showed no signs of abating. He had
sensed its coming soon after he had left Croatoan. It could
not have come at a worse time.

Now, watching intently for the least sign of change in
Laura's breathing, he sent a silent plea to the spirit of old
Soconme, a great healer who had been his mother's teacher.
He tried to recall what little of the white man's medicine he
had learned at their schools. He would need all the wisdom
of both worlds this night if his little sparrow were to survive.

The bleeding had stopped. The wound looked clean
enough, for the rain had washed her until her skin was pale
as cold ashes. The blade had passed between the bones of
her foot. The wound had bled freely—too freely. Even if she
survived the loss of so much blood, without a poultice to
draw out the poisons before the wound healed over, she
might sicken with fever.

He must take her to his people. As soon as she was strong
enough—as soon as the storm blew itself out, he would take
her to Num Peree, to his own lodge, where he would ask
Mary Brown Bear to look after her. Mary was wise in her
knowledge of herbs and healing potions.

But first Laura needed strength. Judging from the deep
hollows around her eyes and under her cheeks, she had eaten
little or nothing since she had been captured.

How long ago that had been, he had no way of knowing.
It made no difference—she needed food. She needed
warmth so that she could rest and food so that she could regain her strength, and he had neither to offer her.

All through the night he held her close against him, shel-
tering her body with his, lending her his own warmth. Fingers of wind found their way between the logs where the
chinking had been lost. Stormwalker cursed his own short-
sightedness in not coming prepared. He had neither hides

nor blankets to cover her with. He had no kettle to make broth, no meat, no honey.

Lying beside her on the earthen floor, her slender back tucked securely against his warm belly, Stormwalker stared over her head into the darkness. He had not dared linger in the clearing to search for his weapons, which Three Turtle had taken from him. His only purpose had been to get his woman as far away as possible before the mad dog changed his mind and came back for her.

Stormwalker, the great teacher, he thought mockingly. The learned man who would one day bring to his people the knowledge that would enable them to live in the changing world. Stormwalker, son of the great *werrowance* Kinnahauk, who might one day be called upon to lead his people because his sister, White Swan, had married a white man.

"See me now, oh, Great Spirit. In your wisdom, keep safe this woman and her son, who have done nothing to offend you. Do not let my sins fall upon her head. She does not know of my love. I am not worthy of hers, for I let her son be taken from her. See me now, O Great Spirit. I am weak. Lend me your strength. I will not use it unwisely. I will not seek to rise above others. I will cleanse my heart of hatred if it displease you, but if you would have me fight your enemies, lend me your strength."

With a heavy sigh, Stormwalker closed his arms around Laura, chafing warmth into the smooth skin of her arms. He had forced her to drink water before she slept, but it was food she needed. She needed *him*, and suddenly he felt strength and purpose flow through him, wiping away the horrendous effects of the two-day race from Croatoan to the mainland. She *would* live. He would *will* her to live!

But in the black hours before dawn, after the storm had beaten itself out and moved northward, the doubts crept in again. And if she lives, he thought, what will you tell her of her son? That he has been sold to the treacherous Coranine at Raruta? That he may even now be dead?

If there had been any other way, Stormwalker would never have told Three Turtle that the boy was his son. It had been a gamble, for mad as he was, it could have served to

enrage the man who despised all whites and half bloods.
Little Thunder showed no signs of his mixed blood, but it
was there. Could a father love one part of his son and despise the other? Could he kill one part of his son and let the
other part live?

It was a gamble, one Stormwalker had been forced to
take. There had been a time when Three Turtle had loved a
younger sister. He had played with the children at feasts and
gatherings, showing no sign of the twisted man he would
one day become.

Stormwalker could only hope that a shred of honor remained in the man who had once been his friend.

Chapter Seventeen

Eyes closed tightly, Laura turned her face away from the smell of food. How could she think of food when her baby was gone? Little Thunder had been taken away from her and she would never see him again. Her own son! How could God allow such a thing to happen?

"Open your eyes, Laura. I have brought you food."

She opened her eyes and stared dully up from her pallet at the tall man who stood over her. Why was Stormwalker here with her in a dark, fetid room, when Little Thunder was lost? Why wasn't he out searching instead of badgering her to eat? It was as if nothing had happened. As if they were back on the island.

Almost absently, she studied Stormwalker's straight black hair, his proud, angular features. For a little while she had almost forgotten that he was one of the wild'uns. How strange—could he still be in sympathy with Three Turtle after all that had happened? He had said they'd once been friends. They were both wild'uns.

Her gaze moved over his dark features, his glossy black hair...so different from her own. Different from the Harkers and the Packwoods, from everyone she knew. Except for his eyes....

But then, only one part of him was wild. The other part was as English as she was.

"Please," she whispered. "I want my baby."

"I will find him, Laura," Stormwalker heard himself promising, wondering even then if it would be possible.

"But first you must eat and gain strength so that I can take you to a safe place."

"A safe place? Where is that? My home? That's where that animal took us!" Her voice was too shrill, her eyes too wide.

"I will take you to a safe place, Little Sparrow, but first you must eat, for it is half a day's journey from here." It was half a day's journey for a running man. For a man carrying a woman over fallen trees and flooding creeks, it would be longer. "I would have made broth, but I had no kettle." He proffered the haunch of a rabbit he had snared at first light and then roasted over a small fire while she slept.

"How can you think of food when my child is in danger? He may even be dead for all you know!"

Laying aside the meat, Stormwalker gathered her stiff body into his arms and held her until her weak struggles ceased. He had not felt so helpless since the night he had come upon her in the throes of childbirth. "*Sehe*, Little Sparrow. Soon I will find your son, but first I must carry you—"

"You don't need to carry me anywhere, I can look after myself! Go after them! You should never have let them go!" Wild with anxiety, she could not have known the great pain inflicted by her unjust words.

Stormwalker fought for control of his emotions but soon the hurt gave way to anger. Did not the foolish woman know that to have gone after her son, leaving her unattended, could have meant her death? A woman of his own kind would have accepted what he had done, knowing that at the proper time, he would do all in his power to restore her child to his arms.

But not this buzzing hornet. She demanded of him that he take leave of his own senses and do her bidding. She demanded that he—

She *demanded*! The women of his people did not demand. How was it possible that such a small, unreasonable creature could have captured him so easily? She had neither danced for him nor sung for him. She had not wooed him with soft glances and softer sighs. She had cooked no food for his lodge nor had she worked his hides, much less had she made him a fine shirt.

In no way had she proven herself worthy, yet she had taken root deep inside his spirit and now he feared he would never be free of her. Leave her alone and untended? How could he leave her, not knowing if she would starve, if her wound would grow angry, if her hiding place would be discovered and she would be taken prisoner again—or worse?

His only hope lie in making her see that his way was best. "Three Turtle was once an honorable man," he reminded her, knowing he must convince her that her son was in no real danger.

In convincing her, he could only hope to convince himself. Three Turtle was no longer sane. The seed of madness had been planted years before, when a white trapper had raped and murdered Makes Wind and Six Toes. It had remained hidden for years, until Hancock had incited his band of Tuscaroras along with others to rise up against the white man.

War was its own madness, Stormwalker thought. Aloud he said, "Only the Great Spirit can say who will live and who will die, but surely not even Three Turtle could kill his own son, Laura."

She seemed to grow quieter in his arms, as if suddenly too weary to fight him. Or as if his words had finally impressed her.

If only he could convince himself of their truth.

A deep sadness welled up inside him as his gaze lingered on her bruised face. The sight of her wide gray eyes and her soft, vulnerable mouth made him want to hide her away somewhere where pain and sorrow could never find her, a place where she would know only joy and pleasure.

It could not be. He must find a way to restore her son to her arms and then, for a brief moment, he would share in her joy. But she would return to her own people and he to his.

Stormwalker fought against the despair that threatened to overcome him. He could not afford to weaken now, for there was much to be done. When he spoke again, his voice was stiff and without expression. "Three Turtle will not harm your son. He has heard my words. I do not know if he will believe them, but if he were going to kill your son, he would have done so where we both could see. Instead, he took him away. He will not injure Little Thunder, Laura. Of that I am certain."

The Great Spirit alone knew how very uncertain of that he was, but he had to say something to take away the haunted look in her eyes before it destroyed him.

The storm had moved on during the night, leaving the river overflowing its banks until half Ned Gray's old fields flooded. Stormwalker knew that the creeks between there and Num Peree would be flooded, as well, and difficult to cross without going miles out of the way.

It would have to be the island again. The journey by boat would be easier by far, but before he dared risk even that, he must find some way to make Laura take nourishment.

"I have brought a squirrel," he said a few hours later, rousing her from a restless sleep.

She blinked sleepily and then her face took on its familiar belligerence. "What will my baby eat? Will that filthy creature suckle him—or will he force him to eat grubs and rattlesnake? He needs me! My baby needs me—he's scarcely more than a month old!" Sitting up, she lifted her heavy breasts and cradled them in her palms, and to his great shame, Stormwalker suddenly knew an unworthy desire to remove her hands and replace them with his own.

Abruptly he turned and left her, after first placing the roasted squirrel on a large oak leaf beside her. He suspected she would ignore it as she had ignored his other offering of food, but he had to try.

She was crying. Her sobs, her soft pleas, followed him outside, but he forced himself to ignore them. She must be made to eat. He had seen too many creatures slowly starve when taken into captivity, and the same wild look was in her eyes.

* * *

The sun was directly overhead when next Stormwalker slipped inside the dark musty shed. He grunted when he made out the haunch of squirrel swarming with ants. Tossing it outside, he raked the top layer of dirt along with it.

She was asleep, lying on her side on the bed he had fashioned from pine boughs and moss. Taking care not to waken her, he lay down beside her, moving closer until her back was curved against his front.

With a sigh that only hinted of the torment he was beginning to feel whenever he touched this woman, or even gazed on her, he stared unseeingly out the wide opening, telling himself he was only lying with her to lend her the comfort of his body. He, too, was tired, for he had not slept in three nights. Another two hours and the tide would turn, making the river easier to cross.

His eyelids drooped. He vowed to stay awake in case she should need him, but his strength was not equal to his will. He smoothed her torn gown over her limbs, wishing his own garment would cover her—wishing he could have given her a fine doeskin gown like those his mother wore.

Not that she would wear such a garment, he mused sleepily. She would much prefer all the layers upon layers that her kind favored—the skirts and overskirts, with poufs and kerchiefs and aprons and such....

After a few moments he shifted to relieve the growing heaviness between his thighs. His last waking thought was that at the first opportunity he would buy her another gown if he had to go all the way to Bath Towne to do it. Until then, he would try not to see the pale soft flesh revealed through the tatters of her ugly garment.

Sometime later, Laura blinked her eyes at the chinks of red-gold light that fell through the roof of the tumbledown shed. She was alone. Sitting up, she yawned widely, flexed her stiff shoulder and drew her foot up to examine it, pleased to discover that it was no worse than before. If her wound had been going to fester, she was reasonably certain it would have shown signs of trouble by now. Stormwalker had taken great care to cover the entire floor of the shed with a thick layer of brush so that it had remained clean.

Her belly growled noisily and as if on cue, Stormwalker ducked through the square doorway. Laura's gaze flew to his hands, which were empty, and she knew a moment's regret for having declined the feast he had offered her earlier.

"Come, it is time to return to the island."

"The island! But I thought we would go after Little Thunder. You promised!"

Ignoring her words, he knelt and swept his arms under her, lifting her as if she weighed no more than a child. Instinctively, Laura clutched his shoulders to keep from falling. "Stormwalker, you promised! We must go after Little Thunder. The rain's ended and my foot is almost well now." Both her eyes and her words pleaded with him, willing him to respond.

In a shed constructed for oxen, Stormwalker could barely stand upright. Head lowered to accommodate the sagging roof, his mouth was a mere breath away from hers. He fought against a sudden fierce compulsion to touch her lips with his, to tell her in his own way what he could not say in words.

Instead he ducked outside, breathing deeply, as if to draw strength. "Are you hungry?"

"No, damn you, I will *not* eat until we find my son!"

Face hardening, he nodded and set off at an easy lope in the direction of the river. She would not eat? Then he would wait until she was too weak to defy him and he would force food between her lips.

She would not listen to his words of reason? Then he would speak no more until she grew tired of silence and pleaded for the sound of his voice.

"Where are you taking me?"

"I have spoken. Be quiet now, woman. The voice of the river is too loud and I have other things to think on."

Suddenly aware of the rushing sound of the water, Laura fell silent. But that did not mean her anger left her. She was seething. It was not enough that her son, the most precious thing in the world, had been taken from her to live like a savage in some verminous heathen encampment. It was not enough that she was being ignored and jostled as if she were no more sensible than a sack of grain.

But what bothered her even more at this moment was her terrible awareness of the arms that held her and the cool, damp flesh against which her cheek was pillowed. She was ashamed to admit that as distraught as she was, she was not above being stirred by Stormwalker's arms, by the scent of his skin and by his great strength. How could a man be so gentle and caring one moment and so stubbornly, persistently *maddening* the next?

Laura wrapped herself in anger, as if seeking refuge, for to admit to any other emotion under the circumstances was unthinkable. Little did *he* care that her son had been wrenched from her very arms! He was no more civilized than the rest of the savages! W..y, he wasn't even breathing hard after running all this distance carrying her in his arms, and for some reason that irritated her beyond bearing.

But in spite of her spurious anger, she could not help but admit that he had taken particular care not to jostle her foot.

Not wanting to soften toward him, she said sharply, "Your canoe will be filled with water—that is, if it hasn't washed away."

Carefully, Stormwalker settled her on a dry patch of riverbank while he went about shoving his canoe back in the water. "As you see, it was neither," he grunted. "I came back while you slept and dragged it up onto the bank, lashing it bottom up to a tree."

"Always so perfect. Is there anything you don't know? Anything you can't do?" Pushing away his hands, she hopped to the edge of the water and grasped the rough sides of the canoe, climbing clumsily into the narrow craft. From there she glared at him while he knelt on the bow and shoved them away from the bank.

"I am far less than perfect, Laura Gray," he said quietly as he set them on course with a deft turn of his paddle. "There are many things I do not know. There are many things I cannot do, but this I promise you. When you are safe and well, I will go after Little Thunder. I will bring him back to you." If the Great Spirit be willing, he finished silently.

"How can I convince you that I am safe and well?" Lacking the strength to do otherwise, Laura settled herself as comfortably as possible and closed her eyes. Within moments she was asleep, unaware of the deep blue eyes that swept the horizon again and again, returning each time to gaze at her unguarded face.

Nor did she awaken until the long, narrow craft nudged the bank. Opening her eyes, she struggled to sit up. "Where are we? Have you found him yet...? Oh..." Disappointment weighted her voice as she looked around to see the familiar shore.

Stormwalker knew a moment's strong irritation. Could the woman think of nothing but her son? He, too, loved the boy. Had he not brought him into this world? He would have given his life if he could have spared the child a moment's pain, but pain was a part of living. One must learn to accept what one could not avoid.

"On the day when you are strong enough to care for yourself, to gather food and prepare it so that you do not starve before I return, then will I leave you to find your son."

It was not the gathering of food that concerned him, for he would leave her with enough to last her for many days. The fighting still went on. With both sides suffering great losses, no one was safe. She must be strong enough to evade danger, but there was no way he could prepare her for that without frightening her.

Avoiding her accusing eyes, Stormwalker leaped over the side and shoved the heavy canoe higher onto the bank. He lifted her out and glanced over his shoulder from force of habit to see what he had left behind.

There was nothing. Three Turtle had taken his knife, his tomahawk and his bow. He was without weapons of any kind until he could replace them. "Come, there is time before dark to try for a fish."

"Food! Is that all you can think of?"

His arms tightened perceptibly as he set out toward the cabin. "If you would regain your strength so that I can leave you, woman, you must eat," he said with rapidly eroding patience.

"I'm strong as an ox, you great bloody savage! I keep telling you that! If you won't go, I'll only wait until you're asleep and go after him myself." Tears of weakness and frustration suddenly filled her eyes and she wiped them away impatiently.

Stormwalker stepped easily over the fallen log that lay halfway along the shore. "How will you know where to find him?"

"Where does Three Turtle live? Do you know?"

"Yes."

She clutched his hair, forcing his head to one side. "Then tell me! At least you can tell me that much."

"His village is called Seconiac. It lies in that direction." He pointed to the northeast. "It is surrounded by great swamps. You would be lost or killed by one of the creatures that live there before you even came in sight of his village. It is not easy for a man to find unless he knows the land well. For a white woman alone, it would be impossible."

"Then how—" Tears threatened her again, and Stormwalker hardened his heart. She must not try to go alone. If she died, as surely she would, the sun would go from his sky.

"I have given you my promise, woman. I will search for your son. But a mother who has been killed by a bear or an alligator, or sold into slavery, or murdered for her golden hair will be of no use to Little Thunder."

She shuddered in his arms and his eyes narrowed on hers, as if he could force his will on her. "You must be strong for your son, Laura Gray." *And for me,* he added silently. *One of us must keep our wits about us, and I fear, Little Sparrow, that you have scattered mine.*

Thinking to distract her as they neared the cabin, he said, "I have thought much about this matter, Laura Gray. The difference between the white man and the red is that the red man seeks visions to tell him what the future will hold. The white man seeks no visions. Instead, he seeks to shape the future to suit his own needs."

He could have argued the matter from either side, but she remained silent. Her head was now leaning against his shoulder and he gloried in the small weight of it.

And the half blood, he asked himself mockingly. What does he seek? He sought visions and then wondered if he could believe in them. He tried to shape the future of his people and then wondered if the future he had chosen for them would destroy them.

Laura muttered something—he failed to catch her words, but he had little doubt as to their meaning. Smiling, he strode into the clearing.

And there his smile left him. One wall of the cabin was gone. The chimney was still standing, though several of the rocks from the top had fallen onto the dangerously sagging roof. The entire southwest side was gone, swept away by the tides that had covered all but the highest knoll in the center of the island.

"Put me down," Laura demanded, and this time he obeyed. Together they surveyed the damage. Stormwalker would not allow her to go inside. Leaving her there beside the fresh pond, which was no longer quite so fresh, he feared, with the intrusion of water from the brackish sound, he stood just outside what once had been the doorway.

"Can you reach the kettle? I could parch some yaupon for tea."

"The kettle is gone. There is nothing left, Laura. Tonight you will sleep under the stars, as I do. Tomorrow I will build you another shelter."

"But how will I make tea? How will I cook broth?"

"Patience, Little Sparrow. You have much to learn."

That night they divided the bony shad, which was all Stormwalker was able to catch before dark using the spear he had managed to sharpen with Laura's rusty knife. That, at least, had not been swept away, for it had somehow become impaled between two rocks of the hearth.

The following day he set about teaching her, giving her no time to dwell on the fate of her son. After first dressing her foot with some gray substance that she thought it best not to ask about, he wrapped it in leaves and bound it tightly with supple vines so that it would not separate and begin to bleed again.

Of the same vines, which had been stripped of blossoms, he wove a net and set it where the river current swept between the island and the mainland. Later that day, he showed her how to wrap a fish in layers of leaves so that in cooking, the juices would be miraculously doubled. He taught her that a bed of the wild grass under the stars was no great hardship when one was weary beyond belief.

Laura learned that a blanket was not necessary to ward off the bone-leaching cold that came with the dew just before morning. Stormwalker, who had lain within arm's reach all night, had somehow managed to come close enough while she was sleeping so that the heat of his body burned along her back. His arm lay across her waist, his forearm curling up over her own so that his hand fell heavily against her breast.

That must be what had caused this awful ache in her breasts, Laura thought groggily as she carefully lifted his arm away and sat up.

It was scarcely daylight. Birds noisily searched for food among trees that had been swept bare of fruit, grasses that had been swept bare of seeds. Off the tip of the island, an osprey soared high and then plummeted, rising a moment later with a wriggling fish in his talons.

She was hungry—that must be why she was so miserable. But for a moment she forgot even her misery as she gazed down at Stormwalker's sleeping face. She had never seen him this way before. He looked younger, somehow. Neither hard nor soft, neither red nor white, his beauty defied description. It was more than the fact that his features were proud and perfectly formed, his body lean and hard. He was as neatly made as any man she had ever seen. Why, compared to Coby Packwood, he was . . .

There was simply no comparison, either in looks or in character. Coby, for all his stout blond handsomeness, was mean-spirited and invariably cruel to those he considered his inferiors. As for Stormwalker—her gaze moved slowly over his short, but remarkably thick lashes, his well-shaped forehead, his narrow, high-arched nose and his lips.

His lips. While time hung suspended between night and day, Laura's mind began to stray. How strange that a mouth could speak so harshly and yet bring such astounding pleasure when applied softly against...

Her fingers lifted to touch her own lips and her imagination took wing. In that brief moment, in spite of her pain and anxiety, in spite of all that had happened, she felt a strange shivery feeling begin to grow deep inside her body.

Stormwalker's lashes twitched, indicating that he was not asleep, as she had thought. She turned away, her face flaming. At least he had not opened his eyes and caught her staring at him.

"I would appreciate it," she snapped, "if you would see to erecting some sort of shelter today. I find I lack the stomach to sleep outside like a common—"

"Squaw?" he finished silkily, still without opening his eyes. "Perhaps the word you were seeking was *savage*."

She jerked herself away and in doing so, jarred her swollen breasts. A low cry of distress escaped her and instantly he was awake. Rising to his knees, he studied her hunched shoulders. "What is it, Laura? Are you ill? Is your foot fevered?"

"No," she whispered. "Leave me alone!" How could she tell him what hurt? She didn't know, herself. At least, she knew *what*, but she didn't know why or how to make the pain stop.

Silently, she rocked back and forth. She was going to burst wide open and die, and there wasn't a thing she could do about it.

"Is it your belly? The fish we ate—"

"It's not my belly!"

"Is it your head? Sometimes before a storm, sometimes afterwards, my mother's head will—"

"It's not my head!" she cried softly. "It's this! These!" Twisting around, she lifted her breasts in her hands, too miserable to be embarrassed by the torn and faded gown that now barely covered her. "They *hurt!*"

Neither of them moved for an eternity. Stormwalker was as pale as it was possible for him to be, given his coloring. He swallowed hard, and then he reached out a tentative finger and touched one of her swollen breasts. Her gown was wet and circled with rings where it had been wet before and had dried.

She flinched at his touch but did not draw away, and he placed his palm over the full surface, shocked at the heat and the hardness.

Something terrible was happening to her. Had she been injured there as well? He knew nothing of fevers of the breast.

"Please," she whispered, "can't you do something? It aches so!"

"Laura, I am not sure—that is, I have never—umm..."

"You had never brought a child into the world before, but you did it. Can't you *please* think of something before I die? Why is this happening to me?"

Taking a deep breath, Stormwalker drew on all the wisdom at his command and found it lamentably lacking. "I—um, I believe it to be caused by milk." It was all he could think of, though it made little sense.

"Milk!" she screeched.

He snatched back his hand, but then replaced it, taking care not to add to her discomfort with his touch. Hard, lumpy and fevered. Many of the wisest among shamans would split open her breasts to let the devils out, but he had enough of the white man's knowledge to know that the shamans had sometimes been overzealous in their efforts to cure.

And sometimes totally wrongheaded.

"The milk was given to you to feed your son. Now that he no longer needs it, it does not know where to go. It gathers there and waits to be suckled."

Laura drew in a deep, shuddering breath. "When a cow comes fresh, her milk comes down. When the calf is taken away..."

Searching her face, he waited. When she did not go on, he prompted her. "Yes? When the calf is taken away?" His people did not keep cows, but they could be little different from any other animal in that respect.

"Then we milk them," she whispered, her gray eyes wild and wide as they stared into his.

Chapter Eighteen

There was no longer any question of going after Little Thunder immediately. Laura could not have borne the trip and Stormwalker would not have left her. He did his best to reassure her, borrowing heavily from the stoicism of a people who had suffered great losses and survived against great odds.

She was in agony. The wet moss helped for a little while, but soon it grew warm from the heat of her fevered breasts, and Laura would find herself weeping silently as she watched Stormwalker go about constructing a shelter of bowed saplings and bundles of rushes.

He was careful to hold any conversation between them to impersonal matters as he removed the warm damp moss and replaced it with more that had been wet and allowed to stand until it grew even cooler.

"My people on Croatoan build their lodges from rushes," he told her, avoiding her eyes as he went about the intimate task.

Laura didn't care if they built them of beans and barley. She only knew she was ill. She might even die, and then who would look after her baby?

"Little Thunder would—" she began, when Stormwalker went on speaking as if he had not heard her.

"Those of my people who live on the mainland in the village of Num Peree build their lodges from the bark of cypress or the tulip tree. After they have peeled the bark from the tree, they split the trunk in half and heap coals upon the flat side, burning and then scraping away the charred wood until it is hollowed along the full length.''

She groaned at the weight of the wet moss.

Steeling himself against the pain he felt for her, Stormwalker forced himself to go on as if she were no more to him than a fellow warrior who had been wounded in a hunt and must be cared for. "Our boats are not so fine as yours, yet some of them can carry forty men." Carefully, he angled the fan of palmetto fronds so that they shaded her face. "I will tell you about the—"

"Am I going to die?"

One look at his stricken face and Laura's worse fears were confirmed. Reaching up, she grabbed him before he could turn away. "Don't lie to me! Tell me the truth. Am I just going to go on swelling with milk until I burst wide open and die? Because if I am, I want you to carry me out in the water and leave me. Stormwalker, if you're my friend, you'll do it. I'd rather—I'd rather dr-drown."

"You will not die," he declared, his voice so low and fervent she almost believed him. "Laura, there is one way to relieve the fullness. If there were another child, he could . . . But there is only me. Will you let me do this for you?"

Blue eyes, narrowed with determination, burned into gray eyes that were wise with apprehension. "You mean—" she whispered, and without replying, he lifted the moss from her breast and began to peel back her wet bodice. "Oh, please— I would sooner die!"

Stormwalker did not offer her the option. Taking great care not to press upon the tender, blue-veined flesh, he placed his lips gently over the rose-colored bud and began to suckle.

Tears streamed down her face unheeded. At her sides, Laura's small fists curled and uncurled as the unbearable pressure began to ease. Never had she been so mortified in her entire life—not even when Stormwalker had delivered her baby. She had known nothing of what was happening then, being out of her mind with pain at the time.

She was aware now. Terribly aware. And as the pain left her, she became acutely conscious of the feel of his hot wet mouth on her breast, suckling so persistently. The first few times had been painful. Now there was only a shivery feeling that was almost...enjoyable.

Unconsciously, she tightened her thighs, drawing her knees together. Her heels dug into the soft earth and she sighed deeply.

Instantly he lifted his face. His eyes were narrowed, his cheeks strangely flushed as he stared down at her. "Did I hurt you?"

"No. Oh, no—please. Can you— That is, if it's not too...too—"

He knew what she wanted, knew, too, that she felt uncomfortable at having him perform the intimate service. Yet he had performed another far more intimate service, one that had affected him more deeply than anything in his entire life.

He had helped a new spirit come into the world and draw its first breath. To his amazement, it had not been a shameful thing to be carried out among women and whispered of thereafter, but a glorious thing that should be celebrated by all.

He had brought the child into the world and it had become his own, even though he had not fathered it. Now he knew more surely than he knew his own name that he wanted to father a child on this woman—many children, who would bear her likeness as well as his own. And he wanted to be with her when her time came, to help draw them through from the spirit world into this world of the flesh, to guide them in all the ways a father guides his children, to teach them all the things they must know to live in an increasingly troubled world.

"No more now," he said gently. He touched each of her breasts, finding them still firm but less fevered. The hardness was gone. "When they swell again, I will suckle until they are only half filled. With time they will fill less until one day they will fill no more."

He cursed himself for his unthinking words. "Your son," he said quickly, "will soon fill them again with his vigorous hunger."

Her son, he thought, could be eating venison and corn by the time they saw him again, but she did not need to be reminded of that.

Over the following days Laura regained her strength, and with it, her impatience. Her foot was healing cleanly with no sign of infection, and her breasts, thanks to Stormwalker's careful attention, grew smaller and more comfortable each day.

"Please, can we go today?" she would ask each morning.

"Can you walk for two days? Can you run if it becomes necessary? If I fall, will you be able to carry your son to safety?"

And knowing she could not, she would subside.

The new shelter was completed, and Laura pronounced herself delighted, although there was no hearth. But then, she had no kettle, so the small smokeless fire Stormwalker built in the clearing each morning served all purposes.

The days passed comfortably enough, except for her abiding anxiety. Stormwalker was a skilled fisherman, even in the broad of summer when fish were not so plentiful. Last year's crop of acorns was gone, washed away by the storm, and this year's crop had not yet ripened. With no acorns and no corn, there was no bread. She was heartily sick of fish, but what small game the island provided was apt to be wormy this time of year, and Stormwalker refused to leave her to go to the mainland for supplies.

In truth, she did not much want to be left behind. She would never forget looking up to see that hideous figure silhouetted in her doorway. Stormwalker had finally convinced her that Three Turtle believed her dead and would not come for her again, but there were others who hated the English as much.

Little Thunder. A hundred times each day she thought of him, wondered about him—where he was, what he was eating, if he were well.

Stormwalker always seemed to know. As soon as she grew still, her eyes focused somewhere beyond the horizon, he would be beside her with some small word of comfort, of reassurance.

"He fares well, Laura. The People—" he might say, and by now she knew that the People meant any who were not white skinned. "The People love children above all. Each child has many parents, for all will take them in, sharing whatever they have for the sound of a child's laughter."

And then he would commence to distract her with a tale. To her amazement, she had learned that he had traveled far more than she, among her own people as well as his. He had even attended schools with the sons of gentlemen in Virginia and the Massachusetts colony.

"But how...? I mean, I didn't know they allowed, um—"

"Wild'uns?" Stormwalker had long known of her father's term for his people and found it amusing. "I went as John Walker, with a white linen shirt and hard shoes and my hair all nicely redded with bloodroot, so that I was deemed no more uncivilized than any other trapper's son come in from the wilds."

His broad smile was new to her, and she found that she looked for it—courted it, even. "Did you stay long?"

"Long enough," he allowed. "Your people's notion of education is different from ours. I stayed in the Northern Colonies long enough to take instruction in all your sciences and your history, which seems to me to be only one side of a story with many sides. In Virginia I learned something of astronomy, of geography, of algebra and surveying and navigation."

Laura's mouth was agape. She had learned only letters and a bit of ciphering, which was deemed sufficient for any woman. "Why didn't you tell me?"

"I am telling you now, am I not?"

"Yes, but—"

He waited with characteristic patience. Discerning her discomfort at finding his schooling far greater than her own, he said, "Truly, it is no great thing, Laura Gray. I learned of your Latin language, yet it does little but fill space in my head. I learned of your poets, yet I believe our song-singers to be far more skilled. As for your navigation, my people have been traveling great distances since before the Time of The Grandfathers without those things which your seamen deem necessary."

"Yes, but— Then why did you bother to attend?" she asked, stung by his disdain of the wonderful schools she had heard of but never even seen.

"I learned much of value. I learned that the wonders my mother spoke of are but a small part of the wonders to be found across the Great Sea. I learned that wisdom is not confined to the ancients of any one people. I learned that there are winds of change that no man can foresee and that no man can escape."

Laura toyed with a torn strip of cloth from the hem of her gown. She was going to have to find something else to wear, or else she would find herself going as naked as any savage before the summer was ended. "If you learned so much, why did you bother to come back? Why not stay and learn all there was to know?"

Stormwalker did not miss the envy in her voice. Edward Gray had not been a wealthy man. He had owned no slaves, but had depended on his wife and daughter to help work his land. Even had he been among the wealthiest of planters, he would not have wasted an education on a daughter. Few white men did.

He had much to teach her, Stormwalker mused with a slow smile of satisfaction. They would spend long days in exploring and sharing ideas and long nights in exploring and sharing the many ways a man and a woman could give and receive pleasure. They would love Little Thunder no less for the love they shared with the sons and daughters that would follow....

A bleak look of emptiness replaced the smile as his dream faded. The choice was not his to make. He must heal the woman and restore her son to her arms, and then he must return her to her own kind. If only his father had not chosen to marry a white woman—yet no woman was more loved and respected among his people.

They were still resting beneath the palmetto shelter he had fashioned outside the new lodge. Laura's bodice had been stretched to cover the fresh layer of damp moss. Her hair, burnt gold by the sun, fell over her shoulders, and her eyes were the soft gray of a summer rain. Her lips moved, but Stormwalker had not heard her words. Lost in her rare beauty, he could almost forget who she was, and why she was there.

"Well, do they?"

Recalling his thoughts, he said, "I was not attending."

A cloud passed over the sun and her gaze wandered beyond him, to the distant northeast shore. "It's not important," she said wistfully. "I only asked if many of your people were sent to schools."

He knew well where her thoughts were straying. His own, as well, were with the boy night and day. Deliberately seeking to distract her, he answered in more detail than he would have. "Not many. A few were chosen as young men to go and learn from your teachers. When they were returned to us, they could no longer run, they were unable to live in the woods, unable to bear the heat or the cold, ignorant of all means of taking game and fish and of building a lodge. Some could not even speak their own language well, for it was not permitted in your schools, thus they were returned to us fit neither for hunters nor warriors nor councillors." He cast her a rueful glance. "I fear I was much the same, to my father's great disgust."

The admission brought a smile to Laura's face that lightened his spirits enormously. He would have painted himself a complete fool to have made her laugh.

She is kind and faithful, both fierce and tender in her love. She is brave enough to have risked her own life to save mine, and against all reason, I would have her for my wife. Yet neither white man's teaching nor red man's wisdom can tell me how this may be.

Before the day had ended, Stormwalker found himself agreeing to go after Little Thunder on the following morning. He agreed only to go—he did not tell Laura that she would not be going with him. Time enough for that when they reached the mainland.

Several times during the day he had suckled her breasts to give her ease. She could not bring herself to ask him or even to speak of it, yet he knew by the drawn look on her face when the pain became too great.

Thinking to relieve her of her embarrassment, he said, "Do not think of me as a man, Laura, but as a friend."

Her breath hung suspended. Their eyes caught and held. In that moment, each of them was acutely aware that their relationship had long since passed beyond the bounds of friendship.

During the day, while she watched the clouds moving across the sky or the gulls diving for fish, it had been bad enough. At night, with only the starlight and the soft lapping of the water for company, the intimacy was unbearable.

With a tenderness she had come to expect from him, he folded back her bodice, removed the poultice of moss and bathed her gently with cool water.

"At least I can do that," she protested, her face burning in the darkness.

"*Sehe*, Little Sparrow," he whispered, and she knew by now that he had only told her to hush. She hushed, for she had come to look forward to these moments, even as she dreaded them.

By the time his lips came down on her tender flesh, she thought she would die—not with pain, but with something akin to the prickle she always felt at the first flash of lightning in a summer storm.

Sometimes he had held her afterward, neither of them speaking. More often he would slip away and not return until daylight. Sometimes when she had not been able to sleep, she had lain awake wondering where he was, why he held her, why he left her—what he was thinking during the times she would see him staring out at the empty horizon.

Was he, too, thinking of Little Thunder?

Or was he missing his own people? Perhaps he missed Kitappi. Perhaps he was longing to be shed of her so that he could return to Kitappi.

Tonight—their last night on the island, if Stormwalker kept his promise—he held her. And when he held her, she couldn't think—all she could do was feel. And wonder what it was she was feeling and why she had never felt this way before.

Holding the woman in his arms, Stormwalker lay awake and struggled with his own demons. It had been a mistake to bring her here, yet what else could he have done? She could not have borne a longer journey.

It had been a mistake to have stayed with her, yet he could never have left her. And now he feared he would not be able to take her to her own people and leave her there, even though he knew he must.

Whether fishing or working on one of the wooden utensils he had fashioned for her, he had kept careful watch, making note of how many canoes passed the island and how many fishermen. There had been fewer canoes since they had returned, and in none of them were the men painted, which was an encouraging sign.

The war had been doomed from the beginning, pitting a well-armed-and-fed garrison against scattered bands of warriors, many of whom did not know how to use the muskets that they had managed to acquire, many of whom were hungry—and some of whom already suffered from one of the many fevers that could sweep through a village like wildfire, killing its entire population.

Stormwalker had been relieved when Kokom had ordered his people to remain close. There was always the danger of fever, but there was an even more pervasive danger now. Few whites could tell the difference between the peaceable Hatorask of the Algonquin family and Hancock's warring band of Tuscarora, comprised of Indians from the Mattamuskeet, the Pamticoe, the Neuse, the Coree and the Bay tribes. One red man was like another in the eyes of most white men. It was one of the reasons Kokom had sent Kitappi to stay on Croatoan. Though for the most part there was little mingling among the two peoples there, they at least knew and respected one another.

Small merchant ships still passed in and out of the mouth of the river, which was also an encouraging sign. Yet the supplies they brought would only prolong the fighting.

Now, in the darkness, with a long and dangerous journey ahead of him, he could not sleep. The woman's breath was soft and warm on his chest, for she had turned to him in her sleep and he could not move away, even though he knew he should.

The scent of crushed wildflowers was strong in his nostrils, and his arms tightened. Her face was close, so close that he could feel the heat of her cheek burning his chest.

Leave her, eppesyau rockumme*! Leave her while you still can!*

But it was already too late, for she was stirring in his arms. As the gray light of dawn crept above the horizon, Laura opened her eyes. "Is it time?" she whispered.

"It is time," he replied, and his hand reached out to touch her warm golden hair. She lifted her face and her eyes widened. Once more in that magic moment when time hung suspended between day and night, all cares fell away. Her heart leaped wildly in her breast as she watched his face move down toward her own.

The whole world was caught up in that dark, angular face. And then it blurred and the world became a pair of intensely blue eyes. At the last moment, they, too, disappeared. Later, she never knew if he had closed his eyes or she had closed her own. She only knew that when his lips touched hers, her soul lifted clean out of her body and soared like a spirit set free.

Neither of them moved. With his lips firm, yet incredibly gentle, on her own, she could not have moved if her life had depended on it. The scent of woodsmoke, leather and herbs stirred her senses, and she wrapped her arms tightly around him.

Somehow, her bodice had come open, the moss falling away, and her breasts, tingling now rather than aching, were pressed against Stormwalker's hard chest.

He was sleek and bare, his powerful muscles flexing as he moved over her. Supporting his weight on his arms, he lifted his head to gaze down at her in the gray morning light, and instinctively she lifted her head, seeking...

And instinctively, he gave her what she sought. This time, there was little gentleness. Stormwalker had held back the fire for too long. His lips parted and he tasted her innocence, broaching it with his tongue. He felt her startled reaction and fought for control over his own raging desires.

Tenderly, he began to soothe her, for she had stiffened momentarily, as though with fright. His tongue played gently about the edges of her small white teeth when he wanted desperately to plunge and devour. He stroked her shoulder when he wanted only to rip the ugly threads of her wretched gown from her body and gaze on her beauty and see the sun warm her pale breasts and her soft belly before he covered them with his own body.

Laura's small hands fluttered helplessly before settling on his back. Overwhelmed by her own feelings, she was terrified, yet she did not want it to end.

As if sensing her fears, he reassured her. "I will never hurt you, Little Sparrow," he whispered, his lips moving over her cheek to her temple. "Know that I would leave this place and never return before I would hurt you, my heart's *wittapari*." He brushed each eyebrow with his lips, and then kissed her closed eyes, first one, then the other. "You know this to be true, do you not?"

She swallowed hard. "I don't even know what you said, much less if it—if it's true or not," she whispered.

He smiled, and it was the most beautiful smile in all the world, that much she did know. "I only said you were the sun and moon of my heart because I could think of no other words to describe the way I am feeling."

Beyond speech—beyond all thought—she closed her eyes and waited for the world to end, as surely it must. No mortal was made to endure such feelings.

With a reverence she could hardly countenance, he unlaced her bodice and slipped it off. He could have told her that there had been little need for him to suckle her these past few days, for her milk had not returned. Yet, to his great shame, he had not done so. Nor had he given up the pleasure of spreading cool moss over her breasts, allowing his knuckles to brush against her softness. Allowing himself the pleasure of watching her eyes widen and darken when he touched her sensitive nipples.

He would take her gently, he vowed silently. And only once, because he loved her so and he was weak as the broken stems of the grass she had plucked and tossed aside. He would love her well and then he would take her to his people and leave her there while he went in search of her son.

And then as John Walker, so that she would not be shamed, he would take her to her own people and leave his heart in her keeping forever.

Chapter Nineteen

Outside the shelter, long fingers of golden light reached above the horizon. The air was redolent of juniper, sweet myrtle and pine. From deep in the woods there came the sad *coo-whee-coooo* of a mourning dove.

Laura made no sound of protest when Stormwalker lifted her up and slipped her ragged bodice over her head. She wore no petticoat, for that had long since been worn out. For all the lingering heat, she felt a chill shiver along her skin when he carefully removed her skirt.

When she saw him fold the stained and faded garment and lay it carefully aside, she could have wept. How could any man be so gentle and yet so strong? How could any man, wild or not, be so splendid?

Little wonder she had come to care for him. He had found her when she had no one else, when she would have died without help. He had cared for her as tenderly as he would one of his own, and if he wanted her now, why then, she was his. For as long as he wanted her.

Kneeling before her with one hand on the band that held his single garment, he whispered, "Are you afraid?"

"No, I'm not afraid, but . . ."

"Laura, if you do not want this, it will not happen."

"I do! Please, I—I really do. It's just that. . ." She stared at him as if her eyes could never get their fill of his proud face with the haughty nose, the startlingly blue eyes, his hair, so dark and glossy. . . and his mouth.

She stared at his lips as if willing them to return to hers. Had she only imagined the way he had made her feel when his mouth had covered hers? Gazing at the curved bow of his short upper lip and the fullness of his lower one, she fancied she could feel the magic beginning all over again.

"We will go slowly, sun of my heart." He came down beside her then and placed a hand upon her thigh. In a soft voice that set up trembling echoes inside her—a voice she followed easily as it slipped from one language to another, he began to describe in exquisite detail all the ways in which he wanted to touch her, to pleasure her.

Laura's eyes closed against the sensual images his words evoked. Muscles that had been clenched against the unknown began to ease as she felt a warmth kindle deep in the pit of her belly. Tongues of flame began to lick along the ticklish pathways of her limbs.

"Is this a part of it?" she asked. "This aching?"

"Yes, my *wattapi*." The hand that had been stroking the underside of her knee, slowly started working its way upward. "Is it not sweet?"

She nodded quickly, and his palm began to move in a small circle, widening until his fingers brushed the floss that covered her most secret place.

Laura shuddered as his other hand came into play, settling gently on her belly to caress the small dimple of her navel. "I cannot—please, you must stop! I cannot bear it!"

The tenseness in Stormwalker's loins urged him hurry, but his heart whispered that he must go slowly if he would erase all her fears, if he would heal her with his love.

"Is this a part of it, too?" she asked. "This—touching?"

"It is. Do you like the touching?"

"It frightens me."

"Then I will touch you in a way that will not frighten you," he murmured, and before she knew what he was about, he had lowered his head and placed his mouth on her breast, the one hand still on the cleft between her thighs.

Lightning stabbed at her again and again. Her eyes grew wide, and she pushed at his shoulder even as her hips surged against his hand. "You have to stop now! Something's happening to me, and I don't know what it is!"

He lifted his head, but she could not meet his eyes. Her body was trembling so that she could scarcely lie still. "Please, just go and leave me here," she cried, frightened and embarrassed by what was happening to her.

"Laura, hear me well—what you are feeling is what a woman is meant to feel when she lies with a man. Give yourself up to my keeping. I would never hurt you nor would I speak falsely to you."

"You don't understand," she wailed.

"I understand. Do you think I feel nothing? I have but to touch you—I have but to look at you and my body begins to change. Sometimes the change comes so quickly that I must walk away to keep from frightening you."

"There, you see? I told you it was something awful! You're frightened, too!"

He laughed, but the sound was not at all convincing. Laura glanced at him from the corner of her eyes, wondering how she had come to find herself in this awful condition. "If you were truly my friend—" she began, but he placed a finger across her lips.

"Shhhh, Little Sparrow. *Sehe*, my *wattapi*—for all that has happened to you in the past, you know less than nothing."

"You're truly not afraid?"

His smile would have melted the hardest heart, and hers was already far gone. "I am truly not afraid. The changes in your body and mine are caused by the same sweet spell. Your heart beats so, does it not?" He placed a hand upon her breast, which was shuddering with every beat of her pounding heart. Then, smiling, he reached for her hand and placed it on his own chest. "See? We are much the same."

Laura longed to ask if he felt the strange, almost painful throbbing in his loins. She had thought it must have something to do with her having so recently given birth, but that had been ages ago.

Tilting her head, she cast a sidelong glance down his body in an effort to see if he, too, was wet there, but she could see only the apronlike garment he wore, which seemed oddly misshapen. Too embarrassed to ask about it, she drew in a deep, shuddering breath and stared up into his smiling face, and gradually, she began to smile, too.

"You are not frightened of me, are you, Little Sparrow?"

She shook her head. Truly, she was not. If she was frightened, it was of herself, not of him.

"Give me your hand."

Trustingly, she placed her hand in his. He kissed her fingertips, and then he placed her hand over his apron, and her eyes widened at what she felt there. The same rigid rod she had felt once before when he'd caught her bailing her boat and carried her out into the water. "What is it? Does it hurt?"

Eyes sparkling, he told her that it did, indeed, hurt, and she began to stroke it, but after a moment, he groaned and pulled away.

"Oh, I'm sorry," she whispered. "I didn't meant to—"

"No, no—you did nothing wrong. I—*cottchee-wa*, Laura! Did your mother never tell you of the way men are made?"

She shook her head. "When she thought I would marry Coby, she told me they were different and that she would tell me more after the corn was in, but then there was the bean field to do, and then the weeds to chop, and Pa and I were clearing another field . . ."

With an inarticulate cry, Stormwalker lay down and drew her on top of his body, laughing unsteadily when she grabbed at his shoulders to keep from falling off. "I knew there was much we would one day learn from one another, little dove, but I did not think this would be one of those things."

And then he proceeded to tell her how a man and a woman came together and of the wonderful way their bodies were fashioned so that when the time came, they fit together like a knife in its sheath.

"But why am I—that is, why do I feel this—uh—this way? Down there, I mean?"

Turning so that they lay side by side, he reached down and touched her there, dipping his fingers gently into the welcoming dampness between her thighs. "That is the way a woman is made so that she will feel no pain, only pleasure."

"Are you sure?" she asked anxiously.

"Have I not studied in the finest schools in the white man's English America? Have I not sat at the feet of the wisest among all seers and shaman? Tell me if my touch brings you pleasure." He began to stroke, his sensitive fingers unerringly finding the target.

Laura gasped, her eyes widening until he could see the whites all around their gray centers. She clutched his arm and tried to drag it away, and then suddenly, she was holding him there.

His own control eroded almost beyond bearing, Stormwalker forced himself to wait until he felt the beginning of her shuddering release and then he mounted her.

This time it was he who cried out. Her tight inner heat was such that he was forced to remove his mind to a different plane in order to control his need.

Using a slow, swinging motion of the hips, he set a pace that would deepen her pleasure without robbing his shaft of its strength. But all too soon, his control was tried beyond endurance. Her soft whimpering cries drove him too close to the edge. Her body arched and bowed as her coming drew near, and he quickly prepared himself for the challenge.

Head thrown back, he tensed his buttocks and began to thrust ever deeper, riding a furious race that swept her along with him, carrying them both far beyond the outer boundaries of reason, where they hovered for a lifetime before slowly drifting back into this worldly realm.

When next Laura opened her eyes, the golden fingers had reached out until the whole eastern sky was molten with color. One of Stormwalker's thighs held her captive, and she lay loosely encircled by his arms. For a long moment she studied his closed eyes and wondered how any man could be so powerful and yet so vulnerable.

His regular breathing told her he was asleep. She gazed down the length of his body, her eyes lingering on the soft man-flesh. Now that she had known its power, her body hungered to know it once more.

She reached out and touched him there lightly, feeling protective and protected all at once. And then she snatched back her hand, shamed by her own boldness.

Laura's tentative touch awakened Stormwalker, and he lay still, longing for it to continue. She had touched him so few times voluntarily that he hungered for more. "You can touch me if you wish, Laura Gray."

She gasped.

But this must be the last time, whispered the Voice That Speaks Silently.

"That cannot be," Stormwalker muttered under his breath, and she turned toward him then.

"Cannot be? I'm sorry—I don't understand."

He attempted a smile to put her at her ease. "I only meant that I cannot sleep when you lie beside me."

The Voice whispered again, reminding Stormwalker of his promise to take her to find her son. By now they should have been well on their way. Closing his mind to reason, he drew her into his arms once more. The last time, mocked the Voice. This must be the last time, for such a woman could have no place in his life.

Abruptly, he stood and drew her up, holding both her hands in his. "We will bathe," he said, leading her outside.

Sunlight fractured into a million rainbows on each drop of dew as he led the way along the path to the offside shore. The air was so rich and clean, Laura felt as if she could have floated on that alone.

They had never bathed together before, Laura having always waited until Stormwalker was away fishing or hunting before wading out on the other side of the island to cleanse herself as best she could in the brackish water. She had quickly discovered that if she waited until the outgoing tide, the water would be fresh, though it was far cooler and more refreshing on an incoming tide.

Taking her hand, he led her out until the water lapped about his hips and waist. At first she had felt shy, turning away and attempting to cover herself, but he would have none of that. His patience quickly won out, and soon she was sporting about as if she had swum naked with a man every day of her life.

And then he began teaching her to take pleasure in her own body. One moment he would have her shouting with laughter, the next gasping with the most exquisite sensations. He lifted her up in his two hands to lap the sparkling drops of water from her body and then lowered her so that she floated across his arms, her hair flowing out like seaweed as the cool morning breeze tightened the tips of her breasts.

Standing her before him, be bathed her with a caressing hand until she would have collapsed had he not caught her to him. Stepping back, she reached out to him hesitantly and discovered to her delight that her touch had the same mystical power over his body that his did over hers. His chest was hard and flat, like thick tiles hung from a mighty frame. The muscles of his flat belly were bunched in two rows that bulged smoothly under his taut copper skin. As for his thighs...

She sighed. So much to discover. So much to explore....

Head thrown back, Stormwalker closed his eyes and groaned. Capturing her curious fingers, he held them captive. If only, he thought, this moment could last forever....

But once more the Voice intruded, reminding him that his duty lay elsewhere. Reaching deep inside himself, he found the control to turn her toward the shore. She had forgotten....

No, that was not true. Neither of them had forgotten, they had merely stolen this one moment for themselves. It was over now. It would not come again, he promised himself, but that was before she stepped in a place where silt had made the bottom treacherous.

Grasping his arm, she cried out and without thinking, he swept her into his arms and strode toward the shore.

Still holding her, he demanded, "Did your foot give way? Have you injured it again?"

"No, I—it was nothing. I stepped in a muddy place and started to sink, that's all."

But it was more than enough. The heat of passion had been kindled until now it burst out of control. Still holding her in his arms, Stormwalker turned her so that her thighs slipped easily around his waist, and to her intense delight, Laura discovered that making love was not something that could only be done when a man and a woman lay together in the darkness.

They breakfasted on a shad that had been taken from the net and dressed, stretched onto a green board and then propped before the fire to roast. Neither of them noticed the lack of salt, the lack of bread, the lack of anything to drink other than the flat-tasting rainwater that had collected in a hollow log at the edge of the forest.

Stormwalker broke off choice bits of meat, skillfully removing the bones, and held them for her to eat from his fingers. His eyes were luminous as he watched her every move. Slowly, she became aware of his gaze and her hands grew still. She waited for him to speak.

The silence drew out immeasurably as their eyes held. To Laura's amazement, she felt the now familiar bonds of pleasure begin to tighten around her all over again, to lift her higher and higher until...

"How do you do that?" she gasped when she could finally speak. "How did you make me—how could you make it...? You aren't even *touching* me!"

Stormwalker gave her his rare, sweet smile. "The wisdom of my people has been handed down since before the Time of the Grandfathers. I do not know where it began. I only know that it is more powerful than anything learned at your schools." There was both pride and modesty in his voice, and when he held out his arms, she fell into them willingly.

But he only held her. After a long moment, he said evenly, "It is time now. Come—we must go."

It took but a few moments to collect their possessions. Halfway along the clearing, Laura turned back and stared at the chimney rising above the strange shelter. Part cabin, part rush lodge and part sun shade, it had served her well. Something told her that no matter what happened, some-day—somehow—she would return to this place.

Turning away, she followed Stormwalker, who had waited for her. They reached the canoe in silence, and in silence, Laura climbed into the shallow craft and took her place.

They had traveled for perhaps an hour, with Laura's thoughts now completely focused on the mission ahead, when their attention was captured by a graceful sloop heading out from Thomas Harding's shipyard in Bath Towne. With a deft twist of a blade, Stormwalker steered the dugout closer to the southernmost bank of the river, and he, too, watched until the ship had gone past them.

Neither of them spoke of the curious stares from several crew members aloft and at the railing. Or of the rude calls that carried across the water.

Laura's face flamed. She dared not look at Stormwalker for fear he would read her shame and mistake it for shame at being seen with him. Shame was the last thing she felt for this man who had come to mean more to her than any other man ever had. The shame she felt was for her own kind—for any poor soul who knew no better than to measure a man's worth by the color of his skin and the language he spoke.

As she herself had done on more than one occasion, she knew to her great shame.

"Stormwalker," she began, but he abruptly stood and turned them toward shore, which was quite nearby then. Reaching up, he grabbed the overhanging limb of a gum tree and guided the dugout to a small notch in the muddy bank that looked as if it had been made to fit the bow of the canoe.

"Walk carefully," he said, helping her out as if she were no more to him than a paying passenger. "There will be water snakes along the path."

Deeply wounded by what she deemed his sudden loss of interest in her, Laura snapped, "Then why not leave them to it and walk somewhere else?"

He was three strides ahead of her, having left the canoe in the water without dragging it up on the bank. Now he turned, and for the first time since they had left the island, she saw him smile. "Because you, Little Sparrow, would soon wander into a bog and be swallowed up. Stomp your feet as you go and the snakes will move aside. I cannot say as much for the mosquitoes."

"Which never bother you, of course," she muttered, slapping her neck.

"Never." Ignoring her sarcasm, he grinned over his shoulder. "Bear oil and essence of wax-berry leaves. My mother began tanning my hide with those while I was still on my cradle board."

At the mention of his mother's attentions, Laura's thoughts flew once more to Little Thunder. She hurried ahead and caught at Stormwalker's arm. "Stormwalker, are you *sure* you know where he is?"

"Little Thunder? No, Laura, I am not certain. I will search first in the most likely place and go on from there. There is no other way."

"Are we close? To the most likely place, I mean." She hurried along beside him, favoring her injured foot, ignoring the swarms of insects, the sweltering heat and the slap of branches and vines against her arms, her legs and her face.

She had nearly reached the end of her patience when, to her amazement, he turned and took her into his arms, holding her so tightly she could scarcely breathe. When she lifted her face to protest, he kissed her with a fierceness that would have been shocking had she not . . . *liked* him so very much.

Their eyes met and clung, and Stormwalker read all the bright expectations in hers, and his heart constricted painfully for what he was about to do.

"How will we do it?" she demanded, and without waiting for him to answer her first question, she rushed. "Will there be guards? Lookouts? Are Three Turtle's people all as vicious as he is? You know, I could have sworn you said his village lay to the northeast, but the river flows—well, ne'er mind, you've studied navigation.''

Without pausing for breath, she continued. "What is our plan? Are we going to discover which house is his and hide nearby in the woods until we see him leave? Surely he doesn't stay inside all the time. Perhaps he's left my baby in the care of someone else—an old woman or perhaps a young girl. Perhaps you could distract them while I—''

"Laura.''

"Perhaps we could—''

"Laura!'' She blinked, her small chin dropping so that he could see the row of small white teeth that showed above her soft pink bottom lip. "I am taking you to a village called Num Peree. There you will wait with my friends until I find your son.'' He braced himself for her outburst, which was not long in coming.

"I refuse to—''

"Hear me out.''

"I will *not* stay behind while you—''

"Quiet, woman! Among my people, when a man speaks, a woman heeds and obeys.'' Some *few* women heed and obey, he amended silently. Those who are too old or too lazy to do otherwise.

"I am not one of your people,'' she said, enunciating each word very carefully. "I am no squaw to be worked like a dog and then sold to the highest bidder!''

His lips thinned as he fought to control his anger. "I have sold no woman to any man, but hear me now, Laura Gray— if you disobey me in this matter, I will trade you to the first yapping pack of *tauh-he* I meet for no more than the *eppe-syau* that crawl on their filthy hides!''

The threat was absurd enough so that she could not take him seriously. Yet he must make her understand that in this matter, he would prevail. He would go alone; she would remain behind. And since the presence of a white woman in their midst would be a danger to all his village, he must know that she would not cause undue trouble.

"I *will* not—" she began, when something she saw in his eyes stilled her tongue. "I *would* not . . ." she began again, and then paused.

"Yes?"

"Will you—that is, may I know where you're going and when you plan to return?"

Hoping she could not see how relieved he was, Stormwalker drew in a deep breath and expelled it in a long, controlled gust. "The place where the Mattamuskeet reside is near a great body of water called Paquipe, on the north side of the Pamticoe River. There is much bad dust when it is dry, much deep mud when it is wet. The trees are not so large, but they are very dense. There are many bears there. Swamps filled with snakes and alligators surround this place, so that only those who know the way in can safely go there."

"I don't care about bears and snakes and alligators. I only want my baby," she said, her eyes pleading for him to relent.

She could have talked him into cutting out his own heart, but in this matter, Stormwalker knew he must not relent. Aside from the natural dangers, which were no greater than any hunter or trapper faced daily, there was another danger that he did not care to mention. Hancock's war had not yet ended. There would be no predicting what the Mattamuskeet would do if she were to walk into their village, with her golden hair and her pale skin.

"I can go more swiftly alone," he said, and by the look in her eyes, a look born of disappointment, hope and acceptance, he knew he had won. "I will not let you down, Little Sparrow."

Turning away, he set off once more, clearing the path for her to follow. *If our son is alive, I will bring him back to you. This is the gift of my heart,* wattapi.

Chapter Twenty

Stormwalker had been gone two days before Laura admitted, even to herself, that Num Peree was not at all what she had expected of a heathen encampment. In the first place, it was cleaner than Packwood's Crossing. Here, at least, people did not throw refuse out their door for the village dogs to scatter, nor did they go for months and even longer without washing so that one could hardly bear to pass the time of day without fanning one's face with a handkerchief dipped in rose water.

She had been taken directly to the home of the headman, whose name was Kokom and who spoke passably good English. And while the old gentleman, for all his outlandish costume of feathers and beads and tattoos, seemed a decent enough sort, he struck her as a poor choice for a leader. He had made some remark in his own language, and then laughed immoderately. She had looked from one man to the other, seeing a familiar closed look come over Stormwalker's haughty features and wondered if the old man had somehow insulted him.

It had been Stormwalker who had taken her to the lodge where she was to stay, the home of an old woman who spoke not a single word of English.

"This is Runs After Blackbirds. She will look after you until I return."

"But I don't want to stay here. Please, can't I go with you?"

"If you wish me to find your son, you will do as I say," he had retorted, to which she could say nothing. It was true, and she knew it. He could go much faster alone.

"All right, then, go—but please don't leave me here a moment longer than you must, for I won't sleep a wink wondering what's going on and if you're lying dead in the belly of some great beast with an arrow in your gullet."

He had teased her about her wicked imagination, but he had not touched her. She had wanted so much to throw herself in his arms and know the comfort of his strength for one brief moment, but he had turned away without another word.

Stormwalker was different among his own people—more austere. She felt almost as if she didn't know him.

That night she had prayed until her heart was wrung dry. And then, to her great surprise, she had fallen into a deep, dreamless sleep, which could have had something to do with the peculiar tasting tea the old woman had brewed for her. It had smelled of sassafras root, but the taste had been different—not unpleasant, just strange.

The woman continually muttered to herself, chuckling at her own remarks, a habit that Laura found maddening. Just after a midday meal of possum boiled with squash and wild onion, the woman had disappeared inside the lodge where they had slept and returned a few moments later with a pair of small beaded moccasins and a white doeskin gown.

"*Aucummato, yotto-ha.*"

"I do beg your pardon?"

"*Pachee. Pachee!* Ugly!" Which was the first word of English the woman had spoken. She thrust the garments at Laura, and Laura, not wanting to offend her, took them. Perhaps she should have been insulted—she'd never before been called ugly. But she took the things because she was afraid of breaking some obscure rule of propriety.

"She say you must *pachee*—must take. She say she remember yesterday," murmured a soft voice from behind her, and Laura nearly dropped the bundle as she twisted about to stare at the small, moon-faced girl who had come up silently behind her.

The child could hardly be more than ten years old. Her face was shaped like a pumpkin and much the same color, and for all the bright interest in her black eyes, Laura thought she looked embarrassed. "Ask her why she wants me to have these things?" Laura prompted, and the child stepped around in front of her and translated the question in a rush of words that produced a like response from the old woman.

"She say you gown bad. Stormwalker woman dress gooder. She say bride gown too little now. Gown grow small, she grow big. Gown break. She fix. You wear."

That was the beginning of Laura's friendship with Anna Little Crow, who at thirteen was married to White Buffalo, the number-one hunter for the village. It was he who provided meat for the elders and the widows, as well as his own family.

"White Buffalo follow beaver up Eno River. Beaver tail fine meat, you like?"

Never having tasted the delicacy, Laura managed to suppress a shudder. She had seen enough of the flat, scaly, paddlelike tails to know she was not interested in them as food.

"White Buffalo come back soon. We make damn good baby. You teach us eat oyster from knife, no from shell?"

Laura choked on a mouthful of some rank beverage made of ground and fermented acorns. "Teach you what?"

"Stormwalker and T'kiro learn spoon, fork, knife, make picture on bark, picture talk."

Oysters and talking bark? Mystified, Laura could only shake her head. It took several more such exchanges before she understood that Anna was referring to table manners, writing and reading.

"Anna, I'm sorry, but I haven't the least notion of what a 'teekiro' is. As to Stormwalker's table manners, I truly cannot say." In all the time they had been together on the island, they had both eaten with their fingers and thought nothing of it. "Is he—that is, does Stormwalker live here? When he's not traveling, that is?"

"He live here. He live Croatoan. He live with white-eye."
Anna shrugged, which until then had struck Laura as an
essentially English gesture. "He wise man. Keep fever from
this place. You know fever?"

Laura knew fever. Who did not, when yellow fever alone
had killed so many only a year ago. "Is there fever about
now?" Living on the island for so long, she could have no
way of knowing what was going on on the mainland.

The girl only grunted and rolled her eyes. It seemed she
could speak English well enough when it pleased her, but
only when it pleased her. Laura gave up trying to glean any
news from that source. If there was fever, she would hear of
it soon enough. And even if there were, what could she do
other than pray that Stormwalker would stay clear of the
infected towns?

Summoned by Kokom on the morning of the second day,
Laura's first thought was that Stormwalker had returned
with bad news. Heart in her throat, she hurried across the
compound, between the neat rows of lodges, to the large one
set apart.

The old man sat outside, sweat puddling in the hollow
above his paunch. "You sit, woman," he greeted unceremoniously,
and feeling her knees begin to quake, Laura sat.

"Have you heard anything? Has Stormwalker sent
word?"

The old chief ignored her. "Runs After Blackbirds feed
you good?"

"What . . . ? Oh, yes. Very well."

Kokom stroked his smooth jaw, and it struck Laura that
she had never seen hair on the body of any of the wild'uns,
save in that one private part. To her horror, she felt the heat
rise at the thought, and she rushed into speech.

"Possum, I think—and squash. Your gardens are quite
as fine as any I've seen, and your—that is, the—"

"Stormwalker good man, huh?"

"Good?" The old devil knew! Stormwalker had told him
what they had done together—perhaps that was what the
two men had laughed about that first day! And now the old
goat was trying to trick her into confessing so that he could

punish her before Stormwalker got back. He probably planned to sell her as a slave, or—or even kill her!

"I do believe I'll be moving on today, if it's all right," she said, her mind working feverishly. Accordingly to Anna, Kokom hoped for a match between Stormwalker and Kitappi. Anna seemed to think the "teekiro," whatever that was, might prevent it, but that was only the opinion of a foolish girl. At any rate, Kokom would hardly be pleased at Stormwalker's having suddenly turned up with another woman in tow. Particularly a white woman. And particularly if there had been another outbreak of fever. She knew for a fact that while her people could withstand many fevers, the Indians were not so fortunate, the mildest case usually proving fatal.

"Good man, huh? Big. Strong. Make good *tau-batsu*, huh?"

Closing her eyes, Laura fought against the flood of color that stained her cheeks. She didn't even want to know what *tau-batsu* meant. "Yes," she cried desperately. "That is, you're right. He's a—a good man. Honorable, intelligent, kind..." *Pigheaded, passionate, patient and impatient. Loveable and quite maddening.*

Avoiding the old chief's wicked eyes, she managed to compose herself. She had done nothing to be ashamed of—and what's more, she would do it again! "Have you any news? Has Stormwalker sent word?"

Chuckling, the old chief ignored her questions. He nodded several times and said again, "Good man. Son of great chief."

Laura was beginning to wonder if the chief understood English as well as he pretended. Thinking to steer him away from the subject of Stormwalker's goodness, she said, "Yes, well...did you know your daughter was my friend?"

"Salt friend."

Salt friend? There must have been something in her tea, after all. "Umm—yes. Salt friend. Kitappi is my salt friend." The poor old fool seemed harmless enough, but she would just as lief put an end to his roundabout conversation.

"Packwood measure salt, pour out half for Kitappi. Always half for red man. Measure half laudanum, you talk back."

Oh. *That* kind of salt friend. "She told you what happened?"

He snorted. "She tell. Stormwalker tell."

Laura's lips formed a silent O. Did that make her friend or fool in this man's eyes. She was startled to realize that his opinion was beginning to matter to her.

"Packwood great fool. Wise man not steal honey from bee tree at night."

If there was a connection between collecting honey and short-measuring salt and laudanum, she failed to see it—unless Kokom meant that it was foolish to try and rob the daughter of a chief, who would have many friends to defend her.

Or perhaps he meant that Laura would be foolish to try and steal the man of a woman who had many friends to defend her.

"Three Turtle offer bride price for Kitappi," Kokom said with an abrupt change of subject that left her even further at a loss.

"Oh, but surely she wouldn't—I mean, you wouldn't accept such a person. Did Stormwalker tell you—uh—anything?"

"He tell me hell near everything," said the old man with a sly grin that revealed a flawless set of tobacco-brown teeth, minus four.

She wasn't sure what "hell near everything" included and was far too embarrassed to ask, but long before Laura left the chief's lodge, she had begun to suspect that Kokom was not quite so shatter-witted as she had first thought. With his imperfect knowledge of her language, he had deftly led her into disclosing far more than she had intended. She could only hope that he would misunderstand her replies.

Not that Indian men would have the same notion of love that their white counterparts had. After all, they bought and sold women with their so-called bride prices as if they were cattle.

But even if they did, she thought as she returned the shy smiles of the women working outside their lodges, what difference did it make? Stormwalker had never given her any reason to believe he would consider...

And besides, she had a son to raise. Sooner or later, she would have to go back to her own people. She could hardly see a crown prince, or whatever these people called the son of a great chief, settling into a house in town and taking a job as a clerk.

The following day, Laura met Kokom's wife, Gray Otter. She had heard the story from Stormwalker, from Anna and from Kitappi herself, of how Gray Otter had rescued the infant Kitappi from a village that had been swept with fever and had raised her as her own daughter.

She also knew that Gray Otter suffered from a painful wasting disease and was cared for in Kitappi's absence in a separate lodge by a woman who knew about such things.

Even so, Laura was unprepared for the ravaged beauty of the woman who sat propped up in a bed of bearskin robes, shivering despite the great heat.

"Come, come! I know who you are. I know why you are come here," said a weak, nasal voice.

The smell of illness pervaded the small interior as Laura held up the flap and stepped inside. She tried not to breathe, but her heart went out to the frail woman who beckoned her closer with a yellowed, clawlike hand.

"I once knew someone like you." The bitterness in her voice was unmistakable. "I hated her."

Laura took a stumbling step backward, but Gray Otter began to cough and reluctantly, Laura knelt beside the pathetic figure.

"What can I do to help?" she murmured, wanting to go, yet unable to leave if she could bring comfort. The heat was stifling. As if the mid-July sun weren't enough, someone had built a fire in the center of the lodge.

At Gray Otter's instruction, Laura located a small earthen bowl containing a greenish powdery substance. This she sprinkled, as she was told to do, on a flat stone in the midst of the coals, where it immediately began to smolder.

"Ahhh," sighed the older woman, waving the smoke toward her face and breathing deeply. "Now you speak. Why you here? How long you stay? You friend to my Kitappi. You stay to see wedding?"

"Wedding?" Laura repeated. She was growing dizzy as the fumes from the fire added to the effect of the sweltering heat.

"Kinnahauk and Gray Otter marry. No, no—now it is Kitappi and Stormwalker. Stormwalker will build my daughter fine new lodge, big to hold many fine sons. You stay for wedding feast? Good feast, much drink, much dancing, many new baby made."

She cackled with laughter, which turned into coughing, and Laura left as soon as she could, summoning the old nurse, who was smoking a pipe with several other women some distance away.

She felt unclean and then unworthy for thinking such a thing. The old woman was dying! Any decent Christian would be feeling sympathy, not disgust mingled with distrust.

She did feel sympathy—of course, she did. Only there was something about Gray Otter that set her nerves awry. As for the wedding of Stormwalker and Kitappi, once Laura might have credited such a thing, but no more. Both Kokom and Gray Otter—and Kitappi, too, for all she knew—might wish for such a match, but Laura knew in her heart that Stormwalker could not have lain with her the way he had knowing he would soon wed another woman.

"Come we go creek," said Anna, falling in beside her. "First we bathe and then I take you to know Tiree Kiro."

To *meet* Tiree Kiro, Laura corrected silently. She had already met nearly everyone in the village, or so she'd thought. "How did you know I would like to bathe?"

"Gray Otter lodge stink. Too hot."

"She's very ill," Laura murmured, feeling shame wash over her for the uncharitable thoughts that had passed through her head as she'd listened to the poor woman's whining voice go on and on between coughing spells about all the lovely babies Stormwalker and Kitappi would make between them.

"She mean like white-mouth snake," Anna corrected, and laughed immoderately.

They went to the Women's Place, a sheltered pool where the creek widened, and there they undressed and slipped into the clear water. It was warm as fresh-drawn milk, but the air on their wet bodies felt deliciously cool. Laura made an effort to be cheerful, for a long face would not return her baby to her any sooner.

But even as they dressed, she couldn't help but gaze longingly at the children who played in between lodges and garden patches. She had done her best to keep from dwelling on what Stormwalker would find when he reached Three Turtle's village.

If he reached the village.

After her bath, she had put on the doeskin shift Runs After Blackbirds had given her, delighting the old woman into a toothless cackle. Runs After circled round and round her, patting and tugging at the velvet-soft hide. And then she said in perfectly accented English, "Ugly old squaw," and beamed as if she had just paid Laura the greatest kindness.

Impulsively, Laura embraced the old woman. No doubt some thoughtless person had once said that to her, and she, thinking it a compliment, had remembered the words.

It came to her then that she was coming to know these people almost too well. She could not afford to grow fond of them, for she would be leaving in a day or two, at the most.

That afternoon she learned the meaning of a "teekiro." Tiree Kiro, called T'kiro by all, turned out to be a handsome young man, slight of build and diffident of manner, who had been brought to the village by Stormwalker to teach the children. He was surrounded by half a dozen children and had evidently been interrupted in the middle of telling them a story.

It took a moment for Laura to realize that all the children were staring at her hair. One reached out to touch it, and then drew back his hand as if expecting to be punished for his daring.

The young man smiled, his eyes not quite meeting Laura's. "I was telling the children of the legend of the beautiful golden-haired princess who was imprisoned in a tower," he said in a voice that was remarkably like the ones she had last heard in Virginia. Eyes narrowed, she studied him more closely. He was every bit as dark skinned as any Indian she had ever seen, with the same aquiline nose and high cheekbones she had come to expect. His eyes, which he kept averted, almost as if he were too shy to look directly on her face, were the same rich shade of brown as all the others, their whites faintly tinged with red, as was normal among these people. As for his hair, it was thick, glossy and black, without the faintest hint of a curl. He was wearing the same leather apron that all the Indian men wore.

He was an Indian—a wild'un. She was certain of it, yet he spoke with the soft cultured voice of a man who had been raised in one of the wealthy houses of Virginia.

"The—the legend . . . ?" she stumbled, belatedly realizing that she had been staring.

"Of the golden-haired princess. The children believe you are that princess."

Laura reached up to touch her own hair, which she had gathered back with a bit of red cloth Runs After had provided. Golden? She would have thought it more the color of dead grass, but then it had been more than a year since she had held a looking glass in her hand. Still, if it pleased the children to think of it as gold . . .

Her thoughts still pondering the riddle of the man called Tiree Kiro, she knelt and allowed each of the children to feel to their heart's content. Soon they were laughing and trying out their imperfect English on her, and she forgot about a wild'un who spoke perfect cultured English with a faint drawl, and spent a most enjoyable hour, promising to return soon.

"He good man, you think?"

"Tiree Kiro? He seemed quite nice. Where did he learn to speak English?"

"Name T'kiro mean Wolf. He father, mother sold to white peoples live high up in hills." Anna pointed westward. "He father die, he mother go away, take Wolf, give him to mans with many sons live in big lodge. T'kiro learn. Eat oyster from knife. Eat meat from knife. Talk from book."

"Reads," Laura murmured.

Anna frowned at the clumps of wild grass. "From book—not reed. Reed grow by water."

Laura bit her lip to keep from smiling. "I meant a different kind of read. Talking from a book is called reading. Talk from book—read. Do you understand?"

"Huh. You smart woman. When my man come back, put baby in my belly, you teach him this read."

Unsure whether Anna wished her husband or her unborn, and as yet unconceived, child to learn to read, Laura murmured a vague response just as they reached Runs After's lodge. The old woman was removing a blackened earthen pot from the bed of coals, its contents sending up curls of fragrant steam.

The two Hatorask women chatted a moment, and then all three women sat down to a meal of squirrel meat and a lumpy broth that Laura found palatable enough as long as she didn't dwell on the contents. This was followed by a sweet cake with an unfamiliar seasoning.

The old woman sat watching every bite disappear in Laura's mouth, beaming a toothless grin and now and then reaching out to stroke the fringe on the white doeskin gown, which Laura found not at all too hot as she had imagined, but quite comfortable.

"This is good," she said, indicating one of the small cakes.

Immediately, the woman handed her two more. Some words needed no translation.

"Anna, how can I refuse without hurting her feelings? I'm sure she has little enough without another mouth to feed."

The younger woman had no such reservations. Taking one of the proffered cakes, she said, "She has much plenty. What belong to one belong to all. My man give her turtle fat for honey cake. She make good honey cake, you think?"

Turtle fat? Laura's stomach twisted unpleasantly. She had cleaned many a turtle for her mother to make stew, and she well remembered the thick globs of sticky fat that had to be scraped off before the meat could be used. According to all she had heard, neither turtle fat nor venison fat was fit to eat and would sicken a body quicker than rancid meat.

She waited for her belly to turn on her. When nothing happened, she decided that Stormwalker had been right—when it came to knowledge, neither his race nor hers held dominion.

The moon had already begun its descent when two guards converged silently on the figure who approached the palisade. In a low, guttural tone, the younger one, who was called Hooheh Wakena because his only vision had been of a lone pine tree on a creek bank, which was meaningless as far as poor Hooheh had been able to learn, challenged the newcomer.

"Hooheh, have I changed so much or do your eyes grow old before your years?"

"Stormwalker? That you? You been in big fight or you been in big drinking?"

"Neither, my friend. I have been traveling on foot for four days and nights without food or sleep. Is all well here?"

The older man shrugged. "Same as always. Gray Otter more sick. My woman more ugly."

"And—" Stormwalker had been on the verge of asking about the white-eye woman. Instead, he said only, "Are any of our hunters out?"

Both men grunted a negative reply, and Stormwalker looked back along the moonlit path he had followed. "Hear my words. Guard well. Let no one else enter."

"Soldiers?" Hooheh spread his feet and unslung his bow.

"Worse," came Stormwalker's terse reply just before he slipped through the narrow opening in the wall of sharpened stakes.

Chapter Twenty-one

The cook fires had burned to gray ash while the village slept. Stormwalker stood just inside the palisade, surveying the peaceful scene from the shadows. How very different, he thought, from the places he had seen in the days just past. Finding Seconiac deserted, he had set out to follow Three Turtle's people, coming to one after another empty village. Some had been stormed by the soldiers until not a lodge was left standing. Still others had been ominously intact, yet just as deserted.

An owl called softly, and there was a rush of wings, and then all was quiet again. Dappled moonlight shone down on the small lodge of Runs After, where Laura would be sleeping. For a long time, he simply watched.

And then he swore softly under his breath, words he had learned from the sons of wealthy white planters. He would rather have had the flesh flayed from his bones than to go to her bearing the news he had brought.

Tomorrow would be soon enough. Forever would be too soon.

The flap was still up on Kokom's lodge. He would be expecting him. Just how he knew of his arrival, Stormwalker could not have said, but he did not doubt for one moment that the old chief had known he would return this night.

"Ho, friend, are you sleeping?" he asked softly outside the bark-covered *ouke*.

"I have slept. Now I am ready to hear what you have learned."

Stormwalker entered and took his seat on the robe Kokom had spread for his comfort. He accepted a pipe, leaned over to light it from a glowing coal in the fire bowl and drew deeply.

"What of the fighting?" the old chief asked.

"Quiet for the moment. I came across many ruined villages. Seconiac is deserted."

"Barnwell?" The South Carolina colonel had come to be called Tuscarora Jack for his attempts to put down the Tuscarora uprising. It was well known that few in any village he raided escaped his sword, whether men, women or children.

"Something even more deadly than Barnwell. Fever," Stormwalker replied.

Kokom pulled deeply on his blackened clay pipe and allowed the pungent smoke to curl upward toward the opening in the roof. "This I have heard. Two men now guard the gates. I have told them to allow no one to enter. Our hunters go no farther than the river."

Stormwalker knew there was little game left between Num Peree and the river. But there were also no other villages, where pestilence could linger.

"Did you go inside these empty lodges?" Kokom asked after a while.

"I did not. I went first to Seconiac. There were no guards. I climbed a tall cypress and looked down over the palisade, and there was no one about. Outside the village were many new graves."

Kokom thought on this for several minutes. "Some were left to bury the dead."

"There were no carrion birds about," said Stormwalker, answering the unspoken question of what had happened to the grave diggers. "I followed the trail toward the Pungo. On the way, I was warned away from two other villages. Today I met a hunting party who said to me that they had seen two youths and three women from Seconiac who said that all the old ones and all the children, as well as the fighting men who had survived the war, had died of fever."

Both men stared out into the dark village at the neat row of lodges interspersed between well-tended patches of beans and corn and squash. They were both thinking of the woman who slept inside the lodge beside the bean field.

"The white woman's child?"

"Dead. All the children, the hunter said. Along with Three Turtle and all the other fighting men of Seconiac."

"How many villages?"

"Three I saw. Seconiac and two on the Pungo. I have heard of one more on the small water beyond the Paquipe where many are stricken."

"This will slow the fight against the English."

Wearily, Stormwalker shrugged. "It is but another of their weapons, not so swift as the musket nor so pleasurable as rum." For four days he had eaten little and slept less. Suddenly, he was overwhelmed with exhaustion—with sadness. He swore softly under his breath in English, telling himself that it was better than weeping.

Kokom said nothing. If he had been granted his greatest wish, Stormwalker would never have met the white woman. He would have taken Kitappi to his lodge as soon as she became a woman and by now, Kokom would know the joy of teaching his grandsons to hunt and to play.

"Have you told her?"

"I came directly to you. How can I tell her?"

"She is young. She will have many sons. Tomorrow you will take her to her people so that she can find a husband."

Stormwalker's head came up and he stared at the shadowy figure of the old chief. "Is she no longer welcome in your village, Kokom?"

The older man muttered a guttural phrase that translated roughly to "I give up!" "You, who will one day be chief, must find a woman of your own kind to be your wife. Do not insult your people by taking this woman to your lodge and asking them to accept your children, who will be more white than red."

"I have asked nothing of my people!"

"You will take her away, then?"

Stormwalker thought long without speaking. How could he give up his own heart? How could he watch while she took another man as her husband, when she belonged to him? "Why do you say I will one day be chief? My sister, Anna White Swan, has four sons."

"White man's sons! Paugh!"

"Perhaps it is time we learned to live in the white man's world," Stormwalker said quietly. "It will not go away. No matter how we wish it, that will not happen now. They take what they want and feel no guilt. As we once took this land from others who claimed it as their own."

"Old men's tales! There were no others before us. Do not try to outwit me, *yenxau-wha*. I am not yet ready for my song to be sung."

Stormwalker accepted the rebuke without argument. He had been called boy before, though not in many years. "I will think on what you have said, Kokom. But first I must find a way to tell Laura that her son is dead." He smiled then, although in the darkness the old chief could not see it. "The boy would have been tall and strong, Kokom. His fingers—the way he gripped my thumb..." He swallowed hard and turned to stare out into the darkness.

Kokom sighed. "Go to your lodge, my son. You can do nothing until the morrow, unless you would risk the wrath of Runs After Blackbirds for disturbing her rest."

Body aching with weariness, Stormwalker did as he had been bade. His lodge was set somewhat apart from the others, between the beehives and the largest corn patch, at the opposite end of the compound from Kokom's lodge. Not for the first time, he longed for a woman to bathe him, to bring him food and drink—to lie with him and comfort him and drive away his troubled thoughts.

But there was no food, no drink, no bathwater drawn from the river and heated over an open fire—and no woman to warm his mat. There was only one woman he wanted to share his lodge and his love. And, after breaking her heart, he must send her away.

* * *

There had been no rain for a week. The early August heat was oppressive, even in the mornings. Bees drooped in great knots outside the hives, threatening to swarm. The sweet dry scent of corn tassels mingled with the smell of woodsmoke and dust.

Laura opened her eyes and wondered which ached worse, her head or her heart. She shifted to avoid the sunlight that streamed down through the small opening in the roof. Strange that such a contrivance should prove so practical, she thought distractedly. In the summer, it funneled heat out the top of the roof, pulling a draft from underneath the sloping walls that left the interior surprisingly cool. In winter, the draft was choked down so that it kept in the heat from the central fire, yet allowed the smoke to escape.

Last night, too distraught to sleep, she had joined Runs After in her nightly draught of corn beer. Well aged, for it had been made the previous year, the stuff was remarkably strong and foul tasting, but she had slept through the night for the first time since Stormwalker had brought her to this place.

No wonder her head was splitting. Come to think of it, her belly felt none too fine, either.

Groaning, she struggled to sit up, a fragment of thought nagging at her. She had a dim recollection of having reached a decision on something she must do—something concerning the garrison at Bath Towne.

Oh, yes, that was it. She had decided to take matters into her own hands instead of waiting forever for a man who might or might not even return. Surely the soldiers could find her son. What else were they there for, if not to protect the citizens of North Carolina?

"*Coosauk.*" Runs After ducked inside the lodge and held out a blackened bowl of steaming broth that smelled strongly of wild onions. "*Coosauk—patchee, patchee.*"

Laura turned away from the strong smell. If memory served her, *coosauk* was a kind of pea—or was it a feather? "I don't want to *patchee*, Runs After. Thank you all the same, but I don't feel like eating."

"*Coosauk* ugly, Laura *patchee*, heh?"

Raking an unsteady hand through her hair, Laura reluctantly held out her hands. Whatever it was, the sweet old soul considered it ugly, which in her mind meant fine, pretty, good. One swallow probably wouldn't kill her, Laura thought.

It was a broth made of peas and some kind of meat. At any other time she might have welcomed it, but at the moment, she felt dreadful. All in the world she wanted right now was to go outside and pour a gourdful of cold water over her head.

Still wearing the rumpled white doeskin, her hair a wild tangle about her head, Laura stumbled outside and practically fell over Stormwalker.

He caught her by the shoulders. Seeing her sudden pallor, he lowered her gently to the ground. "What is it? Have you heard? Who told you?" He could not believe Kokom could have done such a thing, yet how else could she have known?

He should not have slept so far into the morning. He should have come to her last night, as soon as he returned.

"Laura—Little Sparrow, listen to me. I know Three Turtle. In spite of what you believe, he would have cared for your son to the end as tenderly as any father ever cared for a child."

Her eyes widened. Only then did he become aware of the look of horror that spread across her small, pale face. "No," she whispered, shaking her head from side to side. She grabbed at his shoulders, her nails biting through the skin. "No! It isn't true! You're lying to me—you want me to think he's dead, but he's not! I know he's not dead! I *know* it, do you hear me?"

"Laura!" Glancing up in consternation at the old woman who had come waddling out of the lodge at the first sound of distress, he shook his head. "I thought she knew," he said in English, and then, in his own tongue, "Have you not heard of the fever? Has no one told you that many have died? The entire village of Seconiac perished, except for two youths and three women."

After a hurried exchange that passed completely over Laura's head, the old woman nodded and went back inside. Stormwalker lifted Laura, who was staring dry-eyed at nothing at all, and walked through the compound, oblivious to the curious eyes. Waving off the two guards, he left the village, but instead of taking the path that led to the creek, he turned and followed another, less-traveled path.

Presently, he came to a dark pond surrounded by lush tangles of grass threaded with nodding wildflowers. Overhead, a giant oak tree spread its arms. Kneeling, he lowered Laura to the bed of grass and began to speak in a slow, unaccented voice.

"I know of this fever, Laura. It is swift and merciless, yet the young ones do not suffer as the old ones do. They go quickly, for they lack the strength to fight. Before the fever struck, Little Thunder would have been loved and cared for by all who came to know him." Stormwalker could only pray it was so. He had seen soldiers impale infants of his own people on their swords. He had known of white-skinned children whose lives had been cruelly ended by red-skinned warriors.

At least one among the Mattamuskeet, who were at war with the English, had known of Little Thunder's mixed heritage, which meant he would have enemies, as well as friends, on both sides.

Laura began to sob, great, wrenching heaves that brought no comfort. Soon Stormwalker's eyes were wet, as well, but he held her, staring at the blurred image of a small purple flower until he could bring his emotions under control.

"Who could have resisted such a child, my Little Sparrow? They would have held him and sung to him and played with him, even as you would have done, my love—as I once did. He knew naught but love, and then he slept. In time you will—"

"Where?" she demanded harshly. "Where did you find him? How do you know all this?"

He told her of his journey, leaving out nothing. She heard him out without interrupting. "Few are spared when fever strikes a village. The well survive only by leaving behind those who are ill. I have seen a father remove a child from the arms of its stricken mother, leaving her to die untended."

"How cruel! That is inhuman!"

"Would you have him sacrifice the child, as well?"

She fell silent. For a long time, neither of them spoke. Now and then she sobbed, and the sound of it twisted his heart until it was all he could do not to touch her, to hold her, to make promises that no man could keep. But her eyes, though still swollen, were quite dry now. Her small chin no longer trembled uncontrollably.

She sat apart from him, and he watched as she fought against accepting this latest in a long list of cruel blows. She was wearing a gown he recognized as being a wedding dress. Did she know? Probably not. Nor would she care, for at this moment, she cared for nothing except the fate of her son.

Stormwalker had never felt more helpless in his life. It was not a feeling he cared for. How could he have lived so long and not have learned the pain of loving? To love a woman— to love a child, brought a kind of agony that no man could withstand.

With no conscious decision, he made up his mind. He would allow his Little Sparrow her period of mourning, which had begun when Three Turtle had stolen the boy and run off with him. After that, he would ask his father to summon a council of the old ones. He would tell them what was in his heart. If in their wisdom, they asked of him that he send this woman away, he would leave his people and live among hers, renouncing his heritage.

"Will you take me to Bath Towne?" Laura asked suddenly, her voice empty of all feeling.

"When you are stronger," he said gently.

"Now! This very day!" Her chin went up a notch and he was reminded of the very first time he had ever seen her. Her defiance then had been aimed at a stubborn taproot.

This time it was aimed at him. "Tomorrow," he said, keeping his voice carefully even. "You have had a great blow. You must not force yourself to—"

"I might have known you wouldn't dare risk showing your face near the garrison. Did you even go as far as Three Turtle's village?" Stormwalker reeled from the unexpected blow. Before he could respond, she continued, her voice too fast, too shrill. "I know what you did—you skulked about in the woods for a solid week, taking your ease, and then you brought back that wicked tale to explain why you had failed!"

Before he realized what she was about, she had jumped up and began running toward the woods. Scrambling in undignified haste, Stormwalker caught up with her just as she left the all-but-invisible path. He caught at her arm and swung her about, his eyes blazing into hers as a clean, sharp anger overtook other, less bearable emotions. "You will *do as I say*, woman! Are you deliberately trying to lose yourself in a bog? Is that it? I can recommend one which has swallowed many an unwary trapper."

"Take your hands off me, you—you savage!"

"A savage would not have endured your vile tongue as patiently as I have done!"

"Patiently!" Her eyes blazed and then, to his astonishment, she crumpled to the ground, and this time when she began to weep, her sobs held a note of acceptance. She turned to him blindly when he knelt before her, and lifting her in his arms, he carried her back to the village, ignoring the stares of his people.

He took her directly to his own lodge and reaching back, let fall the flap that covered the entrance. There he held her until her sobs dwindled down to the occasional hiccup. When her breathing became slow and even, he laid her carefully on his sleeping mat, removed three bark squares near the ground and then adjusted the opening overhead so that air would funnel through, but the sun would not.

"Kokom," he said to the old chief a short while later, "I will leave on the morrow to take the woman to her people."

"You will go as John Walker?"

"It would be best."

"Will you return?"

Stormwalker stared at the squash patch, where two young girls were working. "I cannot say."

"If there is fever in the town?"

"Then I will not."

"I could send her with Yah-testea Roo-iune."

"Blue Blanket is a good hunter. You will need him when winter comes."

"I do not know if we will live until winter comes. I had a vision while you were away. It is strange. I do not know what it means, but I saw many wolves. Perhaps only wolves will sleep in our *oukes* and feast on our corn and our beans."

Stormwalker managed a smile he was far from feeling. "I fear it is but another rum vision. You should stick to the corn beer. It is kinder to the gut."

Wolves, he thought. His sister had dreamed of wolves. A dream that came three times was held to be a vision among his people, although many did not feel that way. Many thought that only a man who had fasted and bled could have a true vision, but Stormwalker knew that women had powers unknown to men.

"Tell me your vision," he said.

Kokom was well within his rights to refuse, but there were few left of his people in whom he could confide. He needed his old friend Kinnahauk, but in his absence, Stormwalker would do as well.

"The male was larger than the rest, yet not so much larger than his mate. Three times I saw this pair, and each time they were surrounded by pups, yet, it was the male who held the attention of the pups. The female stood off to one side, as if her duty had ended."

He took a long pull on his pipe and drew the smoke into his lungs. It was expelled in slow curls as he resumed the telling of his vision. "The pups began to grow until they were large, some even larger than their sire. Yet, instead of leaving the pack to seek their own territory, as is the way of such creatures, they remained with the old ones."

Stormwalker turned over the image in his mind. It was much like the image Anne had related to him before he had

left Croatoan. A pack, somehow different from other woll
packs, the old sire smaller than his offspring, yet maintain
ing his dominance.

What could it mean? "I will think on your vision, old
friend. If I am able to return, I will speak to you again on
this matter. If there is fever in the town, I will returr
until all danger is passed. Keep your guards posted. Let no
one inside until you are certain they are not bringing dan
ger with them."

Kokom sighed. "Few men remain here. I have kept only
four hunters and four youths to serve as guards. Five of our
young braves left two days ago to stay on Croatoan until al
danger has passed. I would not have us become a village o
old men, women and children."

It had been a wise move on Kokom's part, this Storm
walker recognized. Yet it left the ones remaining in a vul
nerable position.

"I will take the woman, and then I will return," he said
"Even wars and fevers cannot last forever."

Wolves, he thought as he returned to his own lodge
Could it be true? Would the day soon come when wild red
wolves would roam freely in this place that had come to be
his home?

Chapter Twenty-two

That night, Stormwalker held Laura while she slept, his mind too troubled to give him rest. He knew she could not have meant the things she had said by the pond. It had been her grief speaking, not her heart. He had seen women rend their skin, break out their teeth and pull out their hair over the loss of a beloved child. It was not hard to understand how someone who had suffered as Laura had suffered, first from the loss of her parents and the brutal attack on her own body, and then from the loss of her son, could turn against someone close to them, as if pain inflicted could somehow lessen their own burden of suffering.

It was true that he had not seen the body of the child. He could not swear that Little Thunder had perished when fever had swept through the village, yet if he told her that, she would insist on going there and searching in every lodge to find some sign.

She would sicken and die for her trouble, and he could not bear to lose her.

A mocking voice responded, *How can a man lose what he has never truly possessed?*

For a little while he had managed to convince himself that she could live as he lived, moving freely from place to place, taking what he required from the land without thought for the future. Or that he could live as she did—in one of her towns, shut up in an airless box, wearing long shirts and coats in the broad of summer or grubbing up full grown trees in an effort to tame that which was never meant to be tamed, planting the same crops on the same ground year after year until the earth turned cold and barren.

Could there by any future for two people from such different worlds, where hatred had outstripped understanding?

Tomorrow he would take her to the garrison. Beyond that day, he would not think. If the soldiers offered to go in search of Little Thunder, he would say nothing. Let them search—it could do no harm. If she needed to hope, he would not take that from her.

As if his heavy sigh had aroused her from her deep sleep, Laura stirred in his arms. Suddenly—and most inappropriately—Stormwalker's body reacted to her nearness, to the soft swell of her buttocks pressed against his groin.

She turned over onto her back, and the arm that had held her against his chest fell across her breast. Every muscle he possessed tensed until he could scarcely breathe.

"Little Sparrow, are you awake?" he whispered after a moment. Her breathing was slow, but it was also uneven. His hand curved over her soft breast and he heard the slight sibilant sound of her gasp. She was awake.

One of his knees was drawn up so that it pressed against her thigh and he straightened his limbs out slowly, his hand never moving from its soft cushion. Edging closer, he felt his thrusting manhood brush against her hip. She had slept in the doeskin gown. Such a gown was never meant to be slept in. It would be difficult to remove, but suddenly he knew that he would remove it. Neither grief nor anger would keep him from claiming what he so desperately needed this night.

Or from giving her a brief surcease. He must touch her once more, feel her against him—feel himself inside her body. The world offered no certainties. If they parted tomorrow, he might never see her again—he must take care that he did not leave her with child!

With child . . . *his* child! At the thought of his seed growing in her body, his control nearly was lost.

Slowly, without forcing her to confess to being awake, Stormwalker set about removing the soft garment. It seemed determined to fight him at every step, dragging over her naked skin, clinging to her hips and then her shoulders. How could she even pretend to be asleep when he was forced to support her on one arm and drag the wretched thing over her head with the other, nearly smothering her in the process?

At last she lay naked in his arms. Lying on his side so that they were face-to-face, he took a moment to bring himself under control. It was then that the moon came out from behind a cloud, pouring its light through the small opening overhead.

"Your eyes gleam like the eyes of a forest creature," he whispered. "How long have you been awake?"

"Since just before you started trying to bundle me up in my gown like a shoat on the way to market. Did you plan to let me sleep while you had your way with me?"

"Is my way not your way, as well?" he countered, and suddenly, he could no longer see her eyes. Either she had closed them, or the moon had gone back behind its cloud.

"Please—do we have to talk?"

"Would you rather sleep?"

"I would rather . . ." she whispered. And then, in a little rush, "I would rather— Make me forget, Stormwalker, just for a little while." Trembling, she pressed against him, the sweet heat of her body burning his skin. Her eyes were open once again, clinging to his in the near darkness, and then he saw nothing more, for they were too close. Warm hands searched—and found. Hungry lips lifted—and met.

As she began eagerly to stroke him, Stormwalker was startled, and then profoundly moved by her passion, even though he knew it had little to do with him as a man. She needed to be reminded in the most basic of ways that she was capable of feeling more than pain and grief.

Tenderly, he nuzzled the sweet curve between her neck and her shoulder. He remembered the way she had been the first time he had ever seen her—an innocent, untouched by sorrow. Now she was a woman, profoundly changed by all that had happened to her, yet still the same golden girl he had glimpsed so long ago.

And suddenly, he needed her as he had never needed her before.

Lifting his hand, he cradled her breast with reverence and passion, and Laura strained upward, moaning and burying her hands in his soft hair as his tongue began to tease at her nipple. Quickly, his delicate strokes had created a desperate need for more, and she pressed him to her in silent command.

His hand found the shallow valley of her waist, and slipped down across the subtle swell of her belly as one fingertip lingered to explore her tiny navel. His thumb began a slow, sensual circling of the delicate bones that rimmed her womanhood, and then he dipped lower still, until he found what he sought.

She was burning—moist and hot—and his own body grew painfully rigid. He throbbed against her, needing desperately to thrust deeply into the well of her womanhood, yet he forced himself to wait. In the silence of the night, he rocked her against his hand until she whimpered with desire. His loins were on fire now, the blood thundering through his body until he thought he might perish with his own great need, yet he would not end this sweet torture—not yet. The dawn would intrude soon enough, but he would hold it at bay yet a while longer.

"Please..." she gasped, tugging at his arm. He knew what she wanted. His own body cried out for the same release.

As the moon lifted above a bank of low-lying clouds, Stormwalker ended the self-inflicted torment of denial. Moving swiftly, he thrust himself fiercely into her fire and heard his voice cry out in the night.

She was weeping. Perhaps he wept, too. He only knew that they rose together with a swiftness they had never before achieved—above the moon, above the stars—into the golden splendor of life itself.

Together they soared, clinging, weeping, crying out against the fate that had brought them together only to tear them apart.

Finally, exhausted, they slept in each other's arms. He had ridden her hard and she had demanded still more of him. It was as if she knew, even as he did, that this night must last them a thousand lifetimes.

He took her once more in the night, and again just as the sun broke above the eastern shore. And then he slipped out and moved silently to the creek that flowed nearby. After bathing himself, he carried water for her.

Neither of them spoke more than was necessary. It was as if they were afraid of what might be said. As if not voicing their fears made them less real.

By the time the tall young man wearing buckskin trousers and a white linen shirt, escorting a young woman in a strange assortment of garments, slipped through the gate of the palisade, the sun was already well above shoulder level.

Laura had watched in silence while Stormwalker applied the red mudlike substance to his hair, dulling it and changing the color. Finally, she had been forced to speak.

"Why? It is truly an ugly color. It does not become you at all."

He had sent her a rueful smile as he rinsed the stuff from his hands. "Would you have me suffer under a wig? Not in the broad of summer, *wittapi*—even the beasts of the forest have enough sense to shed their long winter coats when the heat is enough to parch an acorn on the tree."

He'd removed a wrinkled white shirt from a bundle that she had thought contained only dressed hides and slipped it over his bare chest. It was plain, of the sort that any poor landowner might possess, yet on him, it looked finer than anything worn by the wealthiest planter in all the land. "I'll cut a poor figure beside you," she'd said, as he struggled to fit on a pair of brown buckskin shoes with small red heels and a pewter buckle.

"You will do well enough. Anna Little Crow has found you something that is not quite so remarkable to wear." He indicated a small bundle against one wall, and Laura glanced at it without bothering to look closer. "Go ahead— we must leave as quickly as possible, before there is too much traffic about."

Reluctantly, Laura unfolded and examined the odd assortment of garments. She would much rather have worn the soft doeskin gown, which was by far the most comfortable thing she had ever worn, except perhaps for her shift, when she had been alone on the island.

A short while later, she had said her goodbyes, embracing her plump and garrulous hostess and touching hands with a tearful Anna. Dressed in the awful green-and-tan striped gown that had been made to fit someone twice her size, and that a hundred years before, from the style, she was draped with bits and pieces that bore only the slightest resemblance to panniers, stomacher, cap and apron.

They had reached the canoe and were well upriver before Laura brought herself to remark on Stormwalker's changed appearance. "I remember you now, you know. That day outside the store. It was you, wasn't it?"

"Who went inside to find you a kerchief and returned with a square of silk, only to discover that you had taken wing? Yes. That was a trapper who is sometimes called John Walker."

She said nothing for a while, and Stormwalker bent to his task of sending them upriver toward the garrison at Bath Towne. It was not a journey he wished to make, yet he had promised. In truth, he knew of no other course to take.

"Why?" she asked after so much time had passed that he had set his mind on other matters.

"Why what?"

"Why are you dressed like that now? You've already split a seam at your shoulder."

"Better a split seam than a split gullet. Do you think the men in your English garrison can be counted on to ask questions first and shoot later when they see a naked savage with a yellow-haired paleface woman?"

To that she had no reply. Neither of them spoke for the remainder of the journey. With the outgoing tide, Stormwalker skirted the bank in order to avoid the swiftest current, but the going was still difficult for one man.

They passed two sloops taking advantage of the wind and the tide on the outward journey. No one showed any particular interest in a woman and a white-shirted man, his hair glinting red beneath a black beaver hat.

Laura grudgingly accepted the wisdom of Stormwalker's disguise, but she resented it. Even as she watched the powerful muscles of his shoulders bunch and gather with each stroke of the paddle, she resented the hold he had over her. Those same hard and callused hands that gripped the ashwood paddle so surely, wielded a magic she could not fight, a magic that had made her forget for a little while what she had lost—and how little she had left to live for.

"Harding's boatworks is beyond the next point," Stormwalker said, breaking into her thoughts.

Startled, for she had not noticed how much time had passed while she had been lost in memories of the three of them together on the island, Laura stared at the tall masts above the roofs of the warehouses. It had been two—no, three years now since she had last seen Bath Towne. Even then it had been a handsome place, with neat houses behind picket fences and a new church and public buildings. The women had gone about in gowns finer than any she had seen since leaving Virginia.

Gazing down at her bare feet and her drab borrowed costume, Laura suddenly knew a desire to turn back to the safe comfort of Runs After's unpretentious lodge. Poverty was no great shame, but she didn't even possess a petticoat to hold her skirts away from her body. Her limp cotton gown was so thin she could practically see through it, and it had been torn and clumsily mended so many times it was hard to discern the original design.

"Perhaps we should wait until the sun is not so high," she said as Stormwalker swung the canoe toward the low, marshy bank. The sun was already touching the tops of the distant pines.

"We will go now. I do not care to approach your town in the darkness. There has been more fighting in recent weeks."

Her head came up at that. "Where? Who?"

"A renegade band of Coranine who defy even Hancock to control them."

"I don't mean that—I mean whose houses were raided? Was anyone hurt?"

Stormwalker sighed, wishing he had never brought up the matter. He had been more concerned with the villages that had been raided in retaliation. "If you wish to speak to the captain, perhaps you had better step out and allow me to secure the canoe."

"Storm—"

"John," he said softly, his eyes burning through her as she crouched half in and half out of the dugout. "Unless you want my blood on your hands, you will call me John Walker while we are among your people."

By then the guard, a stripling no more than sixteen years old, was close enough to challenge them. His voice broke as he did so, which only made him all the more belligerent.

Stormwalker slipped easily around Laura, standing between her and the unsteady barrel of the boy's flintlock. "I am John Walker, come to seek council with your captain."

"State your business, sir." The boy had halted some fifteen feet away and seemed unwilling to approach closer.

With a blandness that caused Laura to peer at him intently, Stormwalker said, "The woman seeks your help. Her son was stolen and taken to Seconiac on the Paquipe, and we fear for his life." He deliberately pretended ignorance. Few white men had seen the inside of Three Turtle's village—he did not want to arouse suspicion.

"Stolen?" The boy gawked but came no closer. "Mostly they kills 'em. I seen—"

"Your commander, soldier. I would have an audience with him, if you please."

"Yessir, yessir—uh, you'n your missus'll wait here, I'll fetch Cap'n Hazlewood out to speak to you."

They were left to wait while the lad went in search of his commanding officer. Laura leaned closer and whispered, "Do you really believe—"

"Hush."

She noticed that this time he did not warn her to *sehe*, which meant the same thing. He could speak her language as well as she could when he wished to—and probably several more, besides.

Within a very few minutes the lad was back, accompanied by a gaunt, gray-haired man with a tired but distinctly military bearing. "Hazlewood. No strangers admitted—sorry. No one allowed in or out until this bloody fever runs its course. What'd you say your trouble was?"

Laura, small patches of color burning high on her cheeks, pushed in front of Stormwalker and stared at the man, who stood some fifteen feet away. "But you don't understand—my baby, Little—"

Stormwalker moved in front of her and smoothly pushed her behind him. "Little Ned was taken from us by Three Turtle of the Mattamuskeet. Is there anything your men can do?"

Captain Hazlewood removed his dusty cap and scratched his head. "I'm sorry as I can be, Mr.—uh—" the guard stepped closer and supplied the name, and the captain went on "—Mr. Walker. I know you and your wife must be worried plumb sick, but there's not a solitary thing I can do right now. I can't even let you inside the garrison. Like I say, town's sealed off until this fever runs its course. Governor Hyde's a'ready dead, and Tom Pollack's not likely to last out the day. Try to look on the good side if it'll help—the Indians is dropping like flies. They can't throw it off once it hits 'em. War'll be over a sight quicker, and no more ammunition wasted on the treacherous bastards, beggin' your pardon, ma'am."

Laura's hand slipped into Stormwalker's and he gripped it hurting hard, unaware of what he was doing. They watched silently as the officer turned and stalked back inside the gates. The young guard seemed overly occupied with examining his weapon. He did not look up again.

After a long moment, Stormwalker took Laura's arm and led her back toward the river. "Come, Little Sparrow. We will go now."

His eyes burned with hatred as he felt his last hope disappear like a wisp of fog under a burning August sun. Until that very moment he had not even known it was there—the one small hope.

But how could there ever be a future for him and this woman when such hatred existed between their two people?

A good thing had come from the fever—Indians dying—treacherous bastards dropping like flies.

A good thing!

His eyes burned fiercely in his hard face as he helped Laura back into the dugout and shoved it away from the bank. They would have to travel hard to reach Packwood's Crossing by morning. Laura needed rest. She was too pale—the haunted look had returned to her eyes.

"It will take hours to reach Packwood's Crossing. If you wish, we can sleep beside the river and make the overland journey tomorrow."

"Packwood's?" She looked puzzled for a moment, as if she had forgotten where they were—and why. "Can't we just go back home?"

Stormwalker frowned. Did she mean to her own home? Had it all been too much for her? Had she forgotten that her own home no longer existed?

While he was pondering how to determine the state of her mind, she said, "I can't go back to Packwood's! I'd sooner go back to the island than have to ask Coby to take me in again, and I don't know anyone else to ask. Stormwalker—John—please..."

She meant Num Peree, he thought in amazement. She had called it *home*. How could he tell her that he was not even certain if Kokom would allow them to enter again? If he were as diligent as Captain Hazlewood, he would turn them away at the gate.

Chapter Twenty-three

Unlike Hazlewood, Kokom did not bar them from reentering the village. Stormwalker, half carrying the exhausted Laura, had sent word through the guard that they had been turned away at the gates of Bath Towne without having come closer than fifteen feet to anyone from the town. Unless it had traveled silently and invisibly through the air to cling to their skins, they carried no taint of fever.

Kokom himself came out to meet them, his eyes bright with questions and concern. Stormwalker quickly explained what had happened, while Laura, who was all but asleep on her feet, leaned against his side, supported by his arm around her waist.

Instead of returning her to the lodge of Runs After, who would be sleeping soundly at this time of night, he took her directly to his own lodge.

"T'morrow," she muttered, struggling tiredly to put together a single coherent thought. Tomorrow she must think about what was to be done. Perhaps Martha Packwood would ... Or Addie Harker...

Laura was asleep before she even settled onto the mat that Stormwalker had unrolled for her. He removed her apron and spread it over her shoulders, smoothing her skirt down over her ankles. For a long moment he knelt beside her, staring into the darkness as he held one small foot in the palm of his hand.

And then he stood abruptly and went outside.

She was back where she belonged, he thought posses-sively, and the primitive side of his nature rejoiced.

But for how long and to what end? countered the part of him that had learned to reason like a white man.

Hazlewood's words echoed again and again in his mind as he lifted his face to the night, absorbing the familiar scene before him. Moonlight fell over the neat dome-topped lodges, silhouetting the tasseling cornstalks that rose be-tween them. He gazed at the large central fire pit that was surrounded by stones, remembering the many feasts and festivals that had centered on its leaping flames. And the funerals.

Overlaying the smell of cold ashes on the still night air was the resinous scent of pine and the dusty-sweet fragrance of ripening corn. He breathed in deeply, as if to rid himself of the stench of hatred.

There had been no real anger behind Hazlewood's words. The captain had merely been stating the position of all whites. It had been that very lack of personal rancor that had impressed Stormwalker with the truth as no amount of fiery rhetoric could have done.

Perhaps it had been different in his father's time, he thought sadly. There had not been quite so many white-eyes spreading out over the country back then, nor had they been quite so bold in their claims.

How could one man and one woman possibly bridge the river of hatred that now existed between their two people?

Over the next few days, Stormwalker treated Laura as if she were a beloved sister, which was both reassuring and in-furiating. Given the choice, she might have lost herself in his lovemaking once more—but she was not given the choice. During the days, he hunted and fished, making up for the absence of so many of the younger men from the village.

At night, he remained outside, talking with Kokom until Laura's eyelids drooped and she was forced to go inside and unroll her sleeping mat. When morning came, he would be gone again—making her wonder if he had come inside at all during the night.

Perhaps he slept elsewhere. Perhaps he resented her being there.

"Perhaps I'll ask if Runs After will let me move in with her again," she suggested one day when he had just come in with four rabbits and was preparing to take his turn guarding the gate.

"And perhaps you will not," Stormwalker replied smoothly. He had been waiting for just such a move on her part. He was surprised that it had not come sooner. "I have brought you to my lodge, which in the eyes of my people means that I have claimed you for my woman."

Laura gasped. "But you've done no such thing! The only reason I'm here is—is . . ."

"Because I brought you here." Arms folded over his chest, Stormwalker watched an array of emotions flicker across her face one after another, his own face remaining unreadable.

"But that was only because—"

"I wanted you here."

"Well, you have a fine way of showing it!" she snapped. The sun beat down on her bare head, turning her hair to molten gold. This was the first time since they had returned to Num Peree that she had shown any emotion at all, and he was delighted, even if it was primarily anger, and that directed at him.

"Would you have had me make love to you each night?"

Her mouth gaped open as she struggled to contain her indignation. "Don't be ridiculous! That's the last thing I— the *very* last thing—of *course* I don't want you to make love to me!"

He didn't even smile, although he wanted nothing more than to gather her into his arms and prove to her what a monstrous lie she had just uttered. "Then would you have me declare my love and promise never to make love to you again?"

"No! Certainly not—I mean, yes—I mean...you're being absurd!"

Eyes glittering in an otherwise impassive face, Stormwalker continued to regard her until she flounced off, all steam and protests, to skin the rabbits he had taken in his traps. Only when he was certain she would not look back did he allow his feelings to rise to the surface.

Caution. Joy. Doubts—hopefulness. In spite of everything, she still wanted him. It seemed that, against all reason, the more he stayed away, the more powerful that wanting became.

He knew she cried in the night. That first night, he had come to the door of his lodge and heard her sobbing in her sleep, and it had near unmanned him. His first impulse had been to go to her, to hold her and comfort her in whatever way he could.

But he knew how that would end. They would make love and he would be drawn deeper under her spell, and she in turn, would be drawn closer to him. It was not enough. Reason told him that such a match could not be, yet his heart told him it was far too late to turn away.

For both their sakes, as well as the sake of his people, Stormwalker had forced himself to go slowly. He had held out for four days, using the only means he could think of. He had spent the days away from the village and each night he had helped guard the gate and then shared T'kiro's lodge.

They had talked until late that first night. Stormwalker had discovered that his young friend had, indeed, lost his heart to Kokom's daughter. Stormwalker had thought perhaps Kitappi had exaggerated T'kiro's affection for her, as she was inclined to believe all men her slaves.

As most of them were, Stormwalker admitted freely. Certainly the young teacher was under her spell.

"Have you spoken to Kokom?" he asked. The two men sat outside the small lodge that had been assigned to T'kiro, smoking the milder tobacco that the younger man favored.

"Do you think he would accept my small store of books as a bride price?"

"Would you give them?"

"And many more. If I possessed the finest plantation, the fastest ship and the greatest store of gold ever a man could claim, I would gladly offer it all for Kitappi. But I have nothing to trade for bearskin robes or horses or such things. I have no gold.''

''Few men do,'' Stormwalker reminded him dryly.

''No peak,'' T'kiro continued, referring to the small beads made of hard clam shells that were used for exchange in the absence of gold, even by the English.

''You have something even more valuable,'' Stormwalker reminded him. ''Kitappi cares for you. She spent hours on the journey to Croatoan praising your beauty, your virtue and your wisdom. She told me you have captured the hearts of the children as no one has done before, and that even the old ones have come to respect you.''

T'kiro dug his heel into the soft earth, unable to look up. His face, normally the color of a well-tanned buckskin, took on an unnatural ruddiness. ''She is the daughter of a chief. I am but the son of a slave.''

''Paugh! That means nothing. You are what you have made of yourself. Only that. All of that.''

''Do you think Kokom would hear me out without ordering my death?''

Stormwalker hid a grin. If it meant his daughter's happiness, the old man would give her willingly, with or without the bride price. But he asked only, ''Is she not worth the risk?''

''A hundred times over!''

''Then go to him, you great fool—tell him you will pay her bride price in grandsons. That should cool his hot head quickly enough.''

On the fourth night, Stormwalker waited until the village was quiet before slipping out to bathe in the creek. He had watched Laura go earlier in the day with Anna Little Crow and two other young women. They had been chattering in a mixture of both languages, and Laura had actually smiled once or twice before they had been lost to his sight.

Since they had returned from Bath Towne, she had not spoken again of returning to her own people. Not that he had given her the opportunity. Only now would he admit that he had deliberately stayed away, hoping she might discover how easy it would be to live among his people.

One damned sight easier, he told himself wryly, than it would be for him to live among hers. His mother had found it comfortable enough to live among her husband's people. And though Kinnahauk took her to Bath Towne, and even to Virginia when she insisted on it, she was always eager to return to Croatoan, claiming that her head hurt from the constant clatter of cart wheels and horses and the prattle of too many tongues.

Laura was not asleep when Stormwalker entered the lodge. She had opened the flap in the roof to its widest and tied back the door flap so that a small current of air funneled through the lodge, carrying away the day's heat and replacing it with the cool, sweet night air.

"You are not sleeping yet?" he asked, suddenly uncomfortable at what he had come to do.

"Do you need something? Can I get it for you?" And then, as if she, too, were uncomfortable, she hurried on. "Stormwalker, I'm right sorry for putting you out this way. Honestly, I wouldn't mind moving in with Runs After again. She doesn't snore so awfully bad—at least not all night long. It's only toward morning, when—"

"*Sehe.* If I did not want you in my lodge, Little Sparrow, you would not be here. Know that. I brought you here so that all would know what was in my heart."

"Your...heart?" she whispered.

He slapped his naked chest. "That part of me that does not know the meaning of reason—that does not care that you are of one people and I am of another—that our two people are at war. That my father has four grandsons who are more English than Hatorask, and I would give him four more of the same."

Laura had been kneeling on the sleeping mat when Stormwalker had stepped into the lodge. Now she stared up at him, her face unreadable in the dim light. She could not have spoken if her life had depended on it.

"Laura? Did you hear what I said? Do you not know what I want from you?"

"My—me?"

Taking time only to close the flap, he came inside and knelt beside her. Smiling softly in the half-light, he said, "Your—you."

After a long, breathless silence, he drew her gown over her head. She was wearing the doeskin shift again, having returned the ugly green gown to its owner, who considered it a great treasure, although she would never have dreamed of wearing it.

Neither of them spoke as Stormwalker removed his own single garment. Their eyes clung together as his hands moved over her shoulders, down her arms, to claim her hands and bring them to his chest.

She was trembling. This time, it was different. Laura could not have said just how she knew, but it was there, all the same—the unspoken love. The commitment. This time would be a beginning, not an ending.

He loved her gently at first, telling her with his touch that she was more precious to him than his own life—that without her there could be no life, only barren existence.

All too quickly, passion took control, driving them toward a mindless, heedless summit where they dwelt together for a sweet eternity, their bodies clasped in the most intimate embrace of all.

And then he told her with his lips. Kissing first one eyelid and then the other, he whispered the words she had unconsciously needed to hear for so long. First in her language, then in his.

And Laura repeated the words. In his language—stumblingly—and in her own.

Rolling onto his back, he carried her with him so that when he chuckled, she held on to his shoulders to keep from tumbling off.

"What's so funny?" she demanded.

"You have just called me a musket."

"I did no such—not unless you called me one first."

He bit her throat ever so gently, so that she shuddered at the sensations that raced down her body. "I only called you the sun of my heart, my *wittapare*."

Laura tilted her head back to allow him better access to the sensitive places on the sides of her throat. "And I—ahhhh...and I said—"

"That I was your *wittape*—your musket."

As she felt his thrusting manhood harden against her belly, a smile spread slowly across Laura's face. Eyes sparkling, she whispered, "I think perhaps I have a truer understanding of your language that either of us suspected, don't you?"

Through the night they loved and whispered and laughed. That night, Laura did not cry. Toward morning, she finally fell asleep, sated and content in the arms of the man she had come to love so dearly. Tomorrow no longer seemed quite so desolate.

It was during the afternoon of the following day when the commotion arose outside the gates. Laura had slept late and then spent an inordinate amount of time at the creek, bathing and smiling at nothing at all while Anna Little Crow chattered on at her usual pace.

"Someone's coming," Anna said.

"Here?" Laura scrambled toward shore and snatched up her shift, tugging it down over her wet body. The soft doeskin resisted her efforts, and by the time she had finally managed to cover herself, Anna was beside her, wrapping a long-fringed shawl loosely around her body and tying it above the breast with a narrow thong.

"Not here, foolish *auhaun*—outside the gates."

Laura would take issue with being called a foolish goose another time. If there was trouble, she did not want to be caught outside the gates. "Hurry, Anna!"

The other woman only laughed. "It is only the hunters returning." At Laura's nervous look, she said, "Why do you run like a frightened rabbit? We have nothing to fear. The white soldiers are all huddled in their forts and everyone else is hiding from the fever. Who would...?"

By now they had come up from the creek and were in sight of the palisade gate. It was Laura who saw him first—what appeared to be a drunken man carrying a bundle under one arm. He was staggering toward the guards, who were backing away, their weapons drawn.

Anna Little Crow stopped in her tracks and caught at Laura's arm. "Wait," she said softly. "If he is drunk, they will shoo him away. If he is our enemy, they will kill him. But if he is—"

At that moment, the stranger, who was rail-thin and of a peculiar yellowish color, swayed on his feet and dropped, throwing his bundle forward. The guards looked at each other. Anna took a step back, still clutching Laura's arm.

And then, suddenly, Laura was running. The bundle had cried out, and then begun to whimper. Before anyone could stop her, she had fallen on her knees and was gathering up the pitiful bundle of filthy-looking skins.

"Oh, God, please, oh please, oh please," Laura whispered over and over as she stripped off the mangy-looking hide to bare the small naked body.

Anna was screaming at her. Both guards were shouting. There was a commotion just inside the gates, and then Kokom stepped outside, an armed man on either side of him.

Laura ignored them all. "My sweetest, please—it's all right, you're home now, please stop crying, love..." Frantically, she examined him. He was thinner—much thinner, but there was no mistaking that tiny nose, the pointed little chin and those great shining eyes. She had known from the moment she had heard that pitiful cry! "Little Thunder, my own sweet baby, don't cry. Mama has you now, it's all right," she crooned. On her knees, she held the pathetic infant tightly to her breast, her eyes defying anyone there to try and remove him from her arms.

No one was paying the slightest bit of attention to the fallen stranger. All eyes were on Laura. And on the baby she held on to as if he were her only means of salvation.

And then, suddenly, Stormwalker was there. He had come up quietly behind them, having been out hunting. After pausing just long enough to size up the situation, he stepped forward.

"No!" someone screamed. It was Anna Little Crow. "Don't go any closer—he has the fever!"

Laura heard the voices, but the words had no meaning. Her baby was back.

"Stormwalker, the woman must go." That was Kokom.

Dimly, Laura was aware that they were speaking of her. She kissed the top of Little Thunder's head. His hair, though matted and filthy, had grown while he had been gone—it was as black as Stormwalker's, with scarcely any skin showing through, she thought proudly. And he was taller, too.

And then the voices all around her changed. For the first time since she had gathered her son into her arms, Laura became fully aware of what was taking place. Still on her knees, she turned slowly to look at the fallen man. It was Three Turtle, and he was quite obviously dead, his eyes open and staring, a trickle of spittle drying at the corner of his mouth.

She shuddered. And then her eyes were drawn beyond, to the man standing some ten feet away. *Stormwalker*. As if suddenly waking to find herself still in the midst of a nightmare, Laura cried out to him. "Stay away! Don't come any closer—you can't help him now. No one can!"

"Laura, get up off your knees," Stormwalker said calmly. He began to walk toward her. From the gate, where practically everyone in the village had gathered to watch, no one spoke. Anna had hurried to join those watching from a safe distance, and she cried out now.

"Laura, I will place food outside the gate for you."

Laura looked from Anna to Stormwalker. She could not go back, of course. To do so would be to bring almost sure death to everyone in the village. She must get away before anyone else was endangered. As for Three Turtle, they must deal with his corpse as best they could, or leave him to the carrion eaters to dispose of. She no longer cared for anything now that her baby was back.

Eyes cast downward, she stood and began backing off to one side, leaving a clear path for Stormwalker to reach the gate. She dare not look at him for fear he would read what was in her heart.

Goodbye, goodbye—I leave all my love in your keeping.

It was the sudden murmur from the gate that caused her to look up. Her eyes widened, and she clutched Little Thunder so tightly he began to whimper again. "No, please—you can't," she whispered as Stormwalker deliberately paced off the distance that separated them. All her instincts cried out against what he was doing, even as her heart rejoiced. "Stay away from me! I don't need you. I don't want you!" she cried. If he would not protect himself, then she must do it for him. "I can't stand the sight of you! Go away!" She continued to back away from him, praying she wouldn't trip and fall.

Still he came after her, his eyes never leaving her face.

It was the bramble thicket that trapped her, snagging in the fringe of her shift. With one hand she tried to free it, and while she was still caught, Stormwalker stepped forward and removed Little Thunder from her arm.

"Oh, God, no," she breathed. "Please give him back or I'll die." She remembered hearing him tell of how a father would sometimes tear a child from the arms of his mother when fever raged through a village. "Please, please—I'll do anything!" She was practically screaming at him by now.

"*Sehe*, woman! I would not rob you of your son," said Stormwalker, as though reading her fears.

But that was not the worst of her fears. "Give him back— you must! Stormwalker, my baby could have the fever, too, and if you get it—if anything were to happen to you, I couldn't bear it, don't you understand?"

"I have chosen," he said calmly. Turning to face his people, Stormwalker looked first at Kokom and then at young Tiree Kiro, the wolf who even now gathered the pups around him—the wolf who would some day lead his people.

And then, deliberately, he kissed the child on the top of his downy crown and gathered the woman to his side.

"I have chosen," he told Kokom.

Laura, too, turned to face her friends. Distraught though she was, it was impossible to miss the sorrow on their faces. Kokom's eyes, even from this distance, looked suspiciously wet. Runs After was wailing softly and Anna Little Crow was wringing her hands in a way that reminded Laura of her own mother.

"Where will you go?" Kokom called, his voice rougher than usual.

"To the island," Stormwalker replied. "When enough time has passed, I will take Laura and our son to Croatoan."

"You will return to us."

"If it be the will of Kishalamaquon."

"You will return to us," repeated Kokom, as though the matter were settled.

Laura was openly weeping now as she looked out across the clearing toward the circular wall of peeled stakes. These were her friends. Her people.

She looked up at Stormwalker. "Are you sure?" she whispered. "There might still be time..."

"I have always been sure. There is a voice inside me that speaks only the truth. It told me long ago, but I, with my white man's schooling, thought I knew best."

"And did you?" She smiled tearfully.

"Come, let us go while there is still light. In time, even you will come to understand that reason is no match for the Voice That Speaks Silently."

Epilogue

It is hard to recall a time when there was no fighting and no fever," said Bridget Abbott to her husband, Kinnahauk. The sun setting over the calm sound cast a warm light over her face, making her look far younger than her years.

"Did you say no fighting, woman? What is that I hear coming from the shore?"

Bridget laughed and lifted her new granddaughter over her shoulder, patting her tiny back until she released a bubble of air. Cradle boards were all very well for mothers, but grandmothers could do without them.

"I believe Little Thunder has claimed the pony that Wetkes thought was his."

"It is for the horse to choose. If a man cannot control his own horse, then he is not much of a man."

Bridget slanted a teasing look at her husband who, for all his years, could still outride any Croatoan brave. "The last time I heard those words, it was not a horse you were speaking of, but a wife."

Kinnahauk grinned. "That was for the ears of our new granddaughter." He reached for the infant, who gazed up at him from eyes that were as startlingly blue as her father's. "Although it is not too soon for young Mary Elk to learn the proper place of a woman."

"Which is, as we both know, wherever that woman wishes it to be." They had spoken these same words many times before, for such gentle teasing was a game they both enjoyed.

"Englishwomen have not been properly taught, as I learned to my great sorrow."

Bridget bumped against him playfully with her shoulder, which delighted their granddaughter, who thought it all a game for her benefit.

Freeing his braid from the child's tiny fist, he added, "As my son is now learning."

"Are you sorry?" Bridget asked, her eyes growing thoughtful as she watched the pair walking slowly along the shore, arms entwined and heads close together.

"That he did not take Kitappi to his lodge? How can I regret our son's happiness? The Voice spoke—"

"And being a wise young man, he paid heed."

"As did I, Wauraupa Shaman . . . as did I."

The look that passed between them spoke of a bond that had only grown stronger and more precious with time. Both had sensed between Stormwalker and Laura a bond equally strong.

"The school goes well. Stormwalker has persuaded three youths from Raruta and another from Seconiac to study with Tiree Kiro until the Moon of the Falling Leaves."

"If those people are wise, they will allow their girls to go and study, as well."

"Woman, you will not be satisfied, will you?"

"You must admit that Laura has taught our girls well. That girl can spin and weave better than I ever could. Don't you like the fine linen shirt she made for you, old man?" Bridget knew he had not yet worn it, for he preferred his familiar buckskin, but he had laid it away in a special place, along with the tokens he treasured most.

Without bothering to reply, for his woman knew his mind better than he did himself, Kinnahauk rose to meet his new daughter, of whom he had grown exceedingly fond, and his son, Stormwalker, who carried the boy, Little Thunder, on his shoulders. "Come and sit with us for a while," he said, as the dark-haired Mary Elk lifted her arms to be taken by her mother. "I would hear more of your plans for the future."

Seated under the sprawling live oak tree, four people gazed out across the sound, to the place where the sun was sinking in a fiery show of glory.

"Ah, the future..." said Stormwalker, his gaze following his young son as he ran to join the other children at play.

* * * * *

Author's Note

According to John Lawson, English gentleman and surveyor general of North Carolina from the year 1700 until 1711, "They (the Indians of North Carolina) are really much better to us than we have been to them, as they always freely give us of their victuals at their quarters, while we let them walk by our doors hungry, and do not often relieve them. We look upon them with disdain and scorn, and think them little better than beasts in human form; while with all our religion and education, we possess more moral deformities and vices than these people do."

Baron Christopher de Graffenried, who secured a tract of land at the junction of the Neuse and Trent rivers for settlement by a colony of Swiss and Germans, spoke of "the harsh treatment of (by) certain surly and rough English inhabitants who deceived them in trade, would not let them hunt about their plantations, and under this excuse, took away from them their arms, munitions, pelts or hides, yes, even beat an Indian to death."

Lawson and de Graffenried were captured by the Tuscaroras in September 1711. Lawson was killed. De Graffenried was later released. On the twenty-second of that month, the Indians launched a series of attacks in what later became known as the Tuscarora Wars.

It ended in March 1713, with a raid by a Colonel Moore on Hancock's fortified town at Catechna in what is now Greene County.

De Graffenried wrote that ''The savages showed themselves unspeakably brave, so much so that when our soldiers had become masters of the fort and wanted to take out the women and children who were underground, where they had been hidden along with their provisions, the wounded savages who were groaning on the ground still continued to fight.''

The Tuscarora were routed with losses that were described by Moore as, ''Prisoners 392, Scolps (scalps) 192 out of ye sd. fort—And 166 kill'd and taken out of ye fort.''

COMING NEXT MONTH

#49 FREEDOM FLAME—Caryn Cameron

For Merry Morgan, the chance to be George Washington's spy seemed the remedy to her dull existence. Her contact, Darcy Mont, was rude, arrogant—and irresistible. But the mysterious Frenchman harbored secrets that threatened to keep them apart forever....

#50 HEAVEN AND EARTH—Kathleen Eagle

Jed West rued the day he laid eyes on her. He'd had his fill of the white man's world, and besides, Katherine Fairfield was a missionary—not a woman. But even while he scorned her piety, he yearned to love her with all the passion that burned between them.

AVAILABLE NOW:

#47 STORMWALKER
Bronwyn Williams

#48 DRAGONFIRE
Patricia Potter

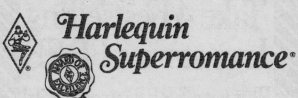

Harlequin Superromance

A June title
not to be missed....

Superromance author Judith Duncan has created her
most powerfully emotional novel yet, a book about
love too strong to forget and hate too painful to
remember....

Risen from the ashes of her past like a phoenix,
Sydney Foster knew too well the price of wisdom,
especially that gained in the underbelly of the city.
She'd sworn she'd never go back, but in order to
embrace a future with the man she loved, she had to
return to the streets...and settle an old score.

Once in a long while, you read a book that affects you
so strongly, you're never the same again. Harlequin is
proud to present such a book, STREETS OF FIRE by
Judith Duncan (Superromance #407). Her book merits
Harlequin's AWARD OF EXCELLENCE for June 1990,
conferred each month to one specially selected title.

S407-1